МИХАИЛ ШОЛОХОВ

ТИХИЙ ДОН

РОМАН В ЧЕТЫРЕХ КНИГАХ

*

КНИГА ВТОРАЯ

ИЗДАТЕЛЬСТВО ЛИТЕРАТУРЫ НА ИНОСТРАННЫХ ЯЗЫКАХ
МОСКВА

MIKHAIL SHOLOKHOV

AND QUIET FLOWS THE DON

A NOVEL IN FOUR BOOKS

✳

BOOK TWO

FOREIGN LANGUAGES PUBLISHING HOUSE
MOSCOW

A TRANSLATION FROM THE RUSSIAN
BY STEPHEN GARRY

REVISED AND COMPLETED
BY ROBERT DAGLISH

PART FOUR

I

Nineteen-sixteen. October. Night. Rain and wind. Woodland. Trenches on the edge of an alder-grown marsh. Barbed-wire entanglements in front. A freezing slush in the trenches. The wet sheet-iron of an observation post gleams faintly. Lights here and there in the dug-outs.

At the entrance to one of the officers' dug-outs a thick-set officer halted for a moment, his wet fingers slipping over his greatcoat fasteners. He hurriedly unbuttoned them, shook the water from the collar, wiped his boots on the heap of straw trampled into the mud at the entrance, and only then pushed open the door, stooped, and entered the dug-out.

A yellow band of light streaming from a little paraffin lamp gleamed oilily on his face.

An officer in an open jacket rose from a wooden bunk, passed his hand over his rumpled grey hair and yawned.

"Raining?"

"Yes," the visitor replied, and removing his greatcoat, hung it together with his sodden cap on a nail by the door. "You're warm in here. Worked up a good fug."

"We lighted the stove a little while ago. The trouble is that the water is oozing up through the floor. The rain will drive us out, blast it. What do you think, Bunchuk?"

Rubbing his hands, Bunchuk stooped and squatted down by the stove.

"Put some planks down over the floor. We're fine and dry in our dug-out. We could walk about with bare feet. Where's Listnitsky?"

"He's asleep. He came back from a round of the sentry posts and lay down at once."

"All right to wake him up?"

"Go ahead. We'll have a game of chess."

Bunchuk brushed the rain from his heavy brows with his index finger, examined the finger attentively, and called quietly:

"Yevgeny Nikolayevich!"

"Sound asleep," sighed the grey-haired officer. "Yevgeny Nikolayevich."

"Well?" Listnitsky raised himself on his elbow.

"Have a game of chess?"

Yevgeny dropped his legs from the bed, and rubbed hard at his chest with his soft white palms.

As the first game was nearing its end two officers of the Fifth Squadron, Captain Kalmykov and Lieutenant Chubov, entered.

"News!" Kalmykov cried as he crossed the threshold. "The regiment will probably be withdrawn."

"Where did you hear that?" the grey-haired officer, Junior Captain Merkulov, smiled sceptically.

"Don't you believe me, Uncle Pyotr?"

"To tell the truth, no."

"The commander of the battery just informed us over the telephone. How did he know? Well, he only returned from the divisional staff yesterday."

"It would be wonderful to have a bath," Chubov said, with a note of ecstasy in his voice, and slapped his shoulders as if flaying himself with birch twigs.

"We could do with a tub in here, we have plenty of water," Merkulov smiled.

"You're damp in here, gentlemen, very damp," Kalmykov grumbled, looking around the timbered walls and the muddy floor.

"We've got the marsh right at our side."

"Thank the Almighty that you *are* in the marsh, and as comfortable there as if you were in Abraham's bosom!" Bunchuk interposed. "In other districts they're attacking, but here we fire one round a week."

"Better to be attacking than rotting in this hole."

"They don't keep the Cossacks to get them wiped out in attacks. Why try to appear naive, Merkulov?"

"Then what are we kept for, in your opinion?"

"At the right moment the government will play its old game of maintaining itself on the backs of the Cossacks."

"Now you're talking heresy," Kalmykov waved his hand.

"Heresy? Why?"

"Because it is."

"Rubbish, Kalmykov. You can't deny the truth."

"What kind of truth. . . ."

"Why, everybody knows it's the truth. Why don't you admit it too?"

"Attention, gentlemen!" Chubov shouted, and bowing theatrically, pointed to Bunchuk. "Cornet Bunchuk will now begin to interpret the Social-Democratic dream-book!"

"Are you trying to play the clown?" Bunchuk smiled ironically, meeting Chubov's glance with his hard stare. "Well, it's up to you. Every man to his trade. I'm telling you that we haven't seen war since the middle of last year. As soon as the trench warfare began the Cossack regiments were distributed in sheltered spots, and are being kept there quietly until the right moment arrives."

"And then?" Listnitsky asked as he gathered up the chess-men.

"And then, when unrest sets in at the front— and that is inevitable; the soldiers are beginning to get fed up with the war, the growth of desertion shows that—then the Cossacks will be called upon to suppress the revolts. The government holds the Cossacks like a stone in its hand. At the right moment it will attempt to break the head of the revolution with that stone."

"Aren't you letting your imagination run, my dear fellow? Your assumptions are rather shaky," Listnitsky objected. "To begin with, it's impossible to predict the course of events. How do you know about the coming unrest and so on? But let us suppose that the allies shatter the Germans and the war ends brilliantly, then what role will you assign to the Cossacks?"

Bunchuk smiled drily. "It doesn't look like coming to an end at the moment, least of all a brilliant one."

"The campaign is going slowly. . . ."

"It'll go even slower," Bunchuk assured him.

"When did you get back from leave?" Kalmykov asked.

"Two days ago."

Bunchuk rounded his lips, puffed out a ball of smoke and threw away the butt of his cigarette.

"Where did you spend it?"

"In Petrograd."

"Well, what's the news from the capital? Ah, what the devil wouldn't I give to spend one short week in Petrograd!"

"You'd find little to comfort you," Bunchuk said, weighing his words carefully. "There's a shortage of food. In the workers' districts there is hunger, discontent, and seething unrest."

"We shan't come happily out of this war. What do you think, gentlemen?" Merkulov looked round questioningly.

"The Russo-Japanese war gave birth to the Revolution of 1905. This war will end with a new revolution, and not only revolution, but civil war."

Listnitsky made an indefinite gesture as though about to interrupt him, then rose and paced up and down the dug-out, frowning. With restrained anger in his voice he said:

"I'm astonished to find such characters among us officers as this fellow," he pointed to Bunchuk. "I'm astonished, because to this very day I cannot clearly gather what is his attitude to his country, and to the war. The other day he spoke very vaguely, yet sufficiently clearly to let us understand that he wants to see us defeated. Did I understand you correctly, Bunchuk?"

"I'm in favour of our being defeated."

"But why? In my view, no matter what your political views may be, to wish the defeat of your own country is state treason. It is dishonourable to any decent man."

"Do you remember how the Social-Democratic members of the Duma agitated against the government, in that way contributing to the country's defeat?" Merkulov intervened.

"Do you share their views, Bunchuk?" Listnitsky asked.

"If I say I'm in favour of our being defeated it's obvious that I do, and it would be absurd for me, a member of the Russian Social-Democratic Labour Party, not to share the view of my fellow Party members in the Duma. I am very

13

surprised that you, Yevgeny Nikolayevich, with your education, are so ignorant politically."

"First and foremost I am a soldier devoted to the monarchy. I am revolted by the very sight of 'socialist comrades.' "

"First and foremost you're a blockhead, and after that a self-satisfied military brute," Bunchuk thought, and hid a smile.

"In the army one is placed in an exceptional situation," Merkulov said as though apologizing. "We have all held ourselves aloof from politics, we live on the outskirts of the village, so to speak."

Captain Kalmykov sat stroking his drooping whiskers, his fierce Mongolian eyes gleaming. Chubov lay on a bed, staring at a drawing by Merkulov fastened to the wall. It was of a half-naked woman with the face of a Magdalene, smiling languorously and wantonly as she gazed at her bare breasts. With two fingers of her left hand she was drawing aside one nipple, and the little finger was held back cautiously. Under her half-closed eyelids lay a shadow softened by the warm glow of her eyes. One slightly raised shoulder held up her slipping chemise, and a soft shade of light lingered in the hollows below her collar-bones. There was so much natural grace and real truth in her

pose, so unexpectedly beautiful were the soft tones, that Chubov involuntarily smiled, delighting in the masterly sketch, and not following the drift of the conversation at all.

"That's fine!" he exclaimed, tearing his eyes away. His remark came at a very inopportune moment, for Bunchuk had just said:

"Tsarism will be destroyed, you can rest assured."

Rolling a cigarette, and smiling caustically, Listnitsky stared first at Bunchuk, then at Chubov.

"Bunchuk!" Kalmykov exclaimed. "Just a second, Listnitsky! Bunchuk, listen! Let us admit that this war will be transformed into a civil war. Then what? You'll overthrow the monarchy. But what sort of a government do you propose to set up in its place?"

"The government of the working class."

"A parliament, do you mean?"

"More than that," Bunchuk smiled.

"Well, what then?"

"A workers' dictatorship."

"Now we've got it! But the intelligentsia, the peasantry? What part will they play?"

"The peasantry will follow us, and part of the intelligentsia also. The others . . . well, this is what we'll do with them." With a swift movement he screwed up a paper in his hand,

and threw it away, saying through his teeth: "That's what we'll do!"

"You're flying high . . ." sneered Listnitsky.

"We'll be landing high," Bunchuk retorted.

"Better spread some straw in case you don't."

"Why the devil did you volunteer for the front, and even work your way up to officer's rank? How can you reconcile that with your views? Incredible! Here's a man against the war, against the destruction of his, what do you call them, class brothers, and he's an officer!" Kalmykov slapped the legs of his boots and laughed with genuine amusement.

"How many German workers have you slaughtered with your machine-guns?" Listnitsky inquired.

Bunchuk drew a large packet of papers from his pocket and rummaged among them, standing with his back to Listnitsky. Then going to the table he spread open a newspaper yellow with age and smoothed out the creases with his big sinewy hand.

"How many German workers have I killed? That's . . . a question. I came voluntarily because I'd have had to come in any case. I think the knowledge I have gained here in the trenches will be of some service later on . . . later on. Listen to this." And he read Lenin's words:

Take the modern army. It is one of the good examples of organization. This organization is good only because it is *flexible* and is able at the same time to give to millions of people a *single will*. Today these millions are living in their homes in various parts of the country; tomorrow a call for mobilization is issued, and they gather at the appointed centres. Today they lie in the trenches, sometimes for months at a stretch; tomorrow they are led to the attack in another formation. One day they perform miracles hiding from bullets and shrapnel; tomorrow they perform miracles in open combat. Today their forward detachments lay mines under the earth; tomorrow they move forward scores of miles, according to the advice of flyers above the earth. When, in the pursuit of a single aim, animated by a single will, millions change the forms of their intercourse and their actions, change the place and the method of their activities, change their tools and weapons in accordance with changing conditions and the requirements of the struggle—this is organization.

The same holds true of the working-class struggle against the bourgeoisie. Today there is no revolutionary situation. . . .

"But what do you mean by 'situation'?" Chubov interrupted.

Bunchuk stared at him as though he had only just been awakened from sleep, and rubbed his prominent forehead with his thumb knuckle, trying to grasp the question.

"I asked, what do you mean by 'situation'?"

"I understood all right, but it's difficult for me to explain." Bunchuk smiled a simple, child-like smile. It was strange to see it on his big, moody face. It was as though a young silver hare had skipped across an autumnal, rain-swept field. "A situation is a position, a combination of circumstances. Am I right?"

Listnitsky shook his head vaguely. "Read on."

Today there is no revolutionary situation, the conditions that cause ferment among the masses or heighten their activities do not exist; today you are given a ballot paper —take it. Learn to organize in order to be able to use it as a weapon against your enemies and not as a means of getting soft parliamentary jobs for men who cling to their seats in fear of having to go to prison. Next day the ballot paper is taken from you, and you are given a rifle and a splendid quick-firing gun constructed according to the last word of engineering technique—take this weapon of death and destruction, pay no heed to the sentimental snivelers who are afraid of war; too much has been left in the world that *must* be destroyed by fire and iron in order that the emancipation of the working class may be achieved; and if anger and desperation grow among the masses, if a revolutionary situation arises, prepare to create new organizations and *utilize* these useful weapons of death and destruction *against your own* government and *your own* bourgeoisie. . . ."

Bunchuk was interrupted by a knock and the entry of the sergeant-major of the Fifth Squadron.

"Your Honour," he turned to Kalmykov, "an orderly from the regimental staff."

Kalmykov and Chubov threw on their great-coats and went out. Merkulov sat down to draw. Listnitsky continued his pacing up and down the dug-out, fingering his moustache and deep in thought. Shortly afterwards Bunchuk also took his departure. He made his way through the slippery mud of the trenches, his left hand holding the edges of his collar to-gether, his right keeping down his greatcoat. The wind streamed along the narrow trench, cling-ing to the ledges, whistling and eddying. His face wore a vague smile. When he reached his dug-out he was again wet through with the rain, and smelling of decaying alder-leaves. The commander of the machine-gun detachment was asleep, his swarthy face still showing the traces of three sleepless nights spent at cards. Bunchuk rummaged in the kit-bag he had kept since the days of his service as a private, ar-ranged a pile of papers close to the door, and set fire to them. He put two tins of meat and sev-eral handfuls of revolver bullets into his pock-ets, then went out again. The wind caught at the momentarily opened door, sent the grey ash of the burnt papers flying, and blew out the smok-ing lamp.

After Bunchuk's departure Listnitsky strode up and down for some time in silence, then went across to the table. Merkulov was still drawing, and from under his pencil-point the face of Bunchuk, wearing his customary dry smile, was beginning to stare from the white square of paper.

"He's got a strong face!" Merkulov remarked, turning to Listnitsky.

"Well, what do you think?" Yevgeny asked.

"The devil knows!" Merkulov replied, guessing the significance of the question. "He's a strange fellow. He's given himself away completely now, but previously I didn't know how to decipher him. You know he enjoys tremendous popularity with the Cossacks, especially among the machine-gunners. Have you noticed that?"

"M'yes," Listnitsky answered, a little indefinitely.

"The machine-gunners are Bolsheviks to the last man. He's certainly succeeded in winning them over. I was astonished when he showed his hand today. What did he do it for? He knows that none of us can share his views. Yet he gives himself away like that. And he isn't a hothead either. He's dangerous."

Still pondering on Bunchuk's strange behaviour, Merkulov pushed away his drawing and began to undress. He hung his wet stockings over the stove, wound up his watch, and lay down, smoking a cigarette. He quickly fell asleep. Listnitsky sat down on the stool Merkulov had vacated, and on the other side of the drawing of Bunchuk wrote in his flowing hand:

"Your Excellency,

"The suppositions which I previously communicated to you have now been completely confirmed. In a talk today with the officers of our regiment (in addition to myself, Captain Kalmykov and Lieutenant Chubov of the Fifth, and Junior Captain Merkulov of the Third Squadron were present) Cornet Bunchuk, for reasons which I have to admit I do not fully understand, explained the tasks which he is carrying out in accordance with his political convictions, and undoubtedly on the instructions of his party. He had with him a number of papers of an illegal nature. For instance, he read us an extract from the illegal paper *Communist* printed in Geneva. Without doubt Cornet Bunchuk is carrying on underground activities in our regiment (we may suppose that this is why he joined the regiment as a volunteer) and the machine-gunners have been the first object of his attentions. They have been demoralized. His dangerous influence is beginning to tell on the morale of the regiment. There have been cases of refusal to carry out orders, as I have already informed the special department.

"He has only just returned from leave (in Petrograd), bringing back with him a large quantity of subversive literature. He will now endeavour to carry on his work with greater intensity.

"On the basis of the foregoing I have come to the conclusion: 1. That Cornet Bunchuk's guilt is fully established (the officers present during the conversation will confirm my words under oath). 2. In order to stop his revolutionary activities it is necessary to arrest him immediately and bring him before a field court martial. 3. The machine-gun detachment must be broken up immediately, the more dangerous being removed and the others either sent to the rear or scattered through other regiments.

"I beg to assure you of my sincere desire to serve my country and the monarchy. I have sent a copy of this letter to S. T. Korp.

"Captain Yevgeny Listnitsky

"Sector No. 7. October 20, 1916."

Early next morning Listnitsky sent his report by orderly to the divisional staff, and after breakfast went out into the trenches. Beyond the slippery parapet of the trench a mist hovered over the marsh, hanging in shreds as though caught on the barbs of the wire entanglements. The bottom of the trench was covered with an inch-thick layer of liquid mud. Little brown streams trickled out of the embrasures. The Cossacks, in wet, mud-plastered greatcoats, were boiling pots of tea on sheet-iron from the parapet, smoking and squatting on their heels, their rifles propped against the walls of the trench.

"How many times have you been told not to light fires on the sheet-iron? Don't you understand, you swine?" Listnitsky shouted as he came up to the first group of Cossacks.

Two of them rose unwillingly; the others continued to squat and smoke, the edges of their greatcoats gathered up under them. A swarthy, bearded Cossack, with a silver earring dangling from his ear, replied as he thrust a handful of brushwood under the pot:

"We'd be very glad to do without the sheet-iron. But how are we to light a fire otherwise, Your Honour? Look at the mud."

"Pull that iron out at once!"

"What, are we to sit here hungry? Is that it?" a Cossack with a broad pock-marked face asked, frowning and not looking up at the officer.

"I tell you to pull that iron out!" With the toe of his boot Yevgeny kicked away the burning brushwood from under the pot.

Smiling angrily and confusedly, the bearded Cossack poured the water out of the pot, muttering:

"You've had your tea, boys. . . ."

The Cossacks stared silently after the captain as he strode off. Tiny flames gleamed in the bearded Cossack's eyes.

"The haughty bastard!"

Another Cossack gave a long sigh and slung his rifle on his shoulder.

In the sector manned by the First Troop Listnitsky was overtaken by Merkulov. He came up panting heavily, his new leather jerkin creaking; his breath reeked of home-grown tobacco. He called Yevgeny aside and said hurriedly:

"Heard the news? Bunchuk deserted last night."

"Bunchuk? Wha-at?"

"Deserted. . . . Understand? The commander of the machine-gun detachment, who is in the same dug-out, told me he didn't return after leaving us. So he must have cleared out as soon as he left our dug-out. What d'you think of that?"

Listnitsky stood polishing his pince-nez and frowning.

"You seem to be disturbed." Merkulov stared inquisitively into his face.

"I? Are you out of your senses? Why should I be disturbed? I was only taken aback by the unexpected news."

II

The next morning the sergeant-major came into Listnitsky's dug-out with a worried look on his face, and after much humming and hawing, informed him:

"This morning, Your Honour, the Cossacks found these papers in the trenches. It's a bit awkward. . . . And I thought it best to report to you. . . ."

"What papers?" Listnitsky asked, rising from his bunk.

The sergeant-major handed him some crumpled type-written leaflets. Listnitsky read:

WORKERS OF ALL COUNTRIES, UNITE!

Comrade Soldiers,

Two years this accursed war has lasted. Two years you have rotted in the trenches, defending other men's interests. Two years the blood of the workers and peasants of all nations has been poured out. Hundreds of thousands of killed and wounded, hundreds of thousands of widows and orphans: these are the results of this slaughter. What are you fighting for? Whose interests are you defending? The tsarist government has sent millions of soldiers into the firing line in order to seize new lands, and to oppress the peoples of those lands as it already oppresses enslaved Poland and other nationalities. The world industrialists will not share the markets where they could dispose of the output of their plants and factories, will not share the profits; instead they are dividing the markets by armed force, and you, ignorant people, in the struggle for their interests, are going to your death, and are killing toiling men like yourselves.

Enough of shedding your brothers' blood! Awake, toilers! Your enemy is not the Austrian and German soldiers, just as deluded as you, but your own tsar, your own industrialist and landowner. Turn your rifles against them. Fraternize with the German and Austrian soldiers. Across the wire entanglements which separate you as though you were animals stretch out your hands to one another. You are brothers in labour, the bloody calluses of toil are still on your hands; you have nothing to divide. Down with the autocracy! Down with imperialist war! Hurrah for the unity of the toilers of the whole world!

Listnitsky read the leaflet with rising anger. "Now it's begun!" he thought, gripped by a senseless hatred and overwhelmed with his presentiments. He at once communicated the discovery by telephone to the regimental commander.

"What are your instructions in the matter, Your Excellency?" he asked.

"Take the sergeant-major and the troop officers and carry out an extensive search at once. Search everybody, not excluding the officers. I'll ask the divisional staff today when they propose to relieve the regiment. I'll hurry them up. If you find anything in the course of the search inform me at once."

"I think it's the work of the machine-gunners."

"You do? I'll order the commander at once to search his Cossacks."

Assembling the troop officers in his dug-out, Listnitsky informed them of the regimental commander's order.

"How monstrous!" Merkulov exclaimed indignantly. "Are we to search one another?"

"Your turn first, Listnitsky," a young lieutenant remarked.

"No, we'll throw dice for it."

"Alphabetically."

"Joking aside, gentlemen," Listnitsky interrupted. "The old man has gone too far, of course; the officers in our regiment are as pure as Caesar's wife. There was only Cornet Bunchuk, and he's deserted. But we must search the Cossacks. Someone fetch the sergeant-major."

The sergeant-major, an elderly Cossack with three Crosses of St. George, entered. He coughed and glanced from one to another of the officers.

"Who are the suspicious characters in the company? Who do you think could have left these leaflets about?" Yevgeny demanded.

"There are none in our company, Your Excellency," the man replied confidently.

"But the leaflets were found in our sector. Have any men from another company been in our trenches?"

"No, sir."

"We'll go and search every man." Merkulov waved his hand and turned towards the door.

The search began. The Cossacks' faces expressed every shade of feeling. Some frowned in amazement, others looked at the officers in alarm, yet others laughed as the officers rummaged in their miserable belongings.

"What are you looking for? Has something been stolen? Perhaps we've seen it somewhere," a smart-looking sergeant remarked.

The search yielded almost no results. Only one Cossack had a crumpled copy of the leaflet in his greatcoat pocket.

"Have you read this?" Merkulov demanded.

"I picked it up for a smoke," the Cossack smiled without raising his downcast eyes.

"What are you grinning at?" Listnitsky shouted furiously, turning livid and striding towards the man. His short golden eye-lashes blinked nervously under his pince-nez.

The Cossack's face became serious, and the smile vanished as though swept away by the wind.

"Excuse me, Your Honour. I can hardly read. I picked it up because I have no paper for cigarettes, and I saw this lying about, so I picked it up." The man spoke in a loud, aggrieved, almost angry tone.

Listnitsky spat and turned away, the other officers trailing after him.

The next day the regiment was withdrawn and stationed some ten versts behind the front line. Two men of the machine-gun detachment were arrested and court-martialled, some of the others were transferred to reserve regiments, and some sent to other regiments of the Second Cossack Division. After a few days' rest the regiment was brought into comparatively good order. The Cossacks washed and cleaned themselves up thoroughly, and even shaved. Nor did they have to resort to the method used in the trenches, which consisted of setting fire to the hair on the face, and as soon as the flame began to burn the cheek, passing a wet towel over it and wiping off the burnt hair. This method had come to be called "singeing the pig," since the time when a troop barber had asked one of his clients: "Shall I singe you like a pig, or how?"

The regiment rested, and the Cossacks outwardly seemed light-hearted and in splendid fettle. But Listnitsky and the other officers knew that the mood was only superficial and fleeting, like a fine day in November. As soon as any rumour of a return to the front ran through the regiment the expressions changed, and discontent, strain, and morose unfriendliness rose uppermost. The mortal weariness and strain made themselves felt and engendered moral instability and apathy. Listnitsky knew well how terrible a man can be when, dominated by such a mood, he struggles to some purpose.

In 1915 he had seen a company of soldiers sent five times into attack, suffering terrible losses and still receiving again and again the command to renew the offensive. The remnants of the company at last arbitrarily withdrew from the sector and marched towards the rear. Listnitsky's squadron had been ordered to stop them, and when, spreading out in a line, the Cossacks attempted to halt the movement, the soldiers opened fire. Not more than sixty of them were left, and Listnitsky had noted the senselessly desperate bravery with which these sixty defended themselves, falling under the

Cossacks' sabres, marching on to death, to destruction, resolved that it mattered not where death came to them.

The incident now came to him as a formidable reminder, and Listnitsky anxiously studied the Cossacks' faces anew, wondering whether they, too, would turn round one day and retreat, restrained by nothing but death. And as he noticed their tired, sullen glances he had to admit that they would.

The Cossacks had changed radically since the early days of the war. Even their songs were new, born of the war, and expressing a sombre joylessness. As he passed by the spacious shed of the factory in which his squadron was quartered he most frequently heard one yearning, indescribably mournful song. Listnitsky would stop to listen, and the simple sorrow of the song would move him strongly. A string was tautened with the increasing beat of his heart, and the low timbre of the voice plucked the string, setting it vibrating painfully. Listnitsky would stand a little way off, staring into the autumnal gloom of the evening, and feel his eyes moisten with tears.

Only once during the whole time the regiment was resting did Listnitsky hear the brave words of an old Cossack song. He was returning from his usual evening stroll, and as he passed the shed noisy laughter and the sound of half-drunken voices reached his ears. He guessed that the quartermaster-sergeant, who had been to the neighbouring town for provisions, had brought back some illicit spirits and had treated the Cossacks. And now they were quarrelling and laughing at something or other. He heard their wild and piercing whistle and the strong melody of the song when still some way off. A long vibrating whistle spiralled upwards and was smothered in a roar of at least thirty voices. One of the youngsters evidently was dancing on the wooden duckboards and letting out short ear-splitting whistles. The clatter of his heels was drowned by the singing.

Listnitsky involuntarily smiled, and tried to bring his steps into time with the rhythm. "I don't think the infantry yearn for home so strongly as the Cossacks," he thought; but cold reason objected that the infantryman was no different. Yet undoubtedly the Cossacks reacted more painfully to the enforced sitting in the trenches, for the very nature of their service had accustomed them to constant movement. And for two years they had been engaged in trench warfare, or marking time in fruitless attempts to advance. The army was weaker than ever before. What it needed was a strong hand, some resounding success, a big stride forward that would shake it up. Of course, there had been periods in history, periods of long and protracted war, when the morale of the most reliable and well-disciplined troops had been known to falter. Suvorov, even he had experienced.... But the Cossacks would hold out; even if they did break down, they would be the last to do so. They were a little nation in themselves, war-like by tradition, and not factory or muzhik riffraff.

As though deliberately to undeceive him, a strained voice began to sing another song. Other Cossacks took it up, and once more Listnitsky heard the Cossacks' yearning translated into song.

> The young officer prays to God.
> The young Cossack asks to go home.
> "Oh, young officer,
> Let me go home,
> Let me go home
> To my father and mother,
> To my father and mother,
> And to my young wife."

On the fourth evening after he had deserted, Bunchuk came to a large merchant town situated in the front-line area. Lights were already gleaming in the windows. Frost had coated the puddles with a fine crust of ice and the footsteps of occasional passers-by could be heard from afar. Bunchuk listened alertly as he made his way through the back-streets, avoiding the lighted thoroughfares. On entering the town he had nearly run into a patrol and now he proceeded with wolf-like caution, sidling along by the fences and keeping his right hand in the pocket of his unbelievably filthy greatcoat—the result of a day spent lying buried in a chaff heap.

An army corps was based in the town; several units were quartered there and, knowing that he was in constant danger of running into a patrol, Bunchuk never relaxed his grip on the serrated butt of the revolver he carried in his greatcoat pocket.

On the other side of the town Bunchuk paced up and down a deserted side-street, glancing into gateways and studying the outlines of every mean dwelling. After about twenty minutes he approached a small shabby house on a corner, peeped through a chink in the shutters and, smiling to himself, resolutely entered the gate. His knock was answered by an elderly woman in a shawl.

"Does Boris Ivanovich live here?"

"Yes. Come in, please."

Bunchuk edged past her into the corridor. The latch clanked coldly behind him. In a low-ceilinged room lighted by a small oil-lamp an elderly man in military uniform was seated at a table. He rose, peering in the dim light, and held out his arms to Bunchuk with restrained joy.

"Where have you come from?"

"The front."

"Well?"

Bunchuk hesitated, then smiled, and touching the other's army belt with his finger-tip, said softly: "Have you a room?"

"Yes, indeed. Come in here."

He led Bunchuk into an even smaller room, gave him a chair in the darkness and, after closing the door into the next room, drew a curtain over the window and said:

"Are you through?"

"Yes."

"How are things out there?"

"All ready."

"Reliable fellows?"

"Very."

"You had better take your things off, then we'll have a talk. Let me have your greatcoat. I'll bring you something to wash in."

While Bunchuk was washing over a greenish copper bowl, the man in uniform stroked his short-clipped hair and spoke in a quiet tired voice:

"At present they are far stronger than we are. We have got to grow, to spread our influence, to work without pause explaining the true causes of the war. And we are growing. You can be sure of that. Everything they lose comes over inevitably to us. A mature man is unquestionably stronger than a boy, but when he grows old and flabby, the lad can make short work of him. And in this case we are dealing not only with the flabbiness of old age, but with a progressive paralysis of the whole organism."

Bunchuk finished washing and, as he wiped his face on a rough towel, he said:

"Before I left, I told those officers my opinions. It was rather funny, you know.... They will certainly shake up the machine-gunners, one or two of the lads may even get a court martial, but there's no evidence, so what can they say? I hope they will scatter them into different units; that will play into our hands. Let them sow the seed for us. There are some fine chaps there. Hard as flint!"

"I have had a note from Stepan. He's asking for someone who understands military matters. You'll go, but what about papers? Will you manage it?"

"What's the job?" Bunchuk asked and stood on tiptoe to hang the towel on a nail.

"Instructor for the lads." His host smiled. "Don't you grow at all?"

"No need to," Bunchuk retorted. "Specially for a man in my position. I ought to be the size of a pea-pod so as not to be noticed."

They talked until the sky greyed in the east. A day later, Bunchuk, his looks changed beyond recognition by fresh clothes and make-up, with a set of papers bearing the name of private 441 of the Orshansky Regiment Nikolai Ukhvatov, invalided out of the army owing to a wound in the chest, walked out of town in the direction of the station.

III

The area from Vladimir-Volhynsky to Kovel in Volhynia was held by the Special Army. The "Special Army" was really Number Thirteen, but as even generals of high rank suffered from superstitious prejudices it was called the "Special Army." During the last days of September, 1916, plans were made for an advance in this area, and the way was prepared with artillery operations.

An unusually heavy force of artillery was concentrated in the area. For nine days hundreds of thousands of shells of various calibre pounded the zone held by two lines of German trenches. On the very first day of the bombardment, as soon as the shelling became intense, the Germans withdrew from their first line, leaving no one behind except the observers. A few days later they abandoned their second line and retired to a third.

On the tenth day units of the Turkestan Rifle Corps started to advance. They adopted the French method of attacking in waves. Sixteen waves splashed out of the Russian trenches. Swirling and thinning, boiling up round ghastly heaps of shattered barbed wire, the grey human tide rolled forward. And from the German side, from behind the charred stumps of alder-trees and hillocks of sand came a crackling, blazing, continuous roar of firing. Occasionally the crash of a battery broke through the din, then everything was drowned in a solid wave of sound, accompanied by the furious chattering undertone of the German machine-gun fire.

Over an area about a mile wide the mutilated sandy earth was lashed into a whirlwind of black explosions, and the attacking waves broke, foamed, splashed out of the shell-craters and crawled onwards.

Faster and faster came the black spurts of bursting shells, the rending whine of shrapnel rose to a crescendo, and the machine-gun fire slashed the earth with increasing intensity. The attacking troops were mown down even before they reached the wire. Only the last three waves out of the whole sixteen got as far as the entanglements and no sooner did they reach the mangled barrier of twisted wire and scorched posts than they broke against it and fell back in streams and trickles.

Over nine thousand lives were splashed out that day on the grim sandy soil near the village of Svinukhi.

Two hours later the attack was renewed. Units of the 2nd and 3rd divisions of the Turkestan Rifle Corps advanced. On the left flank, units of the 53rd Infantry Division and the 307th Siberian Rifle Brigade filed along the communication trenches; on the right moved battalions of the 3rd Grenadier Division.

The commander of the 30th Army Corps of the Special Army, Lieutenant-General Gavrilov, received orders from staff headquarters to transfer another two divisions to the area. In the night, the 320th Chembarsky, the 319th Bugulma and the 318th Chernoyarsk regiments of the 80th Division were withdrawn from their positions and replaced by Latvian infantry and fresh units of local volunteers. Although the operation took place at night, the previous evening one of the regiments had been demonstratively moved in the opposite direction and only when it had marched a distance of twelve versts along the line of the front did it receive the order to turn back. The regiments marched in the same direction but by different routes.

Before being transferred, the 318th Chernoyarsk Regiment had been stationed at a small town on the river Stokhod. In the morning, after the first march, the regiment was distributed through a forest in abandoned dugouts, and here for four days they were instructed in the French method of attack, advancing in half-companies instead of battalions. The grenadiers were taught to cut barbed wire with the greatest possible speed and received additional practice in throwing hand grenades. Then they marched on again. For three days they passed through forests, through glades, along wild woodland paths scarred with the marks of cannon wheels. A light, patchy mist, stirred by the wind, clung to the tops of the pines, flowed through the clearings and hovered like a kite over the blue-green of the steaming marshes. A drizzling rain fell continually, and the men were wet through and sullen. They reached a village not far from the zone of the offensive, and rested for a day, preparing for the mortal journey.

At the same time a special Cossack squadron,

accompanying the staff of the 80th Division, was moving towards the scene of the battle. In the squadron were third-reserve Cossacks from Tatarsky village, and the Second Troop was entirely composed of them. There were the two brothers of one-armed Alexei Shamil, the former mill engine-man Ivan Alexeyevich, Afonka Ozerov, the former ataman Manitskov, Gavrila Likhovidov, the life and soul of the squadron, and many others. Likhovidov was a wild-looking Cossack, famous for the way he unprotestingly endured the beatings he frequently received from his seventy-year-old mother and his wife, a woman of no great beauty but of indomitable temper.

Early on the morning of October 3rd the squadron entered a village just as the First Battalion of the Chernoyarsk Regiment was preparing to march out. The soldiers were running out of the abandoned, half-ruined huts and lining up in the street.

A small dark-skinned corporal was standing near the leading platoon. He was taking chocolate out of his map-case and unwrapping it. The corners of his rosy lips were smeared with chocolate. As he walked down the line his long mud-caked greatcoat dangled between his legs like a sheep's tail. The Cossacks came down the left side of the street. Ivan Alexeyevich, the engine-man, was on the outside file in one of the ranks of the Second Troop. He was marching with his eyes fixed on the ground, trying to avoid the puddles. Someone called to him from the ranks of the infantry, and he turned his head and passed his eyes over the soldiers.

"Ivan Alexeyevich! Old friend. . . ."

A little soldier broke away from his platoon and came running awkwardly towards him, throwing his rifle back over his shoulder. But the sling slipped and the butt jangled against his mess tin.

"Don't you know me? Forgotten me already?"

With difficulty Ivan Alexeyevich recognized the little soldier, whose mouth and chin were covered with a bristling, smoky-grey beard, as Knave.

"Where've you sprung from?"

"I'm in this regiment, the 318th Chernoyarsk. I never expected to meet any of my old friends here."

Still gripping Knave's dirty little hand in his own bony fist, Ivan Alexeyevich smiled gladly and with emotion. Knave, hurrying to keep up with his long stride, began to trot, looking up into Ivan's eyes, while the gaze of his own close-set embittered little eyes was unusually tender and moist,

"We're going into an attack...."

"And so are we."

"Well, how are you getting on, Ivan Alexeyevich?"

"There's nothing to tell."

"The same here. I haven't been out of the trenches since 1914. Never had a home or family of my own, but I've got to fight for someone."

"D'you remember Stockman? He was a good fellow, our Osip Davidovich! He'd tell us what it was all about. He was a man, if ever there was one...."

"Do I remember him!" Knave cried, shaking his tiny fist and crinkling his little bristly face into a smile. "I remember him better than my own father. Never had much use for my father. You never heard how he got on, did you?"

"He's in Siberia," Ivan Alexeyevich sighed.

"What?" Knave asked, bobbing up and down beside his tall friend, and cocking his foxy ear.

"He's in prison. For all I know he may be dead now."

Knave walked along without speaking for a moment or two, now looking back to where his company was assembling, now gazing up at Ivan's stern chin and the deep round dimple right under the lower lip.

"Good-bye!" he said, releasing his hand from Ivan's. "I don't suppose we'll be seeing each other again."

With his left hand the Cossack removed his cap, and bending down, he put his arm round Knave's stringy shoulders. They kissed each other firmly, as though saying good-bye for ever, and Knave dropped back. His head suddenly sank on his breast, so that only the dark rosy tips of his ears emerged from his grey greatcoat. He turned back, huddled up and stumbling over his feet.

Ivan Alexeyevich broke away from the rank, and called with a quiver in his voice:

"Hey, brother! Brother! You were bitter, weren't you! D'you remember? You were a strong one ... eh?"

Knave turned his tear-stained face, and beat his fist on his bony breast through his open greatcoat and torn shirt.

"I was! I was hard! But they've crushed me now.... They've driven the old horse to death!"

He shouted something else, but the Cossack squadron turned into a side-street, and Ivan lost sight of him.

"That was Knave, wasn't it?" asked Prokhor Shamil who was marching behind.

"That was a man," Ivan Alexeyevich replied

heavily and his lips trembled as he tugged at his rifle sling.

As the Cossacks marched out of the village they began to fall in with wounded, at first in ones and twos, then in groups of several at a time, and finally in crowds. Several carts filled to overflowing with serious cases dragged slowly along. The nags pulling at the traces were terribly emaciated. Their skinny backs bore the marks of incessant whipping, and in places the bones showed through the wounds. They hauled the carts with difficulty, snorting and straining, their foam-crusted muzzles almost touching the mud. Occasionally one would stop, her sunken flanks heaving impotently and her head hanging despondently. A blow of a whip would stir her from the spot, and she would drag on again, swaying from side to side. All round the carts wounded men were clinging, dragging themselves along.

"What regiment are you from?" the squadron commander asked a soldier who looked more amiable than the others.

"Turkestan Corps, 3rd Division."

"Wounded today?"

The soldier turned away without answering.

The Cossack squadron turned off the road and entered the forest. The infantry companies of the 318th Chernoyarsk had left the village and were trudging up behind them. In the distance, against the hazy washed-out sky hung the yellowish-grey blob of a German balloon.

"Look, lads, there's a marvel for you!"

"Like a sausage."

"That's where he's watching the movements of our troops from, the bastard."

"Did you think he got up so high for nothing?"

"Whew, what a height!"

"Even a shell wouldn't reach him."

In the forest the first infantry company overtook the Cossacks. Until evening they were huddled together under the streaming pines. The rain leaked under their collars and wandered down their backs; they were forbidden to light fires, but in any case it would have been difficult to do so in the rain. As dusk was falling they were led off into a communication trench. Not very deep, hardly more than a man's height, it was flooded with water and smelled of slime, of sodden pine-cones and the velvet-soft scent of rain.

The Cossacks with the skirts of their greatcoats gathered up were squatting on their haunches, smoking and keeping up a grey ragged thread of conversation. The Second Troop shared out the ration of tobacco they had received before leaving and bunched together round their troop sergeant. He was sitting on an abandoned drum of wire, talking about General Kopylovsky, killed the Monday before, in whose brigade he had served during peacetime. He did not have time to finish his story for the troop commander gave an order and the Cossacks jumped up drawing greedily at their cigarettes for a last smoke even at the cost of burning their fingers. From the trench the squadron was led on again through the darkening pine forest. They marched along endeavouring to encourage one another with jest. Someone began to whistle.

In a small glade they came upon a long row of corpses. The bodies lay flung down shoulder to shoulder, in various, frequently horrible and indecent postures. A soldier armed with a rifle, a gas-mask hanging from his belt, stood guard over them. The damp earth had been churned by hundreds of boots and cart wheels. The Cossacks passed close to the bodies, and they caught the heavy, cloying odour of decay already coming from them. The squadron commander halted the squadron, went with the troop officers up to the soldier, and stood talking to him for a minute or two. Meanwhile the Cossacks broke rank and went over to the bodies, removing their caps and staring down at the figures with that feeling of secret, fluttering fear and curiosity which all living beings experience before the mystery of the dead. The bodies were those of officers, and the Cossacks counted forty-seven of them. The majority were youngsters between twenty and twenty-five years of age, judging by their looks. Only the one on the extreme right, who was wearing the epaulettes of a captain, was elderly. His mouth was wide open, concealing the mute echoes of his last cry in its depths; above it hung heavy black whiskers; the broad brows frowned across his deathly pallid face. Some of the dead wore dirt-bespattered leather jerkins, others greatcoats. Two were bare-headed. The Cossacks stared long at the figure of one lieutenant, handsome even in death. He lay on his back, his left arm pressed against his chest, his right flung out and holding a pistol in an everlasting grip. Evidently someone had tried to take the weapon away—his broad yellow wrist was scratched—but the steel had fused to his hand, and they would never be separated. His cap was pushed back on his curly flaxen hair. His face was pressed cheek downward to the earth, as though fondling it, and his orange-bluish lips were sadly, amazedly twisted. His right-hand neighbour lay face downward, his greatcoat hummocked on his back, its backstrap torn away, revealing strong legs with tautened muscles in khaki-coloured trousers and short chrome-leather boots, the heels twisted to one side. He had no cap, nor had he the upper part of his cranium, for it had been cut clean away by a shard of shrapnel. In the empty brain-pan, framed by damp strands of hair, glimmered rose-coloured rain-water. Next to him lay a stout little officer in an open leather jerkin and a torn tunic. His lower jaw rested crookedly on his bare breast; below the hair of his head glimmered a narrow white band of forehead with the skin burned and shrivelled into little tubes. Between the brow and the jaw were merely pieces of bone and a thick black and crimson mash. Beyond these were carelessly gathered pieces of limbs, and the rags of a greatcoat. A crushed leg where the head should have been. Then came a mere youngster with full lips and a childish oval face. A stream of machine-gun bullets had swept across his chest, his greatcoat was holed in four places, and burnt scraps of cotton were sticking through the holes.

"Who ... who was he calling for in his hour of death? His mother?" Ivan Alexeyevich stuttered with chattering teeth, and turned sharply away, stumbling as though blind.

The Cossacks hurriedly returned to their places, crossing themselves and not glancing back. They preserved a long silence as they passed on through the narrow glades, hastening to get away from the memory of what they had seen. After some time the squadron was halted close to a dense network of abandoned dugouts. The officers entered one of the dug-outs with a messenger who had ridden up from the Chernoyarsk Regiment.

Afonka Ozerov gripped Ivan's arm and whispered: "That lad ... the last one ... never even kissed a girl in his life, I reckon. ... And they killed him. What d'you think of that?"

"Where did they get shot up like that?" another Cossack interrupted.

"They were in the attack. The soldier who was guarding them told me," said another, after a pause.

The men stood at ease. Darkness closed over the forest. The wind sent the clouds scurrying, and tore them apart to reveal the lilac points of the distant stars.

Meantime the commander assembled the officers in the dug-out, dismissed the messenger, and opening the packet by the light of a candle stump, read its contents.

At dawn on October 3rd the Germans used asphyxiating gases against the Third Battalion of the 256th Regiment and captured our first line of trenches. I order you to move up to the second line of trenches and, after making contact with the First Battalion of the 318th Chernoyarsk Regiment, to take up your positions in the line and prepare to counter-attack the enemy and drive him out of the first line this very night. On your right flank you will have two companies of the Second Battalion and a battalion of the Fanagoriisk Regiment of the 3rd Grenadier Division.

The officers discussed the situation and smoked. Then the squadron moved on.

While the Cossacks were resting by the dugouts, the First Battalion of the Chernoyarsk Regiment went on ahead. They reached the bridge over the river Stokhod. It was guarded by a strong machine-gun section from the grenadiers. The sergeant-major explained the situation to the battalion commander and the battalion split up into companies after crossing the bridge: two companies moved off to the right, one to the left, and the fourth remained in reserve. The companies advanced in extended line. The dense forest was heavily holed with shells. The men trod cautiously, feeling the path with their feet; occasionally someone would fall and curse under his breath. Knave was in the company on the extreme right, and was sixth from the end of the long file.

Two officers walked past him, talking in subdued tones. The rich mellow baritone of the company commander was complaining:

"My old wound has opened again. Damn that stump. I stumbled over it in the dark, now the wound has burst open and I can't walk. I'm afraid I'll have to go back." The baritone was silent for a moment and then was heard again, softer and softer in the distance: "You take over the command of the First Half-Company. Bogdanov will take the Second, and I ... honest to God, I can't go on. I'll have to return...."

Ensign Belikov's hoarse tenor snapped back at him:

"It's amazing how your old wounds seem to open every time a battle's in the offing!"

"How dare you speak like that, ensign!" the company commander raised his voice.

"Oh, drop it. You can go if you like."

Listening to his own footsteps and to those of the others, Knave heard the crackle of brushwood behind him and understood that the company commander was making for the rear. A minute later he heard Belikov mutter as he went over to the left flank of the company with the sergeant-major:

"They smell it, the scoundrels! As soon as there's fighting they're sick or their old wounds open. And you, a half-baked subaltern, have to take over the command.... The blackguards! I'd just like to ... soldiers...."

The voices broke off suddenly and Knave could hear only the squelch of his own footsteps and a shrill ringing in his ears.

"Hey! Neighbour!" someone suddenly whispered to the left of him.

"What?"

"Going all right?"

"All right!" Knave said, immediately stumbling and sliding back into a shell-hole filled with water.

"It's dark, damn it!" he heard on his left.

They went on for a minute or two, invisible to each other, then unexpectedly the same hissing voice whispered right into Knave's ear:

"Let's go together. It isn't so bad then...."

They went on in silence, setting their waterlogged boots cautiously down on the slippery earth. Suddenly, a horned and spotted moon broke from behind the clouds, breasting the misty waves like a boat; emerging into clear sky, it poured down a flood of uncertain light. The damp pine needles gleamed phosphorescently in its light, and the cones seemed to smell more strongly and the wet soil to breathe a sharper cold.

Knave glanced at his neighbour, who had stopped suddenly and was shaking his head as if from a blow.

"Look!" he breathed.

Three paces away from them under a pine-tree, his legs planted wide apart, stood a man.

"A man!" It was Knave who muttered the words or, at least, thought he did.

"Who's there?" his companion shouted, suddenly flinging his rifle to his shoulder. "Who's there? I'll fire!"

The figure under the pine was silent. His head hung sideways, like a sunflower on its stalk.

"He's asleep!" Knave shuddered and, forcing himself to laugh, stepped forward.

They went up to the standing figure. Knave stretched up and stared. His companion poked the motionless grey figure with his rifle-butt.

"Hey, you, dopey! Having a sleep, mate?" he said mockingly. "Hey, dopey!" His voice broke off. "A corpse!" he cried, backing away.

His teeth chattering, Knave jumped back and the next moment the figure collapsed like a fallen tree on the spot where he had been standing. They turned the body face upwards and only then did they realize that the pine-tree had provided a last refuge for this gas-poisoned soldier of the 256th Regiment in his desperate flight from the death which he carried in his lungs. A tall, broad-shouldered fellow, he lay with his head thrown back, his face smeared with mud from his fall, the eyes pulpy and eaten away by gas; a swollen fleshy tongue stuck out between his teeth like a black lump of wood.

"Come on, for God's sake! Let him lie there!" Knave's companion whispered, grabbing his arm.

In a few paces more they came across another corpse, then another and another. In places the gassed soldiers lay in heaps; some had died sitting on their haunches, some were on all fours, like grazing animals, and at the entrance to the communication trench leading to the second line of trenches a man lay twisted into a ball, his gnawed fist thrust between his teeth in agony.

Knave and his companion ran to catch up with their file. But in the darkness they missed them and somehow got in front. After wandering on for some time they jumped down into a dark cleft of trenches zigzagging off into the darkness.

"Let's search the dug-outs. We may find something to eat," Knave's comrade proposed irresolutely.

"All right."

"You go to the right, I'll take the left. We'll search while the others are coming up."

Knave struck a match and stepped through the open doorway of the first dug-out he found.

But he flew out again as though propelled by a catapult; inside, two corpses lay crossed one on the other. He searched three dug-outs fruitlessly, and flung open the door of a fourth, all but collapsing as he heard a strange metallic voice speaking German:

"Who's that?"

His body tingling, Knave silently jumped back.

"Is that you, Otto? Why have you been so long?" the German asked, stepping out of the dug-out and carelessly adjusting his greatcoat across his shoulders.

"Hands up! Put 'em up! Surrender!" Knave shouted hoarsely, holding his rifle at the ready.

Mute with astonishment, the German slowly raised his hands, turned sideways, and stared fixedly at the gleaming point of the bayonet presented at him. His greatcoat fell from his shoulders, revealing his greyish-green tunic rumpled under the armpits, his big, work-scarred hands trembled above his head, and the fingers stirred as though touching invisible keys. Knave stood without changing his position, gazing at the tall, stalwart form of the German, the metal buttons of his tunic, the short boots, and the peakless cap set slightly on one side. Suddenly changing his attitude, he swayed as though being shaken out of his greatcoat, emitted a curt, throaty sound, neither cough nor wheeze, and stepped towards the German.

"Run!" he said in a hollow, broken voice. "Run, German! I've got no grudge against you! I won't shoot!"

He leaned his rifle against the wall of the trench, and rising on tiptoe, stretched his hand up to the right hand of the German. His confident movements reassured the man, who dropped his hand and listened intently to the unfamiliar intonation of the Russian voice.

Without hesitation Knave gave him his own calloused labour-worn hand, and squeezed the German's cold, limp fingers. Then he lifted the palm. The light of the moon fell on it and revealed the brown calluses.

"I'm a worker," Knave said, trembling as though he had the ague. "What should I kill you for? Run!" He gently pushed the German's shoulder and pointed to the black outline of the forest. "Run, you fool! Our men will be here soon...."

The German stood staring at Knave's outflung hand, his body a little forward, his ears straining to catch the sense of the incomprehensible words. So he stood for a second or two, his eyes meeting Knave's, then suddenly a joyous smile quivered on his lips. Stepping backwards a pace he threw out his arms, squeezed Knave's hands, and shook them, smiling agitatedly and staring into the Russian's eyes.

"You're letting me go? Oh, now I understand.... You're a Russian worker? A Social-Democrat like me? Yes...? It's like a dream. My brother, how can I ever forget...? I can't find words.... But you're a fine brave lad...."

Amid the boiling torrent of foreign words Knave caught the one familiar "Social-Democrat."

"Yes. I'm a Social-Democrat. You've guessed right. And now, run...! Good-bye, brother. Give me your hand."

Instinctively understanding each other, they stood looking into each other's eyes, the tall, well-knit Bavarian and the small Russian soldier. From the forest came the sounds of the approaching file of Russians. The German whispered:

"In the coming class struggle we'll be in the same trenches, won't we, Comrade?" Then he leapt like a grey animal on to the breastwork.

A moment or two later the file of Russian soldiers came up, a Czech reconnaissance party with their officers leading. They all but fired at Knave's companion as he crawled out of a dug-out.

"I'm Russian, can't you see?" he cried frantically, hugging a loaf of black bread to his breast, as he saw the barrel of a rifle pointed at him.

Recognizing Knave, the warrant officer jumped over the trench and jabbed him roughly in the back with his rifle-butt.

"I'll smash you. I'll bust your nose for you! Where have you been?"

Knave stirred limply; even the blow did not produce the desired effect. Staggering forward, he amazed the warrant officer by replying in a good-natured tone, quite unlike himself:

"We got ahead of you. Don't be so rough."

"And don't you muck about! Now you're behind, now you're in front. Don't you know orders? You're not a greenhorn, are you?" After a pause he asked: "Got any tobacco?"

"It's damp."

"Let's have some."

The warrant officer lighted up and went to the rear of the platoon.

Just before dawn the Czech reconnaissance party ran up against a German observation post. The Germans shattered the silence with a volley of shots. At equal intervals they fired two more volleys. A crimson flare over the trenches soared, and its purple sparks had hardly died away when the German artillery opened up. The sound of the exploding shells came from far behind the Russian forces, somewhere by the Stokhod river.

As soon as the first shot was fired, the company, moving up nearly a hundred paces behind the Czechs, threw itself down headlong. The flare shed a ruddy glow over the ground. By its light Knave saw the soldiers crawling like ants among the bushes and trees, no longer squeamish about the mud, but pressing against it in their search for protection. The men crawled into every rut, disappeared behind every tiny earthy mound, thrust their heads into every little hole. Nevertheless, when the stuttering machine-gun fire flooded wildly through the forest like a May downpour, they gave way. Their heads buried between their shoulders, clinging like caterpillars to the ground, moving without bending an arm or a leg, creeping like snakes and leaving traces in the mud behind them, they crawled back. Some jumped to their feet and ran. Lashing up the cones, splintering the pines, the dum-dum bullets skipped and tore through the forest, rending the earth, hissing like serpents.

Seventeen men were missing from the First Half-Company of the Chernoyarsk Regiment when it reached the second line of trenches again. A little way off, the Cossacks of the special squadron were also assembling. They had advanced on the right of the Chernoyarsk Half-Company, had moved cautiously, and might have taken the Germans by surprise, overwhelming the outposts. But when the latter opened fire on the Czechs, the Germans were put on the alert along the entire sector. Firing at random, the enemy had killed two Cossacks and wounded another.

The Cossacks carried back their wounded and dead, talking as they formed up:

"We ought to bury 'em."

"Someone else will do that."

"It's the living we ought to be worrying about, dead men don't need much."

Within half an hour a further order came from the regimental staff. After artillery preparation, the Chernoyarsk Regiment and the special Cossack squadron were again to attack the enemy and to drive him out of the first line of trenches.

The feeble artillery preparation lasted until noon. After posting sentries, the Cossacks and infantry rested in their dug-outs. At noon they began to advance. From the main sector on their left the boom of artillery announced a fresh attack. The Russians were advancing along the whole front.

The Cossacks moved forward in a dispersed

line that joined up on the left with the Cherno-yarsk Regiment. As soon as the ridge of breast-works appeared the Germans let loose a hurricane of fire. The squadron ran forward without shouting, dropped flat, emptied their rifles and ran on again. Fifty paces from the enemy trenches, they dropped down and stayed down. Now they were shooting without lifting their heads. The Germans had fixed wire netting along the whole length of the trenches. Two grenades thrown by Afonka Ozerov bounded off the wires. He raised him-self to throw another and a bullet hit him under the left shoulder and came out through the pelvis. Ivan Alexeyevich lying close by saw Afonka kick feebly, then lie still. Prokhor Shamil, brother of one-armed Alexei, was killed; the third to die was the former ataman Manitskov, and a moment later a bullet struck the Shamils' bow-legged neighbour Yevlanty Kalinin.

In half an hour the Second Troop lost eight men. The captain commanding the squadron was killed, two platoon officers fell, and de-prived of leadership, the Cossacks crawled back. When they got out of the firing zone, the Cossacks gathered in a bunch and found half their number missing. The Chernoyarsk men also withdrew. The First Battalion's losses were even heavier, but nevertheless a fresh order arrived from regiment headquarters: "Renew the attack at once, the enemy must be driven out of the first line of trenches at all costs. The success of the whole operation depends on our regaining our former position."

The squadron spread out in a thin line and advanced again. Under the Germans' murderous fire they dropped flat a hundred paces from the trenches. Again the troops began to dwindle and the fear-maddened men pressed themselves into the earth, not daring to move or lift their heads, stupefied with their horror of death.

Towards evening the Second Half-Company of the Chernoyarsk Regiment crumpled up and ran. The shout of "we're cut off!" reached the Cossacks. They got up and stumbled back, breaking through the bushes, falling, and dropping their weapons. After running to safety, Ivan Alexeyevich slumped down under a shell-blasted pine and tried to recover his breath; then he saw Gavrila Likhovidov coming towards him. He was staggering along drunkenly, his eyes fixed on the ground; one hand was grabbing at the air, while the other seemed to be clawing a cobweb from his face. He had neither rifle nor sword, his straight dark-brown hair was soaked in perspiration and plastered

over his forehead. He stumbled up to Ivan
and halted, squinting vaguely at the ground.
His knees were trembling and slightly bent
and to Ivan it seemed as if he were about to
spring into the air.

Ivan began to say something, but Likhovidov's face was torn by a shudder.

"Wait!" he shouted and squatted on his
haunches, sticking out his fingers and looking
round in alarm. "Listen! I'm going to sing you
a song. The bird of God flew up to an owl and
said:

> *Tell me, tell me, mistress owl,*
> *Who is the biggest, oldest fowl?*
> *Now, the eagle, he's the tsar,*
> *The kite, he's a major,*
> *The ringtail's a captain,*
> *The long-bills are Urals men,*
> *The doves are guardsmen,*
> *The starlings are Kalmyks,*
> *The jackdaws are gypsies,*
> *The magpies are lifeguards,*
> *And the grey ducks are intantry.*

"Here, I say!" Ivan Alexeyevich turned pale.
"Likhovidov, what's the matter? Are you ill?"

"Keep quiet!" Likhovidov went purple in the
face and, again twisting his bluish lips into an
inane smile, resumed his weird chant.

Ivan Alexeyevich jumped to his feet.

"Come on, let's get back to the squadron, or the Germans will grab us! D'you hear?"

Snatching his hand away, Likhovidov went on chanting, warm spittle dripping from his mouth. Then suddenly changing his voice, he broke into a kind of hoarse singing. It was not a song but a rising wolf-like howl that broke from his grinning mouth. Spittle gleamed on his long sharp teeth. Ivan stared in horror at the insanely squinting eyes of this man who a few hours before had been his friend, at the head with its matted hair and wax-like ears. Likhovidov howled out an old Cossack song with a kind of desperate bitterness:

> *Loud the glorious trumpets blow,*
> *Across the Danube Cossacks go,*
> *The Sultan's Turks to put to flight*
> *And free all Christians from his might.*

"Martin! Martin, come over here!" Ivan shouted, noticing Martin Shamil limping past a short distance away.

Martin approached, leaning on his rifle.

"Help me to take him back. See what's happened?" Ivan indicated the madman with his eyes. "It was too much for him. The blood went to his head."

Shamil bandaged his wounded leg with the

sleeve of his vest. Without looking at Likhovidov he gripped his arm; Ivan took the other
and they started off. Likhovidov's cries became
weaker. Shamil frowned painfully and begged
him to stop.

"Don't make so much noise!" he pleaded.
"Stop, for Christ's sake. You've had your fling.
Now stop it!"

The madman went on singing and tried to
wrench himself free from the Cossacks. Now
and then he pressed his hands to his temples,
ground his teeth and, with trembling jaw, let
his head fall on one side under the searing
blast of madness.

IV

Forty versts lower down the Stokhod, there
was heavy fighting. For two weeks the roar of
the artillery had continued without cease. At
night the distant violet heaven was shredded
with dim rainbow beams of searchlights, infect-
ing with inexplicable uneasiness those who
watched from afar the flames and explosions of
war.

Meantime the Twelfth Cossack Regiment was
holding a wild and swampy sector. By day they
fired occasional shots at the Austrians lurking in
the shallow trenches opposite. By night, protect-

ed by the marsh, they slept or played cards. Only the sentries watched the ghastly orange bursts of light where the fighting still raged lower down the river.

On one of those tingling frosty nights when the distant reflections flickered more clearly than usual against the sky, Grigory Melekhov left his dug-out and made his way along a communication trench into the forest, which stood out behind the trenches in grey bristles on the black skull of a low hill. He flung himself down on the spacious, fragrant earth. The air was stifling and oppressive in the dug-out, and brown tobacco-smoke hung like a shaggy blanket over the table around which eight Cossacks were playing cards. But through the forest on the hill-crest a breeze was blowing quietly as though fanned from the wings of invisible passing birds. A mournful scent arose from the frost-bitten grasses. Above the shell-sheared forest hung the darkness; the smoking fire of the Pleiades was burning out in the sky, the Great Bear lay to one side of the Milky Way like an overturned wain with the shaft sticking up; in the north the Pole Star gleamed with a steady, fading light.

Grigory stared up at the star, and its icy light, dim, yet strangely prickling to his eyes, caused cold tears to spring beneath his eye-lashes.

A rush of memory brought all the past years vividly to him. He recalled the night when he had gone to Aksinya at Yagodnoye. He remembered her with sudden pain, the dear yet estranged outlines of her face appearing uncertainly before him. His heart beat faster as he tried to recall that face as he had seen it for the last time, distorted with pain, the livid mark of the knout on her cheek. But memory persistently suggested another face, held slightly on one side, and smiling triumphantly. Now again Aksinya turned her face mischievously and lovingly, looking up at him with fiery black eyes, her wantonly avid, crimson lips whispering something inexpressibly caressing; then she slowly turned her eyes, her head away from him, and he saw the two fluffy curls on her brown neck. How he had loved to kiss them!

Grigory shuddered. For a moment he thought he could even smell the fine, intoxicating aroma of Aksinya's hair, and his nostrils dilated. But no! It was the troubling scent of the fallen leaves. The oval of Aksinya's face faded and passed. He opened his eyes, pressed his palm to the rough skin of the earth, and lay staring unblinkingly beyond the broken pines, at the Pole Star hanging like a blue butterfly in motionless flight.

Other memories obscured Aksinya's features. He recalled the weeks he had spent at Tatarsky with his family after his break with Aksinya; of the nights, Natalya's greedy ravaging embraces, as though she were trying to make up for her previous virgin iciness; during the days the attentive and almost adoring attitude of his family, and the respect with which the villagers greeted their first Cavalier of St. George. Everywhere, even in his own home, Grigory caught sidelong, astonished and respectful glances. They gazed at him as though they could not believe it was the same Grigory who had been such a self-willed and merry lad. The old men talked to him as an equal, and took off their hats when they met him; the girls and women stared with unconcealed admiration at his trim, slightly stooping figure and the cross on his breast. He noticed how obviously proud of him his father was as they walked together to church or to the square. And the subtle, complex poison of flattery, respect and admiration gradually submerged and erased from his consciousness the truth which Garanzha had implanted. Grigory returned to Tatarsky one man, and went back to the front another. His own Cossack traditions, sucked in with his mother's milk and cherished all his life, rose above the greater human truth.

"I knew you'd make a good Cossack, Grigory," old Pantelei, a little drunk, had said, stroking his black and silver beard, as they parted. "When you were twelve months old I carried you out into the yard and sat you bareback on a horse as is the good old Cossack custom. Remember, Mother? And you, you little devil, you just grabbed him by the mane with your little hands; I said then you'd make good. And so you have."

Grigory returned to the front a good Cossack. Mentally still unreconciled to the senselessness of war, nonetheless he faithfully defended his Cossack honour.

1915. May. The 13th German Iron Regiment had advanced over a brilliantly green meadow close to the village of Olkhovchik. The machine-guns chirruped like grasshoppers. A heavy machine-gun of the Russian company positioned along the stream stuttered powerfully. The Twelfth Cossack Regiment bore the brunt of the German attack. Running forward while in the line of Cossacks Grigory glanced back and saw the molten orb of the sun in the midday sky, and another sun in the reedy stream. Beyond the stream, beyond the poplars, were the Cossack horses, and in front was the German line, the yellow gleam of the copper eagles on the helmets. A wind billowed the bluish worm-wood smoke of the gunfire.

Grigory fired unhurriedly, taking careful aim and listening between his shots to the troop commander shouting the range. He cautiously dislodged a ladybird that settled on his sleeve. Then came the attack. With his rifle-butt Grigory knocked a tall German lieutenant off his feet, took three prisoners, and firing over their heads, forced them to run towards the stream.

And in July 1915, with a Cossack troop he had recovered a battery captured by the Aus-trians. During the same battle he had worked his way to the rear of the enemy and had opened fire on them with a light machine-gun, put-ting the advancing Austrians to flight. Then he had taken a corpulent officer prisoner, flinging him across his saddle-bow as if he were a sheep, and had felt the fat sweating body shiv-ering with fear all through the ride.

As he lay on the hill-side Grigory remem-bered particularly clearly one incident in which he had met his deadly enemy Stepan Astakhov. The Twelfth Regiment had been withdrawn from the front and flung into East Prussia. The Cossack horses had trampled the orderly German fields, the Cossacks had fired the German habitations. Along the road they travelled a ruddy smoke had risen, and the charred walls and the tiled

roofs had crumbled to dust. Near the town of
Stolypin the regiment went into attack at the
side of the 27th Don Cossack Regiment. Grigory
caught a momentary glimpse of his brother, of
clean-shaven Stepan and other Cossacks from
his own village. The regiments suffered defeat
and were surrounded by the Germans. When the
twelve squadrons, one after another, were flinging themselves into the attack in order to break
through the enemy ring, Grigory saw Stepan
leap from the horse killed beneath him and spin
round like a top. Fired by a sudden joyous resolve, Grigory reined in his horse, and when the
last squadron had galloped past, all but trampling on Stepan, he rode up to him and shouted:

"Catch hold of my stirrup!"

Stepan seized the stirrup-strap and ran for
half a verst at the side of Grigory's horse. "Don't
ride too fast, not too fast, for the love of
Christ!" he pleaded, panting, his mouth gaping.

They passed successfully through the breach
in the German ring. Not more than two hundred
yards separated them from the forest to which
their squadrons had retreated when a bullet
nicked Stepan's leg, and he fell headlong. The
wind tore the cap from Grigory's head and sent
his hair into his eyes. Brushing it back, he looked
round, and saw Stepan limp towards a bush,
tear off his Cossack cap, sit down, and hurriedly

unbutton his trousers with their scarlet Cossack stripes. The Germans came running out from behind the hill. Grigory realized that Stepan had no wish to die, and so was tearing off his Cossack trousers, knowing that the Germans would show a Cossack no mercy. Answering the call of his heart, he turned his horse round and galloped back to the bush, jumping off while the horse was moving.

"Get on my horse!"

Grigory would never forget the curt sweep of Stepan's eyes as he helped him to mount, then ran at his side, holding on to the stirrup. A stream of bullets whistled over their heads, and from behind them came the sound of the shots, like the splitting of overripe acacia pods.

In the forest Stepan, his face white and twisted with pain, slipped down from the saddle and limped away. Blood was seeping through the leg of his right boot, and at every step a thin cherry-red stream spurted from his broken sole. He leaned against the trunk of a spreading oak and beckoned to Grigory.

"My boot's full of blood," he said, when Grigory went across to him.

Grigory was silent gazing aside.

"Grisha! When we went into the attack today.... Do you hear, Grigory?" Stepan said, attempting to look into his eyes. "When we went into the attack I fired three times at you from behind. . . . But it wasn't granted me to kill you."

Their eyes met. Stepan's keen pupils gleamed unbearably in their sunken sockets. He spoke almost without moving his lips.

"You've saved my life. . . . Thanks. . . . But I can't forgive you for Aksinya. . . . I can't make myself. . . . Don't force me, Grigory. . . ."

"I'm not forcing you," Grigory answered. They parted enemies as before.

In May the regiment with other sections of the Brusilov Army had broken through the front at Lutsk, and had roamed in the enemy's rear, striking and being struck. Near Lvov Grigory had taken over the command of his squadron and captured an Austrian howitzer battery and its crew. One night nearly a month later he had swum across the river Bug to capture a "tongue." He had taken a sentry by surprise and the sturdy, thick-set German and the half-naked Grigory had struggled for a long time in the darkness before Grigory could bind him.

Grigory smiled as he remembered the incident.

And there had been many such incidents during the recent and not so recent fighting.

Grigory had defended his Cossack honour steadfastly, seizing every opportunity of displaying reckless prowess, risking his life in madcap adventures, changing his clothes and going into the enemy's rear, capturing outposts, and feeling that the pain for other men which had oppressed him during the first days of the war had gone for ever. His heart had grown hard and coarse, like a salt-marsh in drought; as a salt-marsh will not absorb water, so Grigory's heart would not absorb compassion. With cold contempt he played with his own and others' lives, and covered himself with glory. He had won four Crosses of St. George and four other awards. On the occasional parades he stood by the regimental banner, seasoned with the powder smoke of innumerable wars. But he knew that he no longer laughed as in former days; he knew his eyes were sunken and his cheekbones stood out sharply; he knew that if he kissed a child he could not look straight into those clear, innocent eyes. He knew what price he had paid for his crosses and medals.

He lay on the hill-side, the folds of his greatcoat tucked under him, resting on his left elbow. His memory obediently resurrected the past, and among the throng of memories some distant incident of his youth was entwined like a fine blue thread. For a moment he rested his mind's eye upon it sadly and lovingly, then returned to the present. In the Austrian trenches someone was playing skilfully on a mandolin. The fine wind-billowed strains hastened across the river, tripping lightly over the earth so often washed with human blood. The stars flamed above, but the darkness was deepening and a midnight mist was bowed over the marsh. He smoked two cigarettes in succession, passed his fingers with a rough fondness over the sling of his rifle, then rose from the hospitable earth and went back to the trenches.

In his dug-out the men were still playing cards. Grigory dropped on to his pallet, tried once more to roam along the time-grown paths of memory, but sleep overcame him even before he could move. In his sleep he dreamed of the parched, interminable steppe, the rosy lilac of the immortelles, the marks of unshod horses' hoofs among the shaggy lilac thyme. The steppe was empty and terrifyingly quiet. He was walking over the hard, sandy ground, but he could not hear his own footfalls, and this alarmed him. . . . He awoke for a moment and raised his head, chewing his lips like a horse that has momentarily caught the aroma of some unusual herb. Then he fell asleep again, untroubled by dreams.

Next day he awoke with an inexplicable feeling of yearning sucking at him.

"What are you looking so sour for today? Dreamed about home last night?" Uryupin asked him.

"You've guessed right. I dreamed of the steppe. . . . I'm so worn out in spirit . . . I'd like to be back home. I'm fed up with the tsar's service. . . ."

Uryupin smiled condescendingly. He had lived continually in one dug-out with Grigory, and had that respect for him which one strong animal feels for another. Since their quarrel in 1914 there had been no conflict between them, and Uryupin's influence was clearly discernible in Grigory's changed character and psychology. The war had strongly modified Uryupin's outlook. Slowly but unswervingly he turned against the war, talking a great deal about traitor generals and the Germans in the tsar's palace. Once he had muttered: "Don't expect any good to come of it when the tsarina herself is of German blood. If she gets the chance, she may sell us to the enemy. . . ." Grigory had tried to explain Garanzha's teaching to him, but Uryupin would have none of it.

"The song's all right, but the voice is a bit hoarse," he had said with a derisive smile, patting his bald patch. "Misha Koshevoi is always crowing about that, too, like a cock on a wall. There's no sense ever comes from these revolutions, only mischief. You remember this, that what we Cossacks need is our own government, and not any other! We need a strong tsar, someone like Nikolai Nikolayevich.* We've got nothing in common with the muzhiks, the goose and the swine are not comrades. The muzhiks want to get the land for themselves, the workers want to have higher wages. But what will they give us? Land we've got in plenty. And what else do we need? Our tsar's a good-for-nothing, there's no use denying it! His father was stronger, but this one will wait till revolution is knocking at the door as it did in 1905, and then they'll all go rolling down to the devil together. We won't gain anything from that; once they've driven the tsar out they'll be coming down on us. First they'll bring up the old grudge against us, then they'll begin to take our land away and give it to the muzhiks. We must be on the look-out."

"You always think along one track," Grigory frowned.

"Rubbish, man. You're young yet, you haven't seen the world. But you wait a little and you'll find out who's right."

* Nikolai Nikolayevich (1856-1929). The Grand Prince, Commander-in-chief of the Russian forces in World War I. During the Civil War he fled abroad, where with the support of Wrangel and the majority of the monarchists, he became one of the pretenders to the Russian throne.

The argument usually ended at that, Grigory lapsing into silence, and Uryupin striving to switch the conversation to something else.

That day Grigory was drawn into an unpleasant incident. At noon the field-kitchen stopped on the farther side of the hill as usual. The Cossacks jostled along the communication trench to the kitchen. Misha Koshevoi went to get the food for the Third Troop, and came back carrying the steaming mess tins on a long pole. He had hardly entered the dug-out when he shouted:

"This isn't good enough, brothers! Are we dogs, or what?"

"What's up?" Uryupin asked.

"They're feeding us on rotten meat," Koshevoi exclaimed indignantly. Throwing back his head of golden hair, he set the tins down on a bed, and with a sidelong glance at Uryupin, exclaimed:

"Smell for yourself what the soup stinks like!"

Uryupin bent over his tin and distended his nostrils. He started back and pulled a wry face. Koshevoi also frowned, and his nostrils quivered in involuntary imitation of Uryupin.

"The meat's off," Uryupin decided.

He pushed the tin away in disgust, and looked at Grigory. Grigory rose from his bed, bent his hooked nose over the soup, then jerked back and with a lazy movement of his foot sent the nearest tin to the ground.

"What did you do that for?" Uryupin asked irresolutely.

"Don't you see what for? Look! Are you blind? What's that!" Grigory pointed to the muddy wash oozing over the floor.

"Here! Worms! My old mother! And I didn't see them! There's a fine dinner for you. That's not cabbage soup, that's noodles. Worms instead of giblets!"

White boiled worms lay limply by the chunk of brick-red meat on the grease-spotted floor.

"One, two, three, four . . ." Koshevoi counted . . . for some reason in a whisper.

For a moment there was silence. Grigory spat through his teeth. Then Koshevoi drew his sabre and said:

"We'll arrest this soup and report it to the squadron commander."

"That's the idea!" Uryupin approved, unscrewing the bayonet from his rifle. "We'll take the soup, and you, Grigory, bring up the rear and make the report."

Uryupin and Koshevoi picked up a pot of soup on a bayonet, then drew their sabres. Grigory followed behind them, and as they passed along the trenches a line of inquisitive Cossacks gathered in a grey-green wave and followed them.

"What's up?"

"An alarm?"

"Mebbe it's something about peace?"

"Huh, peace! Better get something to eat first."

"They've arrested their soup. It's got worms

Koshevoi and Uryupin halted outside the officers' dug-out. Grigory stooped, and holding his cap on with his left hand, entered the "fox-hole."

"Keep back!" Uryupin snapped at a Cossack pushing behind.

After a moment the squadron commander came out, buttoning up his overcoat and looking back at Grigory in astonishment mingled with a hint of anxiety.

"What's the matter, lads?" The officer ran his eyes over the assembled Cossacks.

Grigory stepped in front of him and replied:

"We've brought a prisoner."

"What prisoner?"

"That. . . ." He pointed to the tin of soup at Uryupin's feet. "There's the prisoner. Smell what your Cossacks are being fed on."

His eyebrow rose sharply, twitched and straightened out. The squadron commander studied the expression on Grigory's face attentively; then with a frown he looked down at the pot.

"They've started feeding us on dead horse," Misha Koshevoi exclaimed fiercely.

"Change the quartermaster! He's stuffing himself on kidney soup. And ours has got worms in it," other shouts arose.

The officer waited until the howl of voices had died down, then said sternly:

"Silence! You've said enough! I'll change the quartermaster today. I'll appoint a commission to investigate his activities. If the meat isn't good...."

"Court-martial him!" came a shout from behind, and the officer's voice was drowned in a fresh storm of cries.

The quartermaster had to be changed while the regiment was on the march. A few hours after the Cossacks had arrested the soup and brought it before the squadron commander, the order was received to withdraw from the front and to move by forced marches into Rumania. During the night the Cossacks were relieved by Siberian Sharpshooters. The next day the regiment was mounted and on its way.

Powerful troop formations were being sent to the support of the Rumanians, who had been suffering one defeat after another. The Cossacks realized this on the first day, when the billeting officers who were sent ahead in the evening to the village where the regiment was due to stay the night returned with the news that there was no accommodation available. The village was crowded with infantry and artillery also moving up to the Rumanian frontier, and the regiment was obliged to go on another eight versts to find billets.

The march took seventeen days. The horses were exhausted from lack of fodder. There was no food anywhere in the devastated zone immediately behind the front; the inhabitants had either fled into the interior or hidden in the forests. The gaping doors of the huts revealed bare, gloomy walls. Occasionally the Cossacks would fall in with a sullen, terrified villager in a deserted street, but as soon as he saw the soldiers he hastened to hide himself. Worn out with their unbroken march, frozen, and irritable because of all they and their horses had had to endure, they tore off the straw roofs of the buildings. In villages that had escaped plundering they did not hesitate to steal what miserable food they could find, and no threats on the part of their officers could stop them.

Not far from the Rumanian frontier Uryupin succeeded in stealing some barley from a barn in one of the better-off villages. The owner caught him in the act, but he knocked the peaceable, elderly Bessarabian down and carried the barley to his horse. The troop officer found him filling his horse's basket and with trembling fingers stroking the animal's sunken, bony sides.

"Uryupin! Hand over that barley, you swine! Do you want to be shot!"

Uryupin gave the officer a smouldering sidelong glance and threw his cap down on the ground. For the first time during all his life in the regiment he raised a heart-rending cry:

"Court-martial me! Shoot me! Kill me on the spot, but I won't give up the barley.... Is my horse to die of hunger, eh? I won't hand over the barley, not a single grain!"

The officer stood without replying, staring at the horse's terribly emaciated flanks and shaking his head. Finally he remarked, with a note of perplexity in his voice:

"What are you giving the horse grain for when he's still hot?"

"No, he's cooled down by now," Uryupin replied almost in a whisper, gathering up the grains which had fallen on the ground and putting them back in the basket.

The regiment arrived at its new position in the beginning of November. The winds were howling over the Transylvanian mountains, a freezing mist gathered in the valleys, the forests seared by the first frost smelled strongly of pine needles, and the tracks of animals were frequently seen on the crisp early snow. Terrified by the war, the wolves, elks and goats were abandoning their wild fastnesses and making for the interior of the country.

On November 7th the regiment attempted to storm height "320." The previous evening the trenches had been held by Austrians, but on the morning of the attack they were relieved by Saxons freshly transferred from the Western Front. The Cossacks advanced on foot up the stony, slightly snow-covered slopes, sending the stones rolling down and raising a fine snowy dust. As Grigory strode along he smiled sheepishly, and told Uryupin:

"I feel kind of nervous this morning . . . as though I was going into battle for the first time."

The Cossacks pushed on up the slope in irregular line formation. Not a shot was fired. The enemy trenches were ominously silent.

Behind the breastworks a Saxon lieutenant, with a red weather-beaten face and the skin peeling off his nose, was standing upright and shouting cheerful encouragement to his men and urging them to hold their fire.

The Cossacks quickened their pace. The loose stony ground broke away under their feet. Tuck-

ing in the ends of his weather-stained cowl,
Grigory smiled nervously. His hook-nose and
his sunken cheeks with their black harvest of
whisker were a yellowish blue; his eyes gleamed
dully like splinters of anthracite under his rime-
covered brows. His usual composure had deserted him.

He tried to rid himself of the accursed feeling
of fear which had so unexpectedly returned.
Screwing up his eyes, and directing his unsteady
gaze on the snow-covered crest of the trenches,
he said to Uryupin:

"They're keeping quiet. They want us to
come closer. But I'm scared and I'm not ashamed
of the fact. Suppose we turn back and—run?"

"What are you whining about today?" Uryupin asked in irritation. "It's like card playing.
Lose faith in yourself and you're done for.
You're yellow in the face, Grisha. Either you're
sick or ... you'll get hit today. Look! Did you
see that?"

A German in a short coat and pointed helmet
had suddenly risen to his full height above the
trenches, then disappeared again.

On Grigory's left a handsome blond Cossack
kept pulling his glove on and off as he marched.
He repeated the action continuously, moving his
legs stiffly and uttering affectedly loud coughs.
"Like a fellow going along by himself at night

and coughing to cheer himself up," Grigory thought. Further on he could see the freckled cheek of Sergeant Maksayev, then came Yemelyan Groshev, his rifle with bayonet fixed held firmly at the ready. Grigory remembered that a few days ago Yemelyan had stolen a sack of maize from a Rumanian, and had used that bayonet to prise open the lock of the store-room. Misha Koshevoi was almost level with Maksayev. He was smoking furiously and frequently blew his nose, wiping his fingers on his greatcoat.

"I'd like a drink," said Maksayev.

"My boots are pinching me, Yemelyan," Koshevoi complained.

Groshev interrupted him bitterly:

"Forget about your boots. The Germans will be giving us a burst of machine-gun bullets in a minute."

The very first volley from the enemy knocked Grigory over, and he fell to the ground with a groan. He tried to reach the first-aid dressing in his pack, but the hot blood pouring from his elbow inside his sleeve left him too weak. He lay flat, and shielding his head behind a boulder, licked the downy fringe of snow with his parched tongue, and thirstily caught at the snowy dust with quivering lips. He listened with unusual fear and trembling to the dry, sharp crack of the rifles and the dominating thunder of the guns. Raising his head, he saw the Cossacks of his squadron running back down the slope, slipping, falling, firing at random up the slope. An inexplicable and irrational fear brought him to his feet, and forced him also to run down towards the jagged fringe of the pine forest from which the regiment had opened the attack. Grigory overtook Groshev dragging a wounded troop officer behind him down the steep slope; the officer was staggering drunkenly and leaned on Groshev's shoulder, spitting black clots of blood. The squadron poured in torrents into the forest. On the grey slopes behind them lay little grey bundles of dead; the wounded crawled down unaided, whipped along by the fierce machine-gun fire.

Leaning on Misha Koshevoi's arm, Grigory entered the forest. The bullets ricocheted off the sloping ground. On the Germans' left flank a machine-gun was spitting out a fine hail that sounded like stones flung by a strong hand bouncing off the thin ice of a frozen river.

"They're giving us a warm time!" Uryupin shouted almost exultantly. Leaning against the ruddy trunk of a pine, he fired lazily at the Germans pouring over the ridge of the trenches.

"The fools have got to be taught. They've got to be taught!" Koshevoi shouted, tearing his arm away from Grigory. "The people are swine, swine! When they've poured out all their blood, then they'll learn what they're being shot down for!"

"What are you raving about?" Uryupin frowned.

"If you've got any brains you can understand for yourself. But what can a fool understand? Nothing will make him. . . ."

"Do you remember your oath? Did you take the oath or not?" Uryupin demanded.

Instead of replying, Koshevoi fell to his knees and with fumbling hands raked up some snow. He swallowed it greedily, shivering and coughing.

V

Across the sky, furrowed with a grey ripple of cloud, the autumn sun rolled over Tatarsky. High up a gentle breeze urged the clouds slowly on towards the west; but over the village, over the dark-green plain of the Don valley, over the bare forest it blew strongly, bending the crowns of the willows and poplars, ruffling the Don, and chasing droves of crimson leaves along the streets. On Christonya's threshing-floor it tousled a badly stacked hayrick, tearing away its top and sending the thin ridge-pole flying. Suddenly snatching up a golden load of hay as if on a pitchfork, it carried the burden out into the yard, sent it whirling across the street, and scattered it munificently over the deserted road, finally throwing the untidy bundle on to the roof of Stepan Astakhov's house. Christonya's wife ran out into the yard without her shawl and stood for a minute or two watching the wind lording it about the threshing-floor, then went in again.

Three years of the war had left noticeable marks in the village. Where the houses had been deprived of all male hands the sheds gaped wide open, the yards were shabby, and gradual decay was leaving its traces everywhere. Christonya's wife had only her little nine-year-old son to help her. Anikushka's wife was no use whatever at farm work, and because of her lonely situation paid redoubled attention to her own appearance, painted herself up, and as there were not enough grown-up Cossacks, accepted lads of fourteen or so. Her gates, which someone had once lavishly smeared with tar, still bore the tell-tale traces, testifying to this fact. Stepan Astakhov's house was completely abandoned; the owner had boarded up the windows, the roof was falling in and was overgrown with burdocks, the door lock was rusting, and wandering cattle strayed through the open gate, seeking shelter from the heat or rain in the weedy, grass-grown yard. The wall of Ivan Tomilin's house was falling into the street, being kept from doing so only by a forked wooden prop. Fate seemed to be wreaking its vengeance on the hardy artilleryman for the German and Russian houses he had destroyed.

And so it was in all the streets and alleys of the village. At the lower end only Pantelei Melekhov's house and yard retained their usual appearance; there everything seemed sound and in order, yet it was not entirely so. The iron cocks had fallen from the granary roof, eaten away with age; the granary was sinking on one side; and an experienced eye would have detected other signs of neglect. The old man could not manage everything. He sowed less and less, and only the Melekhov family itself did not diminish. To make up for Pyotr's and Grigory's absence, Natalya gave birth to twins in the autumn of 1915. She was clever enough to please both Pantelei and Ilyinichna by having a girl and a boy. Natalya's pregnancy was a difficult one; there were whole days when she could hardly walk, owing to the tormenting pains in her legs, and tottered about dragging her feet one behind the other. But she bore the pain stoically, and it never found any reflection in her swarthy, lean and happy face. Only by the beads of perspiration that stood out on her temples when the pain was more intense could Ilyinichna guess at her suffering, and tell her to go and lie down.

One fine September day Natalya, feeling her time near at hand, turned to go out into the street.

"Where are you off to?" Ilyinichna asked her.

"Into the meadow. I'll see the cows out."

Groaning and holding her hands under her belly, she walked out hurriedly beyond the village, made her way into a thicket of wild thorn, and lay down. Dusk was falling when she returned by back ways to the house, carrying twins in her canvas apron.

"My dear! You little wretch! What's all this! And where have you been?" Ilyinichna exclaimed when she eventually found her voice.

"I was ashamed, so I went out. . . . I didn't like to . . . in front of Father. . . . I'm clean, Mother, and I've washed them. Take them . . ." Natalya replied, turning pale.

Dunya ran for the midwife, and Darya busied herself lining a sieve. Ilyinichna, laughing and weeping for joy, shouted at her:

"Darya, put that sieve down. Are they kittens, that you want to put them in a sieve? Lord, there's two of them! Oh Lord, one's a boy! Natalya, dear. . . . Make up the bed for her!"

When Pantelei heard that his daughter-in-law had given birth to twins he opened wide his arms in astonishment, then wept happily and tugged at his beard. For no apparent reason he shouted at the approaching midwife:

"No, you old croaker!" He shook his fist in front of the old woman's nose. "You're a liar! The Melekhov line won't die out so soon! My daughter-in-law's got a Cossack and a girl. There's a daughter-in-law for you! Lord, my God! For such kindness how can I repay her?"

Fruitful was that year; the cow gave birth to twins, the sheep had twins, the goats. . . . Astonished at the circumstances, Pantelei reasoned to himself:

"A lucky year this, and fruity too! Everything having twins! What a yield we're getting, oho!"

Natalya kept her children at the breast for twelve months. She weaned them in September, but she did not get really well again until late in the autumn. Her teeth gleamed milkily in her emaciated face, and her eyes, appearing unnaturally large because of her thinness, shone with a warm light. All her life centred round the children. She grew negligent of herself and spent all her spare time with them, washing them, swaddling them, mending for them;

frequently, sitting on the bed with one leg hanging, she would lift them out of the cradle, and with a movement of her shoulders shrug out her full, large melon-yellow breasts, and feed them both at once.

"They've sucked enough at you already. You feed them too often," Ilyinichna would remark, slapping the full little legs of her grandchildren.

"Feed them! Don't spare the milk! We don't want it for cream!" Pantelei would intervene with jealous roughness.

During these years life slowly began to ebb, like flood water in the Don. The days were dreary and exhausting and slipped by, in continual bustling, in work, in petty needs, in little joys and a great, unsleeping anxiety for those who were at the war. Rare letters in greasy envelopes plastered with postmarks arrived from Pyotr and Grigory. Grigory's last letter had fallen into someone else's hands; half of it was carefully obliterated with violet ink, and an incomprehensible sign had been made in ink in the margin of the grey paper. Pyotr wrote more frequently than Grigory, and in his letters to Darya he threatened and adjured her to give up her goings on. Evidently rumours of his wife's unseemly life had reached his ears. With his letters Grigory sent home money, his pay and allowances for his crosses, and promised to come home on leave, but did not come. The two brothers' roads ran in very different directions. Grigory was oppressed by the war, and the flush was sucked out of his face, leaving a yellow jaundice. He could not wait for the war to end. But Pyotr climbed swiftly and easily upward; he wormed his way into the good graces of his squadron commander, was awarded two crosses, in the autumn of 1916 was made a sergeant-major, and he was now talking in his letters of attempting to get himself sent to an officers' school. During the summer he sent home a German officer's helmet and cloak, and his own photograph. His face staring complacently from the grey card looked older, his flaxen moustache twisted up at the tips, and under the snub nose the well-known grin parted his firm lips. Life was smiling on Pyotr, and the war delighted him because it opened up unusual prospects. But for its coming how could he, a simple Cossack, ever have dreamed of an officer's commission and a different, sweeter life? Only in one respect did Pyotr's life have an unpleasant future; ugly rumours concerning his wife circulated in the village. Stepan Astakhov was given leave in the autumn of 1916, and on his return to the regiment boasted throughout the squadron of the splendid time he had had with Pyotr's wife. Pyotr would not believe the stories; his face went dark, but he smiled and said:

"Stepan's a liar! He's trying to gall me because of what Grisha did."

But one day, as Stepan was coming out of his dug-out, whether by accident or design he dropped an embroidered lace handkerchief. Pyotr, who was just behind him, picked it up, and at once recognized his wife's handiwork. Again the old hostility broke out between them. Pyotr watched for his opportunity; death watched over Stepan. If Pyotr could, he would have had Stepan lying on the bank of the Dvina with his mark on Stepan's skull. But before long it happened that Stepan went out on patrol to capture a German outpost, and did not come back. The Cossacks who went with him said one of the Germans had heard them cutting the barbed wire, and flung a grenade. The Cossacks managed to get up to him and Stepan knocked him down with his fist, but a supporting guard opened fire, and Stepan fell. The Cossacks bayoneted the second guard, dragged away the German stunned by Stepan's blow, and attempted to pick Stepan up also. But he was too heavy and they had to leave him. Stepan pleaded: "Brothers, don't leave me to die! Comrades! What are you leaving me for?" But a hail of machine-gun bullets spattered through the wire, and the

Cossacks crawled away. "Brothers!" Stepan called after them, but what of that? Your own skin has to be saved before another's. When Pyotr heard of Stepan's fate he felt relieved, as if he had smeared a painful sore with dripping, but he resolved nonetheless that when he got leave he would have Darya's blood. He wasn't Stepan! He wouldn't stand for that! He thought of killing her, but at once rejected the idea. "Kill the bitch, and ruin all my life because of her? Rot in a prison, lose all I've been working for, lose everything?" He decided merely to beat her, but in a way that would cure her of all desire ever to raise her tail again! "I'll knock her eye out, the snake, then nobody will look at her!" he thought as he sat in the trenches not far from the steep, clayey bank of the Dvina river.

Autumn crumpled the trees and grass, the morning frosts blackened them, the earth grew cold, and the autumn nights darkened and lengthened. In the trenches the Cossacks did their fatigues, fired at the Germans, argued with the sergeant-majors about getting warm clothing, never had enough food, but not one of them stopped thinking of their homeland on the Don, far from this alien unfriendly country.

That autumn Darya made up for all her hungry, husbandless life. One morning Pantelei

Prokofyevich awoke as usual before the rest of the family, and went out into the yard. He clutched his head, overcome by what he saw. The gates had been removed from their hinges and had been flung down in the middle of the road. It was an insult, a disgrace! The old man immediately put the gates back in their place, and after breakfast called Darya outside into the summer kitchen. What they talked about was never known to the others, but a few minutes later Dunya saw Darya run dishevelled and crying out of the kitchen, her kerchief awry. As she passed Dunya she swung her shoulders, and the black arches of her eyebrows quivered in her tear-stained, angry face.

"You wait, you old devil! I'll pay you out for this!" she hissed between her swollen lips.

Dunya saw that her blouse was torn at the back, and a fresh livid weal showed on her bare shoulders. She ran up the steps and whisked into the house, while Pantelei came limping from the summer kitchen, as angry as the devil, and looping up some new leather reins as he walked. Dunya heard her father say: "I ought to have given it you harder, you bitch! You whore!"

Order was restored in the house. For some days Darya crept about quieter than water, humbler than grass, went to bed before anybody else each night, and smiled coldly at Natalya's sympathetic glances, shrugging her shoulders and raising her eyebrows as though saying: "All right, we'll see!" On the fourth day, an incident occurred of which only Darya and old Pantelei knew. Afterwards Darya went about laughing triumphantly, but the old man was embarrassed for a whole week, and as miserable as a guilty cat. He did not tell his wife what had occurred, and even at confession kept the incident and his own sinful thoughts about it a secret from Father Vissarion.

What had happened was this. Pantelei was sure of Darya's complete conversion, and he told his wife Ilyinichna:

"Don't spare Darya! Make her work harder. She'll never go wrong at work, but the filly's getting too fat, all she thinks of is nights out."

He himself made Darya clean out the threshing-floor and stack fire-wood in the back yard, and helped her to clear the chaff-shed. Later the same afternoon he thought he would shift the winnowing machine from the barn into the chaff-shed, and called his daughter-in-law to help him.

Adjusting her kerchief and shaking off the chaff which had worked under the collar of her jacket, Darya came out and passed through the threshing-floor into the barn. Pantelei, in a padded woollen work-a-day coat and ragged trousers, went in front. The yard was empty. Dunya was helping her mother spin the autumn's wool, and Natalya was setting the dough for the morrow's bread. The evening sunset was glowing beyond the village. The bell was ringing for vespers. A little raspberry-coloured cloud hung motionless in the zenith of the translucent sky, the rooks clung like black charred flakes to the bare grey branches of the poplars beyond the Don. In the empty stillness of the evening every sound was sharp and distinct. The heavy scent of steaming dung and hay came from the cattle-yard. Pantelei and Darya carried the faded red winnowing machine into the chaff-shed, and set it down in a corner. He raked away some fallen chaff and turned to go out.

"Father!" Darya called in a low whisper.

He went back to the winnowing machine, asking:

"What's the matter?"

Darya stood facing him with her blouse unbuttoned, her arms were thrown back adjusting her hair. From a chink in the wall a crimson ray of the setting sun fell on her neck.

"Here, Father, here's something.... Come and look," she said, bending sideways and stealthily glancing across the old man's shoulder at the open door. He went right up to her. Suddenly she flung out her arms, and clasping him round the neck, her fingers interlocking, she stepped back, dragging him after her and whispering:

"Here, Father. . . . Here. . . . It's softer. . . ."

"What's the matter with you?" Pantelei asked in alarm. Wriggling his head from side to side, he tried to free himself from her arms; but she drew his head more strongly towards her own face, breathing hotly in his beard and laughing and whispering.

"Let me go, you bitch!" the old man struggled, feeling his daughter-in-law's straining belly right against him. Pressing still closer, she fell backward and drew him down on top of herself.

"The devil! She's gone silly! Let me go!"

"Don't you want to?" Darya panted. Unlocking her arms, she shoved the old man in the chest. "Or perhaps you can't? Then don't judge me! Do you hear?"

Jumping to her feet, she hurriedly adjusted her skirt, brushed the chaff off her back and shouted into the frenzied old man's face:

"What did you beat me for the other day? Am I an old woman? Weren't you the same when you were young? My husband! I haven't seen him for a year! And what am I to do . . .

lie with a dog? A fig for you, one leg! Here, take this!" She made an indecent gesture, and, her eyebrows working, went towards the door. At the door she once more carefully examined her clothes, brushed the dust from her jacket and kerchief, and said without looking back at Pantelei:

"I can't do without it. I need a Cossack, and if you don't want to ... I'll find one for myself, and you keep your mouth shut!"

With her hips swinging she went quickly to the door of the threshing-floor and disappeared without a glance back, while Pantelei remained standing by the winnowing machine, chewing his beard and staring guiltily and disconcertedly around the chaff-shed. "Perhaps she's right after all? Maybe I should have sinned with her?" he thought in perplexity, flabbergasted at what had happened to him.

VI

In November the frost gripped icily. An early snow fell. At the bend by the upper end of the village the Don was frozen over. Occasionally someone ventured over the dove-blue ice to the farther side. Lower down only the edges of the river were sheeted with thin ice, and the stream ran turbulently in the middle, the green waves tossing their grey heads. In the pool below the Black Bank the sheat-fish had long since sunk in a wintry somnolence to a depth of seventy feet. The slimy carp lay near by. Only the pike struggled upstream and darted across the shallows in their chase after whitebait. The sterlet lay on the gravel, and the fishermen were waiting for a hard frost, in order to drag the river for them.

In November the Melekhovs received a letter from Grigory. He wrote from Rumania saying he had been wounded: a bullet had shattered the bone of his left arm, and so he was being sent back to his own district while the wound was healing. A further woe came upon the Melekhov household hard on the heels of the first. Eighteen months previously Pantelei had had need of money, and had borrowed a hundred rubles from Sergei Mokhov, giving him a bill of sale as security. During the summer the old man had been called into Mokhov's shop and had been asked whether he intended to pay or not. Pantelei's gaze had wandered distractedly around the half-empty shelves and the shining counters, and he had hesitated.

"Wait a bit; give me time to turn round a little and I'll pay it back," he had said at last.

But the old man had not been able to "turn round." The harvest had been poor, and the cattle were not worth selling. Suddenly, like snow in June, the bailiff arrived at the village administration office, sent for Pantelei and demanded in so many words:

"Put down a hundred rubles."

A lengthy document lay on the police inspector's desk and there was nothing Pantelei could do but listen as the inspector read:

COURT ORDER

By order of His Imperial Majesty, of the 27th day of October of the year 1916, I, Justice of the Peace of the Seventh Department of the Donets Region, have heard the claim of merchant Sergei Mokhov against Sergeant Pantelei Melekhov in respect of 100 rubles owing by bill of sale to merchant Mokhov. On the basis of articles 81, 100, 129, 133, and 145 of the Civil Code I decree:

Sergeant Pantelei Melekhov shall pay merchant Sergei Platonovich Mokhov 100 rubles by the bill of sale of June 21, 1915, and in addition three rubles costs. Decision taken by default, not final.

On the basis of Clause 3, Article 156 of the Civil Code this order has legal force and shall be put into immediate execution.

The Justice of the Peace of the Seventh Department of the Donets Region, by order of His Imperial Majesty, hereby orders:

The above decision shall be executed in exact accordance with the law by all persons and institutions concerned. The officer charged with the execution of the court's decision shall receive without fail due legal support from all local police and military authorities in the performance of his duty.

When he had heard the order Pantelei asked permission to go home, promising to bring the money the very same day. But he made straight for Korshunov's house. On the square he met one-armed Alexei Shamil.

"Still limping, Pantelei?" Shamil greeted him.

"Same as usual."

"Going far?"

"To Korshunov, on business."

"Oh? You'll find them merry. Their son Mitka has come back from the front, I hear."

"Is that so?"

"So I've been told," Shamil replied, winking with his eye and cheek. Pulling out his pouch, he added:

"Have a smoke, old boy. My paper, your tobacco."

Pantelei lit a cigarette, and stood wondering whether or not to go to see Korshunov. Finally he decided to go, and limped on.

"Mitka's got a cross too. He's trying to catch up with your sons. We've got as many crosses in the village now as sparrows in the bushes," Shamil called after him.

Pantelei walked slowly to the end of the village, glanced through the window of Korshunov's house, and went to the wicket-gate. He was met by Miron himself. The old man's freckled face was shining with joy.

"Heard about our luck?" Korshunov asked, linking his arm in Pantelei's.

"I've just been told about it by Alexei Shamil. But I've come on other business...."

"Let it wait! Come into the house and meet the lad. We've been having a little drink in our joy. The wife has been keeping a bottle for an occasion like this."

"You needn't have told me," Pantelei smiled and twitched his nostrils. "I've smelt it already."

Miron flung open the door and stood aside to let Pantelei in. He stepped across the threshold and at once his gaze rested on Mitka, who was sitting behind the table.

"Here he is, our soldier lad!" Grandad Grishaka exclaimed with tears in his eyes, hugging Mitka's shoulders.

Pantelei took Mitka's long hand in his and stepped back a pace, looking him over in astonishment.

"Well, what are you staring at?" Mitka asked hoarsely, with a smile on his face.

"I can't help looking, I'm so astonished. I saw you and Grisha off at the same time, and you were children. And now look at you! A

Cossack, and fit for the Ataman's Regiment at that."

Lukinichna gazed at Mitka with tear-filled eyes, at the same time attempting to pour out vodka into a glass. Not watching what she was doing, she let it spill over the edge.

"Hey, you idiot! What are you doing, wasting good spirit!" Miron bawled at her.

"To your joy, and to you, Mitka, on your happy home-coming!" Pantelei rolled the bluish whites of his eyes and without pausing for breath drank down the big glass of vodka, his lashes fluttering slightly. Slowly wiping his lips and whiskers with his palm, he fixed his eyes on the bottom of the glass, threw his head back, tossed an orphaned drop of vodka into his gaping mouth, and only then took a breath and bit at a pickled cucumber, blinking beatifically. Lukinichna poured him out a second glass and the old man at once got absurdly fuddled. Mitka watched him with a smile. His cat-like eyes now narrowed into green slits, now widened and darkened. The lad had certainly changed beyond recognition during his years of absence. In this stalwart, black-whiskered Cossack almost nothing remained of the slim youngster who had gone off to do his service three years previously. He had grown considerably, his shoulders had broadened, he had filled out, and certainly weighed no less than five poods. His face and voice were coarser, and he looked older than his years. Only the eyes were the same, just as disturbing and restless.

It was on them that his mother poured out her love, laughing and crying, and passing her wrinkled hand over her son's short stiff hair and narrow white forehead.

"So you've won the cross?" Pantelei said, smiling drunkenly.

"Who hasn't got a cross among the Cossacks?" Mitka frowned. "Kruchkov's got three crosses just for hanging round at headquarters."

"He's proud," old Grishaka hurried to intervene. "He's just like me, the devil. He can't bow his back."

"They don't give them crosses for that," Pantelei replied sharply, but Miron drew him into another room, seated him on a chest, and asked him:

"How's Natalya and the grandchildren? All alive and well? Praise God! You said you'd come on business, didn't you? What is it? Speak up, or we'll be drinking again and you'll be too drunk to talk."

"Give me money! For the love of God! Help me, or I'll be ruined by these . . . by this money matter," Pantelei implored with expansive, drunken abasement. Miron interrupted:

"How much?"

"A hundred."

"A hundred what?"

"A hundred rubles."

"Well, say so then."

Korshunov rummaged in the chest, pulled out a greasy kerchief, untied it, and counted out ten ten-ruble notes.

"Thank you, Miron Grigoryevich. You've saved us from misery."

"No, don't thank me. When it's our own flesh and blood. . . ."

Mitka spent five days at home. He passed his nights with Anikushka's wife, having pity for woman's bitter need and particularly for her, a compliant and simple grass widow. The days he spent wandering among his kinsfolk and friends. Wearing only a light khaki tunic, he swung down the streets with his cap pushed back on his head, vaunting his strength against the cold. One evening he looked in on the Melekhovs. He brought the scent of frost and the unforgettable, pungent smell of the soldier with him into the overheated kitchen, sat talking about the war, the village news, then narrowed his green eyes at Darya and rose to go. Darya flickered like a candle flame when the door banged behind him, and pressing her lips together, was about to put on her kerchief. But Ilyinichna asked:

"Where are you off to, Darya?"

"I want to go outside."

"I'll come with you."

Pantelei sat without raising his head, as though he had not heard the question and reply. Darya went past him to the door, her eyelids drooping over the wolfish gleam in her eyes, her mother-in-law tottering heavily after her. Mitka was coughing and scrunching his feet at the gate. At the sound of the door-latch he turned to come back to the steps.

"That you, Mitka? You haven't lost your way in our yard?" Ilyinichna called slyly. "Fasten the gate behind you or it will be banging all night in this wind."

"No, I'm not lost. I'll fasten the gate!" Mitka replied in a tone of chagrin, and strode straight across the street towards Anikushka's yard.

Mitka lived a carefree, bird-like existence; life today was good, and tomorrow would take care of itself. He was not too keen on soldiering, and though he had a fearless heart to drive the blood in his veins, he did not go out of his way to earn distinction. His army record was far from good. He had been court-martialled twice, once for raping a naturalized Polish woman and once for stealing. During the three years of war he had received innumerable punishments, and on one occasion the field court martial had all but sentenced him to be shot. But he had managed somehow to extricate himself, and although he was one of the worst characters in the regiment, the Cossacks liked him for his gay, smiling nature and his bawdy songs, for his comradeship and straightforward manner, while the officers liked him for his brigand ardour. Smilingly Mitka trod the earth with light, wolfish feet: there was a good deal of the wolf breed in him, in his gait, in the lowering glance of his prominent greenish eyes, even in the way he turned his head. Mitka never twisted his neck, which had been injured by shell blast; if he had to look round he turned his whole body. The muscles were knotted closely on his broad bones and he was light and sparing in his movements; there was an astringent smell of health and strength about him, the smell of good black earth turned up by the plough in a valley. For Mitka life was simple and direct, stretching away before him like a furrow, and he walked along it the absolute master. Just as primitively simple and direct were his thoughts. If you were hungry you could and should steal, even from your comrades; and Mitka stole when he was hungry. If your boots were worn out it was the simplest thing in the world to take a pair from a German prisoner. If you were punished you must make up somehow for your crime; and Mitka did make up for his crimes, going out and bringing back half-strangled German sentries, and volunteering for the most dangerous enterprises. In 1915 he had been all but cut to pieces and taken prisoner; but the same night, tearing his finger-nails, he had broken through the roof of the shed and fled, picking up some wagon harness for a keepsake as he went. And in such ways Mitka got away with a good deal.

On the sixth day Miron drove his son to Millerovo Station, and stood watching as the line of green boxes rattled away, then dug at the platform with his whip, not raising his bleary eyes. Lukinichna wept for her son; old Grishaka coughed and blew his nose into his hand, then wiped his palm on his coat. And Anikushka's grass widow wept as she recalled Mitka's great body, so feverish in its caresses, and as she suffered with the clap she had caught from him.

Time entangled the days as the wind tangles a horse's mane. Just before Christmas a thaw unexpectedly set in, rain fell for days on end, the water raged down from the hills along the dry courses, old grass and mossy slabs of chalk showed green on the bared headlands, the edges of the Don foamed, and the ice turned a cadaverous blue and swelled. An inexpressibly sweet scent rose from the bare black earth. The water bubbled in the wheel-tracks on the high-road. The clayey gullies beyond the village yawned with fresh landslides. The southerly wind brought the heavy scent of rotten grass, and at noon-day tender, dove-blue shadows lurked on the horizon as in springtime. In the village rippling puddles formed round the heaps of ashes thrown out by the fences. The earth melted around the ricks on the threshing-floors, and the cloying sweetness of damp hay pricked the noses of passers-by. In the day-time a tarry water ran off the icicle-hung thatch and down the cornices; the magpies chattered incessantly on the fences, and the village bull wintering in Miron Korshunov's yard bellowed in the premature languor of spring, tore at the fence with its horns, rubbed its glossy chest on an old worm-eaten plough, and trampled the crumbling, watery snow.

The Don broke on the second day of Christmas. The ice floated off down the middle of the stream with a mighty grinding and groaning. Like great sleepy fish the floes flopped out on to the banks. Beyond the Don, urged on by the agitating southern wind, the poplars strained forward in fluttering yet motionless flight.

But towards nightfall the wind began to roar over the hill; the ravens fluttered and squawked on the square, Christonya's pig ran past the Melekhovs' yard with a bunch of hay in its snout, and Pantelei decided that the spring was nipped off again, and a frost would come on the morrow. During the night the wind veered round to the east, a light frost patched the thaw-ravaged puddles with a crystal covering of ice. By the morning the wind was blowing from Moscow, and the frost had set hard again. Winter reigned once more. Only down the middle of the Don the floes glided in great white sheets, and the bared earth smoked frostily on the rise.

Shortly after Christmas the village clerk informed Pantelei at a meeting that he had seen Grigory in Kamenskaya, and that he had been asked to tell his parents that their son would soon be coming to visit them.

VII

With his small, swarthy, hairy hands Sergei Mokhov felt all the pulses of life. Sometimes life played with him, sometimes it hung on him like a stone round the neck of a drowned man. He had seen a great deal. During his lifetime Sergei Platonovich had had many troubles.

Quite a long time ago, when he was still running the elevator, he had bought grain from the Cossacks for next to nothing, and afterwards carted four thousand poods of useless, burnt grain out of the village and dumped it into the river. He remembered 1905 too, when somebody from the village had emptied a shot-gun at him on a dark autumn night. In the course of loss and gain Mokhov had accumulated sixty thousand rubles and deposited them in the Volga-Kama bank, but he scented from afar that times of great commotion were coming. He awaited the dark days, and was not mistaken.

In January 1917, the teacher Balanda, who was slowly dying of consumption, had complained to him:

"The revolution's under our very noses, and here I am dying of a silly, sentimental sort of disease. It's a shame, Sergei Platonovich. It's a shame not to live to see your money-bags ripped open, and you scared out of your soft nest."

"Why's it a shame?"

"Well, isn't it? After all, you know, it would be pleasant to see everything go smash."

"I'm afraid not, my friend. You'll die before that happens!" said Sergei Platonovich, hiding his anger.

In January echoes of the city talk of Rasputin and the tsar's family were still circulating through the villages of the Don. But in early March, Sergei Platonovich was suddenly swept off his feet by the news of the overthrow of the autocracy. The Cossacks received the information with restrained anxiety and expectation. That day the old and young Cossacks crowded around the closed doors of Mokhov's shop. The new village ataman, a red-haired cross-eyed Cossack, was completely crushed by the news, and took almost no part in the animated discussions going on outside the shop; squinting nervously at the Cossacks he occasionally exclaimed disconcertedly: "Well, things have come to a pretty pass! Now what shall we do?"

Seeing the crowd outside the shop, Mokhov decided to go out and talk with the old men. He put on his racoon coat and went down the front steps of his house, leaning on his stick with its modest silver initials.

"Well, Mokhov, you're an educated man, tell us ignorant ones what's going to happen now," Matvei Kashulin asked, smiling anxiously so that little crooked wrinkles appeared round his dew-drop nose.

At Mokhov's bow the old men respectfully removed their caps, and stood back to let him pass into the middle of the group.

"We shall live without the tsar ..." Mokhov began tentatively.

All the old men started speaking at once. "But how, without the tsar?" "Our fathers and grandfathers lived under the tsars. And now isn't a tsar necessary?" "Take off the head, and the legs won't go on living!" "What kind of government will there be?" "Out with it, Sergei Platonovich! Speak up, you needn't be afraid of us."

"Mebbe he doesn't know himself," someone remarked with a smile.

Sergei Platonovich stared stupidly at his old rubber galoshes, and said, spitting out the words painfully:

"The State Duma will govern. We shall have a republic."

"So that's what we've come to, damn it!"

"Now I remember how we served under his late Majesty Alexander the Second," Avdeyich began, but the stern old Cossack Bogatiryov interrupted him severely:

"You've told us that before! Stick to the point."

"Looks like the end of the Cossacks."

"With all these strikes going on we'll have the Germans in St. Petersburg before long."

"If they have this equality, they'll want to make us equal with the muzhiks."

"They'll soon be grabbing our land, eh?"

With a forced smile Sergei Platonovich looked round at the troubled faces of the old men and a sick feeling of depression came over him. With a habitual gesture he parted his greying beard into two, and spoke out, angry at no one knew whom:

"Now you see what they've brought Russia to! They'll make you equal to the muzhiks, deprive you of your privileges, and recall the old affronts into the bargain. Bad times are coming.... It depends on whose hands the government falls into, otherwise we shall be brought to utter disaster."

"If we're alive, we'll see!" Bogatiryov shook his head, and eyed Mokhov distrustfully from under his tufty eyebrows. "You're worrying about your own affairs, Sergei Platonovich, but perhaps we'll be better off?"

"How will you be better off?" Mokhov asked venomously.

"Maybe the new government will put an end to the war. That's possible, isn't it?"

Mokhov waved his hand and shuffled away to his house, thinking disconnectedly of money matters, the mill, and his declining trade; then he remembered that Yelizaveta was in Moscow and Vladimir was shortly to come home from Novocherkassk. The blunt prick of anxiety for his children did not disturb the restless disorder of his thoughts. He reached the porch, feeling that life had all of a sudden grown dark around him, and that his spirit was being eaten away by painful thoughts. Glancing back at the old men, he spat across the railing of the steps, and went along the verandah to his room.

Anna Ivanovna met her husband in the dining-room. Regarding his face with her usual colourless, unemotional gaze, she asked: "Do you want something to eat before tea?"

"Oh, no! How can I eat!" He brushed her aside in disgust. There was a rusty taste in his mouth and his head felt dull and empty.

"There's a letter from Liza."

Anna Ivanovna shuffled into the bedroom (so she had walked since the first days of her married life, overburdened by her numerous household duties) and brought an opened letter.

"An empty-headed frivolous girl, I'm afraid," thought Sergei Platonovich about his daughter for the first time in his life, wrinkling his nose at the scent emanating from the stiff paper envelope. He read the letter hastily, dwelling for a while on the word "mood," pondering over it, seeking in it some hidden meaning. At the end of her letter Liza asked for money. Sergei Platonovich, with that same aching void in his head, read the last lines. Suddenly he wanted to cry. His life rose before him in all its barrenness.

"She's a stranger to me," he thought, "and I to her. She only remembers she's my daughter when she wants money. The dirty little hussy, with her lovers. . . . Yet—as a baby, she had such fair hair, and she was all my own. . . . God! How everything changes! Right down to my old age I've remained a fool. I believed in the possibility of my life getting better, and in reality I'm as lonely as a wayside shrine. I got my money by shady means, but you can't get it by clean. . . . I've squeezed others, and now the revolution is coming, and tomorrow my own servants may turn me out of my house. Curse the lot of them! And my children? Vladimir's a fool. . . . And where's the sense of it all? Nothing matters, perhaps. . . ."

By some vague association he recalled an incident that had occurred at his mill. A Cossack customer had made a fuss about being given short weight, and had refused to pay. The commotion had brought Sergei Platonovich out of the engine room to see what was happening. Having heard the story, he ordered the scalesman to keep the flour. The small thin Cossack tugged at one end of his flour sack, while one of the mill workers, Zavar, a thick-set, barrel-chested fellow, pulled at the other end. When the Cossack pushed him, Zavar raised his arm and struck him a blow on the temple with his great first. The little Cossack fell, then rose to his feet reeling, a raw bruise on his left temple. He took a step toward Sergei Platonovich and sobbed out:

"Take my flour! Gorge yourself on it"—and went away, his shoulders heaving.

There was no obvious reason for Sergei Platonovich to recall this incident and its consequences: how the little Cossack's wife had come to him and asked for the flour; how she had squeezed tears from her eyes in an attempt to gain the sympathy of the other customers.

"What sort of business is this, friends? What right has he to act in this way? Give us back our flour!"

"You go away, Auntie, go away quietly or I'll tear your hair out," Zavar had jeered.

It had been unpleasant and painful to see how Knave, the scalesman, as frail and undersized as the Cossack himself, had jumped at Zavar and been unmercifully beaten by him, later quitting the place altogether.

All this passed fleetingly through Mokhov's mind as he folded the letter and stared ahead with unseeing eyes.

The end of the day left him with a miserable dull pain.

He slept badly that night, turning over and over in the grip of disconnected thoughts and subconscious desires. Next morning, hearing that Yevgeny Listnitsky had arrived home from the front, he resolved to drive to Yagodnoye to find out the real situation, and to relieve his mind of its bitter accumulation of anxious presentiments. So Yemelyan harnessed the horse to the light sleigh and drove his master to Yagodnoye.

The sun was ripening like a yellow apricot above the village, clouds were dying out in smoky wisps above and below it. The keen frosty air was saturated with a rich fruity scent. The ice on the road crumbled under the horse's hoofs, the steam from the animal's nostrils was carried away by the wind and settled in rime on its mane. Soothed by the swift motion and the cold, Mokhov dozed in his seat. But in the village square a crowd of Cossacks in black sheepskins, and flocks of women, wrapped in their otter-trimmed coats, could be seen.

The teacher Balanda stood in the middle of the crowd, holding his handkerchief to his greenish lips, a red ribbon in his button-hole. His eyes burned feverishly as he spoke.

". . . You see, the accursed autocracy has crashed. Now your sons will no longer be sent to put down the workers with their whips. Your shameful service to that vampire, the tsar, has been ended. The Constituent Assembly will govern a new, free Russia. It will build another life, a glorious life."

Behind him, his mistress was pulling his coat-tails and whispering imploringly:

"Mitya, that's enough! Can't you understand that it's bad for you? You'll be spitting blood again, Mitya!"

The Cossacks listened to Balanda, coughing embarrassment and suppressing smiles. But they did not let him finish speaking. A sympathetic bass voice from the crowd interrupted:

"Yes, it'll be a fine life, it seems, but you won't live to see it, poor fellow! Go home now, it's chilly!"

Balanda hastily finished what he was saying, and walked away dejectedly.

Mokhov arrived at Yagodnoye at midday. Yemelyan led the horse by the bridle to the willow mangers by the stables and, while his master climbed out of the sleigh and fumbled under the shirt of his sheepskin for a handkerchief, unharnessed the horse and threw a cloth over its back. He was met at the foot of the steps by a big rusty-coated borzoi hound, who stood in his path, stretching its long legs and yawning, while the other dogs lying around the steps rose lazily behind him.

Sergei Platonovich, alarmed by their numbers, backed away up the steps.

The dry, well-lighted ante-room smelt strongly of dogs and vinegar. From a pair of antlers over a chest hung an officer's Caucasian fur cap, a cowl with a silver tassel, and a Caucasian cloak. As Sergei Platonovich glanced at it, he had the impression for a moment that a tall shaggy figure with hunched shoulders was standing over him. A plump black-eyed woman came out of the side room, gave Mokhov an attentive stare, and without changing the serious expression of her dark attractive face asked:

"You want Nikolai Alexeyevich? I'll tell him."

Sergei Platonovich had difficulty in recognizing Aksinya in this rather plump handsome woman. But she had immediately recognized him, and, compressing her cherry-red lips, with a slight movement of her smooth bare arms held herself unnaturally erect. She entered the hall without knocking and closed the door behind her. After a minute or two she came out again, followed by old Listnitsky. With a grave, welcoming smile he said condescendingly:

"Ah, Mokhov the merchant! What brings you here? Come in." He stood aside, and with a wave of the hand invited his guest into the hall.

Sergei Platonovich bowed with the respect he

had long since learned to adopt towards his social superiors, and went in. Yevgeny Listnitsky came forward to meet him, screwing up his eyes behind his pince-nez.

"This is delightful, my dear Sergei Platonovich! How are you? Not getting old, surely?"

"Why, of course not, Yevgeny Nikolayevich! I still expect to outlive you. But how are you? Safe and sound?"

With a smile that revealed the gold crowns on his teeth, Yevgeny took Mokhov by the arm and led him to a chair. They sat at a small table, exchanging pleasantries and seeking in each other's faces for signs of the changes that had occurred since they had last met. Old Listnitsky told Aksinya to bring in the tea, then came and stood by Mokhov with his hand resting on the table, and asked:

"How are things with you in the village? Have you heard . . . the good news?"

Mokhov looked up at the clean-shaven fold of flesh under the general's chin, and sighed.

"How could one help hearing."

"With what a fatal predetermination things have come to this pass!" The old general took a deep pull at his pipe and his Adam's apple quivered for a second. "I foresaw this at the very beginning of the war. Well, the dynasty was doomed."

"It brings to mind Merezhkovsky ... do you remember, Yevgeny? His story of Peter I and Alexei. After he has been tortured, the tsarevich Alexei says to his father: 'My blood will fall upon your descendants. ...' "

"We haven't any real news of what has happened," Mokhov said agitatedly. He fidgeted in his chair and lit a cigarette, then went on: "We haven't seen a newspaper for a week. And as I heard that Yevgeny Nikolayevich had come home on leave, I decided to drive over and find out what has really happened and what we are to expect next."

The smile vanished from Yevgeny's smoothly shaven face and he replied:

"Menacing events. ... The soldiers are literally demoralized. They don't want to go on fighting, they're tired of it. To tell the truth, this year we simply haven't had soldiers in the accepted meaning of the word. They have become bands of criminals, unbridled and savage. Father simply cannot understand it. He cannot realize the extent to which our army has become demoralized. They arbitrarily abandon their positions, they kill their officers, rob and murder civilians. ... Refusal to carry out military orders is now an everyday occurrence."

"The fish rots from the head," old Listnitsky puffed out with a cloud of tobacco smoke.

"I wouldn't say that," Yevgeny frowned, one eyelid twitching nervously. "I wouldn't say that. The army is rotting from below, disintegrated by the Bolsheviks. Even the Cossack divisions, especially those which have been in close contact with the infantry, are morally unreliable. A terrible weariness and desire to get back home. . . . And the Bolsheviks. . . ."

"What do they want?" Mokhov burst out, unable to contain himself any longer.

"Oh . . ." Yevgeny laughed. "They want. . . . They're worse than cholera germs. Worse in this sense, that they attach themselves more easily to a man, and penetrate right into the very midst of the soldiers. I mean their ideas, of course . . . there's no quarantine that will save you from them. Undoubtedly there are some very clever men among the Bolsheviks. I've come in contact with some of them. Some of them are simply fanatics," and with sudden vicious anger, "but the majority are unbridled, immoral animals. They are not interested in the essence of the Bolshevik teaching, but only in the possibility of pillaging and getting away from the front. Their first desire is to get power into their own hands, and on any conditions to end the 'imperialist' war, as they call it, even by means of a separate peace, and then to hand the land over to the peasants, and the factories to the workers. Of course this is as utopian as it is silly, but it is by such primitive methods that they have succeeded in attracting the soldiers."

Listnitsky spoke with restrained, smouldering anger, twisting an ivory cigarette holder in his fingers. Mokhov listened, his whole body leaning forward as though he were about to jump out of his chair. Old Listnitsky paced up and down the hall, shuffling along in his black, shaggy felt boots and chewing his greenish-grey whiskers.

Yevgeny went on to tell how even before the revolution broke out he had been forced to flee from his regiment, afraid of the vengeance of the Cossacks, and related the story of the events in Petrograd of which he had been witness. For a moment they lapsed into silence. Then, staring at Mokhov's nose, old Listnitsky abruptly asked:

"Well, will you buy the grey horse that you looked over in the autumn?"

"How can you talk about such matters at a time like this, Nikolai Alexeyevich?" Mokhov frowned miserably and waved his hand with a gesture of despair.

In the meantime, Mokhov's driver Yemelyan was warming himself and drinking tea in the servants' quarters, mopping his beet-root cheeks with a red handkerchief, and telling the news of the village. Wrapped in a downy shawl Aksinya stood by the bed, her breast against its carved back.

"I suppose our house has fallen down by now?" she asked.

"No, why should it?" Yemelyan drawled.

"And our neighbours, the Melekhovs, how are they getting on?"

"They're getting on all right."

"Pyotr hasn't come home on leave?"

"I haven't heard tell of it."

"And Grigory?"

"Grigory came home after Christmas. His wife gave him twins last year. He had been wounded."

"Wounded?"

"Yes, in the arm. He was marked all over like a dog after a fight. I don't know whether he had more crosses or gashes."

"And how did he look ... Grisha, I mean?" Aksinya asked. Suppressing a dry sob, she coughed, trying to keep her trembling voice steady.

"Just the same as ever; hook-nosed and dark. A Turk of the Turks, as you'd expect."

"I didn't mean that.... But does he look any older?"

"How should I know? Maybe he's a little older. His wife gave birth to twins. So he can't have aged very much."

"It's cold in the house," Aksinya said with a shiver, and she went out.

Yemelyan poured his eighth cup of tea and watched her go.

"A poisonous, stinking nit if ever there was one!" he snorted. "Not so long ago she was running about the village in peasant sandals, and now she's quite the lady. 'It's cold in the house!' Pah, you lady from the lower end, your mother gave birth to a bitch, she did! I can't stick women like her. I'd show 'em, the carrion...! 'Cold in the house!' The crawling serpent! Pah!"

He was so offended that he could not finish his eighth cup of tea, but got up, crossed himself, and went out, staring arrogantly about him and deliberately soiling the clean floor with his boots. The whole of the journey back he was as gloomy as his master. He poured out the vials of his wrath on the horse, flicking its hind-quarters indecently with the end of the whip, and calling it names. Contrary to his wont, he did not exchange a single word with his master. And Sergei Platonovich also maintained a frightened silence.

VIII

The first brigade of one of the infantry divisions held in reserve on the south-west front, and the 27th Don Cossack Regiment attached to it, were withdrawn from the front before the February Revolution took place, in order to be sent to Petrograd to suppress the disorders which had broken out. The brigade was transferred to the rear, equipped with new winter outfits, fed well for a day, then was entrained and dispatched. But events moved faster than the regiments, and on the very day of departure insistent rumours were circulating that at the headquarters of the commander-in-chief the emperor had signed a decree abdicating the throne.

The brigade was turned back halfway. At the station of Razgon the 27th Cossack Regiment was ordered to detrain. The lines were blocked with transports. Soldiers with red bands on their coats, well-made new rifles of Russian pattern but English manufacture on their shoulders, were scurrying about the platform. Many of them were excited, and stared anxiously at the Cossacks being formed up in squadrons.

The rainy day was drawing to a close. Water was burbling off the roofs of the station buildings. The oily puddles in the permanent ways reflected the grey, soft sheepskin of the sky. The roar of the shunting engines sounded muffled and broken. Beyond the goods warehouse the regiment was met by the commander of the brigade on a raven horse. Steam rose from the horses' legs, which were wet to the fetlock. The crows settled fearlessly in the wake of the column, scratching and pecking at the orange blobs of horse dung.

Accompanied by the regimental commander the commander of the brigade rode up to the Cossacks, reined in his horse, stared hard at the squadrons, and made a speech, stumbling and faltering in his choice of words:

"Cossacks! By the will of the people the reign of the Emperor Nicholas the Second has been ... er ... overthrown. The government has passed into the hands of the Provisional Committee of the State Duma. The army, and you among them, must take this ... er ... news calmly. ... The duty of the Cossacks is to defend their native land from the attacks of external and ... er ... so to speak ... from external enemies. We shall hold ourselves apart from the troubles now begun, and leave it to the civil population to choose a way of organizing a new government. We

must stand apart! For the army, war and politics are ... er ... incompatible. In times when
the foundations are being ... er ... shaken,
we must be as hard. . . ." At this point the
hidebound old brigadier-general, unused to
speech-making, hesitated over the choice of a
simile, while the regiment waited patiently,
". . . as hard as steel. It is your Cossack, military duty to obey your officers. We shall fight
the enemy as valiantly as before, while back
there" (he made a vague sweeping gesture behind him) "let the State Duma decide the fate
of the country. When we have ended the war
we shall take part in the internal life of the
country, but for the present ... we must not,
we cannot betray the army. . . . There must be
no politics in the army."

The Cossacks remained at the station for
some days, taking the oath of allegiance to the
Provisional Government, attending meetings,
frequently consorting with men of their own
locality, but keeping apart from the soldiers
swarming at the station. Among themselves
they discussed the speeches they had heard at
the meetings, distrustfully turning over every
doubtful word, until all of them somehow or
other reached the conclusion that if there was
freedom now, that meant the end of the war.
It became difficult for the officers to struggle

against that conviction, and to maintain that Russia was bound to fight on to the end.

The bewilderment which had taken possession of the higher command of the army had a serious effect on the lower ranks. It was as though the division staff had completely forgotten the existence of the brigade stranded on the line halfway to Petrograd. The soldiers ate up the eight days' rations which had been issued, then crowded to the neighbouring villages. Spirits appeared miraculously for sale, and drunken soldiers and officers became a common sight.

Torn out of the normal round of duties, the Cossacks crowded in their wagons, awaiting transport to the Don. For the rumour that the second reservists were to be demobilized was very persistent. They grew negligent in the care of their horses, and spent the day in the market squares, trading German blankets, bayonets, overcoats and the tobacco they had brought back from the trenches.

When an order arrived for the regiment to return to the front it was received with open discontent. The Second Squadron flatly refused to go, and the Cossacks would not allow the engine to be coupled to the transport wagons. But the regimental commander threatened to have them disarmed, and the agitation died away. The transport dragged slowly towards the front, while in every wagon the situation was excitedly discussed.

"What do you call this, brothers? Freedom? You've got your freedom, but when it comes to the war you've got to shed your blood again!"

"It's the old regime all over again!"

"Why'd we get rid of the tsar, then?"

"It's just the same now as it was under the tsar!"

"The same old trousers, only the fly's in the back."

"That's it."

"How long's this going to last, damn their hides?"

"This is the third year we've had only our rifles to sleep with."

At some railway junction the Cossacks poured out of the wagons as though by previous agreement, and taking no notice of the promises and threats of the commander, began a meeting. In vain did the commandant and the ancient station-master mingle with the grey Cossack greatcoats, imploring them to go back to their wagons and let the lines be cleared. The Cossacks listened with unflagging attention to the speeches of a sergeant and a little rank-and-file Cossack. The latter had difficulty in giving vent to his angry feelings:

"Cossacks! It can't go on like this! They've mucked everything up again! They're trying to make fools of us! If there's been a revolution and all the people have been given their freedom, they ought to stop the war, because the people and us Cossacks don't want war! Am I right?"

"You're right!"

"We're sick of it!"

"We can't keep our trousers up over our bottoms! How can we go on with the war?"

"Down with the war! Let's go back home."

"Unhitch the engine! Come on, boys!"

"Cossacks! Wait a bit! Cossacks! Brothers! You devils! Hold on! Brothers!" the little Cossack shouted away, attempting to raise his voice above the thousand. "Wait! Don't touch the engine! We're only out to stop this fooling. Let his honour the regimental commander show us the document, let us see whether they really want us at the front, or whether it's only another of their little games."

After the regimental commander, almost beside himself, his lips trembling, had read aloud the telegram from the divisional staff ordering the regiment to the front, the Cossacks consented to entrain again.

Six of the Tatarsky men were in one wagon. There were Pyotr Melekhov, Nikolai Koshe-

voi (Misha's uncle), Anikushka, Fedot Bodovskov, Merkulov (a gypsy-looking Cossack with
black curly beard and blazing hazel eyes) and
Maxim Gryaznov, a dissolute and merry Cossack who before the war had been known
throughout the Don district as a fearless horse
thief.

A cross-wind pierced through the wagon, the
horses stood with their blankets over them at
hastily built mangers, damp wood smoked on
a mound of earth in the middle of the floor,
and the pungent smoke was drawn towards
the chinks of the door. The Cossacks sat on
their saddles around the fire, drying their foot-
cloths. Bodovskov was warming his bare feet
at the fire, a contented smile lurking on his angular Kalmyk face. Gryaznov was sewing his
gaping sole roughly to the upper with a waxed
thread. In a voice made husky by the smoke
he remarked to no one in particular:

"When I was a lad I used to climb up over
the stove in winter-time, and my grandmother
(she was over a hundred years old then) would
search for lice in my head with her fingers,
and tell me: 'My little Maxim, my darling!
In the old days the people didn't live like they
do now; they lived well, lawfully, and had no
sorrows. But you, my little child, will live to
see a time when all the earth will be covered

with wire, and birds with iron noses will fly through the air and peck at the people like a rook pecks at a water-melon. And there will be hunger and plague among men, brother will rise against brother, and son against father. There will be no more people left than grass after a fire.' " Gryaznov paused a moment, then continued: "Well, it's all come to pass as she said it would. They've invented the telegraph, and there's your wire. And the iron birds are aeroplanes. And there'll be hunger, all right. My own folk have only sown half their land during these years, and everywhere it's the same. And if the harvest fails, you'll have your famine."

"But brother against brother . . . that's a bit far-fetched, isn't it?" Pyotr Melekhov asked.

"You wait a bit, and the people will come to that too!"

"If there's no one in command, they'll fight each other," Bodovskov interrupted.

"Perhaps we'll have to put them down, the devils."

"You finish with the Germans first," laughed Koshevoi.

"What of it, we'll do a bit of fighting yet. . . ."

Anikushka wrinkled his hairless face into an expression of feigned terror, and exclaimed:

"By our hairy-legged tsaritsa, and how much longer is our bit of fighting to go on?"

"Until you grow a beard, you eunuch," Koshevoi mimicked him.

There was an outburst of laughter, and Anikushka was put to confusion. But in the middle Gryaznov unexpectedly broke out:

"No, we've had enough! We've had more than we can stand! Here we are in misery, perishing with lice, and our families at home are living so hard that if you cut them they wouldn't bleed."

"What are you bellowing about?" Pyotr asked caustically, chewing his whiskers.

"You know what!" Merkulov answered for Gryaznov, burying his smile in his curly beard. "You know what the Cossack needs, what he longs for. . . . You know how it is; sometimes the shepherd drives the herd out to pasture, and as long as the sun hasn't dried the dew off the grass the cattle are all right; but as soon as the sun gets overhead the gadflies begin to buzz and bite. And so it is here." He turned round to face Pyotr. "Then, mister sergeant-major, the cattle begin to bellow and kick. Yes, and you know it! You needn't be uppish! You've driven bullocks yourself. . . . You know how it happens. Some calf sends its tail swishing over its back and off it goes! And the whole herd after it! The herdsman runs to stop them, but they're off like a flood, like we poured in a flood against the Germans. And just you try to stop them then!"

"What's the point of all this?"

Merkulov did not reply at once. He wound a curl of his beard around his finger and tugged it bitterly, then said, serious and unsmiling:

"We've been fighting for over two years . . . that's right, isn't it? It's nearly three years now since they drove us into the trenches. What for, why? No one knows. That's why I say that sooner or later some Gryaznov or Melekhov will break away from the front, and after him the regiment, and after the regiment the army. . . . We've had enough."

"So that's what you're getting at!"

"Yes, that! I'm not blind, and I see that everything hangs by a thread. Only let someone shout 'Shooh!' and everything will fall to pieces like an old coat from the shoulders."

"Go easy," Bodovskov advised him. "Remember Pyotr's a sergeant-major."

"I've never brought trouble on any comrade of mine," Pyotr exploded.

"All right, don't get angry. I was only joking."

Bodovskov looked embarrassed, wriggled the thick-jointed toes of his bare feet, then rose and padded off to the horses.

In the corner, by the bales of pressed hay, a group of Cossacks from other villages was talking in low tones. Presently they struck up a song. Alymov, a Cossack from the Chir, began a jig, but someone slapped him on the back and grunted hoarsely:

"Chuck it!"

Koshevoi called them over to the fire. They fed the flames with bits of wood broken from a station fence and in the warmth of the fire the singing became brighter.

Loaded for battle, the war-horse awaits
At the door of the church where his mas-
ter was wed,
And many's the tear that mother and
grandson
And lovely young wife will soon have to
shed.

But when the Cossack steps forth
In his battle array,
His wife holds the stirrup,
His nephew the lance....

In the next wagon a wheezing accordion ground out a Cossack dance. Army boots pounded the floorboards mercilessly and a cracked voice bawled the words:

> *What a life so full of care,*
> *Tsarist yokes are tight to wear,*
> *They rub the necks of Cossacks fair,*
> *None can breathe a breath of air.*
> *Pugachov* calls the Don countrey,*
> *"Poor folk all come follow me,*
> *Hey, Cossacks, Cossack atamans...."*

Another voice piped up over the first in a high-pitched gabble:

> *The tsar in honest faith we're serving,*
> *For our wives at home we're yearning,*
> *With a wench we'd yearn no more*
> *And for the tsar we'd find a....*

The Cossacks gave up their song and listened with winks and grins of approval to the wild din that grew louder and louder in the next wagon. Pyotr Melekhov could not contain himself and burst out laughing:

"The devils!"

A twinkle came into Merkulov's brown, yellowishly glowing eyes; he leaped to his feet, picked up the beat and tapped rapidly with the toe of his boot, then suddenly stamping

---

* *Yemelyan Pugachov* —leader of the Cossacks and peasants against the tsar in the peasant war 1773-75.

his foot, he flung himself into a light springy dance, squatting and kicking out his legs as he spun round in a circle. Everyone took their turn, warming themselves with the exertion. The accordion in the next wagon had long since died away and now hoarse voices were cursing heavily. But the Cossacks went on with their dance, disturbing the horses, and did not stop until Anikushka in the middle of an astonishing caper accidentally sat down on the fire. Laughing, they picked Anikushka up and by the light of a candle-stump examined his new *sharovari* that were fatally burned at the back, and the scorched tail of his padded jacket.

"Take 'em off!" Merkulov advised sympathetically.

"Are you daft, gypsy? What shall I wear?"

Merkulov rummaged in his saddle-bags and pulled out a long petticoat. They got the fire going again. Merkulov held the petticoat by its narrow shoulder-straps and, choking with laughter, said:

"Here you are! I pinched it off a clothes-line at one of the stations. Thought it would do for foot-cloths. But I won't tear it up. You can have it!"

The cursing Anikushka was forced to don the petticoat and the guffaws were so lusty and deep that heads peered out of the doors of other wagons and envious voices shouted in the darkness:

"What are you up to, you stallions?"

"What are you bellowing at?"

At the next stop they called in the accordion-player and Cossacks crowded in from the other wagons, breaking the mangers and pressing the horses to the wall. In his white petticoat, which must have belonged to a woman of huge proportions, for it was much too long for him, Anikushka danced and whirled in a tiny circle until he dropped with exhaustion.

But above blood-soaked Byelorussia the stars wept mournfully. The smoky darkness sped past into the yawning night. The wind streamed low across the earth, saturated with the bitter scent of fallen leaves, of damp, mouldering clay, of March snows.

IX

Within twenty-four hours the regiment was again close to the front. The transport train was halted at a railway junction. The sergeant-majors brought the order to detrain. The horses were hurriedly led down planks on to the line, there was a scurrying backward and forward after forgotten articles, ragged bundles of hay were flung straight on to the damp sand.

An orderly from the regimental commander called out to Pyotr Melekhov as he passed.

"The commander wants you at the station."

Adjusting a strap on his greatcoat, Pyotr went slowly towards the platform. "Anikushka, keep an eye on my horse," he asked as he went by.

Anikushka stared silently after him, anxiety mingling with the usual expression of boredom on his sullen face. As Pyotr walked along, staring at his muddy boots and wondering why the regimental commander had sent for him, his attention was attracted by a small group gathered at the end of the platform by the hot-water shed. He went up and listened to the conversation. A score of soldiers stood surrounding a tall, ruddy-faced Cossack who was standing with his back to the shed in an awkward, hunted attitude. Pyotr stared at his bearded face, at the number 52 on his blue, sergeant's shoulder-straps and felt sure he had seen the man before somewhere.

"How'd you manage it? And you with a sergeant's stripe too!" a volunteer infantryman with a freckled intelligent face questioned him maliciously.

"What's the matter?" Pyotr asked inquisitively, touching the shoulder of a man standing in front of him.

The soldier turned his head and answered unwillingly:

"Caught a deserter ... one of your Cossacks."

Pyotr tried to recall where he had seen the Cossack's broad ginger-eyebrowed, ginger-moustached face before. The prisoner made no reply to the importunate questionings of the volunteer, but sipped hot water out of a copper mug made from a shell case, and chewed at a dry biscuit soaked in the water. His prominent widely spaced eyes narrowed as he chewed and swallowed, and his eyebrows quivered as he glanced about him. An elderly, thick-set soldier stood on guard with rifle and fixed bayonet at his side. The Cossack finished his drink, and passed his tired eyes over the soldiers unceremoniously examining him. His blue, childishly simple eyes suddenly hardened. Hurriedly swallowing, he licked his lips and shouted in a coarse, deep, inflexible voice:

"Am I an animal? Won't you let a man eat, you swine? Damn you, haven't you ever seen a man before?"

The soldiers burst into a roar of laughter; but Pyotr had hardly heard the first words when, as always happens, he suddenly remembered the man's name, and how he and his father had bought a three-year-old bullock from him at the annual Yelanskaya fair before the war.

"Fomin! Yakov!" he shouted, pushing his way through the crowd.

The man put the mug down with a clumsy, bewildered movement, and, gazing at Pyotr with smiling, embarrassed eyes, replied as he chewed:

"I can't say I know you, brother!"

"You're from Rubyezhin, aren't you?"

"Yes. And you're from Yelanskaya, aren't you?"

"No, from Vyeshenskaya. But I know you all right. You sold my father a bullock at the market five years ago."

Still smiling the same childish smile, Fomin tried to remember.

"No, I've forgotten it. I can't remember you," he said with evident regret.

"You were in the 52nd?"

"Yes."

"You ran away? How could you, brother?"

Fomin took off his fur cap and fished out an ancient pouch. He bent and slowly pushed his cap under his arm, tore off a corner of paper, and only then fixed Pyotr with a stern, moistly glittering gaze.

"Couldn't stand any more, brother," he said gruffly.

Pricked by the man's stare, Pyotr coughed and bit at his yellow whiskers.

"Well, finish your talk, or I'll be getting into trouble through you," the escort sighed, picking up his rifle. "Come on, old man."

Fomin hurriedly pushed the mug into his pack, said good-bye to Pyotr with eyes averted, and with a lumbering bear-like gait accompanied his escort towards the station commandant's office.

Pyotr found the regimental commander with the two squadron commanders bent over a table in what had once been the first-class buffet.

"You've kept us waiting, Melekhov," the colonel frowned with tired, irritable eyes.

Pyotr listened to the information that his squadron was being placed at the disposition of the divisional staff, and that it was necessary to keep a sharp watch on the Cossacks, informing the squadron commander of any noticeable change in their attitude. Pyotr stared unwinkingly at the colonel's face, listening attentively, but Fomin's moistly glittering eyes and the quiet "couldn't stand any more, brother," remained ineradicably in his memory.

He left the warm, steaming buffet and went back to the squadron. As he approached his wagon he saw a group of Cossacks gathered around the squadron smith. He promptly forgot Fomin and their conversation and hastened his steps, intending to have a word with the smith about the re-shoeing of his horse. The petty cares and anxieties of the daily round rose uppermost. But it was only for a moment. From behind a wagon came a woman decked in a white, fluffy shawl, and dressed differently from the women in Byelorussia. The strangely familiar shape of her figure fixed Pyotr's attention. The woman suddenly turned her face towards him, and hastened in his direction; there was a slight swaying movement in her shoulders and her slim, youthful body. And, although not yet close enough to distinguish her features, by that light, hip-swinging walk of hers Pyotr recognized his wife. A pleasant, prickly cool penetrated to his heart. His joy was the greater because unexpected. Deliberately slowing his steps, so that the others should not think he was particularly pleased, he went to meet her. He embraced Darya, kissed her the customary three times, and was about to ask her something. But his deep, inward agitation broke through to the surface, his lips trembled, and he lost his voice.

"I wasn't expecting you," he choked up at last.

"My dear! How you've changed!" Darya clapped her hands. "You're quite a stranger! You see I've come to visit you. They didn't want to let me go at home. But I thought I must go and see my dear one." She tumbled out the words, pressing against her husband and gazing at him with moist eyes.

The bunch of Cossacks round the wagons stared at them, grunting and winking.

"Pyotr's happy all right!"

"My old wolf-bitch wouldn't come to visit me!"

"She's got a round dozen back there without you."

"He might take pity on us and lend his wife to his own troop for a night."

"Come on, lads, it gives me a pain to watch 'em."

At that moment Pyotr forgot that he had made up his mind to punish his wife ruthlessly, and he caressed her in front of everybody, stroking the arches of her eyebrows with his great, tobacco-stained finger, and rejoicing. Darya also forgot that only two nights previously she had slept in a wagon with a veterinary surgeon of the dragoons, who had been on his way from Kharkov to rejoin his regiment. The surgeon had had an unusually fluffy, black moustache; but that had been two nights ago, and now with tears of sincere joy in her eyes she embraced her husband, gazing at him with true, clear eyes.

X

On his return from leave Yevgeny Listnitsky did not report to his old regiment, from which he had so shamefully been forced to flee even before the February Revolution, but went straight to the divisional staff. The chief of staff, a young general from a famous Don Cossack noble family, willingly arranged for his transfer to the 14th Don Cossack Regiment.

"I know you will find it difficult to work in your old surroundings, Captain," he told Listnitsky, taking him into a private room. "The Cossacks feel hostile towards you, your name is odious to them, so naturally it will be wiser for you to join the 14th Regiment. The officers there are an exceptionally fine lot and the Cossacks are more reliable, duller. Most of them are from the southern stanitsas. You will find it easier there. Aren't you the son of General Listnitsky?" the chief of staff paused and on receiving confirmation of his inquiry, continued: "For my part I can tell you that we value your kind of officer. Even among the officers, the majority are double-dealers nowadays. There is nothing easier than to change one's faith, and even to serve two faiths at the same time," the chief of staff concluded bitterly.

Listnitsky was glad of the transfer. The same day he travelled to Dvinsk, where the 14th Regiment was stationed, and reported to the regimental commander. He was satisfied to find that the majority of the officers were monarchists, while the Cossacks, Old Believers for the most part, were by no means revolutionary-minded. They had sworn the oath of allegiance to the Provisional Government very reluctantly, without understanding or wishing to understand the events seething around them. Cringing and peaceable Cossacks had been elected to the regimental and squadron committees. Listnitsky breathed more easily in his new situation.

Among the officers he encountered two former members of his old Guards Regiment, who held themselves aloof; the remainder were exceptionally united and at one together, and talked openly of restoring the monarchy.

The regiment had been stationed some two months in Dvinsk, becoming a united unit, well-drilled and rested. Previously the squadrons had been attached to infantry divisions and had wandered about the front from Riga to Dvinsk, but in April a careful hand had brought the squadrons together, and the regiment was now prepared for anything. Under the officers' strict supervision, the Cossacks spent their days at exercise, fed their horses well, and lived a temperate, sluggish existence, removed from all outside influence. Only a few vague rumours circulated among them as to the real purpose of their regiment, but the officers talked openly of their intention, guided by reliable hands, of reversing the course of history in the not distant future.

The front loomed near at hand. A little further west the armies panted in a mortal fever; there was a shortage of military supplies and food. With innumerable hands the soldiers reached out to the phantasmal word "peace." The army took a mixed attitude towards the provisional head of the republic Kerensky, and spurred on by his hysterical appeals, suffered huge losses in the June offensive. In the armies a ripened anger flowed and bubbled like water in a spring.... But in Dvinsk the Cossacks lived peaceably, quietly, and the miseries they had endured at the front were overgrown in their memories. The officers regularly attended their meetings, lived well, and ardently discussed the future of Russia.

So it was until the early days of July. On the third the order came to advance without losing an instant. The regiment moved towards Petrograd. On the seventh the hoofs of the Cossack horses were clattering over the cobbled streets of the capital.

The regiment was quartered in houses on the Nevsky Prospect, and Listnitsky's squadron was assigned to an empty commercial building. The Cossacks had been awaited with impatience and joy by the counter-revolution; the care which the city authorities had taken to fit up the quarters assigned to them bore eloquent witness to that. The walls gleamed with fresh whitewash, the clean floors shone, a smell of fresh pinewood came from the newly-erected bunks; it was almost comfortable in the light, tidy semi-basement. Listnitsky, frowning under his pince-nez, carefully examined the quarters and decided that they could hardly have been better. Satisfied with his inspection, he turned towards the door leading to the yard, accompanied by the little, elegantly dressed representative of the city administration who had been assigned to welcome the Cossacks.

But here an unpleasant incident occurred. As he grasped the door-knob, he saw a drawing, scratched on the wall with some sharp instrument, of a dog's head and a broom.* Evidently some of the workers who had repaired the building knew for whom it was intended.

"What's this?" asked Listnitsky, his eyebrows twitching.

The city representative glanced at the drawing out of his sharp mouse-like eyes, and gasped. The blood rushed to his head so violently that even his stiff collar looked pink.

"I beg your pardon, Captain, a vile hand. . . ."

"I hope that this emblem was drawn without your knowledge."

"Why, what do you think? How else could it have been done? It's a Bolshevik trick, performed by some scoundrel. I shall at once order them to whitewash the wall again. The devil! I'm terribly sorry that this stupid business has occurred. Believe me, I feel ashamed that people can be so vile. . . ."

Listnitsky began to feel genuinely sorry for this depressed, confused citizen. Softening his ruthlessly cold gaze, he said quietly:

* A dog's head and a broom were attached to the saddles of the *Oprichniki*, the notoriously brutal armed forces of Ivan the Terrible, as a symbol that they would sink their fangs in the tsar's enemies and then sweep them away.

"The artist didn't hit the mark—the Cossacks don't know enough Russian history. But it doesn't follow from this that we can encourage such an attitude towards us...."

The representative tried to scratch out the drawing with his firm polished nail, smearing his expensive English coat with the white dust as he rose on tiptoe trying to reach the drawing. Listnitsky was polishing his pince-nez and smiling, but a bitter feeling gnawed within him.

"So this is how they greet us, this is the other side of the medal. But does all Russia really regard us as *Oprichniki*?" he thought as he crossed the yard towards the stables, listening inattentively to the chatter of the city representative.

The sun's rays fell obliquely into the deep broad well of the yard. People were leaning out of their windows, watching the crowd of Cossacks below. When they had led their horses to the stables, the Cossacks squatted down in the shade of the walls.

"Why don't you go to your quarters, lads?" Listnitsky asked.

"Plenty of time for that, Captain."

"We'll get fed up with the place soon enough."

"We'll go when the horses are stabled."

After Listnitsky had inspected the warehouse allotted for stables, he turned towards the city representative and, trying to recover his former hostility towards him, said:

"Come to an agreement with whoever is in charge of these matters and have something done about this. We must have another doorway made in these stables. Three doors for a hundred and twenty horses are not enough. If there were an alarm it would take us half an hour to get the horses out. It's strange that this circumstance was not taken into consideration beforehand. I shall have to report the matter to the regimental commander."

Having received an assurance that not one but two doors would be fitted immediately, Listnitsky thanked the representative curtly for the trouble he had taken, appointed orderlies and went upstairs to the rooms temporarily assigned to the company officers.

He walked up the back stairs, unbuttoning his tunic and wiping the perspiration from under the peak of his cap, gratefully aware of the cool dampness of the rooms. There was no one in the officers' quarters except Junior Captain Atarshchikov.

"Where are the others?" Listnitsky asked, dropping on to a camp bed and throwing out his legs heavily in their dusty boots.

"They're gone out to have a look at Petrograd."

"Why didn't you?"

"Oh, I didn't think it was worth it. Going out as soon as you arrive. I've just been reading about what happened here a few days ago. Interesting!"

Listnitsky lay silent, feeling the damp sweat of his shirt cooling pleasantly on his skin. Worn out with his journey, he was disinclined to rise and wash, but mastering his lassitude, he rose at last, and called his batman. He changed his linen and washed thoroughly, snorting with satisfaction and rubbing his fleshy sunburnt neck with a fluffy towel.

"Wash yourself, Vanya," he advised Atarshchikov, "it works wonders.... Well, what's in the papers?"

"Yes, perhaps I shall wash. Not bad, you say? What's in the papers?—a description of the Bolshevik demonstrations, government measures.... Read it!"

The wash had freshened Listnitsky, and he was about to pick up the newspaper when an invitation came for him to call on the regimental commander. Rising unwillingly from his bed, he put on a clean, though rather crumpled tunic, fastened on his sword and went out on to the Nevsky Prospect.

Crossing the street, he turned and glanced back at the building where the squadron was billeted. Outwardly it looked no different from the others, a five-storied building faced with rough smoke-darkened stone, in a line of other buildings of the same kind. Lighting a cigarette he strolled along the pavement. A dense throng foamed with men's straw hats, bowlers and caps, and the elegantly simple hats of the women. Occasionally the democratic green cap of a soldier appeared and disappeared, engulfed in the flood of colours.

A fresh, stimulating breeze was blowing from the sea, but it broke against the blocks of buildings and was scattered into feeble gusts. Clouds were floating southward over the steely, violet-tinted heaven; their milk-white masses were sharply and distinctly serrated. A steaming sultriness heralding rain hung over the city. The air was scented with the smell of warm asphalt, petrol fumes, the nearby sea, the indefinite aroma of perfume, and the myriad other odours characteristic of every large city.

As he walked slowly down the street smoking, Listnitsky noticed the respectful side glances of the passers-by. At first he felt slightly embarrassed on account of his crumpled uniform and soiled cap, then he decided that a man from the front need not feel ashamed of his appearance, especially as he had only just come off the train.

The sun-blinds of the shops cast lazy, olive-yellow patches on the pavement. The wind sent the blinds billowing and bellying, and the patches stirred, dodging away from the feet of the passers-by. Although it was afternoon, the Nevsky was crowded with people. With joyous satisfaction Listnitsky, grown unaccustomed to cities during the years of war, drank in the myriad-voiced roar intermingled with the sound of laughter, the motor-horns, the shouts of the newspaper sellers. Feeling at home in this crowd of well-dressed, well-fed people, nevertheless he could not but think: "How satisfied, how glad and happy you are now! All of you: merchants, stock-brokers, officials, landowners, people of blue blood! But how did you feel only three days ago, when the rabble and the soldiery were pouring in a molten stream along this very street? Truly, I am glad for you, yet not glad. And I don't know how to rejoice in your well-being...."

He tried to analyse his mingled feelings, to find their source, and had no difficulty in deciding that he thought and felt like this because the war and all he had had to live through had drawn him apart from this crowd of well-fed, satisfied men and women.

"What about him, for instance," he thought, as his eyes met those of a plump, rosy-cheeked young man. "Why isn't he at the front? I suppose he's the son of a factory owner or some prosperous merchant, and has got out of military service, the scoundrel! Doing his bit on the home front? What does he care for the country, living on the fat of the land, likes having his women in comfort. . . .

"But whose side are you on anyhow?" he asked himself, and smilingly decided: "Why, of course I'm with these. There is a particle of me in them and I myself am a particle of their collectivity. Everything that is good and bad in my class exists to some extent in me. Perhaps I have a slightly thinner skin than that fat pig, perhaps I feel things more acutely and that's why I'm honest and go to the front instead of 'working for the defence.' Perhaps that's why I threw myself on the snow this winter, in Mogilev, and wept like a baby when I saw the deposed emperor leaving headquarters, when I saw his sorrowful lips and inexpressibly helpless hand thrown across his lap. . . . I am honest in my non-acceptance of the revolution. I can't accept it. Both my heart and my mind revolt against it. I would lay down my life for the old, lay it down without posing, simply, like a soldier. . . . But are there many who'd do the same?"

His face paled as he recalled with agitating distinctness a late afternoon in February, the governor's house in Mogilev, the damp iron railings, the snow-covered ground, the rosy glow of the sunlight, the sun lowering behind a misty veil. . . . On the other side of the Dnieper the sky had been azure, scarlet, rust-golden. . . . Every stroke on the horizon was so ethereal that it was painful to look at it. Near the gate a small crowd of officers and civilians were gathered. A limousine appeared. Baron Fredericks and the tsar could be seen through the window leaning back on cushions. The tsar's face was ashen, violet-hued. Tilted over his pale forehead he wore the black lamb's-wool hat of the Cossack Guards.

Listnitsky had almost run past the crowd, who had stared after him in amazement. He had seen the tsar's hand drop from the black rim of his cap as he answered the salute, he had heard the burr of the motor, and the humiliating silence with which the crowd had seen off their last emperor. . . .

He went slowly up the steps of the house in which the regimental staff was quartered. His cheeks were still quivering and his eyes were red and swollen. On the second floor landing he smoked two cigarettes in succession, then, wiping his pince-nez, mounted the stairs two at a time to the third floor, where the staff was quartered.

The regimental commander opened a map of Petrograd before him, and pointed out the area in which Listnitsky's squadron was to guard the government offices. He specified the buildings one by one, and informed him with the utmost detail of the time and manner of posting the guards. He concluded with:

"In the Winter Palace, Kerensky...."

"Not a word of Kerensky!" Listnitsky muttered fiercely, turning deathly pale.

"Yevgeny Nikolayevich, you must take yourself in hand."

"Colonel, please...."

"But my dear...."

"Please!"

"Your nerves...."

"Am I to send our patrols in the direction of the Putilov Works immediately?" Yevgeny asked, breathing heavily.

The colonel bit his lips, smiled, shrugged his shoulders and replied:

"At once! And they must be commanded by a troop officer."

Listnitsky turned and went out, crushed by the memory of all that he had experienced and his conversation with the colonel. Almost directly outside the main door he saw a patrol of the Fourth Don Cossack Regiment. Wilted flowers drooped wanly from the snaffles of the officer's horse, and the man's flaxen-moustached face wore a half smile.

"Hurrah for the saviours of our country!" a sententious elderly gentleman shouted, stepping off the pavement and waving his hat.

The officer courteously saluted, and the patrol trotted on. Listnitsky stared at the agitated face, the slobbering lips of the civilian who had cheered the Cossacks, at the man's carefully tied, coloured cravat, and frowning, slipped with drooping shoulders into the gateway of his squadron quarters.

XI

General Kornilov's appointment as commander-in-chief of the south-western front was highly approved by the officers of the 14th Cossack Regiment. They spoke of him with esteem and respect as a man of iron character, and undoubtedly capable of getting the country out of the mess into which the Provisional Government had plunged it. Listnitsky especially welcomed the appointment. Through the younger officers of the squadron and trusted

Cossacks he tried to find out how the lower ranks reacted to it, but the information he obtained hardly pleased him, for the Cossacks were either silent or replied apathetically:

"Makes no difference to us."

"Who knows what he's like?"

"If he tried to bring peace, then of course. . . ."

"We shan't get anything out of his promotion."

Within a few days, rumours were circulated among the officers that Kornilov was putting pressure on the government to restore the death sentence at the front, and to introduce other emergency measures on which the fate of the army and the successful prosecution of the war depended. It was said that Kerensky was afraid of Kornilov and would probably try to have him replaced by a more compliant general. So the government communiqué of July 19th, appointing Kornilov supreme commander, came as a great surprise. Soon after this, Junior Captain Atarshchikov, who had numerous acquaintances in the Chief Committee of the Officers' Alliance, informed them, quoting reliable sources, that Kornilov in his report to the Provisional Government was insisting that the following measures be adopted: the establishment of courts martial throughout the country, having jurisdiction over the troops in the rear and the civil population, with the right to inflict capital punishment; the reintroduction of the disciplinary powers of the higher officers; the limitation of the activities of the soldiers' committees, and so on. On the evening of the same day Listnitsky, in conversation with other officers of the regiment, put the question bluntly to them: Whose side were they on?

"Gentlemen!" he said, restraining his agitation, "we are living like one family, we know each other well, yet so far a number of important questions have remained unsettled among us. And now that we are clearly moving towards a clash between the supreme command and the government, we must settle the question of whose side we are on. Let's talk like comrades, hiding nothing from one another."

The first to reply to his invitation was Junior Captain Atarshchikov:

"For General Kornilov I am ready to shed my own blood, and other people's too. He is a man of absolute honesty, and he alone is capable of putting Russia on her feet. Look what he's done already with the army. Thanks to him the hands of the commanders have been untied somewhat, whereas before it was continual committees, fraternizations, desertions. How can there be any discussion about it? Every decent man will support Kornilov!"

He spoke fierily, and, when he had ended, looked round the group of officers and tapped a cigarette challengingly on his case. Atarshchikov had unusually slim legs and was disproportionately broad in the shoulders and chest; on the lower lid of his right eye there was a large brown mole. It prevented the upper lid from closing properly and at first sight this gave the impression that his eyes were constantly veiled with a contemptuously expectant sneer.

"If we've got to choose between the Bolsheviks, Kerensky, and Kornilov, of course we're for Kornilov."

"It's difficult to judge what Kornilov wants: is it the restoration of order, or the restoration of something else...."

"That's no answer! Or if it is, it's a silly one! What are you afraid of, the restoration of the monarchy?"

"I'm not afraid of that; on the contrary."

"Well then, what are you arguing about?"

"Gentlemen!" the speaker was Dolgov, who had only recently been promoted from sergeant-major to cornet for his distinguished ser-

vices. He spoke in a firm well-weathered voice.
"Why wrangle about it? Say frankly that we
Cossacks must cling to General Kornilov as a
child clings to its mother's skirt. If we break
with him, we're lost. Russia will rake us up
like dung. The position is clear: where he goes,
we go also."

"That's exactly it!" Atarshchikov exclaimed,
clapping Dolgov delightedly on the back, and
fixing his laughing eyes on Listnitsky, who was
smiling and anxiously straightening the creases
in his trousers.

"Now, gentlemen!" he raised his voice. "Are
we for Kornilov, or aren't we?"

"Why, of course we are."

"Dolgov has cut the Gordian knot at a
stroke."

"All the officers are for him!"

"To our dear Lavr Georgievich, a Cossack
and a hero, hurrah!"

Laughing and clinking glasses, the officers
drank their tea. The tense feeling which had
prevailed was dissipated, and the conversation
turned to the events of the past few days.

"We're all for the commander-in-chief, but
the Cossacks are a bit down in the mouth,"
Dolgov remarked irresolutely.

"In what way, 'down in the mouth'?" Listnitsky asked.

"Why, they're in the dumps, and that's all there is to it. The swine want to go home to their wives. They're sick of living hard."

"It's up to us to carry the Cossacks with us," another officer declared, bringing his fist down with a bang on the table. "That's what we're officers for."

"The Cossacks must have it explained to them patiently whose side they should take."

Listnitsky rattled his spoon against his glass, and when he had secured attention, said deliberately:

"I beg you to remember, gentlemen, that our work at the moment consists in explaining to the Cossacks the true state of affairs. We must get the Cossacks away from the influence of the committees. That means bringing about a change of character as great as the change most of us had to induce in ourselves since the February upheaval—if not greater. Formerly, in 1916 for instance, I could thrash a Cossack, and risk his sending a bullet through my back in the next battle. But since the February Revolution we have had to act differently, because if I struck some idiot the rest would have killed me on the spot without waiting for a convenient opportunity. And now the situation has changed again. Now we must," Listnitsky emphasized the word, "fraternize with the

Cossacks. Everything depends on that," he declared emphatically. "You know what is happening at present in the First and Fourth regiments?"

"It's appalling!"

"Exactly. Their officers continued to cut themselves off from the Cossacks with the old barriers, and as a result the Cossacks have come under the influence of the Bolsheviks almost to a man, and 90 per cent of them have become Bolsheviks themselves. It's clear that we shall not be able to avoid the menacing events that are coming. July 3rd and 5th* were only a harsh warning to all who are heedless. . . . Either we shall have to fight with Kornilov, or the Bolsheviks will bring about another revolution. They are having a breathing-space, concentrating their forces, and meantime we are slacking. How can we let things go on like this? It's trustworthy Cossacks that we need in the coming upheaval."

"That's true, Listnitsky."

"Very true!"

"Russia has one foot in the grave. . . ."

"Do you think we don't understand that? We do, but at times we're powerless to do any-

---

* Mass armed demonstrations of workers, soldiers and sailors in Petrograd against the Provisional Government.

thing. Order No. 1* and *Okopnaya Pravda*** are sowing their seed."

"And we are admiring the shoots instead of trampling them underfoot or burning them out!" Atarshchikov shouted.

"No, we're not admiring them, we're simply powerless!"

"You're wrong, Cornet! We're just negligent!"

"That's not so!"

"Prove it!"

"Quiet, gentlemen!"

"The *Pravda's* been destroyed. But Kerensky wakes up when everything's over...."

"What is this, a market-place? We'll get nowhere like this!"

By and by the disorderly shouts subsided. One of the squadron commanders who had been listening to Listnitsky with a great deal of interest begged for silence.

"I suggest we give Captain Listnitsky an opportunity to finish."

"Go ahead."

---

* Order No. 1 (March 1, 1917) of the Executive Committee of the Petrograd Soviet introduced elective organizations within the army, whose task it was to supervise the actions of the old tsarist officers.

** *Okopnaya Pravda* (*Trench Truth*), a Bolshevik daily paper, published in 1917.

Listnitsky, rubbing his angular knees with his fists, went on:

"I say that when the coming struggle arrives ... the civil war, I mean—and I've only just begun to realize that it's inevitable—we shall need trustworthy Cossacks. We must fight to win them away from the committees which are inclining them towards the Bolsheviks. That is a vital necessity! Remember that in the event of fresh disturbances the Cossacks of the First and Fourth regiments will shoot down their own officers. . . ."

"That's true; they won't stand on ceremony."

". . . And by their experience—a very bitter one—we must profit. Every second Cossack of the First and Fourth regiments—they're no longer Cossacks for that matter—will have to be hanged, we may have to get rid of the lot. The weeds must be cleared from the field! And we must save our own Cossacks from mistakes for which they would afterwards have to pay."

After Listnitsky one of the squadron commanders, an elderly officer who had been in the regiment nine years and had been wounded four times in the war, spoke of the difficulties of service in the Cossack regiments before the war. The Cossack officers had been kept in the background, grudged all amenities; promotion had been slow and for the majority of regular officers the rank of colonel had been the highest they could aspire to; and in his view this explained the inertia of the Cossack leaders at the time of the tsar's overthrow. But even so it was necessary to support Kornilov at all costs, and to maintain closer contacts with him through the Council of the Alliance of Cossack Troops and the Chief Committee of the Officers' Alliance. "Let Kornilov become dictator!" he ended. "For the Cossacks that will be salvation. Perhaps we shall be better off under him than under the tsar."

It was long after midnight. Night hung over the city in a simple white drapery of cloud. Beyond the window the black needle of the Admiralty spire loomed amid a yellow flood of lights.

The officers sat talking till dawn. It was decided to have talks with the Cossacks three times a week on political subjects, and the troop officers were to occupy the troops daily with gymnastics and reading, in order to fill up spare time and to win the Cossacks away from the disintegrating atmosphere of politics. Before breaking up, they sang: "The Don's awake and stirring, the quiet and Christian Don," and finished their tenth samovar while toasts were jestingly proposed amid a clinking of glasses. Just before the end Atarshchikov, after a whispered consultation with Dolgov, called out:

"And now, as a dessert, we shall treat you to something in the true Cossack tradition. Quiet, please! And we might have the window open, it's rather thick in here."

Two voices, Dolgov's rough, weathered bass and Atarshchikov's unusually pleasant tenor, joined together, a little uncertainly at first, but finally mingling into a song of overwhelming beauty:

... But our Don is proud, our quiet Don,
our father dear;
Never did he bow to heathen, never asked
of Moscow how to live;
And the Turks—with the sword-point
through the ages did he greet;
And from year to year the Donland steppe,
our motherland,
For the Virgin pure and its own true faith,
Yea, for the Don so free, with murmuring
wave,
battled with its enemies. ...

Atarshchikov sat with his hands crossed on his knees, singing without faltering, his face unusually stern. Towards the end of the song Listnitsky noticed a tear running down his cheek.

After the officers of the other squadrons had departed, Atarshchikov came and sat down on Listnitsky's bed, and fiddling with the faded blue braces on his broad chest, whispered:

"You know, Yevgeny.... I'm devilishly fond of the Don, of all that old, age-old style of Cossack life. I love my Cossacks, and the Cossack women. I love it all! I want to weep when I smell the scent of the steppe wormwood.... And when the sunflower blossoms, and the fragrance of the rain-washed grapevines is in the air, I love it all so deeply and painfully.... You understand.... And now I'm thinking: mayn't we be fooling these same Cossacks with all this? Is this the road we want them to take?"

"What are you getting at?" Listnitsky asked cautiously.

Atarshchikov's sunburnt neck looked youthfully fresh and innocent against his white collar. His bluish eyelid hung awkwardly over the brown mole and the half-closed eye gleamed liquidly in the darkness.

"I'm wondering whether this is best for the Cossacks."

"But if this isn't, what is?"

"I don't know.... But why are they so spontaneously turning away from us? The revolution seems to have divided us into sheep and goats; it's as if our interests were divided."

"Don't you see?" Listnitsky began carefully. "Here we get a difference in the understanding of events. We have the greater culture, and can estimate the situation critically, but for them everything is more primitive and simple. The Bolsheviks are continually driving into their heads that the war must be ended, or rather, transformed into civil war. They are setting the Cossacks on us, and as the Cossacks are tired, as there is more of the animal in them, and they haven't that strong moral consciousness of their duty and responsibility to their fatherland which we have, it is natural that they should become favourable soil for these doctrines. After all, what does the fatherland really mean to the Cossacks? It is an abstract conception at the best. 'The Don Province is far from the front,' they reason, 'and the Germans will never get that far.' That's the whole trouble. We must explain to them the consequences that would result from transforming the war into a civil war."

Even while he spoke, Yevgeny felt that his words were not reaching their goal, and that Atarshchikov was closing into his shell again like an oyster. And so it happened. When he had finished, the other man muttered something inaudible, then sat for a long time without speaking, and try as he would, Listnitsky could not discover the secret train of thought he was pursuing. "I should have let him speak his mind out to the end..." he thought regretfully.

Atarshchikov wished him good-night, and without another word went to his own bed. For a moment he had sought a sincere exchange of views, had lifted a corner of that dark curtain of the unknown with which every man veils himself from others, and then lowered it again.

Listnitsky lay smoking for a while, troubled and angered by his inability to get to the bottom of what was disturbing his friend. As he stared tensely into the grey, velvety darkness he suddenly remembered Aksinya, and his days of leave, filled to the brim with her. He fell asleep, soothed by the change of thought and the fortuitous, fragmentary recollection of the women who at various times had crossed his path.

XII

In Listnitsky's squadron there was a Cossack, Ivan Lagutin, who had been one of the first to be elected to the regimental military revolutionary committee. Until the regiment arrived in Petrograd he had not distinguished himself in any way, but at the end of July the troop officer informed Yevgeny that the man was in the habit of attending the military section of the Petrograd Soviet of Workers' and Soldiers' Deputies, was frequently seen talking to the other Cossacks of the troop, and had a bad influence over them. There had been two cases of refusal to undertake guard and patrol duty, and the troop officer attributed them to Lagutin's influence. Listnitsky decided that he must get to know the man better, and find out what he was thinking. It would have been useless and indiscreet to question the Cossack directly so he decided to wait. An opportunity quickly presented itself. A few nights later Lagutin's troop was assigned patrol duty in the streets around the Putilov works, and Listnitsky informed the troop officer that he would take charge on this occasion. He gave instructions to his orderly to get his horse ready, and, having dressed with the help of his batman, went out into the yard.

The troop was already mounted and waiting. He led it out, and they rode along several streets through the misty darkness. Listnitsky deliberately dropped behind, and called Lagutin to him. The man turned his horse and rode up, glancing inquiringly at the captain.

"Well, what's the latest news in the committee?" Listnitsky asked.

"Nothing much just now."

"Where are you from, Lagutin?"

"Bukanovsky."

"And the village?"

"Mityakin."

Their horses were now riding level. By the light of the street lamps Listnitsky examined the Cossack's bearded face. A smooth lock of hair showed under his cap, a beard grew wispily on his full cheeks, the intelligent, rather cunning eyes were set deep under heavy arching brows.

"Ordinary enough on the outside, but what's his heart like? Probably hates me, like everything else connected with the old regime ..." Listnitsky reflected and for some reason he suddenly wanted to know about Lagutin's past.

"Are you married?"

"Yes. I've got a wife and two children."

"And a farm?"

"A farm?" Lagutin replied, with a sneer and a note of regret in his voice. "We live from hand to mouth, and our life is one long grind and struggle." He paused for a moment, then added harshly: "Our land is sandy."

Listnitsky had once driven through Bukanovsky, and he vividly remembered the remote, isolated place, bounded on the south by level, worthless marshland, and girded by the capricious windings of the Khoper river. He remembered the green haze of fruit-trees he had seen from a ridge twenty versts away, and the white church-tower rising among them.

"Yes, our soil's very sandy," Lagutin sighed.

"I suppose you'd like to get back home."

"Of course, sir. Of course I'd like to get back as soon as I can. We've had to put up with a lot through this war."

"I'm afraid you won't be getting back yet awhile, my lad."

"I think we shall."

"But the war isn't ended yet."

"It'll be over soon. We'll be going home soon," the Cossack replied obstinately.

"We'll be fighting among ourselves first. Don't you think so?"

Without raising his eyes from his saddle-bow, Lagutin replied after a moment:

"Who are we going to fight, then?"

"We'll have plenty on our hands.... The Bolsheviks perhaps."

Again Lagutin was silent, as though lulled into a doze by the firm, rhythmic clatter of the hoofs. Then he slowly answered:

"We haven't any quarrel with them."

"But what about the land?"

"There's enough land for everybody."

"Do you know what the Bolsheviks are after?"

"I've heard a bit. . . ."

"Well then, what ought we to do if the Bolsheviks attack us in order to seize our land and to enslave the Cossacks? You've been fighting the Germans in defence of Russia, haven't you?"

"The Germans are different."

"And the Bolsheviks?"

"Well, sir," Lagutin spoke up. Evidently he had come to some decision. He raised his eyes and tried to catch Listnitsky's gaze. "The Bolsheviks won't take my last bit of land from me. I've only got one share, and they won't need that. . . . But . . . only you won't be offended, will you. . .? There's your father now, he has ten thousand dessiatines. . . ."

"Not ten but four. . . ."

"All right, let it be four. That's not a small slice, is it? And where's the right of that? And there are any number like your father all over Russia. Then, sir, you judge for yourself what each mouth craves. You want to eat and everybody else wants to eat. You want to eat, and all kinds of other people want to eat too. You know about the gypsy who thought if he didn't feed his mare she'd get used to going without. Well, she went on getting used to it for nine days and on the tenth she went and died. . . .

Under the tsar everything was wrong, and the poor had a lean time. They gave your father four thousand as his share of the pie, but he can't eat two men's food any more than we plain people can. It's a pity for the people. The Bolsheviks are on the right track, and you talk about fighting. . . ."

Listnitsky listened to him with an agitation which he tried to hide. Towards the end he understood that he was powerless to present any weighty argument against it. He realized that the simple, deadly simple reasoning of the Cossack had driven him into a corner. And because a deeply hidden conviction that he was wrong stirred within him, Listnitsky became disconcerted and angry.

"What are you anyhow, a Bolshevik?"

"The name doesn't matter . . ." Lagutin drawled mockingly. "It's not a question of names, but of right. What the people want is truth, but it's always being buried and earth heaped over it. They say it's been a corpse a long time already."

"So that's what the Bolsheviks have been filling you with. You haven't wasted the time you've spent in their company."

"Ah, Captain, it's life itself that has taught us patient ones, and the Bolsheviks are only setting fire to the tinder."

"You drop those stories," Listnitsky ordered, now thoroughly angry. "Answer me! You were speaking just now of my father's land, and of the landowners' land generally, but that's—private property. If you have two shirts and I haven't even one, then, according to you, I ought to take one away from you?"

Yevgeny could not see the Cossack's face, but from his voice he guessed that he was smiling.

"I'd give up my extra shirt of my own accord. At the front I gave up not an extra shirt, but my very last shirt, and wore my greatcoat against my bare back. But I've never heard of anybody giving away his land."

"What's the matter with you—are you hungry for land? Haven't you enough already?" Listnitsky raised his voice. Breathing heavily, choking, Lagutin almost shouted his answer: "Do you think I'm only thinking about myself? We've been in Poland ... how do the people live there? You saw—or didn't you? And how do the muzhiks live all around us on the Don? I've seen it! It's enough to make your blood boil! Do you think I'm not sorry for them? Mebbe I've bled my heart out for Poles, thinking about the scraps of land they have to make do with."

Yevgeny was about to make a biting reply, but from the looming grey buildings of the Putilov works ahead came a sudden shout of "Hold him!" There was a clatter of hoofs and the sound of a shot. Plying his whip, Listnitsky put his horse to a gallop. He and Lagutin rode up side by side and found the troop halted and gathered at a corner. Several of the Cossacks, their sabres clattering, had dismounted, and in the middle of the ring a man was struggling.

"What's the matter?" Listnitsky thundered, urging his horse into the crowd.

"This bastard has been throwing stones...."

"He struck one of us and ran away."

"Give it to him, Arzhanov!"

The troop sergeant, Arzhanov, was hanging out of his saddle and holding a little man in a Russian shirt by his collar, while three dismounted Cossacks were binding his arms behind his back.

Almost beside himself with rage, Listnitsky shouted at the man:

"Who are you?"

The prisoner raised his head, but in his white face the lips remained pressed firmly together.

"Who are you?" Yevgeny repeated his question. "Throwing stones were you, you scum. You won't speak, eh? Arzhanov...."

Arzhanov leapt from his saddle, let go of the prisoner's collar, and punched him in the face.

"Give it to him!" Listnitsky ordered, turning his horse away.

Three or four of the dismounted Cossacks threw the bound man to the ground and swung their whips. Lagutin flung himself out of the saddle and ran to Listnitsky.

"Captain.... What are you doing...? Captain!" He seized Listnitsky's knee with his trembling fingers and shouted: "You can't do that! He's a man.... What are you doing?"

Yevgeny urged on his horse and made no reply. Running back to the Cossacks, Lagutin grabbed Arzhanov around the waist and tried to drag him away. But the sergeant resisted, muttering:

"Don't take on so! Don't take on! Is he to throw stones and us not say a word? Let me go! Let me go, I tell you for your own good!"

One of the Cossacks bent, and swinging his rifle from his shoulders, brought the butt down against the man's soft body. A low, primitively savage cry crept over the roadway. There was silence for a few seconds, then again the voice rose, but now young and choking, quivering with pain. After each blow he muttered curt exclamations between his groans:

"Swine! Counter ... revolutionaries! Beat on!
O-oh!"

The blows thudded heavily.

Lagutin ran back to Listnitsky, and pressing
against his knee, scratching with his finger-
nails at the saddle, he choked out:

"Let him go!"

"Stand back!"

"Captain.... Listnitsky! Do you hear...?
You'll answer for this!" He turned and ran to
the Cossacks standing apart from the group
around the man. "Brothers!" he shouted. "I am
a member of the revolutionary committee....
I order you to save that man from death...!
You will have to answer for it! It's not the old
days now!"

An unreasoning, blinding hatred carried
Listnitsky away. He struck his horse between
the ears with his whip and rode at Lagutin.
Thrusting his black, well-greased pistol into
the Cossack's face, he roared:

"Silence, traitor! Bolshevik! I'll shoot you!"

With a supreme effort of will he mastered
himself, removed his finger from the trigger,
swung his horse round on its hind legs and rode
off.

A few minutes later the three Cossacks set
out after him.

Arzhanov and Lapin dragged the prisoner

along between their horses. The man's blood-
soaked shirt was sticking to his body. Supported under the armpits by the Cossacks, he
swayed helplessly, his feet dragging over the
cobbles. His bloody head, the face beaten almost to a pulp, hung back loosely between his
raised shoulders. The third Cossack rode some
distance away. At a street corner he saw a
drozhki driver, and standing in his stirrups,
cantered towards him. Expressively striking
his boot-leg with his whip, he gave the man a
curt order, and with servile haste the drozhki
driver drove up to the two Cossacks halted in
the middle of the street.

The next morning Listnitsky awoke with the
feeling that he had committed a great and irreparable blunder. He bit his lips and frowned
as he recalled the scene of the previous night,
and all that had passed between himself and
Lagutin. As he dressed he decided that for the
present Lagutin had better be left alone, in
order to avoid any worsening of relationships
with the regimental committee. It would be
advisable to wait until the other Cossacks of the
troop had forgotten the incident, and then quietly remove him.

"So that was fraternizing with the Cossacks,"
he thought with bitter irony, and for several

days could not shake off the unpleasant impression of the incident.

One fine, sunny day at the beginning of August Listnitsky and Atarshchikov went into the city. Since the conversation after the officers' meeting nothing had happened to resolve the uncertainty which had arisen between them. Atarshchikov kept his own counsel, and whenever Listnitsky attempted to draw him into the open, he dropped the impenetrable curtain which most men habitually wear to protect their true features from other eyes.

It always seemed to Listnitsky that in their dealings with their fellows men hid under their outward appearance other features that were sometimes never disclosed. He firmly believed that once this surface veil was removed, the true, naked, unfalsified core of any man would come to light. He was constantly possessed by a sick longing to know what lay behind these façades, coarse, stern, fearless, arrogant, complacent, cheerful, that different men erected for protection. And now, as he thought of Atarshchikov, he could only conclude that in his struggle to find a way out of the antagonisms dividing the various sections of the nation, Atarshchikov was endeavouring to link up the Cossack aspirations with those of the Bolsheviks. And this supposition led him to cease his attempts to become more friendly with Atarshchikov.

They strolled down the Nevsky Prospekt, exchanging casual remarks.

"Let's go and have something to eat," Listnitsky proposed, indicating a restaurant with his eyes.

"All right!" the other man agreed.

They entered the restaurant and stood looking round rather helplessly. All the tables were taken. Atarshchikov had already turned to leave when a paunchy well-dressed gentleman who had been sitting with two ladies, surveying the officers intently, rose from his table and came towards them.

"I beg your pardon. Won't you take our table? We are just leaving." He smiled, revealing a deficiency of teeth, and motioned them to pass. "I am glad to perform a service to officers. You are the pride of the nation."

The ladies who had been sitting at the table rose. One, tall and dark, patted her hair into place, the other, a little younger, toyed with her sunshade.

The officers thanked the gentleman for his kindness and walked to the window. Through the lowered curtain the broken sun-rays stuck like yellow needles into the table-cloth. The smell of cooking overpowered the subtle perfume of the flowers set out on the tables. Listnitsky ordered some iced beet-root soup, and sat thoughtfully fiddling with the rusty-yellow nasturtium he had taken from the vase. Atarshchikov wiped his perspiring brow with his handkerchief. His drooping, weary eyes, blinking incessantly, watched the sunlight playing on the legs of the neighbouring table. They had not yet finished eating their course when two officers, talking loudly, entered the restaurant. As the first looked for a free table he turned his sunburnt face in Listnitsky's direction, and his black eyes lit up gladly.

"Why, it's Listnitsky!" he cried, and came with confident and unhesitating steps towards him, white teeth glistening under his black moustache.

Listnitsky at once recognized Captain Kalmykov and his companion Chubov. They shook hands heartily. After introducing them to Atarshchikov, Yevgeny asked:

"What fate brings you here?"

Twisting his whiskers, Kalmykov replied:

"We were sent. I'll tell you later. But first tell us about yourself. How do you find life in the 14th Regiment?"

They left the restaurant together. Kalmykov and Listnitsky dropped behind the others, turned down the first side-street and walked along towards a quiet part of the city, talking almost in whispers.

"Our Third Corps is being held in reserve on the Rumanian front," Kalmykov told Yevgeny. "About ten days ago I received instructions from the regimental commander to hand over my squadron to another officer, and to go with Chubov to place ourselves at the disposition of the divisional staff. Wonderful! So we go to the divisional staff. There we are confidentially informed that we are to report at once to General Krymov. So we go to the corps headquarters. Krymov sees me, and as he has been informed which officers are being sent to him, he tells me frankly: 'The government is in the hands of men who are deliberately leading the country to destruction. The group at the head of the government must be replaced, and possibly the Provisional Government will have to be dismissed in favour of a military dictatorship.' He mentioned Kornilov as a probable candidate, and then proposed that I should go to Petrograd, to put myself at the disposition of the Central Committee of the Officers' Alliance. And now several hundred reliable officers are gathered in the city. You can guess what our role is to be. The Central Committee of the Officers' Alliance is working in close contact with our Council of the Alliance of Cossack Troops, and shock battalions are being organized at railway junctions and in the divisions."

"And what will come of it? What do you think?"

"That's the point! But do you mean to say that you, living here, still don't know the situation? Undoubtedly there will be a governmental coup, and Kornilov will seize power. The whole army is on his side. We think there are two equated forces: the Bolsheviks and Kornilov. Kerensky is between the millstones. One or the other will crush him. Let him sleep in the tsaritsa's bed-chamber. He is caliph for an hour. Of course we officers are like pawns on a chess-board; we don't know where the player will move us to. I, for instance, don't understand all that is happening at staff headquarters. But I do know that among the generals—Kornilov, Lukomsky, Romanovsky, Krymov, Denikin, Kaledin—there is some secret understanding. . . ."

"But the army. . .? Will the whole army follow Kornilov?" Listnitsky asked, quickening his steps.

"The soldiers of course won't go. But we must lead them."

"You know that, under pressure from the Left, Kerensky is trying to dismiss the commander-in-chief?"

"He won't dare. Tomorrow he will be on his

knees. The Central Committee of the Officers' Alliance has expressed its opinion quite categorically on that matter."

"Yesterday he received a delegation from the Council of the Alliance of Cossack Troops," Listnitsky said smiling. "They told him that the Cossacks could not even consider Kornilov's dismissal. Do you know what he replied to them? 'It is all a rumour,' he said. . . . 'The Provisional Government has no intention of undertaking anything of the kind.' Trying to reassure the public and at the same time smiling like a prostitute at the deputies of the Soviet."

Kalmykov took an officers' diary out of his pocket and read the telegram aloud:

" 'The Conference of Public Men welcomes you, the supreme commander of the Russian Army. The conference announces that it considers any attempt to undermine your authority in the army and in Russia a criminal act, and joins its voice to that of the officers, the Cavaliers of St. George, and the Cossacks. At this terrible hour of trial the whole of thinking Russia looks to you with hope and faith. May God aid you in your great undertaking of re-creating a mighty army and saving Russia! *Rodzyanko.*' Clear enough? There can be no question of dismissing Kornilov. . . . But did you see his arrival in the city yesterday?"

"I only got back from Tsarskoye Selo last night."

Kalmykov smiled, exposing an even row of teeth and sound pink gums. His slant eyes puckered and broke into a web of fine wrinkles at the corners.

"It was classic! His guard was a squadron of Tekins. There were machine-guns placed in every motor car. And they all rode to the Winter Palace, where Kerensky was. An unequivocal enough warning! You should have seen the faces of those Tekins in their tall shaggy hats! They're worth looking at!"

The two officers walked back to the centre of the city, and took leave of each other.

"We mustn't lose sight of each other, Yevgeny," Kalmykov said as he shook hands. "Difficult times are coming! Keep your feet on the ground or you'll be lost."

As Listnitsky walked away Kalmykov called after him:

"Oh, I'd forgotten to tell you. You remember Merkulov? The artist fellow?"

"Yes?"

"He was killed in May."

"Impossible."

"It was quite an accident. You couldn't have seen a sillier death. A grenade burst in the hands of a scout and blew off the man's arms at the elbow. All we found of Merkulov who had been standing at his side was part of his entrails and a pair of twisted binoculars. For three years death had spared him. . . ."

He shouted something else, but the wind raised the grey dust and only stray syllables reached Listnitsky's ears. Yevgeny waved his hand and strode away, giving an occasional glance back.

XIII

On August 6th, the supreme commander's chief-of-staff General Lukomsky received an order through General Romanovsky, First General of the Headquarters Staff, to concentrate the Third Cavalry Corps and the Native Division attached to it in the Nevel-Velikiye Luki area.

"Why send them to that particular area? Those units are being held in reserve of the Rumanian front," Lukomsky asked in bewilderment.

"I don't know, General. I have conveyed the order exactly as I received it from the commander-in-chief."

"When did you receive it?"

"Yesterday. At eleven o'clock last night the commander-in-chief summoned me to his room and ordered me to report the order to you this morning."

Romanovsky, who had been pacing about near the window, halted in front of the huge strategical map of Central Europe that occupied half of one wall of Lukomsky's room and, examining it with exaggerated attention, said over his shoulder:

"Why don't you ask him? He is in his room now."

Lukomsky picked up the paper, pushed back his chair and walked to the door with marked firmness of tread that distinguishes every corpulent military man in old age. As he showed Romanovsky out, he said, evidently continuing an interrupted train of thought: "Yes. Quite correct."

A tall, long-limbed colonel, whom Lukomsky did not recognize, had just come out of Kornilov's room. He stepped back respectfully to allow Lukomsky to pass and walked down the corridor with a pronounced limp, his shoulder twitching grotesquely, evidently from shellshock.

Kornilov was leaning slightly forward over his desk, his hands pressed outward, speaking to an elderly officer in front of him: ". . .only to be expected. Do you understand me? You will please inform me on your arrival in Pskov. You may go."

Kornilov waited until the door closed behind

the officer, sat down with youthful briskness, and pulling up a chair for Lukomsky, asked:

"Did Romanovsky give you my instructions concerning the transfer of the Third Cavalry Corps?"

"Yes. I have come to talk to you about it. Why did you choose that area?"

Lukomsky studied Kornilov's dark face attentively. It was inscrutable and calm; the familiar lines curved down the cheeks from the nose to the harsh mouth scantily covered with a drooping moustache. The stern expression of the face was relieved only by a lock of hair that fell boyishly over the forehead.

Kornilov cupped his chin in his small dry palm, puckered his glittering Mongolian eyes and, touching Lukomsky's knee with his hand, replied:

"I don't want to concentrate the cavalry specifically behind the Northern Front, I want to have them in an area from which they can easily be transferred to either the Northern or the Western Front. In my view the area I have chosen satisfies that requirement as well as any other. Do you think differently? What?"

Lukomsky shrugged vaguely.

"You have no reason to worry about the Western Front. It would be better to concentrate the cavalry in the Pskov area."

"Pskov?" Kornilov repeated, leaning forward, and drawing back his thin pallid lower lip in a frown, shook his head: "No, the Pskov area won't do."

Lukomsky placed his hands on the arms of his chair with a weary, old-mannish gesture and said, choosing his words carefully:

"Lavr Georgievich, I will give the necessary instructions at once, but I have the impression that you are leaving something unsaid. . . . The area you have selected is very good for concentrating cavalry that might have to be moved to Petrograd or Moscow, but if you dispose your forces in that way, they will be of no use to the Northern Front if only because it will be very difficult to get them there. If I am not mistaken and you are, as I believe, leaving something unsaid, then I must ask you either to send me away to the front or to inform me fully of what you have in mind. No chief-of-staff can maintain his position without enjoying the complete confidence of his superior."

Kornilov bowed his head, listening attentively, but his sharp eye caught the faint flush of agitation that broke out like a rash on Lukomsky's otherwise calm face. He thought for a few seconds before replying:

"You are right. There are certain considerations I have not yet discussed with you. . . . Kindly issue orders for the transfer of the cavalry as I have instructed and immediately summon their commander General Krymov to headquarters. You and I will discuss the subject in detail on my return from Petrograd. Believe me, Alexander Sergeyevich, I have no desire to hide anything from you." Kornilov stressed the final "you" and turned abruptly at the sound of a knock.

"Come in."

Fonvizin, Assistant Commissary to the General Staff, and a stocky, flaxen-headed general entered the room. Lukomsky rose and as he went out he heard Kornilov replying sharply to Fonvizin's question:

"I have no time now to reconsider the case of General Miller. What. . .? Yes, I am leaving. . . ."

When he returned to his own room Lukomsky stood for a long time at the window. Fingering the wedge of his greying beard, he thoughtfully watched the wind stroking the heavy crests of the chestnut-trees and rippling through the bowed sunlit grass.

An hour later the Third Cavalry Corps received an order from the supreme commander's chief-of-staff to prepare to move. The same day General Krymov, who at Kornilov's request had in his time refused an appointment as commander of the 11th Army, was sent a telegram summoning him urgently to supreme headquarters.

On August 9th, Kornilov, escorted by a squadron of Tekins, travelled by special train to Petrograd.

The following day rumours of the supreme commander's arrest or dismissal circulated at headquarters, but on the morning of the 11th Kornilov returned to Mogilev.

Upon his arrival he immediately summoned Lukomsky. Having read the telegrams and communiqués, he straightened the immaculately white cuff elegantly encircling his slim olive wrist and fingered his collar; his hasty movements betrayed unwonted agitation.

"We can now continue our interrupted conversation," he said quietly. "I wish to return to the considerations which prompted me to move the Third Corps towards Petrograd and which we have not yet discussed. You know that on August 3rd, when I was in Petrograd at a cabinet meeting Kerensky and Savinkov warned me not to touch upon any vital matters of defence because, so they say, there are unreliable people among the ministers. I, the supreme commander-in-chief, when I report to the government, am unable to speak of operational plans because there is no guarantee that what I say will not in a few days become known to the German High Command! Is that a government? Can I, after that, believe that such a government is capable of saving the country?" Kornilov walked to the door with firm quick steps, turned the key in the lock and, pacing up and down in front of his desk, said: "It is a bitter and distressing fact that the country is ruled by such worms! Weakness of will, lack of character, lack of skill, vacillation, even treachery, these are the qualities that guide the actions of this 'government,' if one can call it such. With the connivance of individuals like Chernov and others, the Bolsheviks will sweep Kerensky aside. . . . That, Alexander Sergeyevich, is the position of Russia. Guided by the principles we both share, I wish to save our country from fresh upheavals. My main reason for transferring the Third Cavalry Corps is to be able to bring it up to Petrograd by the end of August and there settle accounts once and for all with the Bolsheviks and the workers' rabble. I am entrusting direct command of the operation to General Krymov. I am convinced that, if the situation demands it, he will not hesitate to hang every delegate in the Soldiers' and Workers' Soviet. As for the Provisional Government . . . we shall see about them. I want nothing for myself. . . . We must save Russia—at all costs!"

Kornilov halted in front of Lukomsky and asked abruptly: "Do you share my conviction that only such measures can save the future of the country and the army? Will you stand by me to the end?"

Lukomsky rose and clasped Kornilov's dry hot hand firmly, with deep emotion.

"I share your view completely! I am with you to the end. We must think it over, weigh everything—and strike. Entrust me with the task, Lavr Georgievich."

"I have worked out the general plan. The details will be worked out by Colonel Lebedev and Captain Rozhenko. You are overworked as it is, Alexander Sergeyevich. Believe me, we shall have time in the future to discuss everything and make any changes that may be necessary."

For the next few days Staff Headquarters lived a life of furious activity. Every day officers with sun-tanned weather-beaten faces, in dusty khaki uniforms, came from various front-line units to the governor's house in Mogilev to offer their services; dashingly attired representatives of the Officers' Alliance and the Alliance of Cossack Troops arrived; messengers rode in from Kaledin, the appointed Ataman of the Don Cossack Army.

Various civilians arrived: people who sincerely desired to help Kornilov and restore the old Russia that had collapsed in February 1917; but there were also vultures who, scenting from afar the smell of great bloodshed and guessing whose would be the firm hand that would open the country's veins, gathered at Mogilev in the hope of prey. Such men as Dobrinsky, Zavoiko, and Aladin were reputed to be in close contact with the supreme commander. At General Headquarters and at the headquarters of the Don Cossack Army it was whispered that Kornilov was too trusting and had fallen under the influence of adventurist elements, but at the same time among broad circles of the officers the dominating opinion was that Kornilov was the banner of the restoration of Russia. To this banner there flowed in from all sides fervid supporters of restoration.

On August 13th, Kornilov left for Moscow to attend a State conference.

A warm, slightly cloudy day. The sky seemed to be cast of light-blue aluminium. High overhead hung a fleecy storm-cloud fringed with lilac. On the fields, on the train clattering along the railway line, woods, already brightly feathered with decay, on the pure water-colour outline of a distant birch grove, over all the earth, now clothed in the widow's weeds of approaching autumn, fell a gentle slanting shower glittering with the reflection of a rainbow.

The train cast back the versts, a black trail of smoke behind it. A little general in a khaki tunic with the crosses of St. George on his breast sat at the open window. Half-closing his narrow coal-black eyes, he put his head out of the window and the fresh raindrops lavishly moistened his permanently sunburnt face and drooping black moustache; the wind combed back the lock of hair that fell boyishly over his forehead.

XIV

The day before Kornilov's arrival in Moscow, Captain Listnitsky came to the city with important documents entrusted to him by the Council of the Alliance of Gossack Troops at Petrograd. When he handed the packet over to the staff of the Cossack regiment stationed in Moscow he learned that Kornilov was expected to arrive next day.

At noon the following day Listnitsky was at the station to meet the commander-in-chief. A dense crowd of people, chiefly military, was assembled in the waiting rooms and buffets. A guard of honour from the military academy was drawn up on the platform, and the Moscow women's death battalion was arrayed outside. Kornilov's train arrived at about three o'clock.

A hush fell on the crowd. A band blared out

above the sound of tramping feet. The crowd stirred, then rushed madly on to the platform, carrying Listnitsky with it. Elbowing his way out of the turmoil he saw two ranks of Tekins forming up in front of the carriage of the commander-in-chief. The brightly varnished side of the carriage reflected the vivid red of their long robes. Listnitsky saw Kornilov, accompanied by several officers, alight from the train, inspect the guard of honour, and receive deputations from the Alliance of Cavaliers of St. George, the Alliance of Army and Navy Officers, and the Council of the Alliance of Cossack Troops.

Among those who were presented to the commander-in-chief Listnitsky recognized the Don Ataman Kaledin and General Zaionchkovsky; the officers surrounding Kornilov introduced the others:

"Kislyakov, Deputy Minister of Communications."

"Rudnev, Mayor of Moscow."

"Prince Trubetskoi, chief of the diplomatic chancellery at General Headquarters."

"Privy Councillor Musin-Pushkin."

"The French military attaché Colonel Caillot."

"Prince Golitsin."

"Prince Mansyrev . . ." the obsequiously respectful voices whispered.

As Kornilov approached he was bombarded with flowers thrown by the well-dressed women standing at the end of the platform. A pink blossom caught in his epaulettes and hung there. He brushed it off with a slightly embarrassed, uncertain gesture. A bearded, elderly officer began to stammer out greetings in the name of the Cossack regiments, but Listnitsky could not hear what he said, for the crowd pushed him against the wall and nearly broke the hilt of his sword. After the speeches Kornilov moved on, the way being cleared by officers with joined hands. But the crowd swept them away. Dozens of hands were stretched out to Kornilov. A stout, dishevelled woman hovered at his side, trying to press her lips to his sleeve. At the station entrance Kornilov was lifted shoulder-high and carried out, to a tumult of acclamation. With a strong thrust of the shoulder Listnitsky managed to push aside a dignified elderly gentleman, caught at one of Kornilov's legs, and put it across his shoulder. Unconscious of the weight, panting with agitation and the effort to keep his feet, he moved slowly forward, deafened by the roar of the crowd and the blare of the band. At the station entrance he hastily straightened his tunic, which had rucked up under his belt in the crush. Down the steps they went into the square. In front was the crowd, the green ranks of soldiers, and a mounted Cossack squadron. Listnitsky set his hand to the peak of his cap, blinking his tear-filled eyes and trying to restrain the uncontrollable trembling of his lips. Afterwards he had a confused memory of the clicking of cameras, the frenzy of the crowd, the ceremonial march of the cadets and the little figure of General Kornilov with his slanting jet-black eyes and Mongolian face taking the salute.

The next day Listnitsky returned to Petrograd. He climbed into the upper berth of his compartment, lay down on his greatcoat and smoked, thinking of Kornilov:

"Escaped from the enemy at the risk of his life, just as if he knew the country was so badly in need of him. And what a face! Carved out of rock—nothing superfluous, quite ordinary.... And his character's the same. For him everything must be clear, calculated down to the last detail. When the moment comes he will lead us. How strange, I don't even know who he is. A monarchist? Constitutional monarchy.... If only all of us were as confident of ourselves as he is."

At about the same time, during an interval in the session of the Moscow State Conference, two generals, one short, with a Mongolian face, the other stout, with a thick growth of close-cropped hair on his square head, were strolling up and down one of the corridors of the Bolshoi Theatre, conversing quietly.

"Does this point of the declaration provide for the abolition of committees in the army?"

"Yes."

"A united front and complete solidarity are absolutely indispensable. Without the enforcement of the measures I have indicated there can be no salvation. The army is quite incapable of fighting. Such an army cannot bring victory; it will not even be able to withstand any considerable attack. The divisions have been disintegrated by Bolshevik propaganda. And here in the rear? You see how the workers react to any attempt to apply measures to bridle them. Strikes and demonstrations! The members of the conference have to go on foot ... it's scandalous! The militarization of the rear, the establishment of a harsh, punitive regime, the ruthless extermination of all the Bolsheviks—these are our immediate tasks. Can I count on your support in the future, General Kaledin?"

"I am with you absolutely."

"I was sure of that. Thank you. You see how, when it is necessary to act resolutely and firmly, the government confines itself to half-measures and resounding phrases. They talk about crushing with fire and sword the attempts of those who, like the rebels of the July days, threaten the power of the people. We soldiers are accustomed to acting first and talking afterwards. They do the opposite. Well ... the time is coming when they will taste the fruits of their half-measures. But I have no desire to take part in this dishonourable game. I remain an adherent of the open struggle. I am no double-dealer."

Kornilov halted and, twisting a button of Kaledin's tunic, stuttered in his agitation:

"They've removed the muzzle, and now they're afraid of their own revolutionary democracy and are asking me to move reliable troops nearer to the capital, although at the same time they're afraid to take any real measures themselves. One step forward, one step back.... Only by the complete consolidation of our forces and strong moral pressure can we win concessions from the government. And if not ... we shall see. I shall not hesitate to lay the front open. Let the Germans bring them to their senses!"

"I have discussed the matter with my colleagues. You have the full support of the Cossacks. We have only to agree upon further arrangements."

"I shall expect you and the others in my room after the session. What is the situation on the Don?"

Kaledin's square chin sank to his chest and he stared at the floor morosely. His lips trembled under his broad moustache as he replied:

"I haven't my former confidence in the Cossacks. And it is difficult to judge of the situation at the moment. A compromise is necessary; the Cossacks must concede something to the aliens* in order to retain their support. We are taking certain steps in this direction, but I cannot guarantee their success. I am afraid the clash of interests between the Cossacks and the aliens may lead to an explosion. The land ... all their thoughts centre round that at the moment."

"You must have reliable Cossack divisions standing ready to safeguard yourself. When I return to the staff we shall find some way of sending several regiments from the front back to the Don."

"I shall be very grateful to you if you can."

"Well then, this evening we shall discuss the question of our future co-operation. I firmly believe in the successful accomplishment of our

* The name given to those living on Cossack territory who were not Cossacks.

plan. But fortune is a fickle jade, General. If she turns her back on me despite everything, can I count on finding refuge with you in the Don?"

"Not only refuge, but defence. The Cossacks are famous for their hospitality." For the first time during the conversation Kaledin smiled.

An hour later Kaledin, the Ataman of the Don Cossacks, announced to a hushed audience the historic Declaration of the Twelve Cossack regiments. And now, like a black spider-web, over the Don, the Kuban, the Terek, the Urals, the Ussuri, throughout the Cossack lands from end to end, from one village to another were flung the threads of a great conspiracy.

XV

About a verst from the ruins of a little town that had been wiped out by gun-fire during the June offensive, the monstrously winding zigzag of the trenches ran past a forest. The sector along the outskirts of the forest was held by a special squadron of Cossack cavalry.

Behind them, beyond the impenetrable green of alders and young birches, stretched the rusty mud of peat marsh; the crimson berries of dog-rose bushes shone gaily. To the right, beyond a protruding cape of forest, stretched a shell-holed macadam road, a reminder of paths yet to be trodden in the war. At the fringe of the forest grew miserable, bullet-scarred bushes, and charred trunks huddled forlornly. Here the yellow-brown clay of the breastworks was visible, and the trenches ran like frowns across the open fields into the distance. Behind them even the marsh with its remains of former peat-works, even the broken road were an eloquent testimony to life and abandoned labour; but by the forest edge the earth presented a bitter joyless picture to the eye.

One day in August Ivan Alexeyevich, the former employee at Mokhov's mill, went off to the neighbouring town where the squadron baggage train was quartered, and did not return until early evening. As he made his way into his dug-out he ran into Zakhar Korolyov. Zakhar was almost running, aimlessly waving his arms, his sabre catching in the edges of the sand-bags. Ivan Alexeyevich stepped aside to let him pass, but Zakhar seized him by a button of his tunic, and rolling his jaundiced eyes, whispered:

"Have you heard? The infantry to our right are going away. Maybe they're leaving the front open?"

Zakhar's iron-black beard hung in wild confusion and there was hungry longing in his eyes.

"What do you mean 'leaving the front open'?"

"They're leaving, what for—I don't know."

"Perhaps they're being relieved. Let's go to the troop officer and find out."

Zakhar turned back, and they went along to the troop officer's dug-out, slipping and stumbling over the slippery wet earth.

But within an hour the squadron was relieved by infantry, and was on its way to the town. Next morning they took to their horses and were riding by forced marches to the rear.

A fine rain was falling; the birches were bowed gloomily. The road plunged into a forest, and scenting the dampness and the mouldering, pungent smell of fallen leaves, the horses snorted and quickened their pace. The rain-washed true-love knot hung in rosy beads, the foamy caps of the white clover gleamed an unearthly white. The wind sprinkled heavy granular drops from the trees over the riders. Their greatcoats and caps were dark with wet spots, as though spattered with shot. The smoke of tobacco curled and flowed above the ranks.

"They just get hold of us and shove us from one place to another."

"Haven't you had enough of the trenches?"

"But where are they sending us?"

"Some new position, I reckon."

"Doesn't look like it."

"Come on, boy, let's have a smoke and forget our troubles."

"I carry my troubles in my saddle-bags."

"Can we strike up a song, Captain?"

"Did he say we could. . .? Strike up, Arkhip!"

The damp-sodden voices floated weakly over the wood and petered out. Zakhar Korolyov, who was riding in the same rank as Ivan Alexeyevich, stood up in his stirrups and shouted:

"Hey, you croakers! Is that the way to sing? You ought to be begging outside a church!"

"Sing yourself then."

"His neck's too short, there's no room for a voice in it."

"Scared, eh?"

Korolyov shut his eyes for a moment, then swinging his reins boldly, burst into a stirring song.

The squadron, as though awakened by his echoing first line, took up the tune with a will and the song roared out over the sodden forest.

They passed the whole march in song, rejoicing that they had got away from the "wolves' graveyard," as they called the trenches. The same evening they boarded a train, which dragged towards Pskov. And only some time later did they learn that the squadron was being transferred, together with other sections of the Third Cavalry Corps, to Petrograd to suppress disorders which had broken out. Then the talk died away in the wagons, and a drowsy silence reigned.

"Out of the frying-pan ..." one of them at last expressed the general opinion.

At the first halt Ivan Alexeyevich, who since March had been permanent chairman of the squadron committee, went to the squadron commander.

"The Cossacks are worried, Captain."

The captain stared at the deep dimple in Ivan's chin, and replied with a smile:

"I'm worried myself, my friend."

"Where are we being taken to?"

"To Petrograd!"

"To put down risings?"

"Well, you didn't think you were going to assist in the disorders, did you?"

"We don't want either the one or the other."

"As it happens they're not asking our opinion."

"But the Cossacks. . . ."

"What about the Cossacks?" the officer interrupted him angrily. "I know myself what the Cossacks are thinking. Do you think I like the job? Take this and read it to the squadron. And at the next station I'll talk to the Cossacks."

The commander handed him a folded telegram, and frowning with evident distaste, started eating greasy corned beef from a tin.

Ivan Alexeyevich returned to his wagon, carrying the telegram gingerly in his hand, as though it were a burning brand. "Call the Cossacks from the other wagons."

The train was already in motion, but Cossacks came jumping into Ivan's wagon until some thirty were collected.

"The commander's given me a telegram to read," Ivan told them.

"Let's hear what it says!"

"About peace?"

"Quiet!"

Amid dead silence, he read aloud the manifesto of the commander-in-chief, Kornilov. Then sweaty hands seized the telegram and passed it round.

I, the supreme commander-in-chief Kornilov, before all the nation declare that my soldierly duty, my devotion as a citizen of free Russia, and my supreme love for the country have compelled me in these serious moments of the fatherland's existence to refuse to carry out the instructions of the Provisional Government and, therefore, to retain the supreme command of the army and fleet. Supported in this decision by the commands of all the fronts, I declare to all the Russian people that I prefer death to removal from my post. A true son of the Russian people will always die at his post and sacrifice his life for the fatherland.

In these truly terrible minutes in the life of our fatherland, when the approaches to both capitals are practically laid bare to the victorious advance of our triumphant ene-my, the Provisional Government, forgetting the paramount question of the independence of the country, is frighten-ing the people with the imaginary peril of counter-revolu-tion, which it is furthering by its own inability to govern, its own weakness, its own vacillation.

It is not for me, a blood son of my people, who have given all my life to their service, to refuse to defend the great liberties of my people. An impudent enemy is among us, bringing ruin by bribery and treachery not only to freedom, but to the very existence of the Russian people. Awake, Russian people, and glance into the bottomless pit into which our country is falling!

Avoiding all disturbances, averting all shedding of Russian blood, ignoring mutual reproaches and all my shame and humiliation at their hands, I address myself to the Provisional Government and say: 'Come to me at the staff headquarters, where your freedom and safety are as-sured by my word of honour, and together with me work out and organize such a form of national defence as will safeguard freedom and lead the Russian nation towards the great future worthy of a mighty and free people.'

General Kornilov

At the next station the train was halted for some time. The Cossacks gathered outside their wagons, talking over Kornilov's telegram and another from Kerensky, read by the squadron commander, declaring Kornilov a traitor and counter-revolutionary. The Cossacks discussed the situation in bewilderment and even the officers were confused.

"I'm all muddled," Martin Shamil complained. "Hell knows which of them's in the wrong."

"They're all at each other's throats and we have to suffer."

"They all want to be on top."

"And we Cossacks get the worst of it."

"A fine mess!"

A group of Cossacks came up to Ivan Alexeyevich demanding: "Come to the commander and find out what we are to do."

They went in a body to the squadron commander, and found the officers in conference in his wagon. Ivan Alexeyevich went in.

"Captain, the Cossacks are asking what they are to do."

"I'll be out in a minute."

The entire squadron waited by the end wagon. The commander joined the crowd, made his way to the middle, and raised his hand:

"We are subordinate, not to Kerensky, but to the commander-in-chief and our immediate superiors. That's correct, isn't it? And so unquestionably we must carry out the orders of our superior command and go on to Petrograd. In the last resort we can find out what the situation is when we reach the station of Dno, where we shall find the commander of the First Don

Division. I ask you not to get excited. Such are the times we are living through."

The commander went on to talk about the soldiers' duty, patriotism, and the revolution, seeking to calm the Cossacks and replying evasively to their questions. He achieved his aim. While he was talking to the Cossacks an engine was coupled to the train (the Cossacks never knew that two officers had hastened their departure by threatening the station-master with revolvers) and the men dispersed to their wagons.

The troop train took a day to reach the station of Dno. At night it was held up again while another train carrying the Ussuri and Daghestan regiments went past. The Cossacks' train was shunted into a siding. Guttural voices, the moan of *zurnas* and unfamiliar melodies reached them as the Daghestan wagons rumbled past, here and there a light glittering in the blank darkness.

At midnight the train started off again. The little locomotive stood for a long time at the water pump with sparks falling from its fire-box. The driver leaned out of his cab puffing a cigarette, as if he were waiting for something. A Cossack in the nearest wagon poked his head out of the door and shouted:

"Hey, Ivan, get going or we'll shoot!"

The driver spat out his cigarette, watched it

curve through the darkness, then cleared his throat and said:

"You can't shoot everybody," and turned away from the window.

A few minutes later the engine started with a jerk that set the buffers jangling and raised a clatter of hoofs as the horses strove to keep their balance in the wagons. The train glided past the water pump, past a few lighted windows and dark birch-trees. The Cossacks fed their horses and slept or sat at the half-open doors, smoking and staring out at the sky.

Ivan Alexeyevich lay gazing through the door-chink at the stars flowing past. During the past day he had been thinking over the situation, and had come to the firm decision to prevent the squadron moving further towards Petrograd by all means in his power. As he lay he considered how best to bring the Cossacks round to his own way of thinking.

Even before Kornilov's proclamation he had realized that the Cossacks' road was not that of the commander-in-chief, yet instinct warned him that it was not for them to defend Kerensky either. He turned the problem over and over in his mind, and resolved not to let the squadron get to Petrograd. If a clash had to come with anybody, it must be with Kornilov; yet it must not be in favour of Kerensky, not for his government, but for the one which would arise after him. He was more than confident that the real government he desired would come when Kerensky went. During the summer he had been in the military section of the Party Executive Committee in Petrograd, to which he had been sent by the squadron for advice in regard to a conflict that had arisen with the squadron commander. There he had seen the work of the Committee, had talked to several Bolshevik comrades, and had thought: "Let this backbone be clothed with our workers' meat, and then there will be a government! Die, Ivan, but hang on to that, hang on like a child to its mother's breast!"

As he lay on his horse-cloth, he thought again and again with a great burning affection of the man under whose guidance he had first found his hard new road. As he thought over what he would say to the Cossacks on the morrow, he recalled what Stockman had said about the Cossacks and repeated it to himself with conviction: "The Cossacks are conservative to the backbone. Don't forget that when you are trying to convince one of them of the truth of the Bolshevik ideas, act cautiously, thoughtfully, and adapt yourself to the situation. At first they will be as contemptuous of you as you and Misha Koshevoi were of me, but don't let that trouble you. Chisel away stubbornly—the final success will be ours."

Ivan reckoned he would meet with some objection from the Cossacks when he tried to persuade them not to go with Kornilov. But in the morning when he began to talk to his wagon companions, and suggested that they ought to demand their return to the front and not go on to Petrograd to fight their own brothers, the Cossacks willingly agreed and were fully prepared to refuse to travel further. Zakhar Korolyov and a Cossack named Turilin were closest to Ivan in their outlook, and they spent all day going from wagon to wagon, talking to the others. Towards evening, while the train moved slowly through a way-side station, a corporal of the Third Troop jumped into Ivan's wagon.

"The squadron is detraining at the first stop," he shouted at Ivan. "What sort of committee chairman are you if you don't know what the Cossacks want? We won't go any further! The officers are putting a noose round our necks, and you're neither fish nor flesh. Is that what we elected you for?"

"You should have said that long ago," Ivan smiled.

At the first stop he jumped out of the wagon, and accompanied by Turilin went to the stationmaster.

"Don't send our train any further. We're going to detrain here."

"What?" the man asked in bewilderment. "I have instructions to send you on. . . ."

"Shut up!" Turilin harshly interrupted.

They found the station committee and explained the situation to the chairman, a heavily built, ginger-haired telegraphist. Within a few minutes the engine-driver had willingly shunted the train on to a siding.

Hurriedly laying down planks from the wagons to the permanent way the Cossacks began to lead out their horses. Ivan stood by the engine with feet planted wide apart, wiping the sweat from his smiling face. The squadron commander came running towards him:

"What are you doing? You know that. . . ."

"I know," Ivan interrupted. "And don't you kick up any fuss, Captain." Turning pale, he said distinctly: "You've done enough shouting, my lad. Now we'll do the ordering."

"The commander-in-chief Kornilov . . ." the officer stuttered, turning livid. But Ivan stared down at his boots pressed firmly into the sand of the permanent way, and waving his hand with relief, counselled the captain:

"Hang him round your neck instead of a cross; we haven't any use for him."

The officer turned on his heel and ran back to his wagon. Within an hour the squadron, unaccompanied by a single officer but in perfect order, trotted away from the station in a southwesterly direction. At the head of the First Troop with the machine-gunners rode Ivan Alexeyevich in command, with the stocky Turilin as his assistant.

With difficulty making their way by the map taken from the commander, the squadron reached a village and halted for the night. At a general meeting it was resolved to return to the front, and if anyone tried to stop them, to fight. Hobbling the horses and setting guards, the Cossacks lay down to wait for the dawn. No fires were lit. It was evident that the majority were in a depressed mood; they lay without their usual talking and joking, concealing their thoughts from one another.

"What if they think better of it and go back and submit?" Ivan thought anxiously, as he huddled under his greatcoat. As though he had heard the thought, Turilin came up.

"Are you asleep, Ivan?"

"Not yet."

Turilin squatted down by his side, and lighting a cigarette, whispered:

"The Cossacks are worried. . . . They've done the damage, and now they're afraid. We've cooked up a fine mess for ourselves. What do you think?"

"We'll see," Ivan answered calmly. "You're not afraid, are you?"

Turilin scratched his head and smiled wryly.

"To tell the truth, I am. At first I wasn't, but now I'm a bit scared."

"Not much of a sticker, are you?"

"They've got a lot of power, Ivan."

Neither of them spoke. The lights went out in the village. From somewhere among the marsh willows came the quacking of a duck.

"Calling its mate," Turilin murmured thoughtfully and lapsed into silence again.

The gracious stillness of night enwrapped the meadows. Dew clung heavily to the grass. A breeze brought the mingled scents of the marsh grass and the mouldering rushes, the muddy soil and the dew-soaked grass to the Cossacks' nostrils. Occasionally a horse's hobble jingled, or there was a snort and grunting as one of the animals lay down. Then again the sleepy silence, the distant, hoarse, barely audible call of a wild drake and the nearer answering quack of his mate. The hurried whirring of invisible wings in the darkness. Night. Silence. A misty, meadow rawness. To the west in the nadir hung a rising, heavily violet billow of cloud. And in the zenith, over the ancient lands of Pskov, like a broad, fiery track the Milky Way stretched in unsleeping reminder.

At dawn the squadron set out again. They passed through the village, followed by the slow stares of the women and children driving the cattle to pasture. They mounted a rise flushed brick-red by the dawn. Turilin happened to look back, and touched Ivan's stirrup with his foot. "Look round! There are horsemen galloping after us."

Ivan gazed back at the village, and saw three riders galloping along in a flying cloud of rosy dust.

"Squadron, halt!" he commanded.

With their usual speed the Cossacks ranged themselves in a grey square. When about half a verst away the riders dropped into a trot. One of them, a Cossack officer, pulled out a white handkerchief and waved it above his head. The Cossacks kept their eyes fixed on the approaching horsemen. The Cossack officer in a khaki tunic came on in front, the two others, in Circassian uniform, kept a little behind him.

Riding forward to meet them, Ivan Alexeyevich asked:

"What do you want with us?"

"We have come to negotiate," the officer replied saluting. "Who has taken charge of the squadron?"

"I have."

"I am a plenipotentiary from the First Don Cossack Division, and these officers are representatives of the Native Division," the officer explained, pulling on his reins and stroking the neck of his sweating horse. "If you are willing to enter into a discussion of the situation, order the squadron to dismount. I have to pass on verbal instructions from the commander of the division, Major-General Grekov."

The Cossacks dismounted, and the officers also. Diving into the crowd, they made their way to the middle. The squadron made room for them, and formed a small circle. The Cossack officer spoke first:

"Cossacks! We have come to persuade you to think over what you are doing and to avert the serious consequences of your action. Yesterday the divisional staff learned that you had given way to someone's criminal persuasions and had arbitrarily abandoned your wagons, and we have been sent today to instruct you to return immediately to the station. The soldiers of the Native Division and other cavalry forces occupied Petrograd yesterday; we received a telegram to that effect today. Our advance guard has entered the city, has occupied the government buildings, banks, telegraph, and telephone stations and all the important points. The Provisional Government has fled and is overthrown. Think, Cossacks! If you do not submit to the orders of the divisional commander, armed forces will be sent against you. Your conduct will be regarded as treason, as refusal to fulfil your military obligations. Only if you submit unconditionally can you avoid bloodshed."

As the officers rode up, Ivan Alexeyevich had realized that it would not be possible to avoid entering into discussion with them, for that would have only opposite results to those he desired. When the squadron dismounted he winked to Turilin and quietly pushed close up to the officers. The Cossacks stood with downcast, gloomy faces listening attentively to the captain's words; some began to whisper among themselves. Zakhar Korolyov, his black beard flooding his chest like molten iron, smiled wryly; Borshchev toyed with his whip, glancing aside; Pshenichnikov, the corporal who had suggested they should detrain in the first place, stared straight at the officer with his mouth wide open; Martin Shamil rubbed his cheeks with a dirty fist and blinked rapidly, the yellowish face of another Cossack showing behind him; Krasnikov, a machine-gunner, frowned expectantly; Turilin breathed heavily; the freckled Obnizov pushed his cap on the back of his head and worked his neck about like a yoked ox; the entire Second Troop stood without raising their heads, as though at prayers; not a word was spoken and only the sound of hot laboured breathing rose from the tightly packed crowd. All faces stirred with an undercurrent of confusion.

Ivan realized that the Cossacks were on the point of submitting. A few more minutes and this smooth-spoken officer would win them to his side. At all costs the impression he had made must be dispelled. Ivan raised his hand, and swept the crowd with dilated, strangely white eyes.

"Brothers! Wait a bit!" he cried, and turning to the officer, he asked: "Have you got the telegram with you?"

"What telegram?" the captain asked in astonishment.

"The telegram saying Petrograd has been taken."

"The telegram.... Of course not. What do you want with the telegram?"

"Aha! So he hasn't got it!" The whole squadron heaved a sigh of relief. Many of the Cossacks lifted their heads, and fixed their eyes hopefully on Ivan. Raising his hoarse voice, he seized their attention and shouted mockingly and assuredly:

"You haven't got it, you say? And so we've got to take your word for it? You can't catch us with chaff!"

"It's a trick!" the squadron roared in unison. "The telegram wasn't addressed to me. Cossacks!" the officer pressed his hand persuasively against his chest.

But they would not listen to him. Feeling that he had again won the squadron's sympathy and confidence, Ivan cut like a diamond on glass:

"And even if you had got it, our roads don't run with yours. We don't want to fight our own folk! We won't march against the people. No! We're not fools any longer. We're not going to help set up a government of generals. And that's that!"

The Cossacks shouted their assent: "He's giving it to them!" "That's right, Ivan!" "Send them packing!"

Ivan glanced at the emissaries. The Cossack officer was waiting patiently with lips firmly compressed; behind him the others stood shoulder to shoulder. One of them, a handsome young Ingush, stood with folded arms, his slanting almond eyes glittering; the other, an elderly, grey-haired Ossetian, had his hand resting lightly on his sabre-hilt, and was surveying the Cossacks quizzically. Ivan was on the point of breaking off further discussion; but he was forestalled by the Cossack officer, who, after whispering to the Ingush, cried stentoriously:

"Don Cossacks! Will you allow the representative of the Native Division to speak?"

Without waiting for permission the Ingush stepped forward softly in his heelless boots, fiddling nervously with his narrow silver-mounted belt.

"Brother Cossacks! What's all the noise about? You don't want General Kornilov? You want war? All right. We will give you war. We're not frightened! Not at all frightened! We shall smash you today. There are two regiments at our backs! So!" He began with ostensible calm, but as he went on he poured out his words more passionately, phrases from his own language mingling with his broken Russian. "It's that Cossack there that's upsetting you! He's a Bolshevik, and you're following him! So! Don't I see it? Arrest him! Disarm him!"

He pointed boldly at Ivan Alexeyevich and swept his eyes around the circle, gesticulating fiercely, his face darkly flushed. His companion maintained an icy calm, and the Cossack officer toyed with his sabre knot. The Cossacks were again silent, confused and agitated. Ivan stared fixedly at the Ingush officer, at his flashing animal-white teeth, at the grey streak of sweat across his left temple, and thought regretfully that he had let slip the moment when with one word he could have ended the talk and led away the Cossacks. Turilin saved the situation. Waving his arms desperately, he leapt into the middle of the ring and, ripping his shirt open, roared:

"You crawling snakes! Devils...! Swine...! They wheedle you like whores, and you prick up your ears! The officers will make you do as they want. What are you doing? *What are you doing?* They ought to be cut down, and you stand listening to them! Cut their heads off, let the blood out of them! While you're jawing they're surrounding us. They'll mow us down with machine-guns! You won't be holding meetings long when they start rattling! They're pulling the wool over your eyes until their soldiers arrive. Ha, call yourselves Cossacks? You're a lot of petticoats!"

"To horse!" Ivan Alexeyevich thundered.

His shout burst like shrapnel over the crowd. The Cossacks flung themselves towards their horses. Within a minute the squadron was again drawn up in troop columns.

"Listen! Cossacks!" the captain shouted.

Ivan Alexeyevich unslung his carbine from his shoulder, and putting his finger firmly to the trigger, exclaimed:

"The talk is ended! Now if we have to talk to you it will be in this language!"

He shook his rifle expressively.

Troop after troop they rode off down the road. Looking back, they saw the emissaries mounted on their horses and conferring among themselves. The Ingush was arguing fiercely, frequently raising his hand; the silk lining of his cuff shone snowily white. As Ivan looked round for the last time he noticed this dazzling band of silk, and abruptly before his eyes there appeared the wind-lashed bosom of the Don, its foaming green waves, and the white wing of a sea-gull slanting across their crests.

XVI

By August 29th Kornilov knew from the telegrams he was receiving from Krymov that the attempt to overthrow the government by armed force was a failure.

At two in the afternoon an officer arrived at headquarters with dispatches from Krymov. After conversing with him at some length, Kornilov summoned General Romanovsky. Crumpling a paper nervously in his hand he said:

"Utter collapse! Our trump card is beaten. Krymov will be unable to get his forces to Petrograd in time and our opportunity will be lost. The thing that seemed so easy to accomplish is fraught with a thousand difficulties. . . . Failure is inevitable. Look at the movement of the troop trains!" He held out a map indicating the progress of Krymov's cavalry corps and the Native Division towards Petrograd; a shudder zigzagged across his tired face. "Those damned railway workers are tripping us up at every step. They have forgotten that if we succeed I shall have one in every ten of them hanged on the spot. Read Krymov's report."

While Romanovsky read the report, stroking his bloated face with a large hand, Kornilov wrote rapidly:

Novocherkassk. To Ataman of the Don Cossacks
Alexei Maximovich Kaledin

The significance of your telegram to the Provisional Government has been brought to my knowledge. The patience of the glorious Cossacks has been exhausted in fruitless struggle with scoundrels and traitors, they foresee the inevitable destruction of the country and are ready with arms in hand to defend the life and freedom of the Motherland, which has grown and expanded through their toil and blood. Our relations will be restricted for a time. I beg you to act in agreement with me, as your patriotism and Cossack honour dictate. 29.8.17.

General Kornilov

He finished writing and asked Romanovsky to send the telegram at once.

"Do you want me to send Prince Bagration a second telegram instructing him to continue the journey in marching order?"

"Yes, do."

Romanovsky was silent for a moment, then said in a tone of reflection:

"In my opinion there is no need yet for us to feel pessimistic. You are wrong to anticipate events...."

Kornilov was reaching up and snatching at a butterfly fluttering over his head. His fingers clenched and unclenched and his face was almost tense with expectation. Disturbed by the gusts of air round it, the butterfly made for the open window. But Kornilov managed to catch it and threw himself back in his chair, breathing with relief.

Romanovsky waited for a reply to his remark, but Kornilov responded with a pensive and sombre smile.

"I had a dream last night. I dreamed I was a brigade commander in one of the rifle divisions, directing an offensive in the Carpathians. Our staff stopped at a farm on the road, and an elderly Ukrainian, very finely dressed, came out to greet us. He offered me milk to drink and, doffing his white felt hat, said to me in faultless German: 'Drink, General! This milk has wonderful healing properties.' In my dream it seemed to me that I drank the milk and felt no surprise to find the Ukrainian patting me familiarly on the shoulder. Then we went on through the mountains and it no longer seemed like the Carpathians, but somewhere in Afghanistan, along a kind of goat track.... Yes, that was it—a goat track. Brown pebbles and rocks broke away under our feet and, down below, at the bottom of the gorge we could see a glorious southern landscape flooded with silver sunlight...."

A breeze flowed through the open window disturbing the papers on the desk. Kornilov's misty abstracted gaze hovered somewhere beyond the Dnieper, over the steep slopes and coppery-green meadows.

Romanovsky followed his gaze, then with a faint sigh turned his eyes to the glassily calm, mica-like surface of the Dnieper and the misty fields, exquisitely softened by the approaching autumn.

XVII

The various sections of the army flung by Kornilov against Petrograd were scattered over an enormous stretch of eight railway lines running from the west and south. All the main stations and even halts and sidings were packed with the slowly moving troop trains. The regiments were beyond the moral control of the senior command, and the scattered squadrons lost touch with one another. The confusion was made worse by the changing of instructions while en route and by un-co-ordinated orders, and this intensified the already strained and nervous mood of the troops.

Meeting with the stubborn opposition of the railway workers, overcoming difficulty after difficulty, the Kornilov forces moved slowly on towards Petrograd.

In the small red wagons, half-starved Cossacks from all the Cossack districts and the Caucasian tribesmen of the Native Division crowded beside their half-starved horses. The trains stood for hours at the stations waiting for dispatches, and the men poured out of the wagons and streamed into the waiting rooms, or gathered on the permanent ways, eating everything left by previous trains, stealing from the inhabitants, and pillaging the food warehouses.

The yellow and red trouser stripes of the Cossacks, the dashingly cut tunics of the dragoons, the long waisted coats of the highlanders. . . . Never before had that modest northern landscape seen such a rich array of colour.

Together with the other regiments composing

the First Don Cossack Division, the regiment in which Yevgeny Listnitsky had formerly served was moved up to Petrograd along the Revel-Narva railway line. Two squadrons of the regiment arrived at Narva at five in the afternoon of August 28th. The commander learned that it would be impossible to travel further that night, as the permanent way beyond Narva had been destroyed. A gang of plate-layers had been dispatched to the spot, and if they could restore the line in time the train would be sent on early in the morning. The commander was compelled to accept this. He clambered cursing into his wagon, communicated the news to the other officers, and sat down to drink tea.

The night was overcast. A harsh, piercing wind was blowing from the Gulf of Finland. On the permanent way and in the wagons the Cossacks gathered to talk. At the end of the train a young Cossack voice struck up a song, complaining in the darkness to no one knew whom.

> *Farewell, you city streets and towns,*
> *Farewell, my native village dear,*
> *Farewell, my lassie young and fair,*
> *The azure flower you used to wear.*
> *Once I lay from dusk to dawn*
> *Upon my darling's loving arm,*
> *But now from dusk to dawn I stand*
> *With rifle in my hand.*

A man emerged from beyond the grey bulk of the warehouse. He stopped and listened to the song, looked up and down the track gleaming with yellow patches of light, and strode confidently towards the wagons. His steps echoed hollowly on the sleepers, but were muffled when he walked down the sandy path between the lines. He passed round the end wagon, and the Cossack standing at its door stopped singing and shouted to him:

"Who's that?"

"Who did you expect?" the man answered reluctantly, without stopping.

"What are you wandering about at night for? We'll give you tramps a good hiding!"

The man walked along until he came to the middle section of the train, and thrusting his head through a wagon door, asked:

"What squadron are you?"

"Prisoners!" someone laughed in the darkness.

"No, I'm asking seriously."

"We're the Second."

"And where's the Fourth Troop?"

"The sixth wagon from the front."

Three Cossacks, one squatting and the others standing, were smoking at the door of the sixth wagon. They stared silently at the man coming up to them.

"Hullo, Cossacks!"

"Hullo," one of them replied, gazing into the newcomer's face.

"Is Nikita Dugin alive? Is he here?"

"Here I am," the man squatting answered and rose to his feet, treading out his cigarette with his heel. "But I don't know you. Who are you?" He poked his bearded face forward in an attempt to examine the stranger in a greatcoat and soiled soldier's cap. Suddenly he cried in astonishment: "Ilya! Bunchuk! Where the devil have you sprung from, old boy?"

Gripping Bunchuk's hairy hand in his own and bending over him, he said more quietly:

"These are our fellows, you needn't be afraid. How did you get here? Tell me, the devil curse you!"

Bunchuk shook hands with the other Cossacks, and replied in a strained, thick voice, like the sound of muffled iron:

"I've come from Petrograd, and I've been looking for you everywhere. There's work on hand. We must have a talk. I'm glad to see you alive and well, brother."

He smiled, his teeth gleamed whitely in the grey square of his broad, big-browed face and his eyes glowed with restrained cheerfulness.

"Want to have a talk, do you?" the bearded Cossack's voice went up in surprise. "You, an

240

officer, and you don't look down on our squadron? Thanks, Ilya, lad, the Lord bless you, we don't know what it's like to be treated kindly." There was a note of good-natured amusement in his voice.

Bunchuk replied in the same cordial tone:

"Enough of your joking now! Grown a beard down to your belly and still playing about!"

"I can shave my beard quick enough, but you tell us what's going on in Petrograd. Have the uprisings started?"

"Let's go inside," Bunchuk suggested.

They clambered into the wagon. Dugin prodded someone with his foot, and whispered:

"Get up, my lad! A useful guest has arrived. Hurry up! Get a move on."

The Cossacks stirred and rose. A couple of great hands, smelling of tobacco and horses' sweat, carefully felt Bunchuk's face in the darkness, and their owner asked:

"Bunchuk?"

"That's right. And is it you, Chikamasov?"

"Yes. Glad to see you, friend. Shall I run and fetch the boys of the Third Troop along?"

"That's a good idea."

The Third Troop arrived almost to a man, only two remaining with the horses. The Cossacks went up to Bunchuk and thrust their horny hands into his, bent over him, and examined his face by the light of the lantern. In all their greetings there was a single tone of warm, comradely welcome.

The wagon grew stuffy. Blobs of light danced on the boarded walls, misshapen shadows swayed and spread, the lantern cast a greasy glow through the smoke.

They made him sit down facing the lantern, and crowded around him, those closest squatting on their heels, the others standing in a tight circle. Dugin coughed.

"We had your letter the other day, Ilya, but we still wanted to see you and have your advice about what to do. They're sending us to Petrograd."

"It's like this, Ilya," said a Cossack standing near the door. An ear-ring hung from the wrinkled lobe of his ear; it was the same man whom Listnitsky had once affronted by forbidding him to boil water on the sheet-iron. "All sorts of agitators come along to us and try to get us not to go on to Petrograd, telling us we ought not to fight among ourselves, and all that sort of thing. We listen to them, but we don't trust them too much. They're not our folk. They may be leading us up the garden path for all we know. If we refuse to go to Petrograd Kornilov will send his Native divisions against us, and that will lead to bloodshed too. But you're a Cossack like us, and we have more trust in you, and we're very thankful that you wrote to us and sent us newspapers ... as a matter of fact, we were getting short of paper for making fags. . . ."

"What are you blathering about, you block-head?" another interrupted angrily. "You can't read, and so you think of that. But we aren't all like you. As if we only used the newspapers for making fags! We read them from front to back, Ilya."

"The lying devil!"

"'Short of paper for fags'—a fine way to talk!"

"No, I didn't mean it that way, lads," the Cossack with the ear-ring tried to excuse himself. "Of course, we read 'em first. . . ."

"Did *you* read them?"

"I never got the chance of learning how to read. What I mean is we read 'em together, then used them for fags. . . ."

Bunchuk smiled briefly as he gazed at the Cossacks. He found it difficult to talk sitting down; so he stood up, turned his back to the lantern and spoke slowly and with effort:

"There's nothing for you to do in Petrograd. There aren't any risings there. Do you know what they're sending you there for? In order to overthrow the Provisional Government. And who's leading you? The tsarist general Kornilov. What does he want to kick Kerensky out for? In order to sit in his place. Listen, Cossacks! They want to throw the wooden yoke off your necks, but they'll put a steel one in its place! Of two evils you must choose the lesser. Isn't that so? Think it over for yourselves: under the tsar they put their fists in your face and used you to fight the war. Under Kerensky they're still wanting you to fight, but they don't use their fists on you any longer. But it will be quite different after Kerensky, when the power gets into the hands of the Bolsheviks. The Bolsheviks don't want war. If they were the government there would be peace at once. I'm not on Kerensky's side, the devil take him; they're all tarred with the same brush!" He smiled, wiped the sweat from his brow with his hand and continued: "But I call on you not to shed the blood of the workers. If Kornilov gets into power Russia will begin to wade knee-deep in workers' blood, and it will be harder to tear the power from him and hand it over to the toiling people."

"Wait a bit, Ilya." A little Cossack, as thick-set as Bunchuk himself, emerged from the back rows. The man coughed and rubbed his hands, which were long and like the rain-washed roots of an ancient oak Gazing at Bunchuk with smiling eyes as green and sticky as young leaves, he asked: "You said something just now about yokes. But when the Bolsheviks get the power what yokes will they put on us?"

"What, are you going to put yokes on yourselves?"

"What do you mean, 'put them on ourselves'?"

"Well, under the Bolsheviks who will be the government? You will, if they elect you, or Dugin, or this old boy here. It will be an elected government, a government of Soviets. Understand?"

"But who will be at the top?"

"Why, whoever's elected. If they choose you, you will be at the top."

"Is that true? You're not kidding, Ilya?"

The Cossacks laughed, and all began to speak at once. Even the guard posted at the door left his place for a moment in order to join in.

"But what do they want to do with the land?"

"They won't take it from us?"

"Will they stop the war? Mebbe it's only talk and they'll want us to fight for them."

"Tell us the truth. We're all in the dark here."

"You can't believe strangers. There's a lot of tales flying around. . . ."

"Yesterday a sailor fellow came round crying over Kerensky and we flung him out by the hair. 'You counter-revolutionaries!' he shouted. The fool!"

"We don't know what them long words mean."

Bunchuk turned this way and that, feeling the Cossacks with his eyes and waiting until they were quiet. His first feeling of uncertainty as to the success of his enterprise had gone, and realizing the mood of the Cossacks, he knew for sure that whatever happened the troop train would be halted at Narva. When the previous day he had suggested himself to the Petrograd Regional Party Committee for agitation work among the Cossack detachments he had been quite confident of success, but on his arrival at Narva he had been stricken with doubts. He knew that the Cossacks must be talked to in their own language, and he was afraid he might not be able to do that; for since leaving the front he had mingled only with workers, and had once more thoroughly assimilated their habits and turns of speech. When he spoke to them he had got used to feeling that a word was enough to make himself understood, but here, with his fellow-Cossacks, a different, half-forgotten language was needed, the language of the black earth, a lizard-like agility, a great strength of conviction. It was not enough merely to be able to fan the flames; here the fire had to be kindled in order to destroy the century-old fear of showing disobedience, to tear down the walls of ignorance, to instil the Cossacks with a feeling that they were right, and to lead them forward.

When he first began to speak to the Cossacks he had caught the stumbling uncertainty in his own voice, an affectedness, as though he himself were listening to his own insipid words; he was appalled at the feebleness of his arguments, and tormentedly had racked his brains for words, big, heavy words that would convince and shatter. But only empty phrases had come like soap-bubbles from his lips, while the emasculated, elusive thoughts were entangled in his mind. He stood sweating heavily, breathing heavily, thinking: "I've been entrusted with this big job, and I'm ruining it myself. Can't put the words together ... what's the matter with me? Another man would have spoken a thousand times better. Oh hell, what an idiot I am!"

The Cossack who had asked about the yokes knocked him out of his stupid impotence, and the talk that followed his reply gave him an opportunity to pull himself together. He felt an unusual flow of strength and a rich choice of clear, pointed, cutting words coming to him. He grew enthusiastic, and concealing his agitation under a semblance of calm, dealt weightily and sharply with the questions, guiding the conversation like a rider who has mastered an unbroken horse.

"Tell us, why is the Constituent Assembly a bad thing?" the fire of questions continued. "Your Lenin—the Germans sent him here, didn't they?" "No." "Then where did you get him?" "Bunchuk, did you come of your own free will, or were you sent?" "Who will they give the Cossacks' land to?" "What was so bad about life under the tsar?" "Aren't the Mensheviks also for the people?" "We have our own Army Council and people's government. What do we want Soviets for?"

He dealt with the questions one after another. The little meeting broke up after midnight, having decided to call both squadrons to a general meeting in the morning. Bunchuk spent the night in the wagon, and Chikamasov proposed that he should share his blankets. As the Cossack crossed himself and lay down, he warned Bunchuk:

"You don't seem to worry where you sleep, Ilya.... But, you must excuse us, we're eaten

248

up with lice. If they bother you, you mustn't take offence. We've been so fed up, we've let 'em grow till they're as big as duck's eggs. . . ." He was silent for a moment, then quietly asked: "Bunchuk, what people does Lenin come from? I mean, where was he born, where did he grow up?"

"Lenin? He's a Russian."

"No?"

"It's true; he's Russian."

"No, brother, you're wrong there! It's clear you don't know much about him," Chikamasov said with a touch of superiority in his voice. "Do you know where he's from? He's of our blood. He's from the Don Cossacks, and was born in Salsky District, Velikoknyazheskaya stanitsa ... understand? They say he was in the army as an artilleryman. And his face fits: he's like the lower Cossacks—those big cheek-bones and the same eyes."

"Where'd you hear that?"

"The Cossacks talked it over among themselves. I heard them."

"No, Chikamasov. He's Russian, and was born in the Simbirsk Province."

"I don't believe you. And it's very simple why. There's Pugachov; wasn't he a Cossack? And Stenka Razin? And Yermak Timofeyevich? That's it! There's not a man who has ever raised the poor people against the tsar who wasn't a Cossack. And you say he's from the Simbirsk Province! I'm ashamed to hear such words, Ilya...."

Bunchuk asked with a smile: "So they say he's a Cossack?"

"Yes, and he is a Cossack, only he won't say so at present. As soon as I see his face I shall know." Chikamasov lit a cigarette, and breathed the pungent scent of the uncured tobacco into Bunchuk's face. He coughed thoughtfully. "Of course it's amazing, and we quarrelled and almost came to blows over it. You see, if Lenin is one of us Cossacks, and an artilleryman, where did he get all his knowledge from? Well, they say that he was taken prisoner by the Germans at the beginning of the war, and learned it all there, but when he began getting their workers to revolt and catching their learned men out they got frightened. 'Clear out, you big-head!' the Germans said to him. 'Clear out to your own people, by Christ, you're giving us so much trouble we shall never be able to stop it.' And so they sent him to Russia, because they were afraid he would get their workers to rise. Oho! He's a molar, brother!" Chikamasov said the last words vauntingly and laughed happily in the darkness. "You haven't ever seen him, have you? No? Pity! They say he has an enormous head." He coughed and sent a grey scroll of smoke out of his nostrils. "The women ought to bear some more like him. He'll overthrow more than one tsar! No, Ilya, don't try to argue with me. Lenin is a Cossack. What do you want to doubt it for? Such men never came out of the Simbirsk Province."

Bunchuk remained silent, a smile on his face. He was a long time getting to sleep; the lice swarmed over him, spreading a fiery, tormenting itch under his shirt. Chikamasov sighed and scratched at his side, and the neighing of a restless horse drove away sleep. He turned over and over, and angrily realizing that he was wide awake, began to think of the morrow's meeting. He tried to imagine what form the officers' resistance would take and smiled grimly. "They'll probably run away if the Cossacks make a united protest, but you never know. Better have a word with the garrison committee just in case." Involuntarily he recalled an episode during an attack in 1915, and as if rejoicing to find itself on the beaten track again, his brain insistently began to conjure up fragments of memory: the faces and hideous postures of dead Russian and German soldiers; snatches of talk, colourless, time-faded scraps of scenery; unspoken thoughts; the faint echoes of gun-fire; the well-known sputter of machine-guns and the rattle of the belts; a blaring melody, beautiful almost to pain; the faintly outlined mouth of a woman he had once loved; and then again scraps of the war; the dead; the low-settled mounds of the common graves. . . .

He sat up and said, or perhaps only thought: "Until I die I shall carry these memories, and not I alone but all who come through. Our whole life has been mutilated, cursed! Damn them. . .! Damn them! Not even with death will their guilt be wiped out. . . ."

Then he recalled Lusha, the twelve-year-old daughter of a friend of his, a metal worker killed in the war. One evening he had been walking along a boulevard. The girl—an angular, sickly child—was sitting on a bench, her thin legs flung daringly forward, smoking a cigarette. Her face was faded, her eyes tired, her painted lips, pinched with bitterness at the corners, were prematurely ripe. "Don't you know me, Uncle?" she asked with a professional smile, and rose. Then she began to cry, bitterly and helplessly like a child, stooping, and pressing her head against Bunchuk's elbow.

He gnashed his teeth and groaned, almost choking with the poisonous hatred that filled him. He sat rubbing his chest, feeling that his hatred was seething in his breast like hot slag, preventing him from breathing, and causing a sharp pain under his heart.

He did not drop off to sleep until morning was at hand. And at dawn, yellow and more morose than usual, he went to the railwaymen's committee, persuaded them not to send the Cossack troop train out of Narva, then searched for the garrison committee in order to ensure their assistance.

He returned to the train at eight o'clock, rejoicing vaguely at the probable success of his mission, at the sun pouring across the rusty roof of the warehouse, and the musical, lilting timbre of a woman's voice. A brief but luxuriant rain had fallen late in the night. The sandy earth of the permanent ways was wet and furrowed with the traces of little streams ; it smelled of dampness and still retained the pitted holes of the raindrops on its surface, as though it had had smallpox.

As he passed round the wagons an officer in a greatcoat and muddy top-boots came towards him. Bunchuk recognized Captain Kalmykov, and slowed his steps. As he came up Kalmykov halted and his slanting black eyes gleamed coldly.

"Cornet Bunchuk? Are you still at liberty? Excuse me, I won't offer you my hand. . . ."

He compressed his lips tightly and pushed his hands into his pockets.

"You spoke too quickly; I had no intention of offering you mine," Bunchuk replied mockingly.

"What are you doing here? Saving your skin? Or ... have you come from Petrograd? You're not from friend Kerensky?"

"Is this a cross-examination?"

"It is merely justifiable curiosity as to the fate of a deserter who was once a colleague."

Bunchuk shrugged his shoulders.

"I can reassure you. I have not come from Kerensky," he smiled.

"But surely you are touchingly united, now that danger is facing you. Anyhow, who and what are you? No epaulettes, and wearing a soldier's greatcoat." Kalmykov contemptuously and commiseratingly examined Bunchuk's slightly stooping figure. "A political bagman? Have I guessed right?" Without waiting for an answer he turned on his heel and strode away.

Bunchuk found Dugin waiting for him in the wagon.

"Where have you been? The meeting's already begun."

"What do you mean, begun?"

"Just that. Our squadron commander Kalmykov, who was away in Petrograd, came back this morning and called a meeting of the Cossacks. He's just gone along to talk to them."

Bunchuk waited a few minutes to find out when Kalmykov had been sent to Petrograd. Dugin told him he had been away about a month.

"One of the enemies of the revolution, sent by Kornilov to Petrograd allegedly to study bombing, must be a loyal supporter of his," he thought vaguely as he walked with Dugin to the meeting.

Beyond the warehouse was a dense greygreen ring of Cossack tunics and greatcoats. In the middle, surrounded by officers, Kalmykov was mounted on a barrel, and shouting sharply and emphatically:

". . . carry on to a victorious conclusion. They trust us, and we will justify their trust. I shall now read a telegram from General Kornilov."

With unnecessary haste he pulled a crumpled sheet of paper out of his tunic pocket and whispered to the train commandant.

Bunchuk and Dugin came up mingling with the Cossacks.

" 'Dear Cossacks, friends!' " Kalmykov read expressively and with some fervour. " 'Was it not over the bones of your ancestors that the frontiers of the Russian State widened and spread? Was it not your great valour, your glorious feats, your sacrifices and heroism that made Russia great? You, the free sons of the quiet Don, the handsome warriors of the Kuban, of the foaming Terek, the soaring eagles of the Urals, Orenburg, Astrakhan, Semirechensky and Siberian steppes and mountains, and of distant Transbaikal, the Amur and Ussuri, you have always upheld the honour and glory of your banners, and the Russian land is full of legends of the heroic deeds of your fathers and forefathers. The hour has come when you must rally to the aid of your native land. I accuse the Provisional Government of vacillation, of unfitness and inability to rule, of allowing the Germans to control the internal affairs of the country, as is shown by the explosion in Kazan, where nearly a million shells and 12,000 machine-guns were destroyed. In addition, I accuse certain members of the government of treason. This I can prove. When I attended a cabinet meeting in the Winter Palace on August 3rd, I was informed by Prime-Minister Kerensky and Savinkov that I must not speak my mind because there were disloyal people among the members of the government. It is clear that such a government is leading the country to destruction, that such a government cannot be trusted, and that with such a government unhappy Russia can expect no salvation. ... For this reason, when the Provisional Government, to please our enemies, demanded that I should resign the post of supreme commander-in-chief, I, as a Cossack, true to honour and conscience, felt compelled to refuse this demand, preferring death on the field of battle to shame and betrayal of the Motherland. Cossacks, knights of the Russian land! You promised to rise with me in defence of the Motherland when I should find it necessary. That hour has struck—the Motherland is on the threshold of death! I will not submit to the orders of the Provisional Government and for the salvation of free Russia I oppose the government and its irresponsible counsellors who are selling out the country. Cossacks, uphold the honour and glory, the unexampled valour of your people, and in doing so you will save the country and the freedom gained by the revolution. Obey me and carry out my orders! Follow me! August 28th, 1917. Supreme Commander-in-Chief General Kornilov.' "

Kalmykov paused as he rolled up the sheet, then shouted:

"The agents of the Bolsheviks and Kerensky are preventing the movement of our troops along the railway. We have received instructions from the commander-in-chief that if it proves impossible to travel by rail we are to take to horse and march to Petrograd. We start today. Get ready to detrain."

Roughly working his way through the crowd with his elbows, Bunchuk burst into the middle of the ring, and without approaching the group of officers, shouted stentoriously:

"Comrade Cossacks! I have been sent to you by the Petrograd workers and soldiers. Your officers are leading you on to war with your brothers, to the defeat of the revolution. If you want to attack the people, if you want to restore the monarchy, carry on! But the Petrograd workers and soldiers hope that you will not be Cains. They send you an ardent brotherly greeting and want to see you not as enemies, but as allies. . . ."

He was not allowed to continue. An indescribable uproar arose, and the storm of shouts seemed to tear Kalmykov down from the barrel. He strode across towards Bunchuk, but halted a few steps away and turned to the Cossacks:

"Cossacks! Last year Cornet Bunchuk deserted from the front; you know that. Are we going to listen to this coward and traitor?"

His voice was drowned by a deep bellow from Colonel Sukin, the commander of the Sixth Squadron:

"Arrest him, the scoundrel! We shed our blood while he hid in the rear! Seize him!"

"Wait a bit with your seizing!"

"Let him speak!"

"We don't want any deserters!"

"Go on, Bunchuk!"

"Down with them!" "Give it to them, Bunchuk, give it to them!" a chorus of conflicting shouts arose from the Cossacks.

A tall, bareheaded Cossack, a member of the regimental revolutionary committee, jumped on to the barrel. In fiery words he called upon the Cossacks not to obey the orders of General Kornilov, a traitor to the revolution, and spoke of the ruinous consequences of war with the people. At the end of his speech he turned to Bunchuk.

"And you, Comrade," he cried, "don't think that we look down on you as the officers do. We're glad to see you and respect you as a representative of the people, and because when you were an officer you didn't spit on the Cossacks, but were with them as a brother. We never heard a rough word from you; but don't think that we, uneducated men, don't understand good treatment. Even the cattle understand a kindly word, and we are men. We welcome you, and ask you to tell the Petrograd workers that we shall not raise a hand against them."

There was a roar of approving shouts like the roll of kettledrums. It rose to breaking point, slowly fell, and died away.

Kalmykov again jumped on to the barrel, swaying as he bent his handsome figure towards the Cossacks. Panting and deathly pale, he spoke of the glory and honour of the Don, of the historic mission of the Cossackry, of the blood which officers and men had all shed.

Kalmykov was followed by a Cossack with a tow-coloured head of hair. His malicious attack on Bunchuk was shouted down by the crowd, and they dragged him off the barrel. At once Chikamasov jumped up. With a downward sweep of both arms, as though cleaving a log, he barked:

"We won't go! We won't detrain! Kalmykov says the Cossacks promised to help Kornilov; but who asked us whether we would? We've made no promises to Kornilov! The officers of the Cossack Alliance made the promises. General Grekov wagged his tail, so let him do the helping."

One after another the speakers clambered on to the barrel. Bunchuk stood with his big head bowed, a dark flush in his cheeks, a pulse beating strongly in his face and neck. The atmosphere was charged with electricity. A little more, and some hasty action would have led to bloodshed. But the soldiers of the garrison came along in a crowd, and the Cossack officers abandoned the meeting.

Half an hour later Dugin came running to Bunchuk.

"Ilya, what shall we do? Kalmykov is up to something. They're unloading the machine-guns, and they've sent a horse messenger off somewhere."

"Come on. Collect twenty Cossacks or so. Hurry!"

By the officers' wagon Kalmykov and three other officers were loading machine-guns on to horses. Bunchuk strode up to them, glanced round at the Cossacks behind him, and thrusting his hand into his greatcoat pocket, pulled out a new, carefully cleaned officer's revolver:

"Kalmykov, you're under arrest! Hands up...."

Kalmykov leapt away from the horse, and bent to pull his revolver out of its holster. But a bullet whistled over his head, and in a heavy, ominous voice Bunchuk repeated:

"Hands up!"

The hammer of his revolver slowly rose to the half-cock. Kalmykov watched it with narrowed eyes, and slowly raised his hands, his fingers twitching. The officers unwillingly handed over their weapons.

The Cossacks unloaded the horses and carried the machine-guns back into the wagon.

"Must we surrender our swords?" a young cornet machine-gunner asked respectfully.

"Yes."

"Set guards over these," Bunchuk told Dugin. "Chikamasov, you arrest the other officers and bring them here. Dugin and I will take Kalmykov along to the garrison revolutionary committee. Captain Kalmykov, please step forward!"

"That was smart ... smart!" one of the officers remarked in admiring tones, jumping into the wagon and watching Bunchuk, Dugin and Kalmykov march off.

"Gentlemen! For shame, gentlemen! We behaved like children! No one thought of shooting that scoundrel down! When he raised his revolver against Kalmykov we should have let him have it, and it would have been all over." Colonel Sukin stared at the other officers indignantly, and fumbled with a cigarette in his case.

"There was a whole troop of them. They'd have massacred us," a cornet remarked apologetically. The officers silently lit cigarettes, occasionally exchanging glances. The speed with which Bunchuk had acted had crushed them.

For a little way Kalmykov walked along without speaking, biting the tip of his black moustache. His sharp-boned left cheek burned as though it had been slapped. The passers-by stopped and stared in amazement, whispering to one another. Above the town the evening sky was clouded. Fallen birch leaves, dropped by August in her flight, lay like ruddy ingots along the roads. Rooks were circling around the green cupola of the church. Beyond the station, beyond the darkening fields night had already fallen, breathing coldly; but to the south, torn, leaden-white clouds were still to be seen scudding along. Crossing invisible frontiers, night advanced on the shadows.

By the station Kalmykov swung round and spat in Bunchuk's face.

"Scoundrel...."

Bunchuk dodged the spittle, and raised his eyebrows. His fingers itched to seize his revolver. But he restrained himself and curtly ordered the officer to walk on.

Kalmykov moved on, cursing horribly, pouring out a stream of oaths.

"You're a traitor! You'll pay for this!" he shouted, frequently stopping and turning on Bunchuk.

"Get on! Please ..." Bunchuk urged again and again.

And again Kalmykov would step out, clenching his fists, and straining like an excited horse. They drew near to the water-tower. Grinding his teeth, Kalmykov screamed:

"You're not a party, you're a gang made up of the dregs of society. Who is your leader? The German staff command! Bolsheviks ... ha-ha! Mongrels! Your party can be bought like prostitutes. The cads! The cads, blast them all...! You've betrayed your fatherland! I'd hang you all on one tree.... But the time will come! Didn't your Lenin sell Russia for thirty German marks? He took his bribe and hid himself...."

"Stand up against the wall!" Bunchuk shouted deliberately, panting out the words.

Dugin became excited. "Ilya! Bunchuk! Wait a bit! What are you going to do? Stop!"

His face distorted and livid with rage, Bunchuk leapt at Kalmykov and struck him hard on the temple. He trampled on the cap that went flying from the officer's head, and dragged the prisoner towards the dark brick wall of the water-tower.

"Stand up!"

"What are you going to do...? You...won't dare...don't you dare to beat me!" Kalmykov roared, struggling with him.

As his back struck against the wall, he straightened up, abruptly understanding.

"So you're going to kill me!"

He took a step forward, swiftly buttoning up his greatcoat.

"Shoot, you son of a swine! Shoot...! And see how Russian officers can die...! In the face of death I...."

The bullet struck him in the mouth. The echo of the shot went ringing round the water-tower. Kalmykov clutched at his head with his left hand, stumbled, and fell. He arched his back, spat out blood-stained teeth on to his breast, and licked his lips with his tongue. His back had hardly touched the damp ground when Bunchuk fired again. Kalmykov shuddered convulsively, turned over on his side, then like a drowsy bird huddled his head on his chest and gave a sob.

Bunchuk turned away. Dugin ran after him.

"Ilya.... What did you shoot him for, Bunchuk?"

Bunchuk gripped his shoulders, fixing his hard gaze firmly into the Cossack's eyes, and said in a strangely calm, gentle voice:

"It's either us or them! There's no middle way. Blood for blood. Understand? Such men as Kalmykov have to be wiped out, crushed like reptiles. And those who slobber with pity for them must be shot too. Understand? What are you slobbering for? Pull yourself together! Be hard! If Kalmykov had had the power, he would have shot us without taking the cigarette out of his mouth, and you.... You cry-baby!"

But Dugin's head shook and his teeth chattered, and his big feet in their rust-stained boots seemed to lose all sense of direction.

They walked along the deserted street without speaking. Bunchuk glanced back. The sombre clouds moving towards the east foamed low in the sky. Through a small gap in the clouds the waning, rain-washed moon stared down like a crooked greenish eye. At a corner a soldier and a woman with a white shawl over her shoulders stood pressed to each other. The soldier embraced the woman and drew her towards him, whispering something. But she pushed with her hands at his chest and flung her head back, muttering in a choking voice: "I don't believe you! I don't believe you!" And a soft youthful laugh came from her lips.

XVIII

On the 31st of August, General Krymov, who had been summoned to Petrograd by Kerensky, shot himself.

Delegations and the commanders of the units of Krymov's army began trickling into the Winter Palace to make their submission. Men who only recently had been marching to open war on the Provisional Government now obsequiously bowed and scraped to Kerensky, assuring him of their complete devotion. Morally shattered, Krymov's army struggled in its death-agony. From sheer inertia some sections still rolled on towards Petrograd, but the movement had lost all purpose, for the Kornilov putsch was at an end, the Bengal lights of this outburst of reaction were dying out, and the temporary ruler of the country—no longer quite so sleek of jowl, it is true—was strutting like a Napoleon, and speaking at government meetings of the "complete political stabilization" of Russia.

The day before Krymov's suicide General Alexeyev was appointed commander-in-chief. Realizing the equivocal nature of his position, the scrupulously correct Alexeyev at first categorically refused the post offered to him; but afterwards he accepted, governed solely by the desire to mitigate the fate of Kornilov and those who had been implicated in the organization of his anti-government revolt. Alexeyev entered into direct telephone communication with Kornilov at staff headquarters, trying to ascertain the late commander's attitude to his appointment and imminent arrival. The negotiations dragged on with interruptions until late at night.

The same day Kornilov held a conference of his staff officers and associates. The majority spoke in favour of continuing the struggle.

Kornilov turned to Lukomsky who had remained silent throughout the proceedings.

"Will you give us your opinion, Alexander Sergeyevich?"

Lukomsky spoke in restrained but definite phrases against continuation of the struggle for power.

"Capitulation then?" Kornilov interrupted him sharply.

Lukomsky shrugged.

"The circumstances speak for themselves."

The discussion dragged on for another half an hour. Kornilov, controlling himself with an obvious effort of will, was silent. He dismissed the meeting and an hour later summoned Lukomsky.

"You are right, Alexander Sergeyevich." He

cracked his fingers and, looking aside with a quenched ashen stare, said wearily: "Further resistance would be foolish, and criminal."

He sat drumming his fingers on the desk and seemed to listen to something—perhaps the mouse-like scampering of his thoughts—then asked:

"When will Alexeyev arrive?"

"Tomorrow."

On September 1st Alexeyev arrived at staff headquarters. The same evening, on the instruction of the Provisional Government he arrested Kornilov, Lukomsky and Romanovsky.

Before the arrested generals were taken to the Metropole Hotel, where they were to be guarded, Alexeyev had a personal interview with Kornilov that lasted twenty minutes. He left the room deeply shaken, scarcely able to control himself. When Romanovsky tried to see Kornilov he found his path barred by Kornilov's wife.

"I'm sorry but he asked me not to let in anybody at all."

Romanovsky glanced hurriedly at her troubled face and turned away, blinking rapidly and with bluish patches under his eyes.

The next day the commander-in-chief of the South-Western Front, General Denikin, together with generals Markov, Vannovsky and Erdeli, were arrested at Berdichev. So the Kornilov revolt came to an inglorious end, as history ordained it. But in its end it engendered a new revolt, for surely it was during the "Kornilov days" that the first beginnings of the plans for the coming civil war and the extended attack on the revolution were born.

XIX

Early one morning at the end of October, Captain Listnitsky received instructions from the regimental commander to take his squadron on foot to the Winter Palace Square. He gave the necessary orders to the sergeant-major, and hurriedly dressed. The other officers rose also, yawning and cursing. They went into the yard. The squadron was drawn up in troop columns. Listnitsky led them at a swift march into the street. The Nevsky Prospekt was deserted. Occasional shots sounded in the distance. An armoured car was driving about the Winter Palace Square, and cadets were on patrol. A desert silence reigned in the streets. At the gates of the palace the Cossacks were met by a detachment of cadets and the Cossack officers of the Fourth Squadron. One of them, the squadron commander, led Listnitsky aside.

"Have you the whole squadron with you?"

"Yes. Why?"

"The Second, Fifth and Sixth squadrons refused to march, but we've got the machine-gun detachment with us. How are your Cossacks?"

Listnitsky waved his hand curtly.

"Bad! But how about the First and Fourth regiments?"

"They're not here. They won't come. You know an attack from the Bolsheviks is expected today? The devil knows what is afoot." He sighed sadly and added: "I'd be glad to get back to the Don and away from all this...."

Listnitsky led his squadron into the palace yard. The Cossacks piled their arms and wandered about the spacious courtyard, while the officers gathered in one corner, smoking and talking.

Some time later a regiment of cadets and the Women's Battalion arrived. The cadets took up their position with machine-guns in the vestibule of the palace. The women crowded in the yard. The Cossacks gathered round them, making rough jests. A sergeant clapped one of the women on the back, remarking:

"It's your job to have children, Auntie, and not mix in men's business."

"Bear children yourself!" the unfriendly "Auntie" snapped back in a deep voice.

"Hey, lassies. You in this too?" Yukovnov, an Old Believer with a taste for the fair sex, teased the women soldiers.

"They need a damn good hiding, the bitches."

"Fine soldiers."

"Why don't they stay at home? Need something better to do."

"Look like soldiers from the front, but from the back they're a toss-up between a priest and the devil knows what. Makes you want to spit."

"Hey, you, shock-troop! Move your arse a bit or I'll move it for you!"

The Cossacks guffawed loudly. But towards noon their gay spirits evaporated. The women broke up into platoons and barricaded the gates with great pine beams. They were commanded by a big woman of masculine build, wearing a medal of St. George on her well-fitting greatcoat. The armoured car drove more frequently around the square, and the cadets carried in boxes of cartridges and machine-gun belts.

"Well, lads, we're in for it now."

"Looks like a fight."

"What did you think they brought you here for? To paw the women?"

Round Lagutin a group of men from his own district was gathered, discussing something.

The officers had disappeared, and there was no one in the yard but the Cossacks and the women. Several abandoned machine-guns stood by the gates, their shields shining wetly.

Toward evening it started to drizzle. The Cossacks began to grumble at being left without food.

"Where's Listnitsky?"

"He's in the palace and the cadets won't let the likes of us in there."

"We'd better send someone for the field-kitchen."

Two men were sent.

"Go without your rifles or you'll get them taken away from you," Lagutin advised.

The Cossacks waited another couple of hours, but neither field-kitchen nor messengers appeared. It turned out later that the kitchen had been turned back by soldiers from another regiment. Just as dusk was falling the Women's Battalion, gathered by the gates, lay down in a long line behind the beams, and began to fire across the square. The Cossacks took no part in the shooting, but stood smoking and getting more and more fed up. At last Lagutin gathered the squadron by the wall, and apprehensively watching the windows of the palace, spoke to the crowd:

"Here's the position, Cossacks! There's no point in us staying here. We must go out, or we'll suffer without cause. They'll begin to shell the palace, and where shall we be then? The officers have vanished. . . . And are we to stop here and die? Let's go home, why should we rub our backs against this wall? As for the Provisional Government. . . . What good have they been to us? What do you think, Cossacks?"

"If we go out of the yard the Bolsheviks will start firing at us with their machine-guns."

"They'll have our blood."

"Why should they?"

"Think it out for yourself."

"No, let's stay here to the end."

"We're like sheep in a pen here waiting for the butcher."

"Do what you like, our troop's going out."

"And we're going too!"

"Send men out to the Bolshies. Let them leave us alone and we'll leave them alone."

The Cossacks of the First and Fourth squadrons came up and joined in the meeting. After a little more discussion three Cossacks, one from each squadron, went out through the gates. After some time they returned, accompanied by three sailors. The sailors leapt across the stockade of beams and strode across the yard. They joined the Cossacks, and one of them, a handsome young black-whiskered sailor, his pea-jacket unbuttoned, his cap thrust to the back of his head, pushed into the middle of the crowd.

"Comrade Cossacks! We, the representatives of the revolutionary Baltic fleet, have come to propose that you leave the Winter Palace. Why should you defend an enemy bourgeois government? Let their own bourgeois sons, the cadets, defend them! Not a single soldier has come out in defence of the Provisional Government, and your brothers of the First and Fourth regiments have joined up with us. All those who want to go with us, step over to the left."

"Wait a bit, brother!" A sergeant of the First Squadron stepped forward. "We'll go gladly, but suppose the Bolsheviks start shooting at us?"

"Comrades! In the name of the Petrograd Military Revolutionary Committee we promise that you will leave in absolute safety. No one will touch you."

Another sailor, stocky and pock-marked, came up and stood with his black-whiskered comrade. He surveyed the Cossacks, slowly twisting his thick bull-like neck, then struck his bulging, tightly buttoned shirt with his fist.

"We'll go with you ourselves! You needn't have doubts, lads. We're not your enemies, and the Petrograd proletarians are not your enemies. Your enemies are these...." He jerked his thumb towards the palace and showed his fierce, close-set teeth in a smile.

The Cossacks hesitated. Some of the Women's Battalion approached and stood listening for a moment, then went back to the gates.

"Hey, you women, coming out with us?" a bearded Cossack shouted after them.

"Pick up your rifles and get moving!" Lagutin said resolutely.

The Cossacks willingly seized their arms and formed up.

"Shall we take the machine-guns?" one of the gunners asked the black-whiskered sailor.

"Yes. Don't leave them for the cadets."

Just as the Cossacks were about to leave the courtyard their officers appeared. They stood in a dense group, staring at the sailors. The squadrons began to march off. The machine-gun detachment went in front with its guns. The wheels scraped and rattled on the wet stones. The sailor in the jacket went with the leading troop of the First Squadron. A tall, fair-browed Cossack tugged at his sleeve and said in a guilty voice:

"Brother, you don't think we wanted to go against the people, do you? They got us here by trickery, but if we'd known we wouldn't have come." He shook his head violently. "Believe my word, we wouldn't! God's truth!"

The Fourth Squadron brought up the rear. The Cossacks paused at the gate, where the entire Women's Battalion was drawn up in a solid mass. A burly Cossack mounted the stockade, and persuasively and significantly shaking his dirty finger, declared:

"You listen to me! We're going out, but you in your women's foolishness are staying here. Well then, no tricks! If you start shooting us in the back we'll turn round and make mincemeat of you. Is that clear? Well then, so long for now."

He jumped down from the stockade and ran to catch up with his troop, occasionally looking back. The Cossacks had almost reached the centre of the square when one of them glanced round and cried out excitedly:

"Look, boys! There's an officer running after us!"

Many of the men turned their heads. A tall officer was running across the square, holding his cap on and waving his hand.

"It's Atarshchikov of the Third Squadron."

"Who?"

"The one with the mole on his eye."

"So he wants to come with us."

"He's a fine chap!"

Atarshchikov ran swiftly after the company, a smile flickering on his face. The Cossacks waved their hands and laughed.

"Run, Cap'n! Quicker!"

From the palace gates came the single dry crack of a shot. Atarshchikov threw out his hands and stumbled, then fell on his back, kicking out his legs and struggling to get up. As though by command the squadrons turned and faced the palace. The machine-gunners trained their guns on the gates. There was a rattle of cartridge belts. But not a soul was visible behind the pine beams. The shot seemed to have swept away the officers and women who had crowded there a minute earlier. The squadrons hastily formed up again and marched away at a hurried pace. Two Cossacks from the last troop, who had gone back to Atarshchikov, caught up with them, and loudly, for all the squadron to hear, one of them shouted:

"They got him under the left shoulder. He's done for!"

The Cossacks' steps rang out firmly and strongly. The black-whiskered sailor gave the order:

"By the left ... quick march!"

They wheeled and marched away, leaving the huddled mass of the palace wrapped in silence.

XX

It was a warm autumn with some rain. The
pallid sun shone rarely over the little town of
Bykhov. In October the birds began their southward flight. Even at night the bitterly agitating
cry of cranes rang out over the cool black
earth. The migrating flocks were hastening
away from the oncoming frosts, from the harsh
northern winds of the upper air.

The generals arrested in connection with the
Kornilov affair had been six weeks awaiting
trial. Meanwhile their life in prison had found
its level and, though perhaps not quite normal,
had acquired a routine of its own. After breakfast the generals went for a walk; when they
returned they attended to their mail, received
visits from relatives and acquaintances, dined,
and after an hour of absolute quiet went to
their rooms to work alone; in the evenings
they usually gathered in Kornilov's room,
where they chatted and conferred until the
small hours.

In the girls' high school that served as their
prison they lived a fairly comfortable existence.

The building was guarded externally by men
of the St. George Battalion, and internally by
Tekins. But the guard, though it did to a certain extent hamper the freedom of the pris-

oners, had one significant advantage in its favour; it was so arranged that, should the prisoners wish it, they could at any moment easily and safely escape. During the whole period of their confinement they remained in free contact with the outside world, exerted pressure on bourgeois circles, covered up the traces of their conspiracy, put out feelers to determine the mood of the officers and, in case the worst came to the worst, prepared their escape.

Kornilov, anxious to retain loyal Tekins for his bodyguard, got in touch with Kaledin, who at Kornilov's demand hastily dispatched several trucks of grain to the Tekins' starving families in Turkestan. To obtain assistance for the families of the officers who had taken part in his attempt to seize power Kornilov sent an extremely sharp letter to powerful bankers in Moscow and Petrograd; fearing embarrassing disclosures, the bankers promptly distributed allowances running into some tens of thousands of rubles. Kornilov remained in active correspondence with Kaledin until November. In a long letter sent to Kaledin in the middle of October he asked about the situation on the Don and what reception he could expect from the Cossacks there. Kaledin's reply was encouraging.

The October Revolution, however, shook the

ground under the feet of the arrested generals. The following day messengers were sent out in all directions and a week later an echo of the alarm felt by someone for the fate of the prisoners could be heard in the letter Kaledin addressed to General Dukhonin, the self-styled commander-in-chief, containing a firm request that Kornilov and his entourage should be released on bail. A similar request was made to headquarters by the Alliance of Cossacks and the chief committee of the Army and Naval Officers' Alliance. Dukhonin hesitated.

On November 1st Kornilov sent him a letter. Dukhonin's marginal notes on that letter show how utterly helpless the high command had become. Having lost all effectual control of the army, it was passing its last days in a state of prostration.

Your Excellency, Nikolai Nikolayevich,

Fate has placed you in a situation where it is incumbent upon you to change the course of events which, largely on account of the vacillation and connivance of the senior commanders, threatens the destruction of the country. For you the moment is approaching when a man must either take a great risk or resign; otherwise the responsibility for the ruin of the country and the shame of finally disintegrating the army will fall on his shoulders.

According to the incomplete and fragmentary information at my disposal, the situation is serious but, as yet, not completely hopeless. Such it will become, however, if you allow headquarters to be seized by the Bolsheviks or voluntarily acknowledge their authority.

The St. George Battalion, half demoralized by propaganda, and the weakened Tekin Regiment which you have at your disposal are by no means strong enough.

Foreseeing the way future events are likely to develop, I think it is essential for you to take measures that, besides ensuring the safety of General Headquarters, will create favourable conditions for the organization of further struggle against the anarchy that threatens to engulf us.

I consider such measures to be the following:

1. One Czechoslovak Regiment and a regiment of Polish uhlans should be immediately transferred to Mogilev.

Marginal note by Dukhonin. Headquarters does not consider these regiments completely reliable. They were among the first to accept a truce with the Bolsheviks.

2. Orsha, Smolensk, Zhlobin and Gomel should be occupied by units of the Polish Corps with artillery support drawn from Cossack front-line batteries.

Marginal note. The Second Kuban Division and a brigade of Astrakhan Cossacks have already been brought up for the capture of Orsha and Smolensk. Undesirable to withdraw the regiment of the 1st Polish Division from Bykhov as this may prejudice the safety of the prisoners. The units of the First Division are considerably weakened and cannot be considered a real force. The Polish Corps has taken a definite line of non-interference in Russian internal affairs.

3. All units of the Czechoslovak Corps and the Kornilov Regiment, as well as one or two of the more reliable Cossack divisions, should be concentrated along the Orsha-

Mogilev-Zhlobin line under the pretext of transferring them to Petrograd and Moscow.

Marginal note. The Cossacks are irreconcilably opposed to fighting the Bolsheviks.

4. All British and Belgian armoured vehicles should be concentrated in the same region and manned exclusively by officers.

5. In Mogilev and one other point in the vicinity, well-guarded stocks of rifles, ammunition, machine-guns, automatic weapons and hand-grenades should be laid up for distribution among the officers and volunteers who are certain to gather in this region.

Marginal note. This may lead to excesses.

6. Reliable communication and accurate agreement should be established with the atamans of the Don, Tersk and Kuban armies and the Polish and Czech committees. The Cossacks have come out firmly for the restoration of order in the country; for the Poles and the Czechs the question of the restoration of order in Russia is a question vitally affecting their own existence.

Every day the news grew more alarming. Discontent was growing in Bykhov itself. Kornilov's well-wishers, who were demanding the release of the arrested generals, drove to and fro between Mogilev and Bykhov in their motor cars. The Cossack Alliance even resorted to veiled threats.

Overwhelmed by the pressure of events, Dukhonin continued to vacillate. On November 18th he gave an order for the prisoners to be sent off to the Don, but then immediately cancelled it.

The next morning a mud-bespattered car drove up to the main entrance of the Bykhov high-school prison. The driver obsequiously threw open the door and an elderly, well-set-up officer emerged from the car. The papers he presented to the officer of the guard bore the name of Staff-Colonel Kusonsky.

"I am from General Headquarters. I have a personal message for General Kornilov. Where can I find the commandant?"

The commandant—Lieutenant-Colonel Erghardt of the Tekin Regiment—took the visitor at once to Kornilov. Kusonsky introduced himself and in a slightly affected tone of urgency reported:

"In four hours Mogilev will capitulate to the Bolsheviks without resistance. General Dukhonin has instructed me to inform you that all prisoners must leave Bykhov at once."

When he had questioned Kusonsky about the situation in Mogilev, Kornilov called in Lieutenant-Colonel Erghardt. Leaning heavily with the fingers of his left hand on the edge of the table, he said:

"Release the generals at once. The Tekins must be ready to leave by midnight tonight. I shall accompany the regiment."

All day the bellows creaked and sighed in the regimental forge; the coals blazed ruddily, hammers clanged and the horses whinnied fiercely at the anvils. The Tekins were shoeing their horses on all four hoofs, repairing their harness, cleaning their rifles and making ready.

During the day the generals left the prison singly. But at the wolfish hour of midnight, when the little provincial town had put out its lights and was fast asleep, horsemen began to ride out of the high-school yard in ranks of three. Their black silhouettes stood out in moulded relief against the steely sky. With their tall sheepskin caps pulled down over their eyes and their dark oily faces muffled in their cowls the horsemen rode along hunched in their saddles like great black birds with ruffled feathers. In the middle of the column, beside the regimental commander, Kornilov sat with drooping shoulders on a tall wiry horse. Now and then he screwed up his face in the cold wind that blustered through the streets of the town, and glanced up, puckering the narrow slits of his eyes at the frosty starlit sky.

The gentle tapping of the fresh-shod hoofs rustled softly through the streets and died away on the outskirts.

XXI

The Twelfth Cossack Regiment had been retreating for two days. Slowly, fighting all the way, but retreating. The baggage trains of the Russian and Rumanian armies rolled over the raised, unpaved roads. The combined Austrian and German divisions embraced the retiring armies with a deep enveloping flank movement, and sought to close the ring.

One evening the news came through that the Twelfth Regiment and the Rumanian Brigade next to it were threatened with encirclement. In the night the Twelfth Regiment, reinforced by a battery of the mountaineers' division, received the order to occupy rear-guard positions in the lower part of the Golsh valley. Setting guards, the regiment prepared for the advancing enemy.

The same night Misha Koshevoi and another, rather a dull-witted fellow from Tatarsky village, Alexei Beshnyak, were sent out to a hidden outpost. They concealed themselves in a gully close to a disused well, and breathed in the rarefied frosty air. From time to time a flock of wild geese sped over the clouded sky, marking their flight with anxious cries. Angry at the order that there was to be no smoking, Misha quietly whispered to his companion:

"It's a queer life, Alexei! Men grope about as though they were blind; they come together and part again, and sometimes they tread on one another.... Here you are living on the brink of death, and you wonder to yourself what it's all about. I don't think there's anything more terrible in the world than another man's soul; do what you like, you can't get to the bottom of it.... Here I am lying by your side, and I don't know what you're thinking, and never did know; and what sort of life lies behind you I don't know, and you know no more about me.... Maybe I'm wanting to kill you now, and here you are giving me a biscuit and haven't any idea of what I'm thinking.... People don't know much about themselves. In the summer I was in hospital. In the next bed to me there was a soldier from Moscow. And all the time he was asking how the Cossacks live, and the Lord knows what else. They believe the Cossacks know of nothing except whips; they think the Cossack is a savage, and that instead of a soul he's got bottle-glass inside him. And yet we're men like them, and we're just as fond of women and girls; we cry over our sorrows, but don't rejoice at others' gladness. What do you think, Alexei? I'm hungry for life; when I remember how many beautiful women there are in the world my heart begins to pinch.... I've got to feeling so tender about women I could love them all till it hurt.... I could lie with them all, tall or short, lean or fat. But it's a fine way life's been arranged for us. They palm you off with one woman and you've got to stick to her till you're dead. How do they expect us not to get fed up with her? And now, to crown it all, they've started a war...."

"They haven't beaten you enough, you bullock," Beshnyak jeered without malice.

Koshevoi threw himself on his back and was silent, staring up at the emptiness of the sky and smiling dreamily, his hands caressing the cold, inaccessibly tranquil earth.

An hour before they were due to be relieved, they were surprised by the Germans. Beshnyak managed to fire one shot, then fell, grinding his teeth, doubled up in agony. A German bayonet slashed through his entrails, pierced his bladder and quivered as it struck against his backbone. Koshevoi was sent down by a butt-end. A stout conscript carried him on his back for half a verst. Misha came to with a feeling that he was choking in his own blood, but when he got his breath back and recovered his strength, he had little difficulty in dropping off the German's back. They fired a volley after him, but the darkness and clumps of bushes helped him, and he escaped.

After the retreat had been stayed and the Russo-Rumanian forces had extricated themselves from the enveloping movement, the Twelfth Regiment was withdrawn to the rear. It was instructed to block the roads, setting outposts on them in order to prevent deserters from getting through. If necessary they were to be halted by fire, and any who were caught were to be sent under guard to division headquarters.

Misha Koshevoi was among the first to be sent on outpost duty. He and three other Cossacks left their village in the morning and took up their positions at the end of a maize-field, close to the road. The road ran along the edge of a wood and vanished into a rolling, well-cultivated valley. They watched in turn. In the afternoon they saw a group of some ten soldiers coming along the road towards them. As they came up to the wood they halted and lighted cigarettes, evidently discussing their route, then went on and turned sharply to the left.

"Shall we shout to them?" Koshevoi asked the others as he rose from the maize-stalks.

"Fire over their heads."

"Hey, you! Stop!"

The soldiers, now some hundred paces away from the Cossacks, heard the shout and halted for a moment, then again slowly moved on.

"Stop!" one of the Cossacks shouted, firing into the air.

With rifles at the trail they ran to overtake the slowly moving soldiers.

"Why the devil didn't you stop? Where are you from? Where are you going? Show us your documents!" the Cossack sergeant in charge of the outpost shouted.

The soldiers halted. Three of them slowly unslung their rifles. One man bent and refastened the wire holding the sole of his boot to the upper. They were all incredibly ragged and filthy. Evidently they had spent the night in the forest undergrowth, for there was a dense brush of brown burrs on their greatcoats. Two of them were wearing forage caps, the others had fur caps with unbuttoned ear-flaps and fluttering strings. His sunken cheeks trembling, a tall, bowed soldier, evidently their leader, shouted in an angry voice:

"What do you want? Have we done you any harm? What are you following us for?"

"Your documents!" the sergeant interrupted, assuming a stern tone.

One soldier, blue-eyed and as ruddy as a freshly-baked brick, drew a hand-grenade from his pocket. Shaking it in the face of the sergeant, he looked round at his comrades and said hurriedly in the Yaroslavl dialect:

"There's my document, my lad! There! That's a mandate for any day in the year. So look out. If I throw it there'll be no collecting the bits afterwards. Get me? Did you get me? Is that clear?"

"Don't play about!" the sergeant frowned and dug him in the breast. "Don't play about and don't try to frighten us, we're frightened enough already. You're deserters, and you've got to come back with us to headquarters. They want to see men like you there."

Exchanging glances, the men unslung their rifles. One of them, dark-haired and lean, who looked like a miner, turned his desperate eyes from one to another of the Cossacks and whispered:

"We'll give you a taste of the bayonet, by God! Clear off! By God, I'll put a bullet through the first one to come near me."

The blue-eyed soldier brandished his grenade above his head; the tall bowed man in front scratched the cloth of the sergeant's greatcoat with his rusty bayonet; the miner shouted an oath and swung his butt-end at Misha Koshevoi. Koshevoi's finger quivered on the trigger of his rifle. One of the Cossacks seized a little soldier by the lapels of his greatcoat and dragged him along at arm's length, nervously looking back at the others in fear of a blow from behind.

The dry leaves rustled on the maize stalks. Beyond the rolling valley emerged a blue, undulating line of hills. Red-brown cows were roaming over the pasture land close to the village. The wind sent a frozen dust whirling beyond the wood. The dull October day was full of a drowsy peace; a blessed calm and silence lay over the sun-sprinkled countryside. But just off the road men were trampling in meaningless anger, preparing to pour out their blood on the fertile, rain-mellowed land.

Their passions died down a little, and the soldiers and Cossacks began to talk more peaceably.

"It's only three days since we were pulled out of the line," Koshevoi said indignantly. "We haven't run away to the rear! And you're deserting, you ought to be ashamed! Leaving your comrades! Who will hold the front? My own comrade was bayoneted at my side, and you say we haven't tasted war! Taste it as we have tasted it!"

"What is there to talk about?" another of the Cossacks interrupted him. "Come on to the staff, and no more argument."

"Stand out of the road, Cossacks! Or we'll shoot, by God we'll shoot!" the soldier who looked like a miner threatened.

The sergeant flung out his arms helplessly:

"We can't do it, brother! Kill us if you like, but all the same you won't get through; our squadron is quartered in that village there...."

The tall, bowed soldier now threatened, now cajoled, now began to plead humbly. In the end he bent down, drew a bottle out of his filthy pack, winked at Koshevoi and whispered:

"We'll give you money, Cossacks; and look.... German vodka.... And we'll collect something more. Let us pass, for the love of Christ. We've got children at home, you know how it is yourselves.... We're worn out, had more than we can bear.... How long are we to stand it? God! Surely you won't stop us?" He hurriedly pulled his pouch out of the leg of his boot, shook two soiled Kerensky ruble notes out of it, and insistently pushed them into Koshevoi's hand. "Take them! Take them! My God...! Don't you worry.... We'll get through somehow. The money is nothing.... We can do without it. Take it! We'll get some more...."

Seared with shame, Koshevoi stepped back, keeping his hand behind him and shaking his head. The blood flushed into his cheeks and tears started to his eyes. "It was Beshnyak's getting killed like that made me mad!" he thought. "Here am I myself against the war, and I'm trying to arrest these men. What right have I got? What am I doing here? What a low swine I am!"

He went over to the sergeant, drew him aside, and said, averting his eyes:

"Why not let them go? What do you think? Let them go, by God!"

His eyes wandering as though he were doing something shameful, the sergeant replied:

"Let them go.... What else can we do with them? We'll be doing the same ourselves soon.... Why try to hide it?"

Turning to the soldiers, he shouted angrily:

"You scum! We treat you decently, with all respect, and you offer us money! Do you think we're short ourselves?" He turned livid and shouted: "Put your pouches away, or we'll take you to headquarters."

The Cossacks stepped aside. The soldiers walked on. Glancing back at the distant empty streets of the village, Koshevoi shouted after the retreating deserters:

"Hey! You fillies! What are you marching along in broad daylight for? There's a wood over there; get into it for the day, and go on at night. Or you'll run into another outpost and they'll take you!"

The soldiers glanced around irresolutely; then, like wolves, they straggled in a dirty grey line towards the aspen wood.

At the beginning of November rumours of the upheaval in Petrograd began to reach the Cossack troops. The staff orderlies, who were usually better informed than the others, confirmed that the Provisional Government had fled to America; Kerensky, they said, had been captured by sailors, who had shaven him absolutely bare, tarred him like a prostitute, and dragged him for two days through the streets of Petrograd.

Later, when the official news arrived of the overthrow of the Provisional Government and the transfer of power to the Bolsheviks, the Cossacks became guardedly quiet. Many were glad, in the expectation that the war would be ended. But rumours that the Third Cavalry Corps was marching with Kerensky and General Krasnov on Petrograd, and that Kaledin was advancing with Cossack regiments from the south, instilled alarm.

The front crumbled to pieces. In October the soldiers had deserted in scattered, unorganized groups; but by the end of November entire companies and regiments were retiring from their positions, sometimes marching with only light equipment, but more frequently taking the regimental property with them, breaking into the warehouses, shooting their officers, pillaging en route, and pouring in an unfettered, stormy flood back to their homes.

In the new circumstances the Twelfth Regiment's task of holding up deserters became senseless. After being flung back into the front in the useless attempt to close the gaps and breaches formed by the infantry abandoning their sectors, it was in December again withdrawn, marched to the nearest station, and loading all the regimental property, machine-guns, reserves of ammunition, and horses into wagons, set off into the heart of struggle-racked Russia.

Through the Ukraine the troop trains of the Twelfth Regiment dragged towards the Don. Not far from Znamenka the Bolshevik Red Guards tried to disarm them. The negotiations lasted half an hour. Koshevoi and five other Cossacks, the chairmen of the squadron revolutionary committees, asked for permission to pass through with their arms.

"What do you want the arms for?" the members of the station Soviet asked.

"To smash our own bourgeoisie and generals with! To twist Kaledin's tail!" Koshevoi answered for them all.

"We won't give up our weapons, they're the Army's," the Cossacks protested.

The trains were allowed to go on. At Kremenchug a further attempt was made to disarm them. They were allowed to pass only when the Cossack machine-gunners set up their guns at the open doors of the wagons and trained them on the station, while one of the squadrons spread out along the lines and made ready to fight. Near Yekaterinoslav not even an exchange of shots with a Red Guard detachment availed; the regiment was partly disarmed, and the machine-guns, more than a hundred cases of cartridges, the field telephone apparatus and several reels of wire were confiscated. To the proposal that they should arrest their officers the Cossacks replied with a refusal. Throughout the journey they lost only one officer, the regimental adjutant; and he was sentenced to death by the Cossacks themselves, the sentence being carried out by Uryupin and a Red Guard sailor.

Towards evening on December 17th, at the station of Sinelnikovo, the Cossacks dragged the adjutant out of the train.

"Is that the one who gave the Cossacks away?" the gap-toothed sailor, armed with a Mauser pistol and a Japanese rifle, asked cheerfully.

"Think we don't know his face? This is him all right!" Uryupin answered panting.

The adjutant, a young junior captain, stared round like a trapped animal, unconscious of the cold that seared his cheeks or the pain of the blow he had received from a rifle-butt. Uryupin and the sailor led him a little away from the train.

"It's devils like him make people rebel, he's the kind that's caused this revolution. . . . Oho, don't shake so much, dearie, or you'll fall apart," Uryupin hissed, and taking off his cap, made the sign of the cross.

"Look out, Captain!"

"Ready?" the sailor asked, toying with his pistol, his lips parted in a broad toothless grin.

"I am."

Uryupin crossed himself once again, glanced sideways at the sailor who had put one foot back and was taking aim, and with a grim smile fired first.

Close to Chaplin, the regiment was accidentally drawn into the fighting which had broken out between the anarchists and the Ukrainians. It lost three men and broke through by sheer force, with great difficulty clearing the lines occupied by the troop trains of a rifle division.

Within three days the first section of the regiment was detraining at Millerovo Station; the other section had been delayed in Lugansk. Half of them broke away and rode straight home from the station, while the remainder rode in good order to Kargin village. There next day they traded their trophies and the horses captured from the Austrians, and shared out the regimental funds and equipment.

Koshevoi and the other Cossacks from Tatarsky village set off home in the evening. They rode up a hill. Below, on the icy-white, winding banks of the Chir, lay the village of Kargin, the most beautiful of all the villages of the upper Don. Smoke was rising in crisp puffs from the chimney of the steam mill, a black crowd of people was gathered on the square, the bell was ringing for vespers. Beyond the slopes of Kargin the crowns of the willows round Klimovsky village could just be seen. Beyond them, on the wormwood blue of the snow-clad horizon, a smoky sunset spread half across the sky in a glittering purple radiance.

The eighteen riders passed by a mound nurturing three wild apple-trees, and at a swift trot, their saddles creaking, rode off to the north-east. The frosty night lurked like a thief behind the ridge of hills. Wrapping their faces in their cowls, the Cossacks now and then urged their horses into a sharp gallop. The horseshoes rang almost painfully clear on the hard road, as it streamed away to the south behind them. On each side of the road an icy crust of snow, pared down by a recent thaw, clung among the grasses, glowing opalescently like liquid fire in the moonlight.

The Cossacks silently urged on their horses. The road flowed away to the south. A forest swathed the east. The tiny tracks of hares showed on the snow at the side of the road. High above the steppe, the Milky Way girdled the sky like a silver-mounted Cossack belt.

PART FIVE

I

The Cossacks began to come home from the front in the late autumn of 1917. Christonya, who had noticeably grown older, and three others who had served with him in the 52nd Regiment returned. Smooth-cheeked Anikushka returned, the artilleryman Ivan Tomilin, and Horseshoe Yakov. After them came Martin Shamil, Ivan Alexeyevich, Zakhar Korolyov, and the tall ungainly Borshchev. In December Mitka Korshunov unexpectedly turned up, and a week later a whole party of Cossacks who had served in the Twelfth Regiment: Misha Koshevoi, Prokhor Zykov, Yepifan Maksayev, Andrei Koshulin, and Yegor Sinilin. Fedot Bodovskov, who had got separated from his regiment, rode straight home from Voronezh on a handsome dun horse taken from an Austrian officer. Afterwards he often told the story of how he had made his way through the villages of Voronezh Province, seething with revolution, and had got away from right under the noses of Red Guard detachments, trusting to the speed of his mount.

Then came Merkulov, Pyotr Melekhov and Nikolai Koshevoi, who had run off from the Bolshevized 27th Regiment. It was they who brought the news that Grigory Melekhov, who had recently been serving in the Second Reserve Regiment, had gone over to the Bolsheviks and remained in Kamenskaya. They had also left behind them Maxim Gryaznov, once a daring horse-stealer, who had been attracted to the Bolsheviks by the novelty of the troublous days and the possibility of an easy life. They told of Maxim that he had acquired a horse of extraordinary ugliness and as extraordinary mettle, that a streak of silver hair stretched right along its back, that it was not particularly tall, but long in the body and as red as a cow. They did not refer much to Grigory. Evidently they were reluctant to, knowing that his road ran counter to that of the village, and that it was doubtful whether they would ever run together again.

The homes to which the Cossacks returned as masters or long-awaited guests were filled with rejoicing, a rejoicing that emphasized more sharply and ruthlessly the deep misery of those who had lost their relatives and dear ones for ever. There were many Cossacks missing, scattered over the fields of Galicia, the Bukovina, Eastern Prussia, the Carpathians, and Rumania —their bodies lying and rotting while the funeral dirge of gun-fire boomed overhead. And now the hillocks of the common graves were overgrown with tall weeds, rain beat down upon them, and the drifting snow enwrapped them. No matter how often the bare-headed Cossack women ran to the corner of the village street and gazed into the distance with shaded eyes, they would never live to see their dear ones come riding home. No matter how much the tears streamed from their swollen and faded eyes, they could not wash away the pain. No matter how much they wept on the anniversaries and remembrance days, the eastern wind would not carry their cries to Galicia and Eastern Prussia, to the sunken hillocks of the common graves.

As the grass grows over the graves, so time overgrows the pain. As the wind blew away the traces of those who had departed, so time would blow away the bloody pain and the memory of those who waited in vain for their dear ones to return, and who would always wait in vain, for human life is short and not long is the time granted to any of us to tread the grass.

The wife of Prokhor Shamil beat her head against the hard ground and gnawed the earthen floor of her hut with her teeth as she saw her brother-in-law, Martin Shamil, caressing his pregnant wife or giving his children presents and dandling them. She writhed and crawled on hands and knees over the floor, while around her her little children clung like a drove of sheep, howling as they watched their mother, their eyes dilated with fear.

Rend your last blouse, dear heart! Tear your hair that has grown thin with your hard and joyless life; bite your lips till the blood comes; wring your work-scarred hands and beat your body on the threshold of your empty home! The master is missing from your house, your husband is gone, your children are fatherless; and remember that no one will caress you or your orphans, no one will press your head to his breast at night, when you drop on to your bed, worn out with weariness; and no one will say to you as once he said: "Don't worry, Aniska, we'll manage somehow!" You will not get another husband, for labour, anxieties, children have withered and lined you. No father will come for your half-naked children. You yourself will have to do all the ploughing and harrowing and pant with the over-great strain. You will have to pitchfork the sheaves from the reaper and throw them on to the wagon, and as you raise the heavy bundles of wheat on the pitchfork you will feel that something is rending under your belly. And afterwards you will writhe with pain, covering yourself with your rags and bleeding.

Turning over her son's old underwear Alexei Beshnyak's mother wept bitter tears as she sniffed at them; but only in the folds of his last shirt, brought back by Misha Koshevoi, could she smell the traces of his sweat. Burying her head in the shirt, the old woman rocked and lamented grievously, patterning the dirty cotton with her tears.

The families of Manitskov, Ozerov, Kalinin, Likhovidov, Yermakov, and many other Cossacks were orphaned.

Only for Stepan Astakhov did no one weep; for there was no one. His boarded-up house, tumble-down and gloomy even in summer-time, was left empty. Aksinya lived in Yagodnoye, and little was heard of her; she never set foot in the village, and perhaps she never wanted to.

The Cossacks of the upper districts of the Don returned home in groups. By December almost all had returned to the villages of Vyeshenskaya District. Day and night the bands of riders passed through Tatarsky in groups of from ten to forty, making their way to the left bank of the Don.

"Where are you from, soldiers?" the old men would go out and ask.

"From Chornaya River; from Zimovnaya; from Dubrovka; from Gorokhovskaya," would come the replies.

"Finished fighting, then?" old men would ask slyly.

Some of the riders, the quiet ones with tender consciences, would smile:

"We've had enough, Dad! We're finished!"

But the more desperate and embittered would curse and advise the old men: "Go and try it yourselves! Why all the questions? There are too many of you busybodies about."

By the end of the winter civil war had broken out close to Novocherkassk, but in the villages in the upper districts of the Don a graveyard silence reigned. Only an internal, hidden dissension raged in the houses, and sometimes broke through to the surface. The old men could not get on with the Cossacks returned from the front.

Of the war which had flared up near the capital of the Don Province the villagers knew only by hearsay. Only hazily understanding the various political tendencies that had arisen, they kept their ears to the ground and waited.

Until January life flowed on peacefully in the village of Tatarsky. The Cossacks who had returned from the front rested at home with their wives and ate their fill, little reckoning that still more bitter woes and burdens than those they had had to bear during the war lurked at the threshold of their homes.

II

In January 1917 Grigory Melekhov was promoted to cornet's rank in recognition of his distinguished services in the field, and was appointed to the Second Reserve Regiment as a troop commander. In the following September he went home on leave, after an attack of pneumonia. He spent six weeks at home, then was passed as fit by the district medical commission and returned to his regiment. After the October Revolution* he was promoted to the rank of squadron commander. About this time his opinions underwent a considerable change, as the result of the events occurring around him and the influence of one of the officers in the regiment, Lieutenant Yefim Izvarin.

* The Proletarian Revolution of November 7 (October 25, old style), 1917.

Grigory made Izvarin's acquaintance the day he returned from leave, and afterwards met him frequently both on and off duty, unconsciously falling under his influence. Yefim Izvarin was the son of a well-to-do Cossack. He had been educated in the Novocherkassk cadets' training college, went straight from college to the Tenth Don Cossack Regiment at the front, served in this regiment for about a year, receiving, as he liked to put it, "the cross of St. George and fourteen fragments of hand-grenade in various convenient and inconvenient parts of the body," and was then transferred to the Second Reserve Regiment.

A man of unusual ability, highly talented, educated considerably above the level of the average Cossack officer, Izvarin was a fervent Cossack autonomist. The February Revolution afforded him opportunities for development, he associated with Cossack separatist circles, and carried on intelligent agitation for the complete autonomy of the Don Region and the establishment of the form of government which had existed on the Don before tsarism had laid hands on the Cossacks. He was well acquainted with history, was ardent yet clear-sighted and sober in intellect, and with compelling eloquence painted a picture of the future free life of the Don Cossacks when they would have their own government, when there would not be a Russian left in the province, and the Cossackry, setting guards along their own frontiers, would talk as equals, without any cap-raising, with the Ukraine and Great Russia, and carry on commerce and exchange with them. Izvarin turned the heads of the simpleminded Cossacks and the poorly educated officers, and Grigory also fell under his spell. At first, heated arguments went on between them, but the semi-literate Grigory was no match for his opponent, and Izvarin easily triumphed in the verbal duels. The discussion usually took place in some corner of the barracks, and the listeners were always on Izvarin's side. He carried the Cossacks away with his arguments and the pictures he drew of the future independent life, which particularly appealed to the innermost, deeply cherished feelings of the prosperous Cossacks of the lower Don.

"But how shall we be able to live without Russia, when we've got nothing except wheat?" Grigory would ask.

Izvarin would patiently explain:

"I am not thinking of an independent and completely isolated existence for just the Don Region. We shall live together with the Kuban, the Terek, and the highlanders of the Caucasus on the basis of federation, that is, association. The Caucasus is rich in minerals; you can find everything there."

"And coal too?"

"The Donets Basin is only a stone's throw away."

"But it belongs to Russia."

"Whom it belongs to and on whose territory it is is a matter of dispute. But even if the Donets Basin goes to Russia we shall lose very little. Our federative alliance will not be based on industry. We are an agrarian country, and that being the case, we shall supply our small industry with coal bought from Russia. And not coal alone. There are many other things we shall have to buy from Russia: timber, metal, manufactured articles, and so on; and in return we shall supply them with good-quality wheat and oil."

"And what shall we gain by being separate?"

"That's simple! In the first place we shall be free from their political protection. We shall restore the order destroyed by the Russian tsars, and turn out all the aliens. Within ten years, by importing machinery we shall raise our agriculture to such a level that we shall be ten times as rich. The land is ours. It was washed with our fathers' blood and fertilized with their bones; but for four hundred years we have been in subjection to Russia, defending her interests and not thinking of ourselves. We have access to the sea. We shall have a strong fighting army, and neither the Ukraine nor even Russia will dare to violate our independence."

A man of average height, handsome figure and broad shoulders, Izvarin was a typical Cossack. He had curly hair the colour of unripened oats, a swarthy face, a sloping forehead, and was sunburnt only on his cheeks and along his bleached eyebrows. He spoke in a high, well-modulated tenor voice, and, when talking, had a habit of suddenly raising his left eyebrow and wrinkling his small hook-nose, so that he seemed to be sniffing at something. His energetic walk, self-confident carriage, and the frank gaze of his brown eyes marked him out from the other officers of the regiment. The Cossacks had a sincere respect for him, more perhaps than for the regimental commander himself.

Izvarin and Grigory had long talks together, and Grigory, feeling that the ground was once again quaking beneath his feet, passed through an experience similar to what he had felt in the Moscow eye hospital when he met Garanzha.

Shortly after the October Revolution he had a long conversation with Izvarin. Torn by contradictory impulses, he cautiously asked the lieutenant what he thought of the Bolsheviks.

"Tell me, Yefim Ivanich, do you think the Bolsheviks are right or not?"

Raising his eyebrow and humorously crinkling his nose, Izvarin replied:

"Are the Bolsheviks right? Ha-ha! My boy, you're like a new-born babe. The Bolsheviks have their own programme, their own plans and hopes. They're right from their point of view, and we're right from ours. Do you know the real name of the Bolshevik Party? No? Well, it's the 'Russian Social-Democratic *Labour* Party.' Understand? 'Labour'! Just now they're flirting with the peasantry and the Cossacks, but the working class is their basis. They're bringing emancipation to the workers, but perhaps even worse enslavement to the peasants. In real life it never works out that everybody gets an equal share. If the Bolsheviks get the upper hand it will be good for the workers and bad for the rest. If the monarchy returns, it will be good for the landowners and suchlike and bad for the rest. We don't want either the one or the other. We need our own, and first of all we need to get rid of all our protectors, whether Kornilov, or Kerensky, or Lenin. We can get along without them on our own land. God save us from our friends and we'll manage our enemies ourselves."

"But you know that most of the Cossacks are drawn towards the Bolsheviks?"

"Grisha, my friend, understand this, for it is fundamental. At the moment the roads of the peasants and the Cossacks coincide with that of the Bolsheviks. That's true, but do you know why? It is because the Bolsheviks stand for peace, for an immediate peace, and at the moment this is where the Cossacks feel the war!" He gave himself a resounding slap on his swarthy neck, and straightening his quizzically lifted eyebrow, shouted:

"And that is why the Cossacks are reeking with Bolshevism and are marching in step with the Bolsheviks. But ... as soon as the war is over and the Bolsheviks stretch out their hands to grab the Cossacks' possessions the roads of the Cossacks and the Bolsheviks will part! That is basic, and historically inevitable. Between the present order of Cossack existence and socialism, which is the final consummation of the Bolshevik Revolution, there is an impassable abyss! Well, what do you say to that?"

"I say that I don't understand anything!" Grigory mumbled. "It's hard for me to make head or tail of it. I'm as lost as if I were in a snowstorm in the steppe."

"You won't get out of it like that. Life itself will force you to make something of it, and will drive you to one side or the other."

This conversation took place at the end of October. In November, Grigory happened to meet another Cossack who played a large part in the history of the revolution on the Don. Grigory met Fyodor Podtyolkov, and once again, after some wavering, the former truth was restored in his heart.

A freezing rain had been falling since midday. Towards evening the weather cleared, and Grigory decided to call on Drozdov, a corporal of the 28th Regiment, who came from his own district. A quarter of an hour later he was wiping his feet on the mat outside Drozdov's door. Drozdov had company: a great, heavily built Cossack with the shoulder-straps of a sergeant-major in the guards' battery was sitting on the camp-bed with his back to the window. He sat with bowed back, his legs in their black cloth trousers set widely apart, his large, hairy hands resting on his broad knees. His tunic fitted him so tightly it looked as if it would burst at the chest. At the creak of the door he turned his short neck, stared coldly at Grigory, and buried the cool light of his eyes in the thick-lidded obscurity of their narrow sockets.

"I want you to know each other! Grigory, this is Podtyolkov from Ust-Khoperskaya, almost a neighbour of ours."

The two men silently shook hands, and Grigory sat down.

Grigory smiled at his host.

"I've marked the floor. Sorry."

"Don't worry. My landlady will put it right. . . . Want some tea?"

Drozdov, small and agile as a lizard, flicked the samovar with a tobacco-stained finger-nail and added regretfully:

"You'll have to drink it cold."

"I don't want any. Don't bother."

Grigory offered his new acquaintance a cigarette. Podtyolkov fumbled a long time with his great red fingers at the closely packed case and muttered: "Damn, can't get hold of it anyhow." Finally he managed to roll out a cigarette, and raised his smiling eyes (even narrower now) to Grigory's face. His easy manner pleased Grigory, who asked: "What village are you from?"

"I was born in Krutovsky, but I've been living in Ust-Klinovsky lately. You've heard of Krutovsky, I reckon?"

Addressing Grigory with no particular formality, he spoke freely and once even laid his heavy hand on Grigory's shoulder.

Podtyolkov's broad clean-shaven face was slightly pock-marked. His whiskers were twisted tightly; his hair was plastered down over his little ears and curled a little over his left eyebrow. He would have made a pleasant impression but for his large, upturned nose and his eyes. At first glance there was nothing extraordinary about his eyes, but as he looked more closely Grigory could almost feel their leaden heaviness. Small, like grape-shot, they gleamed through narrow slits as though from embrasures, and fastened their gaze on one spot with a stubborn persistence.

Grigory stared at the man curiously, noting one characteristic feature. Podtyolkov hardly ever blinked. As he talked he fixed his sombre gaze on his companion, or shifted his glance from one thing to another, but all the time his curly, sun-bleached eye-lashes were drooped and motionless. Only occasionally did he drop his puffy eyelids and suddenly raise them again to take aim once more with those pellet-like eyes.

"Here's an interesting point, brothers," Grigory opened the conversation. "The war will end and we shall begin to live in a new way. The Ukraine will have a separate government, and the Cossack Army Council will rule in the Don."

"You mean Ataman Kaledin," Podtyolkov quietly corrected him.

"It's all the same. Where's the difference?"

"Oh, there's no difference," Podtyolkov agreed.

"We've said good-bye to Mother Russia," Grigory continued his paraphrase of Izvarin's argument, curious to see how Drozdov and this stranger from the guards' battery would react to these ideas. "We shall have our own government and our own style of life. Out with the Ukrainians from the Cossack lands; we'll establish frontier guards and keep the khokhols out! We shall live as our forefathers lived in the old days. I think the Revolution is all to our good. What do you think, Drozdov?"

Drozdov smiled craftily and fidgeted. "Of course it will be better for us. The muzhiks robbed us of our strength, and we couldn't live under them. And all the atamans were Germans: von Taube, von Grabbe, and the devil knows what else. They gave our land to all these staff officers. Now we shall have time to breathe at any rate."

"But will Russia agree to all this?" Podtyolkov asked quietly, addressing no one in particular.

"I reckon she'll have to," Grigory assured him.

"In any case it will be just the same. The same old soup, only thinner."

"How do you make that out?"

"Of course it will." Podtyolkov shifted his pellet-like eyes more swiftly and cast a heavy glance at Grigory. "The atamans will go on just the same as before, oppressing the people who have to work. You will go before some 'Excellency,' and he'll give you one on the snout. A fine life indeed! Better hang a mill-stone round your neck and jump into the river."

Grigory rose and began to pace up and down the room. Finally he halted in front of Podtyolkov and asked:

"Then what are we to do?"

"Finish the job!"

"What job?"

"Once you've started ploughing you must furrow on to the end. Once you've overthrown the tsar and the counter-revolution you must see the government passes into the hands of the people. That story about the old times is all fairy-tales. In the old days the tsars oppressed us, and now if the tsars don't, somebody else will."

"Then what is your way out, Podtyolkov?"

And once more Podtyolkov's heavy, pellet-like eyes darted to and fro, seeking space in the cramped little room.

"A people's government, elected. If you get into the hands of the generals there'll be war again, and we can do without that. If only we could get a people's government set up all over the world, so that the people would not be oppressed and sent to war! But what have we got now? If you turn a pair of old trousers inside out, you're still left with the holes." Podtyolkov slapped his knees loudly and gave a fierce smile, revealing a tight row of small white teeth. "We'd better keep free of the old days, or they'll be harnessing us up so that we shall be worse off than under the tsar."

"And who will govern us?"

"We shall govern ourselves," Podtyolkov replied more animatedly. "We shall have our own government. Only let the Kaledins loosen the saddle-girths a little and we shall soon throw them off our backs."

Grigory halted before the steamy window and stared out into the street, at the children playing, at the wet roofs of the houses opposite, at the pale-grey branches of a bare poplar rising from the fence, and listened no more to the argument between Podtyolkov and Drozdov. He was struggling painfully to see daylight through the jumble of thoughts oppressing him, to come to some decision.

For some ten minutes he stood drawing initials with his finger on the window-pane. Beyond the window the faded, early winter sunset was smouldering behind the roof of the low house opposite. The sun hung as though it had been set edgeways on the rusty ridge of the roof and was about to roll down on one or the other side. Rustling leaves came chasing along the street from the town garden, and a rapidly strengthening wind from the Ukraine stormed through the town.

III

The town of Novocherkassk became the centre of attraction for all who had fled from the Bolshevik Revolution. Important generals who formerly had been arbiters of the destiny of the Russian armies poured down into the lower regions of the Don, hoping to find support among the reactionary Don Cossacks and to use the Don as a base for an offensive against Soviet Russia. On November 2nd General Alexeyev arrived in the town. After talks with Kaledin he set to work to organize volunteer detachments. The backbone of the future Volunteer Army was provided by officers, who had fled from the north, cadets, students, declassed soldiers, the most active of the counter-revolutionary Cossacks, and men seeking adventure and higher pay even in Kerensky rubles.

At the end of November, when Alexeyev had more than a thousand in his detachments, more generals arrived, and on December 6th Kornilov himself appeared in the town. By this time Kaledin had succeeded in withdrawing almost all the Cossack regiments from the Rumanian and Austro-German fronts, and had distributed them along the main railway lines of the Don Province. But the Cossacks, wearied with three years of war and returning from the front in a revolutionary mood, showed no great desire to fight the Bolsheviks. The regiments were left with hardly a third of their normal complement, for the homefires beckoned powerfully, and there was no force on earth that could have restrained the Cossacks from their spontaneous movement towards their native villages. Only three of the Don regiments were in Petrograd and even they did not remain there long.

Some of the particularly unreliable units Kaledin attempted to reform, or to isolate by surrounding them with his staunchest troops. Towards the end of November, when Kaledin made his first attempt to send front-line detachments against revolutionary Rostov, the Cossacks refused to attack, and turned back after going only a short distance. But the widely developed organization for consolidating the fragmentary divisions began to have its results. By November 27th Kaledin had several reliable volunteer detachments at his command, and could borrow forces from Alexeyev, who by this time had collected a few battalions.

On December 2nd Rostov was stormed by White Guard volunteer forces. With Kornilov's arrival there the city became the organizational centre of the Volunteer Army. Kaledin was left alone. He scattered his Cossack units along the borders of the region as far as Tsaritsin and the fringe of the Saratov Province. For his most urgent tasks, however, he used officer-partisan detachments; only on them could the enfeebled Army government rely for everyday support.

Freshly recruited detachments were sent out to subdue the Donets miners. Captain Chernetsov got to work in the Makeyev District, where there were also units of the regular 58th Cossack Regiment. In Novocherkassk various detachments and fighting squads were formed; in the north, officers and partisans were lumped together in the so-called "Stenka Razin" detachment. But from three sides columns of Red Guards were approaching the province. In Kharkov and Voronezh, forces were being assembled to strike a blow against the counter-revolutionaries on the Don. Clouds hung, and deepened, and blackened over the Don. The winds from the Ukraine were already bringing the rumble of gun-fire that accompanied the first clashes.

IV

Billowing yellow-white clouds were floating slowly over Novocherkassk. In the heavens right above the glittering dome of the cathedral, a grey, curly fleece of cloud hung in a blue expanse, its long tail drooping and gleaming a rosy silver.

The rising sun was not bright but the windows of the Ataman's Palace gleamed fiercely in its rays. The sloping iron roofs of the houses glistened, and the bronze statue of Yermak holding out the crown of Siberia was still damp from the rain of the day before.

A platoon of Cossack infantry was marching up the Kreshchensky hill. Sunbeams danced springily on their fixed bayonets. The Cossacks' rhythmic, barely audible tread scarcely disturbed the crystal stillness of the morning, in which the only other sounds were the footsteps of an occasional passer-by and the rattle of a drozhky.

On that morning Ilya Bunchuk arrived in Novocherkassk by the Moscow train. He was the last to leave the carriage, pulling down the edges of his old overcoat, and feeling a little awkward and strange in his civilian clothing.

A gendarme and two girls, both laughing at something, were walking up and down the platform. Bunchuk went out into the town, carrying his cheap, shabby suit-case under his arm. He met hardly anyone, although he crossed the town from one side to the other. After half an hour's walk he halted before a small, dilapidated house. It had not been repaired for years; time had laid hands upon it, and the roof was sinking, the walls were awry, the shutters hung loosely, and the windows squinted. As he opened the wicket-gate Bunchuk ran his eyes over the house and the tiny yard; then he hurried up the steps.

He found half the narrow corridor of the house occupied by a chest piled with lumber. In the darkness he knocked his knee against one corner, but threw open the door, not feeling the pain. There was no one in the first, low room. He went towards the second, halting on the threshold. His head swam with the terribly familiar scent peculiar to this one house. His eyes took in all the room: the icon in the corner, the bed, the table, the small, speckled mirror above it, some photographs, several rickety chairs, a sewing-machine, and a tarnished samovar standing on the stove. With his heart suddenly beating violently, he threw down his suit-case and stared around the kitchen. The tall, green-washed stove had a welcoming look; from behind a blue cotton curtain peeped an old tabby-cat, its eyes gleaming with almost human curiosity, evidently unaccustomed to visitors. Dirty dishes lay untidily on the table, and a ball of wool and four gleaming knitting-needles carrying an unfinished stocking had been left on a stool.

Nothing had changed in eight years. He might have left it all only the day before. He ran out on to the steps. From the door of a shed in the far corner of the yard an old, bowed woman emerged. "Mother! But is it? Is it her?" His lips trembling, he ran to meet her, tearing the cap from his head as he went.

"Who do you want?" the old woman asked in alarm, standing with her palm shading her eyes.

"Mother!" the words burst hoarsely from Bunchuk's throat. "Don't you know me?"

He went stumbling towards her, and saw her sway at his shout, as though under a blow. She wanted to run, but her strength failed her and she came in little spurts, as though battling against a strong wind. He caught her in his arms, he kissed her furrowed face and her eyes, dimmed with fear and gladness, while his own eyes blinked helplessly.

"Ilya! Ilyusha! My little son! I didn't know you.... Lord, where have you come from?" the old woman whispered.

They went into the house. He threw off his borrowed overcoat with a sigh of relief, and sat down at the table.

"I never thought I should see you again.... It's so many years ... my dear.... How could I know you, you've grown so and look so much older."

"Well, and how are you, Mother?" he asked with a smile.

She replied disconnectedly as she bustled about, laying the table, putting charcoal into the samovar. With streaming eyes she ran back again and again to her son to stroke his head and press him to her. She boiled water and herself washed his head, took some clean underwear, yellow with age, from the bottom of the **chest,** gave him a meal and sat until midnight with her eyes fixed on him, questioning him and sadly shaking her head.

Two o'clock had struck in the neighbouring belfry when Bunchuk lay down to sleep. He dropped off at once, and dreamed that he was once more a pupil at the craft school, tired out with play and dozing over his books, while his mother opened the door from the kitchen and asked sternly: "Ilya, have you learned your lessons for tomorrow?" He slept with a fixed, tensely happy smile on his face.

His mother went to him more than once during the night, straightening the blanket and pillow, kissing his great forehead, and quietly going out again.

He spent only one day at home. In the morning a comrade in a soldier's greatcoat and a new khaki cap came and talked with him in undertones; after the man had gone he bustled about, swiftly packed his suit-case, and drew on his ill-fitting overcoat. He took a hurried farewell of his mother, promising to see her again within a month.

"Where are you off to now, Ilya?"

"To Rostov, Mother, to Rostov. I'll be back soon. . . . Don't you fret, Mother . . . don't fret," he cheered her.

She hurriedly removed a small cross from her neck, and as she kissed her son she slipped the string over his head. As with trembling fingers she adjusted it around his neck, she whispered:

"Wear this, Ilya. Defend him and save him, Lord; shield him with thy wings. He is all I have in the world. . . ." As she passionately embraced him she could not control herself, and the corners of her lips quivered and drooped bitterly. Like spring rain one warm tear after another fell on to Bunchuk's hairy hand. He unfastened her hands from his neck and ran with clouded face out of the house.

The crowd was packed like cattle at Rostov Station, and the floors were littered ankle-deep with cigarette-butts and the husks of sunflower-seeds. On the station square the soldiers from the town garrison were trading equipment, tobacco, and the articles they had stolen. A swarming throng of the many nationalities to be found in southern seaport towns moved slowly about, buzzing loudly. Bunchuk pressed through the crowd, sought out the Party Committee room, and made his way upstairs to the first floor. His further progress was barred by a Red Guard armed with a rifle of Japanese pattern. The bayonet was broad and short.

"Who do you want, Comrade?"

"I want Comrade Abramson. Is he here?"

"Third room on the left."

Bunchuk opened the door of the room indicated, and found a short, big-nosed, black-haired man talking to an elderly railwayman. His left hand was under the lapel of his jacket, and his right waved methodically in the air.

"It's not good enough!" the black-haired man was declaring. "That isn't organization! If you carry on your agitation like this you'll get exactly opposite results to those we want."

Judging from the anxiously guilty look on the railwayman's face, he wanted to say something in justification, but the other man would not let him open his mouth. Evidently irritated to the last degree, he shouted:

"Remove Mitchenko from the work at once! This is not to be endured! We cannot allow what is going on among you. Verkhotsky will have to answer for it before the Revolutionary Tribunal. Is he arrested? Yes? I shall insist on his being shot!" he ended harshly. Still not completely in control of himself, he turned his angry face in Bunchuk's direction and asked sharply: "What do you want?"

"Are you Abramson?"

"Yes."

Bunchuk handed him documents from the Petrograd Party Committee, and sat down on the window-ledge. Abramson carefully read the letters, then evidently regretting his rude-ness, gave Bunchuk a sombre smile.

"Wait a bit; we'll have a talk in a moment or two."

He dismissed the railwayman and went out, returning a few minutes later with a well-built, clean-shaven officer of the regular army, bearing the scar of a sabre-cut across his jaw.

"This is a member of our Military Revolu-tionary Committee. And you, Comrade Bun-chuk, are a machine-gunner, aren't you?"

"Yes."

"You're just the man we want." The officer smiled and his scar flushed along its whole length, from his ear to the point of his jaw.

"Can you organize machine-gun detach-ments among the workers in the Red Guards for us? As soon as possible?" Abramson asked.

"I'll try. It's a question of time."

"Well, how long do you need? A week ... two, three?" Smiling expectantly, the other man bent towards Bunchuk.

"A few days."

"Excellent!"

Abramson rubbed his forehead and said with obvious annoyance:

"The detachments of the town garrison are **badly** demoralized, and are not to be relied on.

Like everywhere else, I suppose, Comrade Bunchuk. Our hopes here rest on the workers. The sailors too, but as for the soldiers.... That's why we want our own machine-gunners." He tugged at his black beard, and asked: "How are you off in regard to supplies? Well, we'll arrange that. Have you had anything to eat today? No, of course not."

"He must have starved a bit in his time to be able to tell at a glance whether a man is full or hungry, and he must have known a lot of trouble or horror to collect all those grey hairs," Bunchuk thought with sudden affection as he looked at the dazzling patch of grey on Abramson's beetle-like head. And as he went with a guide to Abramson's room his mind still turned on him: "He's a fine chap, a true Bolshevik! Hard, yet there's something good and human in him. He doesn't think twice about giving the death sentence for some saboteur, yet he can see to the needs of his comrades."

Still under the warm impression of his meeting, he reached Abramson's quarters, handed a note from him to the landlady and had some dinner, then lay down to rest on the bed in the little, book-filled room. He fell straight off to sleep.

V

For the next four days Bunchuk was occupied from early morning till nightfall with the workers assigned to him by the Party Committee. There were sixteen altogether, men of the most varied peace-time occupations, different in age and even in nationality. There were two stevedores, a Ukrainian named Khvilichko and a Russianized Greek Mikhalidi; a compositor Stepanov; eight metal workers; a miner Zelenkov, from the Paramonov mines; a weak-looking Armenian baker Gyevorkyants; a Russianized German, a skilled mechanic, named Rebinder; and two workers from the railway workshops. A seventeenth letter was brought to Bunchuk by a woman attired in a padded soldier's greatcoat and boots that were much too large for her. As he took the sealed letter, he asked:

"On your way back can you call in at the staff for me?"

She smiled, embarrassedly tidied a thick lock of hair that had fallen below her kerchief, and replied nervously:

"I have been sent to you . . ." then, overcoming her momentary confusion, she added ". . . as a machine-gunner."

Bunchuk flushed heavily:

"Have they gone out of their minds? Is it a woman's battalion I've got to organize? Excuse me, but this isn't fit work for you; it's heavy and calls for a man's strength. No, I can't accept you."

Still frowning, he opened the letter and hurriedly scanned its contents. The requisition itself merely stated that the Party member Anna Pogudko had been assigned to the machine-gun section, but attached to it was a letter from Abramson, which read:

Dear Comrade Bunchuk,

We are sending you a good comrade in Anna Pogudko. We have yielded to her insistent demand, and hope that you will make a fighting machine-gunner of her. I know the girl. I can warmly recommend her, she is a valuable worker, and I ask you only to watch one thing: she is fiery and a little exalted in temperament (she hasn't yet outgrown her youth). Keep her from thoughtless actions, and look after her.

The nucleus of your detachment will undoubtedly be the eight metal workers. Of these, pay particular attention to Bogovoi, a very able comrade, devoted to the Revolution. Your machine-gun detachment is international in composition, which is a good thing; it will increase its fighting ability.

Speed up the training. We hear that Kaledin is preparing to attack us.

With comradely greetings,

Abramson.

Bunchuk stared at the girl standing before him. The dim light of the cellar which had been allotted to him for headquarters shadowed her face and concealed its features.

"Oh well!" he said ungraciously. "If it's your own wish . . . and Abramson asks, you can stay."

They crowded around the machine-gun, hung in clusters over it, leaning on one another's backs and watching with inquisitive eyes as under Bunchuk's skilful hands it came to pieces. Then he reassembled it, explaining the nature and function of each part, showing them how to handle it, how to load it, sight it, determine the trajectory and the range. Then he showed them how to protect themselves from the enemy fire, pointed out the necessity of setting up the gun at a point of vantage, and of arranging the ammunition cases correctly.

All seventeen learned quickly, with the exception of the baker Gyevorkyants. No matter how many times Bunchuk showed him, he could remember nothing, and he lost his head, muttering in his confusion:

"Why doesn't it come out right? Ah. . . . I'm a fool . . . this bit ought to be there. . . . But still it isn't right!" he cried in despair. "Why?"

"Here's why!" Bogovoi, a swarthy fellow with blue gunpowder marks on his forehead and cheeks, mimicked him. "It doesn't come out right because you're stupid. Here's what you have to do." He confidently put the part in its proper place. "Ever since I was a boy, I've been interested in military matters." Amid general laughter, he pointed to the blue marks on his face. "I tried to make a cannon, but it blew up and I got the worst of it. That's why I'm so capable now."

And he actually was the first to grasp the technique of machine-gunning. Only Gyevorkyants lagged behind, and his whining, irritated voice was often heard.

"Wrong again, but why? I don't know!"

"What an ass! Wha-a-t an ass! There's only one like that in all Nakhichevan!" the bad-tempered, moist-lipped Mikhalidi said angrily.

"Extraordinarily stupid," the reserved German Rebinder agreed.

"It's different from kneading dough," jested Khvilichko, and all smiled good-naturedly.

But Stepanov shouted with annoyance, his face flushing:

"You ought to show a comrade, instead of grinning at him!"

He was supported by Krutogorov, a great, big-limbed worker with bulging eyes from the railway workshops:

"You stand there laughing, you fools, and the work can wait! Comrade Bunchuk, instruct your waxwork gallery or else send them packing! The Revolution is in danger, and they stand there laughing!" He waved his sledge-hammer fist.

Anna Pogudko inquired about everything with keen curiosity. She pestered Bunchuk, plucked at his sleeve, and could not be displaced from the side of the machine-gun.

"And what would happen if the water were to freeze in the water-jacket? . . . What deviation has to be allowed for in a strong wind?" She plied him with questions, expectantly raising her warmly gleaming black eyes to his.

He felt awkward in her presence, and as though in revenge he grew more exacting with her, and was exaggeratedly cool in his manner. But when each morning punctually at seven she entered the cellar, her hands tucked into the sleeves of her jacket, and shuffling in her great soldier's boots, he was troubled with an unusual, agitating feeling. She was a little shorter than he, with the full, robust figure characteristic of all healthy working girls, perhaps a little round-shouldered, perhaps even plain, were it not for her great, strong eyes, which endowed all her face with a strange beauty.

During the first four days he scarcely had an opportunity to look at her. The cellar was badly lighted, and even if he had had time to study her face he would have felt too uncomfortable to do so. On the evening of the fifth day they left the cellar together. She went in front, but as she stood on the topmost step she turned back to him with some query and Bunchuk gasped inwardly as he saw her in the evening light. She stood waiting for the answer, her head slightly tilted, her eyes fixed on him, her hand brushing back her hair. But he did not catch her question. He slowly mounted the stairs, gripped by a pleasantly painful feeling. She found it difficult to adjust her hair without removing her kerchief, and in her concentration her pink nostrils quivered a little. The lines of her mouth were strong, yet childishly tender. On her raised upper lip there was a fine down, which showed dark against her skin. He bowed his head as though before a blow, and jested theatrically:

"Anna Pogudko, machine-gunner No. 2, you're as beautiful as someone's happiness."

"Nonsense!" she said firmly, and smiled. "Nonsense, Comrade Bunchuk! I was asking at what time we go to shooting practice tomorrow."

Her smile made her appear more simple, approachable and earthly. He stopped at her side, gazing abstractedly down the street to where the stranded sun was flooding everything with a livid hue. He quietly replied:

"Shooting practice? Tomorrow. Which way do you go? Where do you live?"

She mentioned the name of some little street on the outskirts of the town.

At a cross-roads they were overtaken by Bogovoi.

"Bunchuk, when do we get together tomorrow?"

Bunchuk explained as they went along that they were to meet at eight o'clock at Tikhaya Woods. Two of the others would bring a machine-gun in a cab. Bogovoi accompanied them a short distance, then said good-bye. Bunchuk and Anna walked on for some time without speaking. At last she gave him a sidelong glance and asked:

"Are you a Cossack?"

"Yes."

"And you've been an officer?"

"Well, sort of."

"What's your native district?"

"Novocherkassk."

"Have you been long in Rostov?"

"Several days."

"And before that?"

"I was in Petrograd."

"When did you join the Party?"

"In 1913."

"And where is your family?"

"In Novocherkassk," he said hurriedly, and imploringly stretched out his hand. "Stop a bit and let me do some questioning now. Were you born in Rostov?"

"No. I was born in Yekaterinoslav Province, but I have lived here for some time."

"Are you a Ukrainian?"

She hesitated for a moment, then firmly replied:

"No."

"Jewish?"

"Yes. But how did you know? Do I talk like one?"

"No."

"Then how did you guess I was Jewish?"

He reduced the length of his stride in an attempt to fall into step with her, and answered:

"Your ear, the shape of your ears, and your eyes. Otherwise you show little sign of your nationality." He thought for a moment, then added: "It's good that you're with us."

"Why?" she asked inquisitively.

"Well, the Jews have a certain reputation. And I know that many workers believe it to be true—you see I'm a worker, too—that the Jews only do all the ordering and never go under fire themselves. That's not true, and you will prove splendidly that it isn't true. Have you studied anywhere?"

"Yes, I left high school last year. Where did you get your education? I ask because your conversation shows you are not of working-class origin."

"I've read a lot."

They walked slowly. She deliberately took a longer way home, and after telling him a little more about herself, began to question him again about the Kornilov attack, the attitude of the Petrograd workers, and the October Revolution.

From somewhere on the quays came the sound of a rifle-shot, then a machine-gun shattered the silence. She at once asked:

"What make is that?"

"A Lewis."

"How much of the belt has been used?"

He did not reply. He was admiring the orange feeler of a searchlight reaching up from an anchored trawler into the flaming evening sky.

They wandered about the deserted town for some three hours, and separated at last at the gate of the house where she lived.

He returned home glowing with an inward satisfaction.

"She's a fine comrade and an intelligent girl! It was good to have a talk with her. I've grown boorish during these last years; you must have friendly intercourse with people, otherwise you get as hard as soldiers' biscuit," he thought, deliberately deceiving himself.

Abramson, just returned from a session of the Military Revolutionary Committee, began to question him about the training of the machine-gun detachments, and asked about Anna.

"How is she getting on? If she isn't suitable we can easily put her on to other work."

"Oh, no!" Bunchuk said in alarm. "She's a very capable girl!"

He felt an almost irresistible desire to go on talking about her, and mastered his inclination only with a great effort of his will.

VI

On November 25th Kaledin began to fling troops into an attack upon Rostov. Thin lines of Alexeyev's officers' detachment advanced along the railway, supported on the right flank by a denser body of cadets, and on the left by Popov's volunteer detachment. The tiny figures, like little wads of grey, jumped into a ditch, then crawled out and, recovering formation, flowed on again.

The line of Red Guards scattered around the outskirts of the town was restless with anxiety. Some of the workers, many of whom had rifles in their hands for the first time in their lives, experienced fear and crawled about in their black overcoats, regardless of the autumn mud; some raised their heads and stared at the distant, tiny figures of the oncoming Whites.

Bunchuk was in the line, kneeling beside his machine-gun with binoculars to his eyes. The day before he had changed his awkward civilian coat, and in the soldier's greatcoat he now wore felt calm and at ease.

The men opened fire without waiting for the word of command. When the first shot rang out, Bunchuk cursed, jumped to his feet, and shouted:

"Cease fire!"

His cry was drowned in the sputter of shots. He gave up the attempt, and trying to make his voice heard above the noise of firing, ordered Bogovoi to open fire with the machine-gun. Bogovoi set his smiling, ashen face close to the breech, and wrapped his fingers round the trigger. The familiar chatter of the machine-gun penetrated Bunchuk's ears. He stared in the direction of the enemy, trying to make out the accuracy of the fire, then ran along the line towards the other machine-guns.

"Fire!"

"Right-ho! Ho-ho-ho-ho!" Khvilichko roared, turning a scared but happy face towards him.

The lads manning the third machine-gun from the centre were not altogether reliable. Bunchuk ran towards it. He stopped halfway, and bending, stared through the steamy lenses of his binoculars. He could see the huddled grey shapes moving in the distance. The sound of their steady firing reached him. He threw himself down and saw, as he lay, that the range of the third machine-gun was inaccurate.

"Lower, you devils!" he cried, crawling along the line. Bullets whistled dangerously close above him. The enemy was firing as perfectly as if at exercise.

The third gun's muzzle was tilted at a ridiculous angle; around it the gunners lay flat on their bellies. The Greek Mikhalidi was firing without pause, wasting his ammunition. Close to him was the terrified Stepanov, and behind, with head thrust into the ground and back humped like a tortoise, was one of the railwaymen.

Thrusting Mikhalidi aside, Bunchuk took long and careful aim. When the bullets began to spurt once more from the gun, they immediately had effect. A group of cadets who had been coming on at a run turned and fled back down the slope, leaving one of their number on the clayey ground.

Handing the machine-gun over, Bunchuk returned to his own gun, and found Bogovoi lying on his side, spitting out curses and binding up a wound in the fleshy part of his leg. The powder marks showed more clearly on his pale face.

"Keep firing, you devil!" a ginger-headed Red Guard shouted, scrambling to his knees beside him. "Can't you see they're getting nearer?!"

The lines of an officers' detachment were moving across the slope with well-drilled precision.

Rebinder took Bogovoi's place and fired intelligently without wasting ammunition or getting excited.

From the left flank Gyevorkyants came leap-
ing like a hare, dropping at every shot that
passed over his head, groaning and shouting:

"I can't.... I can't.... It won't shoot! It's
jammed!"

Bunchuk ran along the line to the disabled
gun. When still a little way off he saw Anna
on her knees at its side, staring under her palm
at the advancing enemy line.

"Lie down!" he shouted, his face darkening
with fear for her. "Lie down, I tell you!"

She glanced at him and continued to kneel.
Curses as heavy as stones came to his lips. He
ran up to her and flung her forcibly to the
ground.

Krutogorov lay grunting behind the shield.

"It's jammed! It won't work!" he muttered
to Bunchuk, and looking round for Gyevorkyants, burst into a shout: "Now he's run away,
damn him! He got me proper rattled with his
groaning.... He won't let a man work!"

Gyevorkyants crawled up, wriggling like a
snake, mud clinging to the black scrub of his
beard. Krutogorov stared at him for a moment,
then howled above the roar of the firing:

"What have you done with the ammunition
belts? You animal! Bunchuk, take him away,
or I shall kill him!"

Bunchuk examined the machine-gun. A bullet struck hard against the shield, and he snatched his hand away as though he had burned it. He put the gun in order, and himself sprayed the oncoming Alexeyev men with bullets, forcing them to lie down. Then he crawled away, looking for cover.

The lines of the enemy drew closer. Their fire grew heavier. In the Red Guard ranks three men were hit, and their comrades took their rifles and cartridges: dead men have no need of weapons. Before the eyes of Anna and Bunchuk, as they lay at the side of Krutogorov's gun, a young Red Guard was struck by a bullet. He writhed and groaned, kicking the ground, and finally, raising himself on his hands, coughed and gasped for the last time. Bunchuk glanced sidelong at Anna. She was staring unwinkingly at the legs of the dead lad in their ragged puttees, not hearing Krutogorov's shout:

"A belt . . . a belt! Girl, give me a fresh belt!"

By a deep flanking movement the Kaledin troops pushed the Red Guard ranks back. The black overcoats of the retreating workers and the Red Guards' greatcoats began to dribble through the streets of the suburb. The machine-gun on the extreme right flank fell into the hands of the Whites. The Greek Mikhalidi was shot down by a cadet, a second gunner was transfixed with bayonets, and only the compositor Stepanov managed to escape.

The retreat was halted when the first shells began to fly from the Red trawlers in the port.

"Into line ... follow me!" shouted a man Bunchuk recognized as one of the Revolutionary Committee, running forward.

The Red Guards hesitated and turned, then advanced into the attack. Bunchuk had gathered Anna, Krutogorov and Gyevorkyants around him.

Three Red Guards went past them. One was smoking, another was carrying his rifle so that the bolt struck against his knee, the third was intently studying the skirt of his overcoat. A sheepish grin lurked round the tips of his moustache, as though instead of facing death he were returning home from a drinking party with his mates and examining his coat to calculate the degree of punishment he could expect from his quarrelsome wife. Suddenly Krutogorov pointed to a distant fence with little grey human figures assembled behind it.

"There they are!" he shouted.

Bunchuk, crouching, bear-like, swung the barrel round in that direction.

The vigorous chatter of the gun made Anna stop her ears. She sat down, and saw all movement die away behind the fence. After a moment the Whites opened a measured fire, and the bullets sped over them, tearing invisible holes in the misty canvas of the sky. The belt rattled like a kettle-drum as it ran through the machine-gun. The shells fired by the Black Sea Fleet sailors in the trawlers went screaming overhead. Single shots cracked loudly and juicily. The grating howl of the shells flying overhead from the trawlers squeezed the eardrums. Anna saw a Red Guard, a burly fellow in a lambskin cap, with a clipped English moustache, bowing involuntarily to every shell that went over.

"Give it to 'em, Semyon. Give it to 'em!" he was shouting.

The sailors had now got the range, and were carrying on a concentrated fire. Isolated groups of the retreating Kaledin troops were covered by the bursting shrapnel. A shell burst right in the midst of one group, and the brown column of the explosion scattered the men in all directions. Anna dropped her field-glasses and groaned, covering her terror-stricken eyes with dirty palms. A bitter spasm seized her throat.

"What's the matter?" Bunchuk shouted, bending towards her.

She clenched her teeth, and her dilated eyes glazed.

"I can't. . . ."

"Be brave! You . . . Anna, do you hear? Do you hear? You mustn't do that! You mustn't . . ." the authoritative voice of command beat in her ears.

On the right flank some of the enemy had gathered in a valley and on the slopes of a rise. Bunchuk spotted them, ran with the machine-gun to a more convenient spot, and opened fire on the valley.

Rebinder's gun was firing in short bursts. About twenty paces away a hoarse angry voice was shouting:

"A stretcher! Aren't there any stretchers? A stretcher."

"Take aim!" came a long-drawn shout from an infantry platoon officer.

"Platoon, fire!"

Towards evening the first snowflakes began to whirl down over the harsh earth. Within an hour the wet, sticky snow had completely enveloped the field and the muddy-black bundles of the dead. The Kaledin troops withdrew.

Bunchuk spent that snow-blurred night in the machine-gun outpost. Krutogorov with a thick horse-cloth he had found somewhere wrapped round his head chewed away at some stringy meat, spitting and cursing. Huddled in the gateway of the yard, Gyevorkyants warmed his blue hands over a cigarette. Bunchuk sat on an ammunition case, wrapping the trembling Anna in his greatcoat, tearing her damp hands from her eyes and kissing them. Words of unaccustomed tenderness came with difficulty from his lips.

"Now, now, how could you take on so...? You used to be tough.... Anna, listen, take yourself in hand! Anna ... dear.... You'll get used to it. If your pride won't allow you to withdraw, you must be different. You can't look on the dead like that. Don't let your thoughts turn that way! Take them in hand. You see now; in spite of what you said the woman in you is winning."

Anna was silent. Her hands smelled of the autumn earth and of a woman's warmth.

The falling snow wrapped the sky in a dense, gracious blanket. The yard, the fields, the hushed town were wrapped in drowsy slumber.

VII

For six days the struggle continued in and around Rostov. Fighting went on in the streets and at the cross-roads. Twice the Red Guards surrendered the station, and twice they drove the enemy out again. During those six days there were no prisoners taken by either side.

Late one afternoon Bunchuk and Anna were passing the goods station, and saw two Red Guards shoot a captured officer. Bunchuk said almost challengingly to Anna, who had turned away:

"That's sensible! They must be killed, wiped out without mercy. They show us no mercy, and we don't ask for it. So why should we show them mercy? This filth must be raked off the earth. There can't be any sentimental feelings when the fate of the Revolution's at stake. Those workers are right!"

On the third day of the struggle he was taken ill. But he kept on his feet for a whole day, feeling a continually increasing nausea and weakness in every limb. His head rang and seemed unbearably heavy.

The depleted Red Guard detachments abandoned the town at dawn on December 2nd. Bunchuk, supported by Anna and Krutogorov, staggered along behind a wagon loaded with wounded and a machine-gun. He dragged his helpless body along with the utmost difficulty, lifting his iron-heavy feet like a sleep-walker. As from a great distance he could see Anna's worried eyes and hear her voice saying:

"Get into the wagon, Ilya. Do you hear? Do you understand what I say? I ask you to get in; you're ill."

But he did not understand her words, nor did he understand that he was broken and in the grip of typhus. Voices, familiar and unfamiliar, pecked at the outer shell of his consciousness without penetrating; somewhere at a great distance Anna's dark eyes glowed with desperate anxiety, and Krutogorov's beard waved in fantastic patterns.

Bunchuk clutched his head, and pressed his big hands to his burning, flaming face. He felt as though blood were dripping from his eyes, and all the world, boundless and unstable, cut off from him by an invisible curtain, was rearing and lurching under his feet. In his delirium his imagination began to conjure up incredible visions. He stopped again and again, struggling with Krutogorov, who was trying to put him into the wagon.

"No! Wait...! Who are you...? Where's Anna? Give me a bit of earth.... And destroy these.... I order you to turn the machine-gun on them.... Wait! It's too hot!" he shouted hoarsely, tearing his hand from Anna's grip.

They lifted him forcibly into the wagon. For a moment more he could smell a pungent mixture of various scents, and struggled fear-

could not. A black, soundless emptiness closed over him; only somewhere in the heights burned a point of opal and azure blue, and zigzags and fires of ruddy lightning weaved before his eyes.

VIII

Thatch-stained icicles were falling from the eaves and breaking with a glassy tinkle. In the village the thaw blossomed into pools and patches of bare earth. The cattle, still in their winter coats, went wandering with sniffing nostrils along the streets. The sparrows chattered as though it were spring-time, as they pecked among the heaps of brushwood in the yards. Martin Shamil chased across the square after a sleek sorrel horse that had bolted from its stable. Its stringy tail raised high, its unkempt mane tossing in the wind, it bucked and sent the clods of half-melted snow flying from its hoofs, circled round the square, halted by the church wall, and sniffed at the bricks. It allowed its master to get fairly close, glanced askance with a violet eye at the bridle in his hand, and broke again into a wild gallop.

January was indulging the earth with warm, cloudy days. The Cossacks watched the Don in expectation of a premature flood. Miron Kor-

shunov stood in his backyard staring at the
snow deep on the fields, at the icy grey-green
of the Don, and thought: "It'll flood us this
year just like it did last. Snow, snow, nothing
but snow! Must be heavy for mother earth
under that lot."

Mitka, in a khaki tunic, was cleaning out the
cattle-yard. His white fur cap stuck to the back
of his head by a miracle. His straight hair,
dank with sweat, fell over his brow, and he
brushed it away with the back of his dirty
hand. A fluffy goat was stamping by the gate.
A lamb bigger than its mother tried to suck at
her, but she put her head down and drove it
off. A ring-horned black sheep was scratching
itself against a plough.

A big sandy-coated hound lay sprawled on a
thaw-patch near the clay-washed door of the
barn. Nets and fishing tackle hung on the outside walls under the eaves and old Grishaka
stood there, leaning on his crutch and looking
at them; evidently he was thinking of the coming spring and the work of repairing the
nets.

Miron went to the threshing-floor, and with
a thrifty eye estimated the quantity of hay
still left. He began to rake together some
millet straw scattered about by the goats, but
unfamiliar voices reached his ears. He threw

the rake on to the pile and went into the yard.

His feet planted apart, Mitka was standing rolling a cigarette, holding his richly embroidered pouch, the gift of some village sweetheart, in two fingers. With him were Christonya and Ivan Alexeyevich. Christonya was pulling some cigarette-paper out of his cap. Ivan Alexeyevich was leaning against the fence, rummaging in his trouser pockets. His clean-shaven face wore a look of vexation: evidently he had forgotten something.

"Had a good night, Miron Grigoryevich?" Christonya greeted him.

"Praise be!"

"Come and join us for a smoke."

"Christ save you, I've just had one."

Miron shook hands with the Cossacks, took off his red-topped hat, stroked his bristly white hair, and smiled.

"And what may you be wanting with us today, brothers?"

Christonya looked him up and down, but did not reply at once. He slowly ran his tongue along a slip of paper, and after rolling the cigarette, replied:

"We've got business with Mitka."

Grandad Grishaka shuffled by, carrying a fishing-net over his outstretched arm. Ivan and

Christonya took off their caps and greeted him. He carried the net to the steps and then turned back.

"Why are you stopping at home, soldiers? Having too good a time with your wives?" he asked.

"Why, what's up?" Christonya inquired.

"Keep quiet, Christonya! Don't tell me you don't know!"

"God's truth, I don't know!" Christonya vowed. "By the cross I don't, Grandpa!"

"A man arrived the other day from Voronezh, a merchant, a friend or relation or something of Sergei Mokhov. I don't know exactly. Well, he comes and says that strange soldiers, these Bolsheviks, are at Chertkov. Russia is going to make war on us. And you're staying at home! You, too, you young devil. . . . D'you hear, Mitka? Haven't you anything to say? What do you think about it?"

"We don't think about it at all!" Ivan Alexeyevich smiled.

"That's the shame, that you don't think!" old Grishaka waxed indignant. "They'll take you in a snare like partridges! The muzhiks will take you prisoners and smash your snouts for you!"

Miron Grigoryevich smiled discreetly. Christonya rasped his hand over his long unshaven cheeks. Ivan Alexeyevich stood smoking and looking at Mitka. Little fires sparkled in Mitka's cat-like eyes and it was impossible to judge whether those greenish eyes of his were laughing, or burning with unsated spite.

After talking a little longer, Ivan Alexeyevich and Christonya took leave of Miron, and called Mitka to the wicket-gate.

"Why didn't you come to the meeting yesterday?" Ivan asked sternly.

"I had no time."

"But you had time to go along to the Melekhovs!"

With a jerk of his head Mitka brought his hat down over his forehead, and said with restrained anger:

"I didn't come, and that's all there is to it. What is there to talk about?"

"All the men from the front in the village were there except you and Pyotr Melekhov. We've decided to send delegates from the village of Kamenskaya. There's to be a congress of front-line men there on January 10th. We cast lots and it was settled that I, Christonya and you should go."

"I'm not going," Mitka announced resolutely.

"What's your game?" Christonya frowned and took him by the button of his tunic. "Are you breaking away from your own comrades? It's no good."

"He's hand in glove with Pyotr Melekhov," Ivan Alexeyevich said. He touched the sleeve of Christonya's greatcoat and added, turning noticeably pale: "Come on. There's nothing we can do here. So you won't go, Mitka?"

"No! I've said no, and I mean no."

"Good-bye then." Christonya cocked his head on one side. "Good luck to you."

With eyes averted Mitka stretched out his hand and said good-bye, then turned and went to the kitchen.

"The snake!" Ivan Alexeyevich muttered, and his nostrils quivered. "The snake!" he said aloud, staring at Mitka's broad back.

On their way home they informed some of the front-line men that Mitka had refused to go, and that the two of them would set out the following day for the congress.

They left Tatarsky at dawn on January 8th. Horseshoe Yakov had volunteered to drive them to Kamenskaya. His pair of good horses drew them swiftly out of the village and up the slope. The thaw had laid the road bare, and where the snow had gone, the sledge-runners stuck to the earth, and the sledge jerked along, and the horses strained at the traces. The Cossacks walked behind the sledge. His face flushed with the frosty morning breeze, Yakov strode along, his boots scrunching the fine crust of ice. Only the oval scar on his cheek remained a dead blue. Christonya panted up the hill over the crusted snow at the roadside, gasping because of the German poison gas he had drawn into his lungs at Dubno in 1916.

At the hill-top the wind was stronger and the air keener. The Cossacks were silent. Ivan Alexeyevich wrapped his face in the collar of his sheepskin. They drew near to a wood, through which the road climbed on to a mounded ridge. The wind rippled in streams through the wood. The trunks of the antlered oaks were patterned with scaly layers of gold-green rust. A magpie chattered in the distance, then fluttered across the road. The wind was carrying it out of its course, and it flew violently, lop-sidedly, its pied feathers ruffling.

Yakov, who had not said a word since leaving the village, turned to Ivan Alexeyevich and remarked deliberately, evidently giving voice to thoughts he had long been turning over in his mind:

"At the congress try and fix things so there'll be no war. There'll be no volunteers for a war."

"Of course," Christonya agreed, enviously staring after the magpie in its free flight, and mentally comparing the bird's thoughtlessly happy life with human existence.

They arrived at Kamenskaya early in the evening on the 10th. Crowds of Cossacks were making their way through the streets towards the centre of the town. The excitement could be felt everywhere. Ivan and Christonya sought out the quarters of Grigory Melekhov, but learned that he was not at home. The mistress of the house, a stout blonde woman, informed them that he had gone to the congress, and slammed the door in their faces.

When they arrived they found the congress in full swing. The great, many-windowed room could hardly hold all the delegates, and many of the Cossacks were crowded on the stairs, in the corridors, and in adjacent rooms.

"Keep behind me!" Christonya grunted to Ivan, working his elbows vigorously. Ivan followed in the narrow cleft he made.

When they had nearly reached the room where the congress was being held Christonya found his path barred by a Cossack who, judging from his accent, was from the lower Don.

"Not so fast, lad," he snapped.

"Let us through."

"You can stand here. There's no room inside."

"Let us in, you gnat, or I'll smash you!" Christonya boomed, and lifting the Cossack aside with ease, stepped into the room.

A murmur of astonished admiration went up from the crowd round the door. The Cossacks smiled and stared with involuntary respect at Christonya, who was a good head taller than any of them.

They found Grigory by the wall at the back. He was squatting on his haunches, smoking and talking to another delegate. At the sight of his fellow-villagers his drooping raven whiskers quivered in a smile.

"Why, what wind has blown you here? Hullo, Ivan Alexeyevich! How are you, Uncle Christonya?"

"Not so bad," Christonya laughed back, gathering Grigory's whole hand in his own great fist.

"And how's my family?"

"Well. They sent their greetings. Your father ordered you to come and visit them."

"And how's Pyotr?"

"Pyotr ..." Ivan Alexeyevich smiled awkwardly. "Pyotr doesn't mix with us."

"I know. And Natalya? And the children? Did you happen to see them?"

"All well, and they send their greetings. Your dad's offended."

While he talked, Christonya stared at the group sitting behind the table on the platform. Even from the back he could see better than anyone else. Grigory continued to ply them with questions, taking advantage of a short lull in the proceedings. Ivan Alexeyevich gave him the news of the village, and briefly told him of the front-line men's meeting which had sent them to Kamenskaya. He in turn began to inquire about events in Kamenskaya, but someone sitting at the table shouted:

"Cossacks, a delegate from the miners will now speak. Please listen carefully to him, and keep order."

A man of average height stroked his fair hair back and began to speak. The hum of voices died away at once.

From the very first words of the miner's burning, passionate speech Grigory and the other Cossacks felt the strength of his conviction. He spoke of the treacherous policy of Kaledin, who was driving the Cossacks into a war against the workers and peasants of Russia, of the common interests of the Cossacks and the workers, of the aims of the Bolsheviks, who were carrying on a struggle against Cossack counter-revolutionaries.

"We stretch out our brotherly hands to the toiling Cossacks, and hope that in the struggle against the White Guard bands we shall find faithful allies among the front-line Cossacks. At the fronts of the tsarist war the workers and

Cossacks shed their blood together; and in the war against the bourgeoisie that Kaledin is harbouring we must also stand together. And we shall stand together! Shoulder to shoulder we shall go into the struggle against those who have enslaved the toilers for centuries."

"Good for him, the son of a bitch!" Christonya whispered delightedly and squeezed Grigory's elbow so tightly that he grimaced with pain.

"That's right! Aye, that's right!" Ivan Alexeyevich muttered again and again, as he listened with half-open mouth.

When the miners' delegate finished speaking, a tall miner rose, swaying like an ash in the wind, stretched to his full height, glanced over the sea of eyes before him, and waited for the noise to subside. He looked as wiry and tough as a tow rope. The pores of his face were filled with tiny specks of coal dust, and his eyes, which had grown glazed and colourless in the eternal darkness of the earth, had the same coal-like glitter. He shook his closely-cropped head, and raised and lowered his clenched fists as if wielding a pick.

"Who introduced capital punishment for soldiers at the front? Kornilov! Who's helping Kaledin throttle us? Kornilov!" He began to speak faster, choking over his words. "Cossacks! Brothers! Brothers! Brothers! Whose side are you going to join? Kaledin wants us to drink our brothers' blood. No! We'll never do that. We'll crush them! We'll drown them in the sea...."

"The son of a bitch!" Christonya grinned from ear to ear, flung up his hands and guffawed, unable to restrain himself. "That's the stuff. Give it to them!"

"Shut up, Christonya, what's the matter with you? They'll kick you out!" Ivan Alexeyevich exclaimed in alarm.

Lagutin—a Bukanovsky Cossack, the first chairman of the Cossack department of the Central Executive Committee of the Soviets—lashed the Cossacks with burning words, disjointed yet touching them to the quick.

Then the chairman Podtyolkov spoke, followed by Shchadenko, a handsome man with a small English moustache.

"Who's that?" asked Christonya, pointing with his huge paw.

"Shchadenko. A Bolshevik commander."

"And that one?"

"Mandelstam."

"Where's he from?"

"Moscow."

"And who are those?"

Christonya pointed to a group of Voronezh delegates.

"Oh, shut up for a while, Christonya."

"My God, isn't it worth knowing? Come on, tell me, who's that long fellow sitting next to Podtyolkov?"

"Krivoshlykov, from Gorbatov village. Our people are behind him, Kudinov, Donetskov."

"Just one more question. Who's that fellow? No, not that one, the one at the end, with the forelock."

"Yeliseyev. No, I don't know where he's from."

Christonya, satisfied, fell silent and listened to each speaker with unflagging attention and was the first to be heard above the hundreds of voices with his deep thunderous "That's right!"

After the other speakers, a delegate from the 44th Regiment stood up. It took him a long time to force out his clumsy sentences; he would say a word that was like a glowing brand, then stop and sniff his nose. But the Cossacks listened to him with great sympathy, only occasionally interrupting with approving shouts. Evidently his words found a deep response among them.

"Brothers! Our congress must approach this serious business in a way that won't be shameful to the people and so that everything can end quietly and well. What I mean is that we must find a way out without a bloody war. As it is, we've had three and a half years of being buried in the trenches, and if we've got to go on fighting, the Cossacks will be worn to death. . . ."

"That's true!"

"We don't want war."

"We must talk it over with the Bolsheviks and the Army Council."

"We must settle it together, not just anyhow."

The chairman Podtyolkov thundered on the table with his fist, and the roar died away. The delegate of the 44th Regiment went on, plucking at his short beard:

"We must send delegates to Novocherkassk and ask the Volunteers and the partisans to clear out of here. And the Bolsheviks have nothing to do here either. We can settle with the enemies of the working people ourselves. We don't need other people's help, and when we need it we'll ask them to give us help."

"That kind of talk won't do any good!"

"He's right!"

"Wait a bit. What's right about it? Suppose they get us in a corner, where shall we get help then?"

"We ought to set up our own government."

"Easier said than done, that is!"

Lagutin followed the delegate of the 44th Regiment with a challengingly fiery speech. He was frequently interrupted with shouts. The proposal was made to suspend the meeting for ten minutes, but as soon as silence was established Podtyolkov shouted to the excited crowd of Cossacks:

"Brother Cossacks! While we are arguing here, the enemy of the toiling people is not asleep. We would all like the wolves to be full and the sheep whole, but that isn't what Kaledin thinks. We have captured a copy of an order signed by him to arrest all those taking part in this congress. I will read it aloud."

As he read the order, a wave of excitement ran through the delegates, and a tumult arose still greater than before.

Grigory listened in silence, staring at the swaying heads and waving arms of the crowd. In the end he could bear it no longer and, standing on tiptoe, yelled:

"Quiet, you devils! Is this a market-place? Let Podtyolkov speak!"

Ivan Alexeyevich buttonholed one of the delegates and started arguing with him.

Christonya bellowed retorts at a fellow from his own regiment: "We've got to be on the lookout! Don't tell me that stuff! Can't you see we're not strong enough to go it alone!"

At last the roar of voices sank—it was like a wheat-field when the wind drops—and from the platform Krivoshlykov's girlishly thin tones pierced the hush:

"Down with Kaledin! Hurrah for the Cossack Military Revolutionary Committee!"

The crowd groaned. Cries of approval came together in a heavy, lashing braid of sound. Krivoshlykov remained standing with upraised hand. His fingers were trembling a little, like the leaves of an aspen. Hardly had the deafening roar subsided when he cried in the same ringing high-pitched voice:

"I propose that we elect a Cossack Military Revolutionary Committee from among the delegates present, and that it be instructed to carry on the struggle against Kaledin and to orga. . . ."

"A-a-a-ah!" a shout split the air like a bursting shell, sending flakes of whitewash from the ceiling.

The meeting at once began to elect the members of the committee. A small section of the Cossacks, led by the delegate of the 44th Regiment and others, continued to call for a peaceful settlement of the conflict with the Kaledin government. But the majority no longer supported them. The Cossacks had been enraged by Kaledin's order for their arrest, and demanded active resistance to him.

Grigory was summoned urgently to the regimental staff and did not stay to the end of the election. As he turned to go out he asked Christonya and Ivan:

"When it's over come along to my room. I'd like to know who's elected."

Ivan Alexeyevich turned up after nightfall.

"Podtyolkov is chairman, Krivoshlykov secretary," he informed Grigory as he stood on the threshold.

"And the members?"

"Ivan Lagutin and Golovachov, Minayev, Kudinov and some others."

"But where's Christonya?" Grigory asked.

"He went off with some others to arrest the Kamenskaya authorities. He got that worked up he'd fizz if you spat on him."

Christonya did not return till dawn. He stood in the room breathing heavily and mumbling something under his breath. Grigory, lighting the lamp, noticed that his face was bloody and a gun-shot scratch ran across his forehead.

"Who did that to you? Shall I tie it up? Wait a moment, I'll find a bandage." Grigory jumped up and turned out his first-aid kit.

"It'll heal quickly enough, like a dog does," Christonya rumbled. "The military commander fired at me with his pistol. We went along to him like guests, to the front door, and he started fighting. He wounded another Cossack too. I wanted to drag the soul out of him to see what an officer's soul is like, but the other Cossacks wouldn't let me, I'd have felt that soul of his for him, that I would!"

IX

The day after the Kamenskaya congress the 10th Don Cossack Regiment, sent by Kaledin to arrest all the members of the congress and to disarm the most revolutionary of the Cossack divisions, arrived at Kamenskaya, detraining just as a meeting was being held at the station. Podtyolkov was on the platform.

"Fathers and brothers," he was saying, "I'm not a member of any party and I'm not a Bolshevik. I am striving for only one thing: for justice, for happiness and brotherly unity among all workers, so that there will be no oppression, no kulaks, no bourgeois and rich men, so that everyone will live freely and according to his will. . . . The Bolsheviks are trying to get this and are fighting for it. The Bolsheviks are workers, working folk like us Cossacks. Only the Bolshevik workers are more conscious and unified than we are. We've been kept in darkness, but they, in the towns, have learned to understand life better than us. So what it amounts to is that I am a Bolshevik, although I'm not a member of the Bolshevik Party."

The newly-arrived Cossacks, magnificently built men, most of them picked troops, crowded around the meeting, and mingled with the men of other regiments. The yeast of the vigorous agitation which the Bolshevik adherents at once began among them worked quickly, and when the regimental commander called on them to carry out Kaledin's orders they refused.

Meanwhile Kamenskaya was feverish with activity; hurriedy assembled detachments of Cossacks were being sent out to occupy stations; troop-trains were being dispatched. Elections of fresh commanders were taking place in the detachments. Some of the Cossacks, anxious to avoid war, slipped quietly out of the town, while belated delegates from various villages were still arriving. Never before had the streets of Kamenskaya been so animated.

On January 13th a delegation from the Don White Guard Government arrived in the town to open negotiations. It was met by a large crowd at the station. An escort of Cossacks from the Ataman's Lifeguard Regiment conducted it to the post office building, where the Military Revolutionary Committee spent most of the night in session with the government delegation.

Seventeen representatives of the Military Revolutionary Committee were present. Podtyolkov gave a scathing reply to a speech by a government delegate accusing the Committee of betraying the Don and co-operating with the Bolsheviks. He was followed by Krivoshlykov and Lagutin. A speech by Colonel Kushnarev was interrupted by shouts from the Cossacks crowding in the corridor. On behalf of the revolutionary Cossacks a machine-gunner demanded the arrest of the government delegation.

The conference failed to reach any settlement. About two o'clock in the morning, when it was evident that no agreement could be reached, a member of the delegation proposed that the Military Revolutionary Committee should send a delegation to Novocherkassk, in order to come to some final decision on the issue of the future government. The proposal was adopted.

The Don Government delegation departed, and the representatives of the Military Revolutionary Committee set out immediately after it for Novocherkassk. Podtyolkov was at their head. The officers of the Ataman's Regiment, who had been arrested in Kamenskaya, were held as hostages.

X

A snowstorm was raging outside the carriage windows. Wind-driven snowdrifts loomed above sagging snow-fences. The railway cabins, the telegraph poles and all the interminable, dreary,

372

snowy monotony of the steppe sped away to the north.

Podtyolkov, dressed in a new leather jacket, sat by the window. Krivoshlykov, narrow-shouldered and slim as a lad, sat opposite him with his elbows on the table. There was anxiety and expectation in his boyishly clear eyes. Lagutin was combing his rather scanty blonde beard. Minayev, a burly Cossack, was warming his hands on the radiator pipes and fidgeting uncomfortably in his seat. Golovachov and Skachkov lay on the upper bunks talking quietly.

The compartment was foggy with tobacco smoke, and cold. The members of the delegation felt by no means confident of their mission to Novocherkassk. They talked but little, and the silence was dreary. At last Podtyolkov expressed the general conviction:

"Nothing will come of it. We shan't agree."

"Aye, it's a waste of time," Lagutin agreed.

Again they sat silent. Podtyolkov flexed his wrist rhythmically, as though passing a shuttle in and out through a net. Now and then he glanced at his jacket, admiring the soft glow of the leather. They drew near to Novocherkassk. Minayev began to relate:

"In the old days when the Cossacks of the Ataman's Regiment had served their time they'd be equipped to go back home. They'd load their chests, their horses and goods into the train. The train would set out, and just by Voronezh, where the line crosses the Don for the first time, the engine-driver would go slow, as slow as he could ... he knew what was coming. And as soon as the train got on to the bridge ... my grandfathers! What a scene! The Cossacks would go quite mad: 'The Don! The Don! The quiet Don! Our father, our own! Hurrah!' and through the window, over the bridge straight into the water would go caps, old tunics, trousers, shirts, and the Lord knows what else! They would give presents to the Don on their return from service. Sometimes as you looked at the water you would see blue ataman caps floating along like swans or flowers.... It was a very old custom."

The train reduced speed, and finally stopped. The Cossacks rose. As he buttoned his tunic Krivoshlykov said with a wry smile:

"Well, here we are!"

"They aren't putting out the flags for us!" Skachkov tried to jest.

A tall captain threw open the door without knocking, and entered the compartment. He surveyed the members of the delegation with hostile eyes, and said with deliberate roughness:

"I've been instructed to accompany you. Kindly leave the carriage as quickly as possible, Mister Bolsheviks. I cannot guarantee the crowd and . . . your safety."

He fixed his eyes on Podtyolkov, or rather on his leather jacket, then with open hostility snapped: "Out you get. Look sharp!"

"There they are, the scoundrels, the betrayers of the Cossacks!" a long-whiskered officer standing among the crowd on the platform shouted as they got out. Podtyolkov turned pale and glanced back at Krivoshlykov with disconcerted eyes. Krivoshlykov smiled and whispered:

" 'Approval not in praises sweet we hear, but in the vicious howls of spite.' You know that, Fyodor?"

Although he had not caught the final words Podtyolkov managed to return the smile.

A strong escort of officers guarded the delegation. To the very door of the government headquarters they were accompanied by a frenzied crowd demanding that they be lynched on the spot. Not only officers and cadets, but elegantly dressed women and students, and even a few Cossacks, hurled abuse at them.

"This is a downright scandal, this is!" Lagutin turned indignantly to one of the accompanying officers.

The latter glanced at him with a look of hatred, and hissed:

"Thank your God you're still alive. If I had power over you. . . . Damn you, you carrion. . . ."

He was stopped by the reproachful glance of another officer, a younger one.

"What a mess!" Skachkov whispered to Golovachov at the first opportunity.

"Looks as if they're leading us to the gallows."

The hall of the regional government was not large enough to accommodate all the crowd that had gathered. While the members of the delegation were seating themselves on one side of a table as instructed by the lieutenant, the members of the government arrived. Accompanied by Bogayevsky, Kaledin, stooping slightly, approached the table with a firm wolfish stride. He pulled back his chair and sat down, setting his cap, with its officer's cockade, calmly on the table, brushing back his hair and buttoning up the large side-pocket of his tunic. Then he bent towards Bogayevsky who had been whispering something to him. Every movement and gesture expressed resolute, deliberate confidence, and mature strength. His manner was that of a man who had tasted power and in the course of many years had acquired a poise that distinguished him from others. An inferior figure compared with the impressive Kaledin, Bogayevsky seemed more agitated in face of the coming negotiations. He sat whispering, hardly moving his lips, his slanting eyes glittering behind his pince-nez. He betrayed his nervousness by restless movements of his hands, adjusting his collar, feeling his chin, and raising his bushy eyebrows. The rest of the government delegates seated themselves on either side of Kaledin; some of them had been in the delegation to Kamenskaya.

Podtyolkov heard Bogayevsky whisper something to Kaledin. The general looked sharply at Podtyolkov opposite him and said: "I think we can begin."

Podtyolkov smiled, and speaking in a clear voice, stated the reasons for the arrival of the delegation. Krivoshlykov picked up the ultimatum prepared by the Military Revolutionary Committee and stretched it across the table, but Kaledin rejected it with a movement of his white hand, and said firmly:

"There's no point in wasting time while every member of the government separately studies the document. Please read your ultimatum aloud. Then we shall discuss it."

"Read it," ordered Podtyolkov. He held himself with dignity but it was obvious that he, like the rest of the delegation, felt the need for caution.

Krivoshlykov stood up. His girlishly thin

377

voice flowed indistinctly through the crowded hall.

"As from the 10th of January, 1918, all power over the troops in the Don Region is transferred from the ataman to the Don Cossack Revolutionary Military Committee.

"By the 15th of January all troops operating against the revolutionary army as well as all volunteer squads, cadet academies, and schools of ensigns are to be disbanded and disarmed. All members of the above organizations non-resident in the Don Region are to be deported to their places of permanent residence.

"Note: Arms, equipment and uniforms must be turned over to the Commissar of the Revolutionary Military Committee, who will issue permits to leave Novocherkassk.

"Cossack troops will occupy the city of Novocherkassk upon the order of the Revolutionary Military Committee. The credentials of members of the Cossack Army Council are declared invalid as from the 15th of January.

"All policemen stationed in the factories and mines of the Don Region by the Don Government are to be recalled.

"In order to avoid bloodshed the government must announce to all villages and districts of the Don Region that it has voluntarily resigned and is immediately transferring power to the Cossack Revolutionary Military Committee, until a permanent government of the toilers is established in the region."

Hardly had his voice died away when Kaledin asked loudly: "What troops have given you authority for this ultimatum?"

Podtyolkov exchanged glances with Krivoshlykov, and began to calculate aloud:

"The Ataman's Lifeguards, the Cossack Lifeguards, the 6th Battery, the 44th Regiment, the 32nd Battery, the 14th Special Squadron...." As he mentioned each division he bent down the fingers of his left hand, and a jeering titter ran through the hall. Podtyolkov frowned, set his hands down on the table and raised his voice: "The 28th Regiment, the 28th Battery, the 12th Battery, the 12th Regiment...."

"The 29th Regiment," Lagutin prompted him in an undertone.

"... the 29th Regiment," continued Podtyolkov more confidently now, "the 13th Battery, the Kamenskaya Squadron, the 10th Regiment, the 2nd Infantry Battalion, the 2nd Reserves, the 8th Regiment, the 14th Regiment."

When he had finished, Kaledin asked a few unimportant questions, then, leaning forward over the table, he stared at Podtyolkov and demanded:

"Do you recognize the authority of the Council of People's Commissars?"

Podtyolkov finished a glass of water, put the glass back on the table, wiped his whiskers with his sleeve, and replied:

"Only the whole people can answer that."

Afraid that the more simple Podtyolkov might say too much, Krivoshlykov intervened: "The Cossacks will not tolerate any government in which there are representatives of the People's Freedom Party.* But we are Cossacks, and the government should be our own Cossack government."

"How are we to interpret that remark, when Jews and such men are at the head of the Council?"

"Russia has trusted them, and we shall trust them."

"Will you have relations with them?"

"Yes."

Podtyolkov grunted approvingly and supported Krivoshlykov:

"We're not concerned with individuals, we're concerned with an idea."

One of the members of the government asked innocently:

* The Constitutional Democrats, or Cadets, as they were more commonly called.

"Is the Council of People's Commissars working for the good of the people?"

Podtyolkov's searching gaze roved slowly towards him. With a smile he reached for the water-bottle, poured himself another glass of water and drank quickly. He was parched with thirst, as though a great fire were burning within him.

Kaledin drummed with his fingers and asked inquiringly:

"What have you in common with the Bolsheviks?"

"We want to have Cossack self-government in the Don Region."

"Yes, but surely you know that on February 4th a new Army Council is to be called? The members will be re-elected. Will you agree to mutual control?"

"No!" Podtyolkov raised his eyes, and replied firmly: "If you are in the minority we shall dictate our will to you."

"But that will be coercion!"

"Yes."

Bogayevsky turned his eyes from Podtyolkov to Krivoshlykov and asked:

"Do you recognize the Army Council?"

"Only in so far as. . . ." Podtyolkov shrugged his shoulders. "The regional Military Revolutionary Committee will call a congress of representatives of the people. It will work under the control of the military forces. If the congress doesn't satisfy us we shall not recognize it."

"And who are to be the judges in this matter?" Kaledin raised his eyebrows.

"The people!" Podtyolkov threw back his head proudly and his leather jacket creaked as he leaned on the carved back of his chair.

After a short recess Kaledin rose to speak. All noise died away in the hall, and the low, autumn-dull tones of his voice sounded clearly in the silence:

"The government cannot abdicate its powers at the demand of the regional Military Revolutionary Committee. The present government has been elected by all the population of the Don, and only they, and not individual sections, can demand that we abdicate our power. You are blind instruments in the hands of the Bolsheviks. You are doing the will of German mercenaries, not realizing the colossal responsibility to the Cossacks which you are taking on yourselves. I advise you to reconsider the matter, for you are bringing terrible misery on your native land by entering into conflict with the government which reflects the will of the entire population. I shall not cling to my authority. The Great Council of the Don Cossack Army is to be called, and it will decide the destinies of the country. But until it meets I must remain at my post. For the last time I advise you to think over your position."

Speeches were then made by members of the government, Cossacks and non-Cossacks. Bosse, a member of the Socialist-Revolutionary Party, delivered a long oration interlarded with tempting assurances.

A shout from Lagutin interrupted him:

"Our demand is that you should hand over power to the Military Revolutionary Committee! What are you waiting for if the Don Government stands for a peaceful solution of the question. . . ."

Bogayevsky smiled: "That means. . .?"

"You've got to make it public that power has been handed to the Revolutionary Committee. We can't wait another fortnight while your council gets together! The people are wild with anger as it is."

Another member of the government made a long meandering speech; yet another sought an impossible compromise.

Podtyolkov listened to them with irritation. As he glanced at his own supporters, he noticed that Lagutin was pale and frowning, Krivoshlykov had his eyes fixed on the table, Golovachov was bursting to say something. The moment

Krivoshlykov had been waiting for arrived and he whispered quietly:

"Let 'em have it!"

Podtyolkov seemed to have been expecting this. He pushed back his chair and began to speak tensely, stuttering with agitation, seeking words that would drive away all doubts:

"You've got it all wrong! If the Army Government could be trusted I'd willingly give up all our demands. But the people don't trust it! It's not us, it's you who are beginning the civil war. Why have you been sheltering these runaway generals on Cossack land? We won't submit to you. We won't allow it! The facts are in our favour. What action are you taking against the units who don't want to obey you. . .? Aha, that's got you! Why are you sending your volunteers against the miners? Tell me, what guarantee is there that the Army Government will avoid civil war? Aha, you have nothing to say to that! The people and the front-line Cossacks are on our side!"

A laugh ran through the hall like a rustling wind, and angry exclamations against Podtyolkov were heard. He turned his flushed face in their direction, and shouted, making no attempt to hide his bitter anger:

"You're laughing now, but you'll be crying before long!" He turned back to Kaledin, and fixed his pellet-like eyes on him. "We demand that you hand over the government to us, the representatives of the toiling people, and clear out all the bourgeoisie and the Volunteer Army.... And your government must also resign."

Kaledin bowed his head wearily.

"I have no intention of leaving Novocherkassk."

After a short recess the proceedings were resumed by another government speaker:

"The Red Guard detachments are advancing on the Don to destroy the Cossacks! They have ruined Russia with their madmen's rule and they want to do the same here! There has never been a case in history when a bunch of pretenders have ruled the country well and for the people's good. You have been blinded by the madness of others and want to strip us of power and throw the gates open to the Bolsheviks. But we won't let you!"

"Hand over power to the Revolutionary Committee and the Red Guards will stop their offensive," Podtyolkov interjected.

Kaledin gave the floor to a member of the public, Junior Captain Shein. He had risen from the ranks and held all four crosses of the Order of St. George. He straightened his tunic as if on parade and started off at a gallop.

"Why should we listen to them, Cossacks!" he barked, bringing his arm down as if wielding a sabre. "The Bolshevik way is not our way! Only traitors to the Don and to the Cossacks can talk of handing over power to the Soviets and urge the Cossacks to join up with the Bolsheviks!" And pointing straight at Podtyolkov, he leaned forward and shouted: "Do you mean to say, Podtyolkov, that you think the Don will follow a half-educated, illiterate fellow like you? The only followers you'll get will be a band of vagrant Cossacks. But even they'll come to their senses, lad, and hang you for it!"

The assembled heads turned towards him like sunflowers to the sun; a howl of approval went up. Shein took his seat. A tall officer in a short gathered overcoat with lieutenant-colonel's shoulder-straps leaned over and slapped him on the back. Officers crowded round him. A woman's voice cried out hysterically:

"Thank you, Shein! Thank you!"

"Bravo, Major Shein! Bravissimo!" an affected young bass croaked from the gallery, promoting the captain on the spot.

The government speakers went on for a long time trying to talk over the Cossacks of the newly-born Revolutionary Committee. The air grew blue and heavy with tobacco smoke. Beyond the windows the sun was nearing the end of its daily march. Frozen fir branches clung to the outer panes. The people sitting on the window-sills could hear an evening service being sung and, above the moaning of the wind, the hoarse bellow of engine whistles from the station.

At last Lagutin could endure it no longer. Interrupting one of the speakers, he turned to Kaledin:

"Come to a decision: it's time to end this!"

Bogayevsky whispered caustically:

"Don't get excited, Lagutin! Take a drink of water. It's dangerous for family men and epileptics to get excited. And besides, it's not the thing to interrupt speakers; this isn't a Soviet here!"

Lagutin gave him a sharp answer too, but all eyes were on Kaledin again. He was still playing his political game as confidently as ever and still running up against the simple homespun armour of Podtyolkov's answers.

"You said that if we hand over power to you the Bolsheviks will halt their offensive against the Don. But that is only your opinion. How the Bolsheviks will act when they reach the Don, we don't know."

"The Revolutionary Committee is certain that the Bolsheviks will confirm what I've said. Try it out: hand over power to us, turn the Volunteers out of the Don and you'll see–the Bolsheviks will stop the war."

After a moment Kaledin rose. His speech had been previously prepared and he had already ordered Chernetsov to concentrate forces for an advance on the neighbouring station of Likhaya. But he was playing for time, and he ended the conference with a procrastinating suggestion:

"The Don Government will consider the Revolutionary Committee's proposals, and will give an answer in writing by ten o'clock tomorrow morning."

XI

The reply that the Cossack Army Government handed to the delegates of the Revolutionary Committee the next morning read as follows:

The Cossack Army Government of the Don Cossack Army has discussed the demands of the Cossack Military Revolutionary Committee presented by the Committee's deputation on behalf of the Ataman's Lifeguards, the Cossack Lifeguards, the 44th, 28th and 29th regiments, the 10th, 27th, 23rd and 8th units of the 2nd reserve and 43rd regiments, the 14th Independent Squadron, the 6th, 32nd, 28th, 12th and 13th batteries, the 2nd Infantry Battalion and the Kamenskaya Squadron, and the Cossack Army Government hereby states that the government represents the whole Cossack population of the region. As a government elected by the population, it has no right to abdicate its powers until a new Council is called.

The Cossack Army Government of the Don Cossack Army has deemed it necessary to dissolve the former Council and to hold re-elections of the deputies from both stanitsas and army units. The new Council, freely elected (with complete freedom to canvass) by the Cossack population on the basis of direct, equal and secret ballot, will assemble in the town of Novocherkassk on February 4th, 1918, at the same time as a congress of the whole non-Cossack population. Only the Council, a legal institution restored by the Revolution and representing the Cossack population of the region, has the right to remove the Cossack Army Government from office and elect a new government. This Council will at the same time debate the question of the control of military units and of whether there should or should not be volunteer units to defend the government's authority. As for the formation and activities of the Volunteer Army, the present coalition government has already taken the decision to place the Volunteer Army under the control of the government with the participation of the Regional Military Committee.

With regard to the question of withdrawing from the mining area the police that are alleged to have been sent there by the Cossack Army Government, the government declares that this question will be referred to the Council on February 4th.

The government declares that only the local population may take part in the ordering of local life, and therefore, in accordance with the will of the Council it considers it necessary to oppose by every means the penetration into the region of armed Bolshevik detachments desiring to force their way of life on the region. The population, and only the population, must arrange its own way of life.

The government does not desire civil war, at every step it is endeavouring to arrive at a peaceful solution. For this reason it has suggested that the Military Revolutionary Committee should participate in a joint deputation to be sent to the Bolshevik forces.

The government holds that unless alien forces are allowed to enter the region there will be no civil war, for the government is only defending the Don territory, is undertaking no offensive action, does not seek to impose its will on the rest of Russia and accordingly does not desire that any alien body should impose its will upon the Don.

The government will ensure complete freedom of election in the stanitsas and the army units; every citizen will be able to canvass as he wishes and to uphold his own point of view at the elections to the Cossack Army Council.

Commissions of representatives from the various units must be appointed to investigate the needs of the Cossacks in all divisions.

The Cossack Army Government of the Don Cossack Army instructs all units that have sent delegates to the Military Revolutionary Committee to return to their normal task of defending the territory of the Don.

The Cossack Army Government of the Don Cossack Army considers it inconceivable that its own units should act against the government and thus initiate internecine strife on the quiet Don.

The Military Revolutionary Committee must be dissolved by the units that elected it, and in its place, all units should send their representatives to the existing Regional Military Committee, which represents all military units in the region.

The Cossack Army Government demands that all persons arrested by the Military Revolutionary Committee be immediately released; in order that normal life may be restored in the region the administration must be allowed to return to its duties.

Since it represents only an insignificant number of Cossack units, the Military Revolutionary Committee has no right to make demands on behalf of all units, and certainly not on behalf of all Cossacks.

The Cossack Army Government considers it absolutely impermissible that the Committee should have relations with the Council of People's Commissars and receive financial support from it, for this would spread the influence of the Council of People's Commissars into the Don Region—this when the Cossack Council and the Congress of the non-Cossack population of the whole region have acknowledged the power of the Soviets to be unacceptable, as have the Ukraine, Siberia, the Caucasus, and all Cossack forces without exception.

Chairman of the Cossack Army Government, Deputy Ataman of the Cossack Army *M. Bogayevsky.*

Commanders of the Don Cossack Army

Yelatontsev, Polyakov, Melnikov.

Lagutin and Skachkov of the Kamenskaya Revolutionary Committee joined the deputation sent to Taganrog by the Don Government to negotiate with the representatives of Soviet power. Podtyolkov and the other members of the Committee were temporarily detained in Novocherkassk, while Kaledin's forces under Chernetsov, comprising a few hundred bayonets, a heavy battery and two light guns mounted on a railway truck, swiftly occupied the stations of Zverevo and Likhaya and, leaving a small holding force there, continued their advance towards Kamenskaya, occupying that stanitsa on January 17th. A few hours after the capture of Kamenskaya, however, news arrived that Red Army forces had driven the holding forces out of Zverevo and Likhaya. Chernetsov swung his forces round. With a swift frontal attack he knocked out the 3rd Moscow Detachment, gave the Kharkov Detachment a thorough trouncing and threw the Red Guards back to their original positions.

Having restored the situation in the Likhaya direction, Chernetsov seized the initiative and returned to Kamenskaya. On the 19th of January he received reinforcements from Novocherkassk, and the next day decided to advance on Glubokaya.

At a council of war it was decided to take Glubokaya by a wide flanking movement. Chernetsov hesitated to advance along the railway for fear of encountering strong resistance from the units of the Kamenskaya Revolutionary Committee and the Red Guard reinforcements sent up from Chertkov.

That night the flanking movement began; it was led by Chernetsov himself.

They reached Glubokaya before dawn. The column changed formation smartly and spread out in line. Chernetsov gave his final orders, dismounted, and while he stretched his legs, hoarsely instructed a commander of one of the companies:

"Don't stand on ceremony, Captain. Understand?"

His boots crunched on the firm snow; he pushed his grey Astrakhan hat on one side to rub a pink ear. There were dark-blue circles under his light flashing eyes. His lips were pursed from the cold, and his short-clipped moustache was downy with hoar-frost.

Having warmed himself, he leaped into the saddle, straightened the folds of his short officer's coat and, taking the reins with a firm, confident smile, urged on his bay horse.

"Let us begin!"

XII

Just before the congress of front-line Cossacks was held at Kamenskaya Grigory's friend, Junior Captain Izvarin, fled from his regiment. The night before his departure he visited Grigory and hinted vaguely at the step he was about to take.

"I find it difficult to serve in the regiment in the present situation. The Cossacks are wavering between two extremes, the Bolsheviks and the former monarchist system. No one wants to support Kaledin's government, if only because he is behaving like a child with a new toy. What we want is a firm, resolute man who will put the aliens in their proper place. But I think it's better to support Kaledin at the moment, otherwise we shall lose the game entirely." After a silence during which he lit a cigarette, he asked: "I gather you've accepted the Red faith?"

"Almost," Grigory assented.

"Sincerely? Or are you like Golubov, out to get popular with the Cossacks?"

"I'm not in need of popularity. I'm looking for the way out myself."

"You're knocking against a blank wall, you haven't found the way out."

"We shall see...."

"I'm afraid we shall meet as enemies, Grigory."

"A man doesn't recognize even his friends on the field of battle," Grigory smiled.

Izvarin sat talking a little while longer, then departed. Next morning he had disappeared like a stone in water.

On the day of the congress a Cossack guardsman from the Vyeshenskaya District visited Grigory. Grigory was cleaning and oiling his revolver. The guardsman, who had formerly served in Listnitsky's regiment and knew that Listnitsky had taken Grigory's woman from him, had called to tell Grigory that he had seen the ex-officer at the station. Not until he was about to leave, however, did he say casually:

"I happened to see a friend of yours at the station today, Grigory."

"Who?"

"Listnitsky. Remember him?"

"When did you last see him?" Grigory asked sharply.

"About an hour ago."

Grigory sat down. The old pain had seized his heart in a wolf-like grip. He no longer felt the same fierce anger towards his enemy, but he knew that, were they to meet now, when civil war was breaking out, there would be bloodshed between them. The unexpected news of Listnitsky made him realize that the old wound was still unhealed; a mere touch was enough to start it bleeding again. Revenge would have been sweet to Grigory for the bitter wrong Listnitsky had done him, for making his life a husk of what it had been, a wretched hungry yearning instead of the full-blooded joy he had once known.

He was silent for a little and when he felt the flush dying out of his cheeks, he asked:

"Is he coming here, do you know?"

"Shouldn't think so. Probably on his way to Novocherkassk."

"I see."

The guardsman said something else about the congress, passed on the latest news from the regiment and left. No matter how he tried in the days that followed Grigory could not quench the smouldering pain in his soul. He went about in a dazed condition, and more often than usual the memory of Aksinya returned, bringing a bitter taste to his mouth and turning his heart to stone. He thought of Natalya and the children but the joy of that was faded and tarnished with age. His heart was with Aksinya and he still felt the same oppressive and powerful longing for her.

When Chernetsov attacked, the revolutionary forces had to evacuate Kamenskaya in a hurry. The depleted Cossack squadrons crowded pell-mell into the trains, abandoning everything that could not easily be carried away. The lack of organization, of a resolute commander who would assemble and order their really quite considerable forces was making itself felt. During those days a major named Golubov was outstanding among the elected commanders. He took command of the militant 27th Cossack Regiment and at once ruthlessly restored order. The Cossacks obeyed him implicitly, recognizing that he had qualities that the regiment lacked: the ability to weld it into a unit, to allot duties, and to take command. During the evacuation he shouted at the Cossacks who were slow in loading the wagons:

"What's the matter with you? Are you playing hide-and-seek, damn you? Get on with it! In the name of the Revolution I order you to obey immediately. . . . What? Who's that demagogue? I'll shoot him, the scum! Silence. . . ! You're a saboteur and secret counter-revolutionary, and no comrade!"

And the Cossacks did obey. Many of them even liked his hectoring ways, for they still had hankerings after the past. In the old days the biggest bully had always been the best commander in the Cossacks' eyes.

The detachments of the Military Revolutionary Committee retreated to Glubokaya. The virtual command passed into the hands of Golubov. In less than two days he had reorganized the scattered forces and taken the necessary steps to hold Glubokaya. At his demand Grigory Melekhov was placed in command of a detachment consisting of two squadrons of a reserve regiment and one squadron of lifeguards.

At dusk on January 20th Grigory went out to make the round of his outposts, and at the gates of the village ran into Podtyolkov. Podtyolkov recognized him.

"That you, Melekhov?"

"Yes."

"Where are you going?"

"Checking the outposts. Been back long? How did you get on?"

Podtyolkov frowned.

"You can't make peace with men who are sworn enemies of the people. See the trick they played? Negotiate ... and all the while they were egging Chernetsov on. What a swine Kaledin is, eh? Well, I haven't got much time. I must be getting back to headquarters.

He took leave of Grigory hurriedly and strode away.

Even before he had been elected chairman of the Revolutionary Committee he had noticeably changed in his attitude towards Grigory and his other Cossack acquaintances; there was a note of superiority and haughtiness in his voice. Power had gone to the head of the simple-natured Cossack.

Grigory turned up his coat collar and walked on, quickening his pace. The night promised to be frosty, and a light breeze was blowing from the east. The sky was clear. The snow scrunched under his feet. The moon rose slowly, limping, like an invalid going upstairs. Beyond the houses the steppe smoked a dusky lilac. It was the evening hour when all outlines, colours, and distances are obliterated; when daylight is still inextricably entangled with the night, and everything seems unreal and fluid. At this hour even scents have their own more subtle shades.

After making the round he returned to his quarters. His host, a railway employee, prepared the samovar and sat down at the table.

"Are you going to attack?"

"I don't know."

"Or are you going to wait for them here?"

"We'll see."

"Quite right too. I don't think you've anything to attack with, and then it's better to wait. I went through the German war as a sapper, and I know tactical strategy thoroughly. Your forces are small, aren't they?"

"They'll be enough." Grigory endeavoured to avoid the disagreeable conversation.

But the man maintained a zealous fire of questions, hovering about the table and scratching his lean belly under his waistcoat.

"Plenty of artillery? Guns, cannon?"

"You've been in the army; don't you know a soldier's duty?" Grigory said with cold anger, and he rolled his eyes so violently that the man started back. "What right have you to question

as to the number of our troops, and our plans?
I'll have you arrested and cross-examined. . . ."

"Lord. . . . Officer! My dear. . . ." The man
turned pale and almost choked with anxiety. "It
was stupid of me . . . stupid. Pardon me!"

During tea Grigory happened to look up at
the man and noticed him blink sharply, as
though from a flash of lightning; when his eyes
opened again their gaze was affectionate, almost
adoring. His wife and two grown-up daughters
talked in whispers. Grigory did not finish his
second cup and retired to his own room.

Soon afterwards six Cossacks of the 2nd Reserve Regiment, who were also billeted in the
house, returned and sat down to drink tea,
laughing and talking noisily. Grigory was half-
asleep, but he caught snatches of their conversation. One of them was telling of an incident that
had occurred that day:

"I was there when it happened. Three miners
from Gorlovka came along from mine number
eleven and said they had collected a force, but
they hadn't any weapons. So they asked us to
give them what we could spare. And a member
of the Committee . . . I heard him myself," the
narrator raised his voice in answer to some inaudible question, "tells them: 'Go and ask else-
where, Comrades, we haven't any here!' But how
does he make out that we haven't any? I know

we've got reserves of rifles. That wasn't the point. He was jealous of the muzhiks interfering. . . ."

"And quite right too!" another exclaimed. "Give them weapons and they may fight or they may not, but as soon as the question of the land comes up they'll be laying their hands on it."

"We know their kind!" grunted a third.

The first speaker thoughtfully tapped his spoon against his glass, keeping time to his words as he replied deliberately:

"No, that sort of thing won't do. The Bolsheviks will meet us half-way for the sake of all the people, but we aren't real Bolsheviks. All we want is to kick Kaledin out, then we'll start. . . ."

"But look here, lad!" a high-pitched voice remarked with conviction. "Don't you see that we've got nothing to give away? We get perhaps a dessiatine and a half of good land in the share-out and the rest is good for nothing. So what can we give them?"

"They won't take anything from you, but there are others with too much land."

"What about the Cossack Army land?"

"No, thank you very much! Are we to give our own away and then go begging for somebody else's? That's a fine idea!"

"We'll need the Army land ourselves."

" 'Course we shall."

"You're getting greedy!"

"Greedy be damned!"

"Mebbe someone'll think of moving our Cossacks from the upper Don. They've nothing but sand up there."

"True enough."

"It's not our job to work these things out."

"A drop of vodka would help."

"The other day, lads, they broke into the wine stores. One fellow got drowned in a vat of spirit."

"I could do with a drink now. Something to warm your ribs."

As he dozed off Grigory heard the Cossacks settling down on the floor for the night, still arguing about the land and how it should be divided.

They were awakened before daybreak by the sound of a shot right outside the window. Grigory drew on his tunic, fumbling a moment with the sleeve, seized his greatcoat and put on his boots as he ran. Shots rattled out in the street. A cart rumbled by. Someone cried in alarm outside the door:

"To arms. . .! To arms. . .!"

The Chernetsov forces had driven back the outposts and were pouring into the town. Riders dashed past in the grey misty darkness. Infantry ran through the streets, their boots clattering. A machine-gun had been set up at the corner of the street. A line of about thirty Cossacks was drawn up across the street. More were running up. Bolts rattled as they drove cartridges into breeches. In the next street a ringing voice was shouting orders:

"Third Squadron, look lively! Who's that out of line? Atten-shun! Machine-gunners, by the right! Are you ready? Squadron. . . ."

A battery thundered by, the horses galloping, the drivers waving their whips. Machine-guns suddenly started to sputter somewhere close at hand. In the next street a field-kitchen had been overturned in its headlong flight by one wheel hooking against a fence-post. "You blind devil! Couldn't you see it?" roared a mortally terrified voice.

With difficulty Grigory collected his squadron and led it at a gallop towards the station. They found the Cossacks already retreating in a dense stream.

"Where are you going?" Grigory seized one of the foremost by his rifle.

"Let go!" the Cossack jerked his rifle. "Let go, you swine! What's the idea? Can't you see we're retreating?"

"They're too strong for us!"

"Nothing can stop them."

"Where to? Where should we go?" other voices shouted breathlessly.

Close to a long warehouse at the end of the station Grigory tried to deploy his company in extended formation, but a fresh wave of fleeing Cossacks swept them aside. The Cossacks of Grigory's squadron began to mingle with the crowd and fled back with them into the streets.

"Stop! Halt, or I'll fire!" Grigory roared, trembling with fury.

But they paid no attention to him. A hail of machine-gun bullets raked the street. The Cossacks dropped to the road for a moment, crawled closer to the walls, and fled into the side-turnings.

"You won't hold them now, Melekhov!" a troop officer shouted as he ran past. Grigory followed him, gritting his teeth.

The panic which had taken possession of the Cossacks ended in complete and disorderly flight from Glubokaya, most of the equipment being left behind. Only at daybreak was it possible to reassemble the squadrons and throw them into a counter-attack.

Livid and sweating, Golubov, in an open sheepskin jacket, ran along the files of his own 27th Regiment, shouting in a metallic voice:

"Step out! No lying down! March, march!"

The 14th Battery was drawn into position and unharnessed. The commander stood on an ammunition box, staring through his binoculars.

The battle began at six. The mixed forces of Cossacks and Red Guards from Voronezh swept on in a dense mass, trimming the snowy ground with a dark lace-work of figures. A freezing wind was blowing from the east. Under the wind-driven clouds the dawn showed blood-red. Grigory sent off half the Ataman's Squadron to cover the 14th Battery, and led the others into the attack.

The first shell burst well in front of the Chernetsov forces. The tattered orange-and-blue flag of the explosion was flung upward. A second shot was fired. A moment of tense silence, emphasized by rifle-fire, then a distant echo as it burst. The shells began to burst near the enemy lines. Screwing up his eyes against the wind Grigory thought with a feeling of satisfaction: "We've got the range!"

On the right flank were the squadrons of the 44th Regiment. Golubov was leading his own regiment in the centre. Grigory was on his left. Beyond were Red Guard detachments covering the left flank. Three machine-guns had been allotted to Grigory's squadrons. Their commander, a thick-set Red Guard with morose face and broad hairy hands, directed their fire excellently, paralyzing the enemy's attempts at an offensive. He remained the whole time close to the machine-gun that was moving forward with the Ataman's Cossacks. At his side was a stocky woman in a soldier's greatcoat. As Grigory passed along the file of Cossacks he thought angrily: "The skirt-chaser! Going into battle, and he can't leave his woman behind! He should have brought his children and his feather-bed with him too!"

The commander of the machine-gun detachment came up to him, adjusting the revolver strap across his chest.

"Are you in command of this detachment?"

"Yes."

"I'll direct a barrage fire in front of the Ataman's half-squadron. The enemy are preventing their advance."

"All right!" Grigory assented. At a shout from the direction of the momentarily silent machine-gun he turned and heard a bearded machine-gunner roar furiously:

"Bunchuk! We shall melt the gun! We can't go on like this!"

The woman in a soldier's greatcoat was kneeling beside him. Her black eyes, burning under her kerchief, reminded Grigory of Aksinya, and for a second he stared at her with longing, holding his breath.

At noon an orderly galloped up from Golubov, with instructions for Grigory to withdraw his two squadrons from their positions and to encircle the right flank of the enemy, doing so unobserved if possible. He was to strike from the flank as soon as the main forces opened a decisive attack. Grigory at once drew off his squadrons, and after mounting them, led them in a semicircle for about twenty versts along a shallow valley. The horses stumbled and floundered in the deep snow, which sometimes reached to their bellies. Grigory listened to the sound of the firing and looked anxiously at his watch, a trophy taken from the wrist of a dead German officer in Rumania. He directed their course by a compass, but even so deviated rather more to the left than was necessary. They emerged into the open field over a broad down. The horses were steaming with sweat and wet in the groin. Grigory gave the order to dismount, and was the first to climb the hill. The horses were left in the valley. The Cossacks floundered after him up the snowy slope. He looked back, saw more than a squadron of Cossacks scattered over the snowy rise, and felt stronger and more confident. Like most other men, in battle he was strongly possessed by the herd instinct.

Taking in the situation at a glance, he realized that he was late by half an hour at the least.

With a daring strategic manoeuvre Golubov had almost cut off the rear of the Chernetsov forces, sending out flanking detachments on both sides, and was now striking at them from the front. The rifle-fire was rattling like pellets in a frying pan, shrapnel was sweeping the demoralized ranks of the enemy, and the shells were falling thickly.

"Forward!" Grigory shouted.

He struck with his detachment on the flank. The Cossacks advanced as though on parade, but a dexterous Chernetsov machine-gunner sprayed them so efficiently with bullets that they were glad to lie down, after losing three of their number.

In the early afternoon a bullet got Grigory just above the knee. Feeling a burning pain and the familiar nausea from loss of blood, he gritted his teeth. He crawled out of the line and jumped to his feet, shaking his head, half-delirious with the shock. The pain was all the greater as the bullet had not passed out. It had been all but spent when it hit him, and after piercing greatcoat, trousers and skin, it remained cooling in the muscle. The lacerating pain prevented all movement, and he lay down again. As he lay there his mind vividly recalled the attack of the 12th Regiment in the Transylvanian mountains, when he had been wounded in the arm: Uryupin, Misha Koshevoi's face twisted with anger, Yemelyan Groshev dragging the wounded captain after him down the hill. . . .

Grigory's assistant took charge of the squadrons, and ordered two Cossacks to lead Grigory back to the horses. As they sat him on his horse they sympathetically advised him to tie up the wound. Grigory was already in his saddle, but he slipped down, and dropping his trousers, frowning as a shiver coursed through his body, hurriedly bandaged the inflamed, bleeding gash. Then, accompanied by his orderly he rode back by the same circuitous route through the valley, to the spot where the counter-attack had begun. Drowsy with sleep, he stared at the traces of horse-hoofs in the snow, at the familiar outlines of the valley, and the incidents on the hill-side already seemed far away and unimportant.

The rifle-fire continued raggedly, the enemy's heavy battery went into action, and from time to time a burst of machine-gun fire seemed to punch an invisible dotted line for the results of the battle.

For about three versts Grigory rode through the valley. The horses began to tire with the heavy going.

"Make for the open!" Grigory grunted to his orderly, and turned his own horse up the snowy side of the valley.

In the distance they saw the scattered figures of the dead lying like settled crows. On the fringe of the horizon a tiny riderless horse was galloping. Grigory saw the main force of the enemy, shattered and thinned, break away from the battle, turn and retreat towards Glubokaya. He put his bay into a gallop. Some way off were several scattered groups of Cossacks. As he rode up to the nearest of them Grigory recognized Golubov. The commander was sitting back in his saddle. His sheepskin jacket was flung open, his fur cap was pushed back on his head, his brows were damp with sweat. Twisting his sergeant-major whiskers, he shouted hoarsely:

"Melekhov, well done! What, are you wounded? The devil! Is the bone whole?" Without waiting for an answer he broke into a smile. "We've smashed them to bits. To bits! We've smashed the officers' detachment so they'll never be able to rally them again."

Grigory asked for a cigarette. Cossacks and Red Guards were streaming over the steppe. A Cossack on horseback came galloping from a dense crowd in the distance.

"Forty men taken, Golubov!" he shouted when still a little way off. "Forty officers, and Chernetsov as well!"

"You're lying!" Golubov turned anxiously in his saddle, and rode off to meet the prisoners, ruthlessly plying his whip across his white-stockinged horse.

Grigory waited a moment, then trotted after him.

The crowd of captured officers was escorted by a convoy of thirty Cossacks. Chernetsov strode in front of the others. In an endeavour to escape he had thrown away his sheepskin coat, and was wearing only a light leather jerkin. The epaulette had been torn from his left shoulder, and a fresh bruise above his left eye was bleeding. He walked quickly and firmly. His lamb-skin cap, set on one side, gave him a carefree and jaunty appearance. There was not a shadow of fear on his rosy-cheeked face. Evidently he had not shaved for some days, for a growth of fair hair gilded his cheeks and chin. He cast a harsh swift glance at the Cossacks running towards him, and a bitter frown of hate darkened his brows. He struck a match and lit the cigarette held in one corner of his firm lips.

Most of the officers were young, only one or two having traces of grey hair. One, wounded in the leg, lagged behind, and was driven on with a butt-end by a small pock-marked Cossack. Almost at Chernetsov's side was a tall, dashing captain. Two more walked arm in arm, smiling; behind them, capless, came a stocky, curly-haired cadet. Another officer had hurriedly flung a soldier's greatcoat around his shoulders. Yet another was capless, and had an officer's red cowl pulled down over his dark, womanishly beautiful eyes.

Golubov rode behind them. He halted and shouted to the Cossack escort:

"Listen! You will answer with the full severity of the military revolutionary times for the safety of these prisoners. See that they reach staff headquarters unharmed."

He called a mounted Cossack to him, wrote a note and ordered the man to give it to Podtyolkov. Then he turned to Grigory and asked: "Are you going to the staff, Melekhov?"

Receiving an affirmative reply, Golubov rode up close to him and said: "Tell Podtyolkov that I will be responsible for Chernetsov. Understand? All right, off you go!"

Grigory outdistanced the crowd of prisoners and rode off to the Revolutionary Committee staff, which was stationed near a small village. He found Podtyolkov pacing up and down by a machine-gun cart, surrounded by staff officers, couriers, and orderlies. Minayev and Podtyolkov had both only just returned from the scene of battle. Minayev sat in the driver's seat, munching a piece of frozen white bread. Grigory called Podtyolkov aside.

"The prisoners will be here in a minute," he reported. "Did you get Golubov's note?"

Podtyolkov waved his whip violently, and dropping his sunken eyes and flushing darkly, shouted:

"Damn Golubov! It's a fine thing he's asked for! He'll take charge of Chernetsov, will he? Take charge of that counter-revolutionary and bandit! Well, I won't give him up! The best thing is to shoot them all and be done with them!"

"Golubov said he would be responsible for him."

"I won't give him up! I've said that, and I mean it. That's all! He will be tried by a revolutionary court and the sentence will be carried out immediately. As an example to others! You know ..." he spoke more quietly, staring keenly at the crowd of approaching prisoners. "You know how much bloodshed he has caused? Oceans...! How many miners has he had shot?" And again stuttering with fury, he rolled his eyes and shouted: "I won't hand him over!"

"There's nothing to shout about!" Grigory also raised his voice. He was inwardly trembling, as though Podtyolkov had communicated his frenzy to him. "You have plenty of judges here! You go back there!" His nostrils quivering, he

413

pointed behind him to the battle-field. "There are too many of you wanting to settle accounts with the prisoners!"

Podtyolkov walked off, tightly gripping his whip in his hands. From a distance he shouted:

"I've been there! Don't think I've been saving my skin by this cart. You keep your mouth shut, Melekhov! Understand? Who are you talking to? Get rid of those officer ways of yours! The Revolutionary Committee will judge, and not just any. . . ."

Grigory turned his horse towards him, and jumped out of his saddle, forgetting his wound for the moment. But he doubled up with pain and fell headlong. The blood poured from his leg. He rose without assistance, dragged himself somehow or other to the cart, and slumped against the rear spring.

The prisoners came up. Some of the escort broke away and mingled with the orderlies and Cossacks who had been acting as bodyguard to the staff. The fire of battle had not yet burned itself out within them, and their eyes glittered feverishly and angrily as they exchanged opinions on the recent struggle.

Stepping heavily over the deep snow, Podtyolkov went towards the prisoners. Chernetsov, still a little way in front, stared at him with his clear, desperate eyes screwed up contemptuously; he was leaning back nonchalantly on his left leg, biting his lower lip with strong white teeth. Podtyolkov, trembling violently and staring down at the rutted snow, went straight up to him. He raised his eyes, and his stare crossed with Chernetsov's fearless, scornful gaze, and broke it with the terrible weight of its hatred.

"So we've caught you, you swine!" he said in a low, choking voice, stepping a pace backward. A wry, sombre smile gashed his cheeks like a sabre stroke.

"Betrayer of the Cossacks! Hound! Traitor!" Chernetsov spat through his teeth.

Podtyolkov shook his head as though avoiding a blow, his face darkened, and his open mouth gasped for breath.

What followed occurred with astonishing speed. Chernetsov, his teeth bared, his face pale, his fists pressed against his chest, all his body bent forward, strode towards Podtyolkov. Unintelligible words mingled with curses fell from his quivering lips. Only the slowly retreating Podtyolkov caught what he said.

"Your time will come ... you know that!" Chernetsov raised his voice suddenly, so that the words were heard by the prisoners, the escort, and the staff officers.

"You ..." Podtyolkov gasped in a strangled voice, fumbling for his sabre hilt.

There was an abrupt silence. The snow crunched clearly under the feet of Minayev, Krivoshlykov, and half a dozen others who threw themselves in Podtyolkov's direction. But he was too quick for them. Turning his entire body to the right and crouching, he tore his sabre from its scabbard, flung himself violently forward, and struck Chernetsov with terrific force across the head.

Grigory saw the officer shudder and raise his left hand to ward off the blow; he saw the sabre cut through the wrist as though it were paper and come down noiselessly on Chernetsov's thrown back head. First the lambskin cap fell; then, like corn broken at the stalk, Chernetsov slowly dropped, his mouth twisted wryly, his eyes screwed up in agony and frowning as if before lightning.

As the officer lay Podtyolkov hacked him again, then turned and walked away with an aged, heavy gait, wiping his blood-stained sabre. Stumbling against the cart, he turned to the escort and shouted in an exhausted voice:

"Cut them down.... Damn them! All of them! We take no prisoners! In their hearts, in their blood!"

Shots rang out feverishly. The officers turned and fled in a disorderly, jostling mob. The lieutenant with the beautiful, womanish eyes and red cowl ran with his hands clutching his head. A bullet sent him jumping high as though to clear a hurdle. He fell, and did not rise again. Two Cossacks cut down the tall captain. He caught at the blades of the sabres, and the blood poured from his slashed hands over his sleeve. He screamed like a child, fell on his knees, on to his back, his head rolling over the snow, his face nothing but bloodshot eyes and a black mouth lacerated with a cry. The flying blades played over his face, his mouth, but still he shrieked in a voice thin with pain and horror. Straddling him, a Cossack finished him off with a bullet. The curly-headed cadet all but broke through the ring; he was overtaken and struck down by one of the Ataman's Cossacks. The same man sent a bullet through the back of an officer running with his coat flapping in the wind. The officer squatted down and clawed at his chest until he died. A grey-haired junior captain was killed on the spot; as he parted with life he dug a deep hole in the snow with his feet, and would have gone on kicking like a mettlesome, tethered horse had not the Cossacks taken pity on him and ended his agony.

Immediately the slaughter began Grigory had dragged himself from the cart, and fixing his bloodshot eyes on Podtyolkov, had limped swiftly towards him. But Minayev seized him from behind, twisted his arms, tore the revolver out of his hand, and gazing into his eyes with a dull stare, pantingly demanded:

"And what did you expect?"

XIII

The snow-covered hill, dazzlingly bright in the glare of the sun and the blue of a cloudless sky, lay white and glittering like sugar. Below the hill a scattered village lay like a patchwork quilt. To the right, little hamlets and German settlements nestled in blue patches. To the east of the village rose another sloping hill, rent with gullies. Over its brow ran a palisade of telegraph posts. The day was unusually clear and frosty. Pillars of haze smoked in rainbow hues around the sun. The wind was blowing from the north, and driving up the snow from the steppe. But the snowy expanse was clear to the horizon; only to the east, right on the skyline, did a violet haze lurk over the steppe.

Pantelei Prokofyevich had been to Millerovo to bring Grigory home. He decided not to stop at the village, but to drive on to Kashara and spend the night there. He had set out from Tatarsky in reply to a telegram from

Grigory, and had found his son awaiting him at an inn. After being wounded at Glubokaya, Grigory had been a week travelling in a field-hospital wagon to Millerovo. When his leg had healed a little he resolved to go home. He went with feelings of mingled dissatisfaction and gladness: dissatisfaction because he had abandoned his regiment at the very height of the struggle for power in the Don, and gladness at the thought that he would see his own people again. He concealed even from himself his desire to see Aksinya, yet he could not help thinking of her.

His meeting with his father was attended by a feeling of estrangement. Pantelei (Pyotr had been whispering in his ear) stared moodily at Grigory and discontent and expectant anxiety lurked in his eyes. In the evening he questioned Grigory at some length about the events occurring in the Don Region, and evidently his son's replies did not satisfy him. He chewed at his greying beard, stared at his felt boots, and snorted. At first he was reluctant to argue, but flared up in defence of Kaledin, told Grigory to shut up as in the old days, and even stamped with his lame leg.

"Don't try to tell me! Kaledin was in Tatarsky in the autumn. We had a meeting in the square, and he climbed on to a table and talked with the old men, and prophesied like the Bible that the muzhiks would come and there would be war, and if we didn't make up our minds what we were going to do they would take everything from us and begin to live on our land. Even then he knew there would be war. And what do you think about it, you sons of bitches? Does he know less than your lot? An educated general like that, who's led the army, do you think he knows less than you? The men in Kamenskaya are uneducated talkers like you, and they're troubling the people. Your Podtyolkov—who is he? A sergeant-major? Oho! A man of my rank. That's what we've come to!"

Grigory argued unwillingly. He had known beforehand what attitude his father would take. And now a new element had entered into the situation for him: he could not forget, he could not forgive the death of Chernetsov and the slaughter of the officer prisoners without trial.

The two horses easily drew the basket-sleigh along. Grigory's saddled horse was tethered behind. The well-known villages and settlements unfolded along the road. All the way to his own village Grigory was thinking disconnectedly and aimlessly of the recent happenings, and trying at least to discern some landmarks in the future. But his mind could see no further than a rest at home. "When I get back I'll take a little rest, and get my wound healed, and after that . . ." he mentally shrugged his shoulders. "We shall see. Time will show."

He was broken by weariness engendered of the war. He wanted to turn his back upon the whole hate-riddled and incomprehensible world. Behind him everything was entangled, contradictory. The right path was difficult to trace; the ground quaked under his feet as in a bog, the path branched in many directions and he felt no confidence that he had chosen the right one. He had been drawn towards the Bolsheviks, had led others after him, then had hesitated, and his heart had cooled. "Is Izvarin right after all? Who are we to trust?" But when he thought that soon it would be time to get the harrows ready for spring, the willow mangers would have to be woven, and that when the earth was unclothed and dry he would be driving out into the steppe, his labour-yearning hands gripping the plough handles, feeling it pulse and jerk like a live thing; when he remembered that soon he would be breathing in the sweet scent of the young grass and the damp-smelling earth turned over by the plough-share, his heart warmed within him. He longed to clean the cattle-yard, to toss the hay, to smell the withered scent of the clover, the quitch, the pungent smell of dung. He wanted peace and quietness; and so his harsh eyes nursed a constrained gladness as they gazed at the steppe, at the horses, at his father's back. Everything reminded him of his half-forgotten former life: the reek of sheepskin from his father's coat, the homely appearance of the ungroomed horses, and a cock crowing in a farm-yard. Life here, in this retirement, seemed intoxicatingly rich and sweet.

They arrived at Tatarsky towards evening on the following day. From the hill Grigory glanced towards the Don: there were the backwaters fringed with a sable fur of reeds; there was the withered poplar; but the crossing over the Don was not where it used to be. The village, the familiar blocks of farms, the church, the square. . . . As he fixed his eyes on his own home the blood rushed to his head, and a flood of memories overwhelmed him. The well-sweep in the yard seemed to be beckoning to him with its uplifted willow arm.

"Aren't your eyes smarting!" Pantelei smiled, glancing round. Making no attempt to conceal his feelings, Grigory replied: "Yes. . . and how!"

"What a lot home means!" the old man sighed contentedly.

He made for the centre of the village. The horses ran swiftly down the hill, and the sleigh skidded along, bouncing from hummock to hummock. Grigory guessed his father's intention, but he asked nonetheless:

"What are you going to drive through the village for? Make for your own street."

Pantelei turned and winked, smiling into his beard: "I saw my sons off to the war as rank-and-file Cossacks, and they fought their way to officers' rank. Don't you think I'm proud to drive my son through the village? Let them look and be jealous! It's balm for my heart, lad."

In the main street he called to the horses and, leaning out of the sleigh, plied his whip on their flanks; and the horses, knowing they were near home, ran freshly and swiftly as though they felt nothing of the hundred and forty versts they had already covered. The passing Cossacks bowed, the women stared under their palms from the yards and the windows, and the hens scattered squawking over the road. Everything went like clock-work. They drove through the square. Grigory's horse glanced sidelong at another horse tied by Mokhov's palings, snorted, and raised its head high. The end of the village and the roof of Astakhov's house were in sight. But at the first cross-road an accident occurred. A young pig running across the road lost its head, fell under the horses' hoofs, grunted and rolled over, squealing and trying to raise its broken back.

"The devil take you!" Pantelei cried, giving the pig a taste of his whip.

Unfortunately it belonged to Anyutka, the widow of Afonka Ozerov, an ill-tempered and long-tongued woman. She ran out of her yard, and poured out such a stream of curses that Pantelei reined in the horses and turned in his seat.

"Hold your tongue, you fool!" he shouted. "What are you yelling about? We'll pay you for your mangy pig."

"You evil spirit...! You devil! You're mangy yourself, you limping hound! I'll have you before the ataman at once!" she screamed, waving her arms. "I'll teach you to crush a poor widow's animal!"

Pantelei had heard enough, and turning livid, croaked:

"Filthy mouth!"

"You cursed Turk!" the woman replied energetically.

"You bitch, a hundred devils were mother to you!" Pantelei raised his voice.

But Anyutka Ozerova was never at a loss for abuse:

"Foreigner! Whoremonger! Thief! Who stole a harrow? Who runs after the grass widows?" she chattered away like a magpie.

"I'll give you one with this whip, you slut! Close your mouth!" the old man retorted.

But now Anyutka shouted something so evil that even Pantelei, who had seen and heard much in his time, went red with embarrassment and began to sweat.

"Drive on! What did you stop for?" Grigory said angrily as a crowd began to gather, listening attentively to this fortuitous exchange of compliments between old Melekhov and the honest widow Ozerova.

"What a tongue! As long as a pair of reins!" Pantelei spat out despairingly and whipped up the horses as though he intended to ride down Anyutka herself.

When they reached the next turning he glanced round cautiously:

"The way she curses.... What a devil! May you swell and burst, you fat bitch!" he exclaimed with chagrin. "She ought to have been crushed as well as her pig! The bitch could strip the flesh from your bones with that tongue of hers!"

The blue shutters of their own house sped

towards them. Pyotr with bare head and un-
belted shirt opened the gate. There was a
glimmer of a white kerchief, and Dunya, her
black eyes sparkling, ran down the steps.

As Pyotr kissed his brother he glanced into
Grigory's eyes.

"Are you well?"

"I've been wounded."

"Where?"

"Near Glubokaya."

"You needed something better to do! You
should have come home long ago."

He gave Grigory a warm and friendly shake,
and handed him on to Dunya. Grigory embraced his sister's ripened shoulders and kissed
her on the lips and the eyes, then stepped
back in astonishment.

"Why, Dunya, the devil himself wouldn't
know you! Look at the girl you've turned out,
and I thought you would be so plain and
ugly."

"Now, now, Brother!" Dunya foiled his attempt to pinch her, and smiling the same
white-toothed smile as Grigory, ran off.

Ilyinichna brought the children out in her
arms, and Natalya ran in front of her. Grigory's wife had blossomed and improved aston-
ishingly. Her smoothly combed, gleaming
black hair, gathered in a heavy knot at the

back, set off her joyfully flushed face. She cleaved to Grigory, brushed her lips awkwardly several times against his cheeks and whiskers, and snatching her son from Ilyinichna's arms, held him out to her husband.

"Look what a fine son you have!" she cried with happy pride.

"Let me have a look at *my* son!" Ilyinichna excitedly pushed her aside. She pulled down Grigory's head, kissed his brow, and stroked his face with her rough hand, weeping with excitement and joy.

"And your daughter, Grisha! Here, take her!"

Natalya set the girl in Grigory's other arm, and in his embarrassment he did not know whom to look at: Natalya, or his mother, or his children. The little boy, with morose eyes and knitted brows, was cast in the Melekhov mould: the same long slits of black, rather sombre eyes, blue prominent whites, the spreading line of brows, and swarthy skin. He thrust his dirty little fist into his mouth and stared stubbornly and unyieldingly at his father. Grigory could see only the tiny, attentive black eyes of his daughter: the rest of her face was wrapped in a shawl.

Holding them both in his arms, he moved towards the steps; but a stab of pain went up his leg.

"Take them, Natalya!" he laughed wryly and shamefacedly. "Or I shan't be able to get up the steps."

Darya was standing in the middle of the kitchen, tidying her hair. She smiled and came jauntily towards Grigory, closed her laughing eyes and pressed her moist warm lips against his.

"You taste of tobacco!" she raised the delicate arches of her brows humorously.

"Let me have another look at you! My darling, my son!"

Grigory smiled and his heart pricked as he laid his cheek on his mother's shoulder.

In the yard Pantelei in his red-topped cap and red sash was limping round the sleigh, unharnessing the horses. Pyotr had already taken Grigory's horse to the stable, and his saddle to the house, and was saying something to Dunya who had lifted a can of paraffin off the sleigh.

Grigory took off his sheepskin and greatcoat and hung them at the foot of the bed, then combed his hair. He sat down on a bench and called his son:

"Come to me, Misha! Why, don't you know me?"

His fist still in his mouth, the child edged towards him, but came to a halt by the table. His mother gazed fondly and proudly at him from the stove. She bent down and whispered something into her daughter's ear, and gently pushed her forward.

"Go on!"

Grigory gathered them both up, set them on his knees and asked:

"Don't you know me, you wood nuts? Polya, don't you know your daddy?"

"You're not our daddy," the boy said, feeling more confident now that his sister was with him.

"Then who am I?"

"You're some other Cossack."

"And that's that!" Grigory laughed aloud. "Then where is your daddy?"

"He's away in the army," the girl said firmly; she was the more lively of the two.

"That's right, children, give it to him! He's been away all these years and now he thinks everybody ought to know him when at last he comes home!" Ilyinichna intervened with feigned severity, and smiled at Grigory. "Even your wife will be giving you up soon! We were already looking for a man for her!"

"What's this mean, Natalya? Eh?" Grigory turned jokingly to his wife.

She blushed, but overcoming her embarrassment, went across to him and sat down at his side. Her boundlessly happy eyes drank him in, and her hot rough hand stroked his arm, dry and brown.

"Darya, set the table!" Ilyinichna called.

"He's got a wife of his own!" Darya laughed and turned with her jaunty step towards the stove.

She was as slender and elegant as ever. Her lilac woollen stockings clung tightly to her shapely legs, her shoes fitted her feet as though made for her. The flounced, raspberry-coloured skirt was tightly laced, and her embroidered apron was of an irreproachable whiteness. Grigory turned his eyes to his wife, and noticed that she had changed somewhat. She had decked herself out for his home-coming: a blue sateen blouse with lace sleeves tight at the wrists displayed her shapely figure and swelled over her soft large breasts, a blue skirt with a full, crinkled, embroidered hem clasped her waist. Grigory looked at her full shapely legs, her firm belly and her broad bottom, like that of a well-fed mare, and thought: "You can tell a Cossack woman in a thousand. She dresses herself to show everything: Look if you want to, and don't if you don't!' But you can't tell the back from the front of a muzhik woman, she looks as if she's dressed in a sack. ..."

Ilyinichna caught his gaze, and boasted:

"See how officers' wives dress among us Cossacks! They could rub shoulders with any town lady!"

"How can you talk like that, Mother?" Darya interrupted her. "We should look fine among the town ladies! One of my ear-rings is broken, and they were never worth anything anyway," she ended bitterly.

Grigory put his arm across his wife's broad back and thought for the first time: "She's good-looking, anybody can see that. How did she live without me? I expect the Cossacks ran after her, and maybe she ran after one of them. Suppose she did!" At this unexpected thought his heart beat violently, and he stared searchingly at her rosy face, shining and fresh with cucumber pomade. Natalya flushed under his attentive gaze, and whispered:

"What are you looking at me like that for? Glad to see me again?"

"Why, of course!"

He drove away his unpleasant thought, but for a moment he felt a vague, almost unconscious hostility towards his wife.

Pantelei came in coughing, crossed himself before the icon, and croaked:

"Well, good health to you all once more!"

"Praise be, man! Are you frozen? We've been waiting for you. The soup's hot." Ilyinichna bustled around clattering the spoons.

He untied the red handkerchief around his neck, pulled off his sheepskin, shook the icicles from his beard and whiskers, and sitting down by Grigory, said:

"I'm all frozen; but we were warm enough coming through the village. We drove over Anyutka Ozerova's pig. How she came running out, the bitch! How she carried on! 'I'll give it to you,' and 'You're this, that and the other,' and 'You stole a harrow!' The devil knows what harrow!"

He related all the nicknames Anyutka had called him, omitting only her reference to his "whoremongering." Grigory laughed and sat down at the table. Seeking to justify himself in his son's eyes, Pantelei ended fiercely:

"I'd have given her a taste of the whip, but Grigory was with me, and it wasn't a good moment."

Pyotr opened the door and Dunya entered, leading in a handsome young calf by a girdle.

"We shall be having pancakes with cream at Shrovetide," Pyotr cried, gaily thrusting the calf forward with his foot.

After dinner, Grigory untied his kit-bag and

gave out his presents. "That's for you, Mother," he said to her, handing her a warm shawl. Frowning and blushing like a young girl, Ilyinichna took the shawl and threw it around her shoulders. She spent so much time admiring herself in the glass that even Pantelei was riled:

"You old hag, fussing about in front of the glass! Pah!"

"And this is for you, Father," Grigory said hurriedly, unwrapping a new Cossack cap with a high front and a flaming red band.

"God save you! I was needing a new cap. There haven't been any in the shop all this past year. I didn't like going to church in my old one. It was only fit for a scarecrow, but I went on wearing it," he said in indignant tones, looking around as though afraid someone would take away his son's present.

He turned to go to the glass to see how it fitted, but catching Ilyinichna's eyes, wheeled suddenly round and limped to the samovar. He stood before it to try his cap on, setting the peak jauntily to one side.

"What are you doing there, you old fool?" Ilyinichna turned on him. But Pantelei barked back:

"Lord, what a fool you are, woman! This is a samovar, not a looking-glass."

Grigory gave his wife a length of woollen cloth for a skirt; his children received a pound of honey-cake, Darya a pair of silver ear-rings, Dunya material for a blouse, and Pyotr cigarettes and tobacco. While the women were chattering away over their gifts, Pantelei strutted about the kitchen like à lord, with his chest thrown out.

"There's a fine Cossack of the Lifeguard Regiment for you! Took prizes too! Won the first prize at the imperial review. A saddle and all its equipment! That's me. . .!"

Pyotr, biting his wheaten moustache, looked at his father admiringly. Grigory smiled, the men lit cigarettes, and Pantelei, glancing uneasily at the window, said to him:

"Before the relations and neighbours begin to come, tell Pyotr what's happening back there."

Grigory waved his hand. "They're fighting."

"Where are the Bolsheviks now?" Pyotr immediately asked, as he seated himself more comfortably.

"Coming from three sides, from Tikhoretskaya, from Taganrog, and Voronezh."

"Well, and what does your Revolutionary Committee think about that? Why are they letting them come on to our land? Christonya and Ivan Alexeyevich came back and told us all

434

sorts of yarns, but I don't believe them. It's not as they say."

"The Revolutionary Committee is helpless. The Cossacks are running home."

"And is that why it's leaning on the Soviets?"

"Of course that's why."

Pyotr was silent while he puffed at his cigarette, then he looked frankly at his brother.

"And on what side are you?"

"I want a Soviet government."

"The fool!" Pantelei exploded like gunpowder. "Pyotr, you tell him!"

Pyotr smiled and clapped his brother on the shoulder.

"He's as fiery as an unbroken horse," he said. "Can anyone tell him anything, Father?"

"There's nothing to tell me!" Grigory grew angry. "I'm not blind. What are the front-line men in the village saying?"

"What have the front-line men to do with us? Don't you know that fool of a Christonya by now? What can he understand? The people are all lost, and don't know which way to turn." Pyotr bit at his moustache. "Wait and see what will happen in the spring, that's when the trouble will start. . . . At the front we played at being Bolsheviks, but now it's time we came to our senses. 'We don't want anything belonging to anybody else, but don't you touch ours!' that's what the Cossacks ought to say to all who come here grabbing. It's a dirty business that's been going on at Kamenskaya. They've got friendly with the Bolsheviks and they'll set up their system."

"You think it over, Grigory," his father said. "You're not a fool! You must understand this: once a Cossack, always a Cossack. We're not going to be ruled by a lot of Russian peasants. And do you know what the aliens are saying now? All the land ought to be divided up equally among all. What do you think of that?"

"We'll give land to those aliens who've been living on the Don for years."

"Not an inch!" Pantelei snapped his fingers loudly under Grigory's hook-nose.

There was a tramp of feet on the steps outside, and Anikushka, Christonya, and Ivan Tomilin wearing an absurdly tall hareskin hat came in.

"Hullo, Grigory! Pantelei Prokofyevich, what about a drink to celebrate his home-coming?" Christonya roared.

At his shout the calf dozing by the stove started up in alarm, tottering on its still feeble legs and gazing with agate eyes at the newcomers. In its fright it let a fine stream on to the floor. Dunya stopped it with a tap on the back, wiped up the pool and set a dirty pot under the animal.

"You frightened the calf, you trumpet!" Ilyinichna angrily exclaimed.

Grigory shook hands with the Cossacks and invited them to sit down. Soon other Cossacks from the far end of the village arrived. As they talked they smoked so much that the lamp began to sputter and the calf to choke.

"The fever take you!" Ilyinichna cursed them as she sent the guests packing at midnight. "Go on into the yard and smoke, chimneys! Clear out, clear out! Our Grigory hasn't had any rest yet after his journey. Clear off, in God's name!"

XIV

Next morning Grigory was the last to awake. He was aroused by the noisy, spring-like chatter of the sparrows in the eaves and outside the window-frames. A golden drift of sunlight was sifting through the chinks in the shutters. The church-bell was ringing for matins, and he remembered that it was Sunday. Natalya was not at his side, but the featherbed still retained the warmth of her body. Evidently she had not been up long.

"Natalya!" he called.

Dunya entered. "What do you want, Brother?"

"Open the window and call Natalya. What is she doing?"

"She's helping Mother. She'll come in a minute."

Natalya came in, screwing up her eyes in the twilight of the room. Her hands smelled of fresh dough. Without rising he embraced her, and laughed as he recalled the night.

"You overslept yourself?"

"Uh-huh! The night... tired me out," she smiled and blushed, hiding her head against Grigory's chest.

She helped him to dress his wound, then drew his best trousers out of the chest, and asked:

"Will you wear your officer's tunic with the crosses?"

"No, why?" He waved her off in alarm. But she persisted: "Do wear it! Father will be pleased. Why did you win them if you're going to let them lie in the chest?"

He yielded to her entreaties. He rose, borrowed his brother's razor, shaved, and washed his face and neck.

"Shaved the back of your neck?" Pyotr asked.

"Oh, the devil! I forgot!"

"Well, sit down and I'll do it."

The cold lather burned his neck. Reflected in the glass he saw his brother wielding the razor, his tongue sticking out at one corner of his mouth.

"Your neck's got thinner, like a bull's after ploughing," Pyotr smiled.

"You can't expect to get fat on army grub."

Grigory put on his tunic with its cornet's epaulettes and heavy row of crosses, and when he glanced into the steaming mirror he hardly recognized himself: a tall, gaunt officer as swarthy as a gypsy stared back at him.

"You look like a colonel!" Pyotr exclaimed in delight, without the least trace of envy in his voice as he admired his brother. The words pleased Grigory despite himself. He went into the kitchen. Darya stared at him admiringly, while Dunya cried:

"Pfooh! How grand you look!"

At this Ilyinichna could not restrain her tears. Wiping them away with her apron, she replied to Dunya's banter:

"You have children like that, you hussy! I've had two sons and they've both got on in the world."

Natalya did not take her misty, ardently loving eyes off her husband for a moment.

Grigory threw his greatcoat around his

shoulders and went out into the yard. Because of his wounded leg, he found it difficult to get down the steps. "I'll have to use a stick," he thought as he held on to the rail. The bullet had been removed at Millerovo, but the scab had drawn the skin tight and he could not bend his leg properly.

The cat was sunning itself on the ledge of the house wall. Snow was melting into a pool around the steps. Grigory stared gladly and observantly around the yard. Right by the steps stood a post with a wheel fastened across its top. It had been there ever since he was a child; it was used by the women. At night they stood at the top of the steps and placed the milk-jugs on it, and during the day the pots and household utensils dried on it. Certain changes in the yard caught his eye at once: the door of the granary had been washed over with brown clay instead of paint, the shed had been rethatched with rye straw that was still yellow; the pile of stakes seemed smaller—probably some had been used to repair the fence. The hummock of the earth-cellar was blue with ashes; a raven-black cock surrounded by a dozen or so motley hens was perched on it with one leg raised limply. Under the shed the farm implements lay safe from the winter weather, with the side-frames of the wagons sticking out like ribs and some metal part of the reaping-machine burning in a ray of sunlight that pierced through a hole in the roof. Geese were squatting on a pile of dung by the stable, and a crested Dutch gander squinted arrogantly at Grigory as he limped past.

He went over the farm, then returned to the house. The kitchen smelt sweetly of warmed butter and hot bread. Dunya was washing some soused apples on a pattern plate. He glanced at them and asked with sudden liveliness:

"Any salted water-melon going?"

"Step down and get him some, Natalya," Ilyinichna called.

Pantelei returned from church. He divided the wafer into nine parts, a bit for each member of the family, and distributed it around the table. They sat down to breakfast. Pyotr, also dressed up for the occasion, even his moustache greased with something, sat at Grigory's side. Opposite them Darya balanced herself on the edge of a stool. A pillar of sunrays poured over her rosy, shining face, and she screwed up her eyes and discontentedly lowered the black arches of her gleaming brows. Natalya fed the children with baked pumpkin, smiling as now and then she glanced up at Grigory. Dunya sat at her father's side, while Ilyinichna was at the end of the table nearest the stove.

As always on holidays, they ate a hearty meal. The cabbage soup with lamb was followed by home-made noodles, then mutton, a chicken, lamb's foot jelly, fried potatoes, millet gruel with butter, noodles with dried cherries, pancakes and clotted cream, and salted watermelon. After the heavy meal Grigory rose with difficulty, and lay down on the bed breathing heavily. Pantelei was still busy with his gruel; after patting it flat he made a hole in it, poured the amber melted butter into the hole, then started eating the buttery mixture in neat spoonfuls. Pyotr, who was very fond of children, sat feeding Misha, and playfully anointing the lad's cheeks and nose with sour milk.

"Uncle, don't be silly!"

"Why not?"

"Why are you doing it?"

"Why not?"

"I'll tell Mummy." Misha's morose Melekhov eyes glittered angrily and tears of vexation trembled in them. He wiped his nose with his fist and shouted, in despair of persuading Pyotr with fair words:

"Don't do it! Stupid! Fool!"

Pyotr only burst into a roar of laughter and

started feeding his nephew again, one spoonful to the mouth, the next to the nose.

"You're like a child yourself!" Ilyinichna protested.

Dunya sat down by Grigory and told him: "Pyotr's just a big stupid! He's always up to some new trick. The other day he went with Misha out into the yard, and the boy badly wanted to go, and asked: 'Uncle, can I go by the steps?' But Pyotr said: 'No, you mustn't. Go a little farther off.' Misha ran a little away, and asked: 'Here?' 'No, no; run to the barn.' From the barn he sent him to the stable, and from the stable to the threshing-floor. He made the poor boy run and run until he did it in his trousers. And Natalya did go on at him!"

"Let me feed myself!" Misha's little voice rang out like a post-chaise bell.

Pyotr twitched his whiskers in humorous refusal:

"Oh no, my lad. I'm going to feed you."

"I'll feed myself."

"That's what the pigs do in the sty. Have you seen what Granny gives them?"

Grigory listened with a smile to Pyotr and Misha, and rolled himself a cigarette. His father came across to him.

"I'm thinking of driving to Vyeshenskaya today," the old man confided.

"What for?"

Pantelei hiccuped, and stroked his beard:

"I've got some business with the saddler; he's had two yokes of ours to mend."

"Coming back today?"

"Of course. I'll be back in the evening."

After a rest, the old man harnessed the mare, which had gone blind that year, into the shafts of the sledge, and drove off. In two hours or so he was at Vyeshenskaya. He went to the post office, then to the saddler and collected the yokes. Then he drove to an old acquaintance and gossip who lived by the new church. The man, a thoroughly hospitable sort, made him stay to dinner.

"Been to the post?" he asked as he poured something into a glass.

"Yes," Pantelei answered, staring in astonishment at the bottle and sniffing the air like a hound tracking an animal.

"Then you've heard the news?"

"News? No, I've heard nothing. What is it?"

"Kaledin, Alexei Maximovich Kaledin, has gone to his rest."

"What are you saying?" Pantelei turned noticeably green, forgot the suspect bottle and its scent, and threw himself back in his chair. Blinking moodily, his host told him:

"We've had the news by telegraph that he

shot himself the other day in Novocherkassk.
And he was the one real general in all the province. What a spirit the man had! He wouldn't
have let any shame come on the Cossacks."

"Wait a bit! What's going to happen now?"
Pantelei asked distractedly, pushing away the
glass offered him.

"God knows. Bad days are coming. A man
wouldn't put a bullet into himself if the times
were good."

"What made him do it?"

His host, a man as rooted in his opinions as
an Old Believer, waved his hand angrily:

"The front-line men had deserted him, and
let the Bolsheviks into the province; and so
our ataman went. I doubt if we'll find any more
like him. Who will defend us? A Revolutionary
Committee or something has been set up in
Kamenskaya, with front-line Cossacks in it.
And here ... have you heard? We've had an
order from Kamenskaya to get rid of the atamans and to elect Revolutionary Committees
in their place. The muzhiks are beginning to
raise their heads. All these carpenters, smiths
and job-hunters ... they're as thick in Vyeshenskaya as midges in a meadow."

Pantelei sat silent for a long time, his grey
head drooping. When he looked up his gaze
was stern and harsh.

"What is that you've got in the bottle?"

"Spirits. A relation brought it from the Caucasus."

"Well, pour it out, friend. We'll drink to the memory of our dead ataman. May the heavenly kingdom open to him!"

They drank. The daughter of the house, a tall, freckled girl, brought in food. Pantelei glanced at the mare standing morosely by the sledge, but his host assured him: "Don't worry about the horse. I'll see that she's fed and watered."

What with the heated conversation and the bottle Pantelei soon forgot his horse and everything else in the world. He talked disconnectedly about Grigory, fell into an argument with his tipsy host, went on arguing and then quite forgot what it was all about. It was evening when he started to his feet. Ignoring an invitation to stay the night, he decided to set off home. His friend's son harnessed the horse, and his host assisted him into the sledge. Then the man thought he would see him out of the village. They lay down together in the bottom of the sledge with their arms round each other. Their sledge first hooked against the gate-post, then caught in every projecting corner until they drove out into the steppe. There his host burst into tears and deliberately fell out of the sledge. For a long time he knelt on all fours, cursing and unable to rise to his feet. Pantelei whipped the horse into a trot, and saw no more of his host crawling along the road with nose thrust into the snow, laughing happily and hoarsely pleading:

"Stop tickling. . . . Please stop tickling."

Encouraged by the whip, the mare moved on quickly at a blind trot. Soon her master, overcome by drowsy intoxication, fell back with his head against the wall of the sledge, and was silent. The reins happened to fall underneath him, and the horse, unguided and helpless, dropped into an easy walk. At the first fork she turned off the right road and made for a little village. After a few minutes she lost this road also. She struck across the open steppe, was stranded in the deep snow of a wood, and dropped down into a hollow. The sledge hooked against a bush, and she came to a halt. The jerk awoke the old man for a second. He raised his head and shouted hoarsely: "Gee-up, you devil ..." then lay down again.

The horse moved on and got past the wood without mishap, successfully made her way down to the bank of the Don and guided by the scent of smoke brought by the easterly wind, made for the next village.

Some half a verst from the village there is a gap near the left bank of the river. Around the gap springs emerge from the sandy bank, and here the water is never frozen, even in the depth of winter, but lies in a broad, semicircular pool. The road along the river-side carefully avoids the water, making a sharp turn to one side. In spring-time, when the field water pours in a mighty flood back through the gap into the Don, a roaring whirlpool is formed. All the summer the carp lie at a great depth close to the piled drift-wood fallen from the bank.

The old mare directed her blind steps towards the left edge of the pool. When it was some fifty paces away Pantelei turned over and half-opened his eyes. Out of the black heaven the yellow-green, unripe cherries of stars stared down at him. "Night . . ." he reflected hazily and pulled violently at the reins.

"Now! I'll give you one, you old horse-radish!" he shouted at the horse.

The mare broke into a trot. The scent of the nearby water entered her nostrils. She pricked up her ears and turned a blind, uncomprehending eye in the direction of her master. Suddenly the splash of swirling water came to her ears. Snorting wildly, she turned aside and tried to back. The half-melted ice at the edge of the pool scrunched softly under her hoofs, and

the snowy fringe broke away. The mare gave
a snort of mortal terror. With all her strength
she resisted with her hind feet, but her fore-
feet were already in the water, and the thin
ice began to break under her hind hoofs.
Groaning and crackling, the ice gave way. As
the pool swallowed up the mare, she convulsively kicked out with one hind leg and struck
the shaft. At that very moment Pantelei, hearing that something was wrong, jumped from
the sledge and tumbled backward. He saw the
back of the sledge rise, laying bare the gleaming runners as the front was drawn down by
the weight of the mare; then it slipped away
into the green-black depths. The water, mingled with pieces of ice, hissed softly and rolled
in a wave almost to his feet. With incredible
swiftness he crawled backward and jumped to
his feet, roaring:

"Help, good people! We're drowning!"

His drunkenness passed from him as though
knocked out by a hammer. He ran to the pool.
The freshly broken ice gleamed sharply. The
wind drove bits of ice over the broad black
semicircle of the pool; the waves shook their
green manes and muttered. All around was a
deathly silence. The lights of the distant village
shone yellow through the darkness. The stars,

like big, freshly winnowed grain, burned ecstatically in the plush of the sky. The breeze raised the snow from the field, and it flew hissingly in a floury dust into the black depths of the pool. And the pool steamed a little and remained invitingly, eerily black.

Pantelei realized that it was useless and foolish to shout now. He looked around, discovered where he had got to in his drunken stupor, and shook with anger at himself and at what had happened. His knout was still in his hand: he had jumped out of the sledge with it. Cursing terribly, he whipped away at his back with the lash, but felt no pain, for his stout sheepskin softened the blows. And it seemed senseless to undress just for that pleasure. He tore a handful of hair out of his beard, and mentally counting the purchases he had lost, the value of the mare, the sledge, and the yokes, he swore frenziedly and went still closer to the pool.

"You blind devil ..." he said in a trembling moaning voice, addressing the drowned mare. "You whore! Drowned yourself and all but drowned me! Where has the evil spirit taken you? The devils will harness you up and drive you, but they won't have anything to drive you with! Here, take the knout too!" he waved the cherry knout desperately around his head and flung it into the middle of the pool.

It smacked and pierced the water stock first, and disappeared into the depths.

XV

After Kaledin's victory over the revolutionary Cossack troops the Don Military Revolutionary Committee, which had been forced to flee to Millerovo, made haste to clarify its political platform. It sent the following statement to the leader of the operations against Kaledin and the counter-revolutionary Ukrainian Rada.

Kharkov, January 19, 1918. From Lugansk, No. 449, 18:20 hrs.

The Don Cossack Revolutionary Committee requests that you transmit the following resolution to the Council of People's Commissars in Petrograd.

The Cossack Military Revolutionary Committee, in accordance with the resolution of the Congress of front-line men at Kamenskaya, resolves:

1. That the Central Executive Committee of the Soviet of Cossacks', Peasants', Soldiers' and Workers' Deputies and the Council of People's Commissars elected by it be recognized as the central governing power of the Russian Soviet Republic.

2. That the Congress of Soviets of Cossacks', Soldiers' and Workers' Deputies in the Don Region establish a territorial government.

Note: The land question in the Don Region is to be settled by this same Congress.

When this statement was received, Red Guard detachments were dispatched to the assistance of the Revolutionary Committee's forces. As a result, Colonel Chernetsov's forces were smashed and the position of the revolutionary forces was secured. The initiative passed into the hands of the Revolutionary Committee. After taking Zverevo and Likhaya, the Red Guard detachments led by Sablin and Petrov, reinforced by the Cossack troops of the Revolutionary Committee, started an offensive and forced their opponents back to Novocherkassk.

Nearing Taganrog, Sivers' revolutionary forces were defeated by the volunteer detachments under Colonel Kutyopov, losing a cannon, 24 machine-guns, and an armoured car. But on the very day that Sivers' forces were defeated and forced to retreat the workers rose in the Baltic Works in Taganrog, and drove the cadets out of the city.

Sivers rallied his forces, took the offensive and drove the volunteers back towards Taganrog.

Success was evidently favouring the Soviet troops. They were closing in on the Whites on three sides. On January 28th Kornilov sent Kaledin a telegram informing him that the Volunteer Army was evacuating Rostov and moving towards the Kuban.

At 9 a.m. on the 29th, an extraordinary session of the Don Government was held in the Ataman's Palace. Kaledin was the last to arrive. He sank heavily into a chair and drew a pile of documents towards him. His face was drawn and sallow from lack of sleep; there were blue shadows under his faded sombre eyes, and a film of decay seemed to yellow his haggard face. He slowly read Kornilov's telegram, and the reports of troop commanders who were bearing the brunt of the Red Guards' attack north of Novocherkassk. Carefully smoothing out a pile of telegrams with his broad white palm, he said dully, without raising his swollen shadowed lids:

"The Volunteer Army is retreating. We have only 147 bayonets with which to defend the region and Novocherkassk."

His left eyelid twitched, and the corners of his tightly pressed lips quivered. Raising his voice, he continued:

"Our situation is hopeless. The population, far from supporting us, is hostile. We have no troops, and resistance is useless. I want no unnecessary casualties, no unnecessary bloodshed. I propose that we resign and turn the power over to someone else. I for my part resign as Ataman of the Don Cossack Army."

Bogayevsky, who was looking out of the window, straightened his pince-nez, and said without turning his head.

"I resign too."

"Of course, the government resigns as a whole. Now the question is: to whom shall we turn over the power?"

"To the City Duma," Kaledin answered drily.

"We must make it official," said Karev, a member of the government, uncertainly. For a moment there was a deep, awkward silence. The dismal January morning languished outside the misty panes. The city was dreamily silent under the veil of fog and hoar-frost. The ear could not catch the ordinary pulsation of life. The rumble of cannon-fire (the echo of fighting near the village of Sulin) deadened all sounds and hung over the city like a vague, unexpressed threat.

Outside, ravens were croaking hoarsely, sharply. They circled over the white belfry as if it were a carcass. Lilac-hued, fresh snow lay on the Cathedral Square. Now and then someone walked across it and occasional sledges left dark traces behind them. Breaking the strained silence, Bogayevsky proposed that a document be drawn up transferring the power to the City Duma:

"We must get together with the Duma members about this."

"When will it be most convenient for everyone?"

"Later, about 4 o'clock."

The members of the government, as though pleased that the heavy silence had been broken, began to discuss the question of turning over the power, and the time of meeting. Kaledin was silent, quietly, monotonously tapping the table with his finger-nails. Under his shaggy brows his eyes became dull and clouded. Utter weariness, disgust and strain made his glance heavy and repellent.

One of the members of the government was arguing volubly with a colleague. Kaledin interrupted them with quiet fury:

"Gentlemen, be brief. Time is pressing. Russia has perished because of too much talk. I declare a recess for half an hour. Talk things over and ... let's finish this as soon as possible."

He withdrew to his apartments. The others gathered in small groups, conversing quietly.

Someone remarked that Kaledin looked ill. Bogayevsky, who was standing near the window, caught the half-whispered:

"For a man of his calibre suicide is the only possible way out."

Bogayevsky gave a start and walked off rapidly to Kaledin's apartments. He returned soon after accompanied by the ataman. They decided to have a joint meeting with the City Duma at 4 o'clock in order to hand in the document they had drawn up officially relinquishing power. Kaledin rose. The others followed him. As he was taking leave of one of the older members of the government, Kaledin noticed that Yanov was whispering to Karev.

"What's the matter?" he asked. Yanov came up in some embarrassment.

"The government members—the non-Cossacks—are asking for their travelling expenses."

Kaledin frowned and said harshly:

"I have no money. . . . I am sick of all this."

As they were leaving, Bogayevsky, who had overheard the conversation, beckoned to Yanov:

"Come up to my room. Ask Svetozarov to wait in the lobby."

They left immediately after Kaledin, who walked away rapidly, his shoulders bowed. In his room Bogayevsky handed Yanov a wad of money.

"Here's fourteen thousand. Give it to those people."

Svetozarov, who had been waiting for Yanov in the lobby, took the money, thanked him and went towards the door. Just as Yanov was getting his greatcoat from the doorman, he heard a noise on the staircase and looked back. Moldavsky, Kaledin's aide-de-camp, was dashing down the stairs.

"Get a doctor! Quick!"

Yanov dropped his greatcoat and rushed towards him. The aide-de-camp on duty and the orderlies crowding the lobby surrounded Moldavsky.

"What's the matter?" shouted Yanov, paling.

"Kaledin has shot himself." Moldavsky fell sobbing against the balustrade.

Bogayevsky ran up. His lips were trembling as if with ague.

"What happened? What?"

The crowd rushed up the stairs. Bogayevsky was swallowing convulsively, gasping for breath. He was the first to reach the door and throw it open. He ran through an antechamber into the study. The door between the study and the small room adjoining it was wide open. Acrid grey smoke and the smell of cordite hung in the air.

"Oh, oh! A-ah! Alyosha! My own!" the voice of Kaledin's wife was heard, broken, terrible, unrecognizable.

Bogayevsky, tearing open his collar as if it were throttling him, ran into the room. Karev was hunched over the window, his fingers clutching its gilt knob. His shoulder-blades were moving convulsively under his coat, every now and then he shuddered violently. The hollow animal-like wailing of an adult nearly knocked Bogayevsky off his feet.

Kaledin was lying on his back on a camp-bed, his hands folded on his breast. His head was slightly turned to the wall. The white pillow-case contrasted sharply with the moist bluish forehead and cheek resting on it. His eyes were half-closed as if he were day-dreaming, the corners of his stern mouth were twisted in an expression of suffering. His wife was writhing at his feet. Her voice was wild and piercing. On the bed lay a Colt revolver. A thin dark-red rivulet was trickling merrily down the shirt, past the gun.

A coat was carefully hung out across the back of a chair. A wrist-watch lay on the night stand.

Swaying, Bogayevsky fell to his knees, and pressed his ear to Kaledin's warm, soft breast. He smelled the strong vinegary odour of male sweat. Kaledin's heart was still. Bogayevsky, whose whole being at that moment seemed concentrated in his sense of hearing, listened desperately, but all he could hear was the steady ticking of the wrist-watch on the table, the hoarse, choking sobs of the dead ataman's wife and the ominous, mournful croaking of the ravens.

XVI

The first sight to meet Bunchuk's gaze when he returned to consciousness was Anna's black eyes glistening with tears and a smile.

For three weeks he had been delirious. For three weeks he had wandered in another, intangible and fantastic world. His senses returned to him towards evening on December 24th. He stared at Anna with serious, filmy eyes, trying to recall all that was associated with her, but only partly succeeding. Much of his recent past was still inflexibly concealed in the depths of his memory.

"Give me a drink...." He heard his own voice coming from afar, and he smiled with amusement at it. Anna came quickly towards him; she was all aglow with a restrained, inward smile.

"Drink from my hand," she said and drew aside the limp hand he held out for the cup.

Trembling with the effort of lifting his head, he drank, then fell wearily back on to the pillow. He lay staring at the wall, wanting to say something. But his weakness took the upper hand, and he dozed off.

When he awoke it was again Anna's anxious eyes that first met his own; then he noticed the saffron light of the lamp, and the white circle cast by it on the bare planks of the ceiling.

"Anna, come here!"

She approached and took his hand. He replied with a feeble pressure.

"How do you feel?"

"My tongue belongs to someone else, my head belongs to someone else, and so do my legs; and I feel about two hundred years old." He carefully enunciated every word. After a silence, he asked: "Have I had typhus?"

"Yes."

His eyes wandered round the room, and he asked indistinctly:

"Where are we?"

"In Tsaritsin."

"And you . . . how is it you're here?"

"I stayed with you," and as though justifying herself or trying to avert some unexpressed thought of his, she hastened to add: "We couldn't leave you entirely to strangers. So Abramson and the comrades of the Committee asked me to look after you.... And so, you see, quite unexpectedly I had to nurse you."

He thanked her with a look and a weak movement of his hand.

"And Krutogorov?"

"He's gone to Lugansk."

"And Gyevorkyants?"

"He ... he died of typhus."

They were both silent, as though paying respect to the memory of the dead.

"I was afraid for you. You were very ill," she said quietly.

"And Bogovoi?"

"I've lost touch with them all. Some of them went to Kamenskaya. But is it all right for you to talk? And wouldn't you like a drink of milk?"

Bunchuk shook his head. Moving his tongue with difficulty, he continued his questions.

"Abramson?"

"He left for Voronezh a week ago."

He turned over awkwardly; his head swam and the blood rushed painfully to his eyes. Feeling her cool palm on his brow, he opened his eyes. One question was tormenting him: he had been unconscious, and who had attended to his needs? Surely not she? A faint flush coloured his cheeks, and he asked:

"Did you have to look after me all by yourself?"

"Yes."

He turned away to the wall and whispered: "They ought to be ashamed, the rats. Leaving it all to you...."

The fever had left him with the complication of slight deafness. The doctor sent by the Tsaritsin Party Committee told Anna that it would be possible to cure it only when he was thoroughly well again. He made slow progress. He had a wolfish appetite, but Anna strictly apportioned his diet. There was more than one quarrel between them on this account.

"Give me some more milk," he would ask.

"You can't have any more."

"Please ... give me some more. Do you want me to die of starvation?"

"Ilya, you know that I mustn't give you more than a certain amount."

He would lapse into an injured silence, turn his face to the wall, sigh and refuse to talk. Although suffering with tenderness for him, she would not yield. After a little while he would turn back, his face clouded and looking even more unhappy, and plead:

"Can't I have some pickled cabbage? Please, Anna dear.... Listen.... It's all doctor's fairy stories that it's bad for me."

Always meeting with a decided refusal, he sometimes wounded her with harsh remarks:

"You have no right to make fun of me like this. You're an unfeeling and heartless woman. I'm beginning to hate you."

"That would be the best reward I could have for what I have gone through in nursing you," she could not restrain herself.

"I didn't ask you to stay with me. It's not fair to reproach me with that. You're exploiting your position. All right! Don't give me anything. Let me die! It won't be such a great pity!"

Her lips trembled, but she kept her self-control, and patiently endured all. But once, after they had quarrelled over an extra helping of dinner, she noticed with a tightening of her heart that tears were glittering in his eyes. "Why, you're a perfect child!" she exclaimed, and ran to the kitchen to bring back a full plate of patties.

"Eat, eat, Ilya dear. Don't get angry any more. Here's an extra nice one." With trembling fingers she thrust a patty into his hands.

Suffering intensely, Bunchuk attempted to refuse. But he could not hold out; wiping away his tears, he sat up and ate the patty. A guilty smile slipped over his emaciated bearded face, and asking forgiveness with his eyes, he said:

"I'm worse than a child. You see, I almost cried...."

She looked at his terribly thin neck, at the sunken, fleshless chest visible through the open shirt collar, at his bony arms. Troubled by a deep love and pity, for the first time she simply and tenderly kissed his dry, yellow brow.

Only after a fortnight was he able to move about the room without assistance. His spidery legs collapsed under him, and he had to learn to walk.

"Look, Anna, I can walk," he exclaimed, and tried to move more quickly. But his legs could not support the weight of his body, and the floor was slipping from under his feet. Compelled to lean against the first available support, he smiled like an old man, and the skin on his translucent cheeks tightened into furrows. He gave a croaking little laugh, and weak with his efforts, fell back on the bed.

Their rooms were close to the quay. From the window they could see the snowy stretch of the Volga, beyond it the forests sweeping in a dark semicircle, and the soft, undulating outlines of distant fields. Anna often stood by the window, thinking over the strange and violent change that had occurred in her life. In a strange way Bunchuk's illness had brought them very close together.

At first, when after a long and arduous journey they had arrived at Tsaritsin, her life had been burdensome and bitter to the point of tears. Never before had she had to look so closely and nakedly at the reverse side of living with one's beloved. Clenching her teeth, she had changed his linen, combed the insects out of his feverish head, struggled to lift his heavy body and with shuddering and aversion had glanced stealthily at his emaciated, naked masculine form, at the envelope under which the dear life was hardly warm. Everything in her had risen up and revolted, but the external filth could not crush the deeply and faithfully cherished feeling. Under its powerful command she had learned to overcome her pain and incomprehension. And at last all that was left was compassion and a deep well of love which beat and soaked through to the surface.

Once Bunchuk happened to ask her:

"I suppose I'm repellent to you after all this . . . am I?"

"It was a test."

"What of? Your self-control?"

"No. My feelings."

He turned away, and for a long time could not restrain his lips from trembling. They did not refer again to the subject. Words would have been superfluous and colourless.

In the middle of January they left for Voronezh.

XVII

Bunchuk and Anna arrived at Voronezh on the evening of January 16th. They spent two days there, then, learning that the Don Revolutionary Committee and its forces had been driven out of Kamenskaya by the Chernetsov troops, they followed it to Millerovo.

Millerovo was alive and bustling with people. Bunchuk remained there only a few hours, and left by the next train for Glubokaya. The next day he resumed command of the machine-gun detachment, and the following morning took part in the battle which ended in the defeat of the Chernetsov forces.

After Chernetsov had been smashed, Bunchuk unexpectedly had to part with Anna. One morning she came running in from staff headquarters, excited and a little sad.

"Do you know, Abramson's here. He wants to see you badly. And I've some more news. . . . I'm going away today."

"Where to?" he asked in amazement.

"Abramson, several other comrades and I are going to Lugansk on agitation work."

"So you're deserting our detachment?" he asked coldly.

She laughed and pressed her flushed face against his chest.

"Confess! You aren't sad because I'm deserting the detachment, but because I'm deserting you! But it's only for a time. I'm sure I'll be of more service in that work than with you. Agitation's more in my line than machine-guns," she gave him a roguish look, "even under so experienced a commander as Bunchuk."

Abramson came in shortly after. As usual he was active, restless, bubbling with energy. The white lock of his tar-black hair was as dazzling as ever. He was sincerely glad to see Bunchuk.

"Up again? That's fine. We're taking Anna back with us." He screwed up his eyes knowingly. "No objection on your part? None? That's good. I only asked because I thought the two of you got friendly in Tsaritsin."

"I can't deny that I regret parting with her." Bunchuk gave a strained sombre smile.

"You're sorry? Well, that's something. . . . Anna, did you hear?"

He walked up and down the room, picking up a dusty novel from behind a trunk as he passed it, then shook himself and prepared to go.

"Will you be ready soon, Anna?"

"You go, I'll come in a minute," she answered from behind the screen where she was changing her clothes. When she came out she was wearing a soldier's khaki tunic girdled with a leather belt, the pockets stood out a little over her breasts; her old black skirt was patched in places but spotlessly clean. She had recently washed her hair, and it fluffed and broke away from its bun. She put on her overcoat and asked, in a voice which had lost all its previous vivacity and was dull and pleading:

"Will you be taking part in the attack today?"

"Why, of course! Do you expect me to sit doing nothing?"

"I only ask you.... Listen, do be careful. You'll do that for my sake, won't you? I'm leaving you an extra pair of woollen socks. Don't catch cold, and try to keep your feet dry. I'll write to you from Lugansk."

The light suddenly faded from her eyes. As she said good-bye she confessed:

"You see, it's very painful for me to leave you. When Abramson suggested I should go to Lugansk I was delighted, but now I feel it will be empty there without you. Another proof that feeling is only in the way at present, it ties you down.... Well, in any case, good-bye."

She was cold and constrained in her farewell, but he understood that she was afraid of breaking down in her resolution.

He went to the door to see her off. She walked away hurriedly, swinging her shoulders and not looking round. He wanted to call her back, but he had noticed a moist glitter in her eyes as she had said good-bye for the last time, and mastering his desire, he shouted with feigned cheerfulness:

"I hope to see you in Rostov. Keep well, Anna!"

She glanced round over her shoulder, and hastened her steps.

After she had gone Bunchuk suddenly became terribly aware of his loneliness. He turned back into the house, but ran out again at once as though it were on fire. Everything there spoke of her. Everything retained her scent: the forgotten handkerchief, the soldier's pouch, the copper mug, everything her hands had touched.

Until nightfall he wandered about the stanitsa, experiencing an unusual anxiety and a feeling that something had been cut away from him. He could not get accustomed to his new situation. He stared abstractedly into the faces of Red Guards and Cossacks, recognizing some and being recognized by many others. He was stopped by a Cossack who had been in the army with him during the war. The man dragged him to his home and invited him to join in a game of cards with a number of other Red Guards and sailors. Enveloped in tobacco smoke, they slapped the cards down, rustled their Kerensky ruble notes, and cursed and shouted incessantly. Bunchuk longed for air, and went outside. He was saved by having to take part in an attack an hour later.

XVIII

After Kaledin's death a Military Council was summoned on January 29th in Novocherkassk at which General Nazarov was appointed Provincial Ataman. Only a few delegates were present, mostly from the stanitsas of the southern districts. Assured of the support of this depleted Council, Nazarov proclaimed the mobilization of all Cossacks from eighteen to fifty years of age. But the Cossacks obeyed reluctantly, despite threats and the dispatch of armed detachments into the villages to enforce the order.

The day the Council began its work the 6th Don Cossack Regiment under Colonel Tatsin marched into Novocherkassk from the Rumanian Front after fighting its way through the ring of Bolshevik forces. It had been handled roughly at various points on the road from Yekaterinoslav but in spite of this arrived almost in full strength, with all its officers.

The regiment was given a ceremonial welcome. After a thanksgiving service in the Cathedral Square, General Nazarov thanked the Cossacks for maintaining their fine military discipline and for bringing their arms to defend the Don.

Not long afterwards the regiment was sent out to the front and the news reached Novocherkassk that under the influence of Bolshevik agitation the regiment had arbitrarily withdrawn from its positions and refused to defend the army government.

The Council was feeble in action. All felt that the result of the struggle against the Bolsheviks was a foregone conclusion. During the Council sessions Nazarov, formerly an energetic and vigorous general, sat with his head in his hands, as though lost in painful meditation.

The last hopes were collapsing like rotten wood. Already the rumble of artillery could be heard round Tikhoretskaya. It was rumoured that Red Cossack forces under Cornet Avtonomov were advancing on Rostov from Tsaritsin. Captain Chernov's White Guard detachment retreated to Rostov under fire from two sides and Kornilov, realizing that it was dangerous to remain in the town, decided on February 9th to retreat.

All day workers in the Temernik District sniped at the station and the officers' patrols.

Towards evening a long column wound its way out of Rostov, marching heavily over the half-melted snow. An occasional student's greatcoat was to be seen but most of them were officers' uniforms, and captains and colonels were in command of platoons. In the ranks were cadets and officers of all degrees from ensigns to colonels. Behind the numerous wagons of the baggage train came crowds of refugees: elderly, well-dressed men in overcoats and galoshes, and women wearing high-heeled shoes.

In one of the companies of soldiers was Captain Listnitsky. Beside him in the column marched a smart regular officer Staff-Captain Starobelsky, Ensign of the Suvorov Grenadiers Bocharov and Lieutenant-Colonel Lovichev, an aged toothless officer of the line, covered with reddish grey like an old fox.

The evening shadows gathered. There was frost in the air. A damp, salty breeze was blowing from the mouth of the Don. With the firmness of habit Listnitsky trod steadily over the churned-up snow, peering into the faces of those who overtook the company.

Captain Nezhentsev and Guards Colonel Kutyopov, formerly commander of the Preobrazhensky Regiment, his coat flapping open and his cap on the back of his head, went past at the side of the road. Nezhentsev was hailed by Lovichev.

Kutyopov turned his head; he had a great bull-like face with widely spaced black eyes and a broad clipped beard. Nezhentsev also turned and glanced over his shoulder in the direction of the shout.

"Order the first company to quicken their pace! We'll get frozen. Our feet are wet already and marching at this pace. . . ."

"It's nonsensical!" Starobelsky boomed.

Nezhentsev made no reply and walked on, arguing with Kutyopov. A little later they were overtaken by General Alexeyev. The carriage went by in a flurry of snow kicked up by the hoofs of two sleek black horses. Alexeyev, his moustache and eyebrows protruding whitely from his wind-reddened face, was sitting sideways on the seat, holding up his collar against the cold.

Yellow puddles appeared here and there on the heavily trodden road. The going was difficult, and the damp penetrated inside the boots. As he walked Listnitsky listened to the conversation of the men in front of him. An officer in a fur jacket and ordinary Cossack sheep-skin cap was saying:

"Did you see him, Lieutenant? Rodzyanko, the president of the State Duma, and an old man, forced to go on foot...."

"Russia is going to her Golgotha...."

Someone remarked ironically between coughs:

"A Golgotha, truly ... with the one difference that instead of a stony road we have snow, and devilish cold."

"Does anyone know where we shall be spending the night, gentlemen?"

"Yes, I remember, we did a march like this once in Prussia...."

"How will the Kuban greet us...? What...? Yes, of course, things will be different there."

"Have you anything to smoke?" a lieutenant asked Listnitsky. The man removed his mitten and took the cigarette Yevgeny offered, thanked him, and blew his nose on his hand soldier-fashion, afterwards wiping his fingers on his coat.

"You're acquiring democratic habits, Lieutenant," Lieutenant-Colonel Lovichev smiled sarcastically.

"One has to; there's no alternative. What do you do? Have you managed to salvage a dozen handkerchiefs?"

The lieutenant-colonel made no reply. Tiny green icicles were clinging to his reddish-grey moustache. Occasionally he snorted, frowning with the cold which penetrated through his overcoat.

"The flower of Russia!" Listnitsky thought, glancing with keen commiseration over the ranks of the column winding along the road.

A group of horsemen galloped past with Kornilov among them on a tall stallion. His white lambskin cap and short light-green greatcoat with slanting side-pockets bobbed away down the ranks. A throaty cheer from the officers' companies followed him.

"None of this would matter so much if it wasn't for the family...." Lieutenant-Colonel Lovichev gave an ageing cough and glanced sideways at Listnitsky as though in search of sympathy. "I left my family behind in Smolensk," he continued. "My wife and daughter. She was seventeen this Christmas. What do you think of that, Captain?"

"H-m-m...."

"Have you also a family? Are you from Novocherkassk?"

"No, I'm from the Don Province. My father's there."

"How they'll manage without me, I can't imagine ..." Lovichev went on.

He was interrupted by Starobelsky's irritable voice:

"We all have families we've left behind. I can't understand why you keep whining, Lieutenant-Colonel. What people you are! No sooner you have left Rostov...."

"Is that you, Starobelsky? Weren't you in the fighting at Taganrog?" someone shouted from the rear ranks.

Starobelsky turned round and his irritated face broke into a gloomy smile.

"Ah, Vladimir Georgievich, how do you come to be in our platoon? Transferred, eh? Whose toes have you been treading on? I see ... you were asking about Taganrog.... Yes, I was.... Why? Quite so ... he was killed."

As he listened inattentively to the conversation Listnitsky recalled his departure from Yagodnoye, his father, and Aksinya. He was choked by a sudden feeling of yearning. He tramped on, staring at the rifle-barrels and bayonets swinging in front of him, at the sheepskin hats, the peaked caps and the cowls swaying to the rhythm of the march, and thought:

"Every one of these five thousand ostracized beings is like me, and what a charge of hatred and boundless anger each of us carries in his heart. The swine have thrown us out of Russia, and think they will crush us here.

We shall see Kornilov leading us to Moscow yet!"

At that moment he remembered Kornilov's arrival in Moscow and gladly fell to thinking of that day.

Far behind in the rear of the company there was a battery. The horses snorted and the gun-carriages rattled, even the stench of horses' sweat reached Listnitsky's nostrils. The familiar, agitating smell made him turn his head; the leading driver, a young corporal, looked at him and smiled familiarly.

By the 11th of March the Volunteer Army was concentrated in the district of Olginskaya a few versts to the south-east of Rostov. Kornilov delayed any further movement, as he was expecting the arrival of General Popov, the newly appointed Ataman of the Don Cossack Army, who had retreated from Novocherkassk into the steppes to the east of the Don with a detachment of sixteen hundred men, five field-guns and forty machine-guns. Popov, accompanied by his chief of staff Sidorin and a Cossack escort, rode into Olginskaya on the 13th. He reined in his horse on the square in front of the house occupied by Kornilov and, gripping his saddle-bow, heaved his leg over the saddle. He was helped by an orderly, a young Cossack with a raven forelock, dark face and eyes as black as a lapwing's. Popov tossed him the reins and walked with slow dignity towards the porch, followed by Sidorin and other officers. The orderlies led the horses through a side-gate into the yard. While one of them, an elderly bow-legged cavalryman, put on the nose-bags, the black-haired fellow with eyes like a lapwing's had been getting to know the kitchen maid. He had twitted her about something and the girl, a rosy wench with her kerchief tied coquettishly and wearing big galoshes over her bare feet, was making her way past him, slipping and laughing, through a puddle to the barn.

Popov, elderly, dignified, entered the house. In the hall he gave his coat to an attentively efficient orderly, hung up his whip and blew his nose noisily and at great length. The orderly showed him and Sidorin into the drawing-room.

The generals who had been summoned to the conference were already assembled. Kornilov sat at a table with his elbows on a map spread over its top; on his right was Alexeyev, straight, clean-shaven, a whitish grey all over. Denikin with a gleam in his shrewd eyes was discussing something with Romanovsky. Lukomsky, rather like Denikin, was pacing about the room, plucking at his beard. Markov stood by the window overlooking the yard; he was watching the two orderlies tending the horses and exchanging pleasantries with the kitchen maid.

The two newcomers greeted the generals assembled for the conference and went to the table. Alexeyev asked a few unimportant questions concerning their journey and the evacuation of Novocherkassk. Kutyopov entered, accompanied by several line officers whom Kornilov had invited to the conference.

Staring fixedly at Popov, who had seated himself calmly at the table, Kornilov asked:

"General, tell us the size of your detachment."

"Fifteen hundred sabres, a battery, and forty machine-guns with their complement."

"You know the circumstances which compelled the Volunteer Army to evacuate Rostov. We held a conference yesterday, and took the decision to march to the Kuban, in the direction of Yekaterinodar, where volunteer detachments are already in action. We shall take this route." He passed the blunt end of his pencil over the map, and went on hurriedly: "We shall draw in the Kuban Cossacks as we march, shattering the few unorganized and feeble Red Guard detachments which may attempt to impede our movement." He followed Popov's eyes in their narrowed sideways

479

glance. "We propose that you join the Volunteer Army with your detachment and march with us to Yekaterinodar. It is not to our interest to split up our forces."

"I cannot do that," Popov announced sharply and resolutely.

Alexeyev bent a little in his direction. "Why not, if I may ask?"

"Because I cannot abandon the territory of the Don Province and retire into the Kuban. We have the protection of the Don on the north and shall await events in the steppe. We cannot count on any active movement on the part of the enemy, because the thaw will set in soon, and it will be impossible to send artillery or even cavalry across the Don. From the area we have chosen, which is well supplied with forage and provisions, we can develop guerilla activities at any moment and in any direction."

There was impressive assurance in the way he put aside Kornilov's arguments. He stopped for breath, but, seeing that Kornilov was about to speak, obstinately shook his head.

"Let me finish. In addition there is one very important factor, and we of the high command have got to take it into account. That is the attitude of our Cossacks." He held out a soft white hand with a gold ring, deeply embedded in the flesh of the index finger, and, raising his voice a little, went on: "If we retreat to the Kuban there is a danger of our detachment breaking up. The Cossacks may refuse to go. It must not be overlooked that the permanent and the strongest contingent of my detachment consists of Cossacks, and they are by no means so morally reliable as ... as your own men, for instance. They don't understand. They simply won't go. And I cannot risk losing my whole detachment." He rapped out the words and then interrupted Kornilov again: "You must pardon me. I have told you our decision and must assure you that we are not in a position to change it. Of course it is not to our interest to split our forces, but there is one way out of the difficulty. I suggest that, taking what I have said into account, it would be more sensible for the Volunteer Army not to retreat into the Kuban, but to join the Don detachment in the steppe beyond the Don. There it will be able to rest and recuperate and in the spring will be reinforced by fresh volunteers from Russia...."

"No!" exclaimed Kornilov, who the day before had himself been in favour of retiring into the steppes beyond the Don and had contested Alexeyev's opinion to the contrary. "There is no sense in going into the steppe. We have nearly six thousand men...."

"If you are concerned about provisions, I can assure you, Your Excellency, that no region could be better supplied than the trans-Don steppe. Moreover, you will be able to take horses from the private stables there and put part of your army on horseback. You will then have a better chance in a war of movement. You must have cavalry and at present the Volunteer Army is short of it."

Kornilov, that day more than usually attentive to Alexeyev, looked at him, evidently uncertain which course to take, and seeking support from another authority. Alexeyev was listened to with great attention. Accustomed to deciding questions quickly and with complete clarity, the old general expressed himself briefly in favour of the march to Yekaterinodar.

"In that direction it will be easier for us to break through the Bolshevik ring and to join forces with the detachment already in action there," he ended.

"But if we don't succeed?" Lukomsky asked cautiously.

Alexeyev bit his lips and ran his finger over the map. "Even if we're not successful," he said, "we still have the possibility of retreating to the Caucasus mountains and there dispersing the army."

He was supported by Romanovsky. Markov spoke a few fiery phrases. It seemed there was nothing to be said against Alexeyev's weighty arguments, but Lukomsky's words evened the scale.

"I support General Popov's suggestion," he announced, choosing his words slowly and carefully. "A march to the Kuban entails great difficulties that cannot be estimated from here. In the first place, we shall twice have to cross railways. . . ."

All eyes followed the direction of his finger as it moved across the map. Lukomsky went on stubbornly:

"The Bolsheviks will not fail to give us a proper welcome. They will use armoured trains. We have heavy baggage trains and a large number of wounded that can't be left behind. It will all be a tremendous burden on the army and hinder its progress. In addition, I can't understand the readiness to believe that the Cossacks of the Kuban are friendly towards us. If we take as an example the Don Cossacks, who were supposed to be weary of Bolshevik power, we should be doubly cautious and treat all such rumours with a large dose of scepticism. The Kuban Cossacks suffer from the same Bolshevik trachoma that has spread from the former Russian army. They may even be hostile towards us. Finally, I must repeat, my opinion is that we should go east, into the steppes, and when we have recuperated, threaten the Bolsheviks from there."

Supported by the majority of his generals, Kornilov held to his decision to march by a devious route into the Kuban, collecting horses for the equipment of cavalry as he went. The conference broke up. Kornilov exchanged a few words with Popov, coldly said good-bye and went to his room, followed by Alexeyev. Colonel Sidorin went out into the porch, and cried cheerfully to his aide-de-camp:

"The horses!"

A young, blond Cossack lieutenant, holding his sabre as he stepped over the puddles, came up to him. He halted on the lowest step, and asked in a whisper:

"Well, what decision, Colonel?"

"Not bad!" Sidorin replied in an undertone, with jubilation in his voice. "We've refused to march to the Kuban. We're leaving at once. Are you ready, Izvarin?"

"Yes. They're bringing the horses."

The orderlies brought over the horses. The one with the black forelock and eyes like a lapwing's was winking at his companion.

"She's good, isn't she?" he asked with a snort of laughter.

The older man grinned reservedly.

"Good as a horse with ring-worm."

"She might ask you in though."

"Forget it, you jackals. We're in lent."

Izvarin, Grigory Melekhov's old friend, mounted his clumsy white-muzzled horse and gave the order to ride into the street. Popov and Sidorin, accompanied by some of the generals, came down the front steps. One of the escort held General Popov's horse and helped him to find his stirrup. Waving his simple Cossack whip, Popov put his horse into a trot, and behind him, standing in the stirrups and leaning a little forward, came Sidorin, the other officers and the Cossacks.

When the Volunteer Army reached Mechetinskaya after two day's march, Kornilov received further reports concerning the eastern steppes. The reports were unfavourable. Kornilov summoned the commanders of the fighting units and announced his intention of making for the Kuban.

A messenger was sent to Popov with a second invitation to join forces. The reply was the same. With cold politeness Popov refused, writing that his decision could not be altered and that he would remain for the time being in the region east of the Don.

XIX

Golubov's detachment was sent by the Revolutionary Committee in a wide encircling movement to capture Novocherkassk, and Bunchuk went with it. Golubov led the detachment at a swift pace, riding at its head and bringing his whip impatiently down across his horse's croup. At night they entered a stanitsa, and after resting their horses a little, rode out again into the grey starless night, the ice-crusted road crunching under their hoofs. Dawn was breaking when they passed through another stanitsa. The streets were still deserted, but near the square an old Cossack was breaking the ice in a trough by a well. Golubov rode up to him, while the detachment halted.

"Hullo there," the commander greeted the Cossack.

The man slowly raised his mittened hand to his sheepskin cap, and replied in an unfriendly tone:

"Good morning."

"Well, Grandad, have your Cossacks gone off to Novocherkassk? Has there been mobilization in your village?"

Without answering the old man hurriedly picked up his axe and disappeared through the gateway of his yard.

"Forward!" Golubov cried, and rode off cursing.

That same day the Army Council was preparing to evacuate Novocherkassk. The newly-appointed field Ataman of the Don Cossack Army, General Popov, had already withdrawn the armed forces from the town and removed all the military supplies. Meeting with no opposition, Golubov's cavalry entered Novocherkassk unexpectedly. Golubov himself, accompanied by a large detachment of Cossacks, galloped up to the headquarters of the Council. A crowd of gaping sight-seers was gathered at the gate, and a courier was waiting with General Nazarov's saddled horse.

Bunchuk jumped from his horse and seized his light machine-gun. With Golubov and the other Cossacks he ran into the house. At the sound of the door being flung open, the delegates assembled in the spacious hall turned white faces towards the newcomers.

"Stand up!" Golubov commanded tensely, as though on parade ground. Surrounded by Cossacks, stumbling in his haste, he strode to the head of the table. At the authoritative shout the members of the Council rose with a scraping of chairs, only Nazarov remaining seated.

"How dare you interrupt a session of the

Army Council?" the general demanded in an angry voice.

"You are arrested! Silence!" Golubov turned livid. He ran up to Nazarov, tore the epaulettes from the general's uniform, and roared hoarsely: "Stand up, I tell you! Take him away! Who am I talking to? You, brass hat!"

Bunchuk had set up his machine-gun at the door. The members of the Council herded together like sheep. Past Bunchuk the Cossacks dragged Nazarov, the grey-faced Voloshinov, President of the Council, and several others. His sword clattering, his face crimson, Golubov followed them. One of the members of the Council caught at his sleeve.

"Where are we to go, Colonel, sir?"

Another thrust his head over Golubov's shoulder. "Are we free?"

"Go to the devil!" the commander shouted, pushing them away; as he reached Bunchuk he turned on them and stamped his foot. "Clear off to hell! I don't want you! Well, what are you waiting for?"

For some time his weather-beaten voice continued to resound round the hall.

Bunchuk spent the night in his mother's house. Next day the news came that Rostov had been captured. He at once obtained Golubov's permission to go to Rostov, and rode off the next morning.

Arriving in Rostov, he worked for two days in the staff headquarters, and visited the offices of the Revolutionary Committee. But neither Abramson nor Anna was there. At headquarters a revolutionary tribunal had been organized to mete out summary justice to captured White Guards. Bunchuk worked for a day in the court and took part in raids, and on the following day went again, without much hope, to the Revolutionary Committee. As he was going up the stairs he heard Anna's voice coming from a room above. The blood rushed to his heart as he heard her laugh. He slowed his steps, and pushed open the door. The room, which had formerly belonged to the commandant, was thick with tobacco smoke. A man in a button-less greatcoat was writing at a small ladies' desk, soldiers and civilians in sheepskins and overcoats were crowding round him. He saw Anna standing at the window with her back to the door. Abramson was sitting on the window-ledge with hands clasped round his knee, and a tall Red Guard with Lettish features was standing at his side. His little finger cocked, the man was rolling a cigarette and talking; evidently he was telling of some humorous incident, for Anna had her head thrown back in a laugh, and Abramson's smiling face was furrowed like a melon-skin; the Red Guard's massively hewn features glowed with a sharp and rather fierce intelligence.

Bunchuk walked across and laid his hand on Anna's shoulder.

"Hullo, Anna!"

She looked round. The colour flooded her face and flowed down to her collar-bones, and tears started to her eyes.

"Where have you come from? See, Abramson! He's looking like a new coin, and you were anxious about him!" she stammered without raising her eyes. Unable to control her agitation, she turned and walked towards the door.

Bunchuk squeezed Abramson's hot hand, exchanged a few words with him, and then, leaving a question of Abramson's unanswered (he had not even understood its meaning), with a foolish, boundlessly happy smile on his face went to Anna. She had recovered her self-control and welcomed him with a smile, a little annoyed at her own embarrassment.

"Well, and how are you?" she asked. "When did you arrive? Are you from Novocherkassk? Were you in Golubov's detachment? Well, what's the news?"

He answered her questions without removing

his unblinking, heavy gaze from her face. Her own eyes faltered and turned away from his.

"Let's go outside for a minute," she proposed.

As they turned to go, Abramson called after them: "You'll be back soon? I've got work for you, Comrade Bunchuk. We're already thinking of making use of you."

"I'll be back in an hour."

In the street Anna gazed straight into Bunchuk's eyes, and waved her hand angrily:

"Ilya, Ilya, how badly I lost control of myself! Just like a young girl! It was because of the unexpectedness of seeing you, and also because of our half-and-half relation to each other. Really though, what is my relation to you? That of an idyllic engaged couple? You know, at Lugansk Abramson once asked me: 'Are you living with Bunchuk?' I denied it, but he's a very observant man and can't help seeing what's happening right under his eyes. He didn't say anything, but I could see by his look that he didn't believe me."

"But tell me all about yourself."

"Oh, how we made the work go at Lugansk! We gathered a detachment of two hundred and eleven bayonets. We carried on organizational and political activities ... but I can't tell you all about it in two words! I still can't get over

your unexpected arrival. Where are you ...
where are you spending the night?" she asked.

"At a comrade's house." He stammered over
the lie, for he had spent his nights in the staff
headquarters.

"You'll transfer to our house this very day!
Do you remember where I live? You took me
home once."

"I'll find it. But ... isn't it rather crowding
you?"

"Don't be silly! You'll be crowding nobody,
and in any case it isn't worth talking about."

In the evening he collected his belongings in
his capacious soldier's kit-bag, and went to the
street on the outskirts where Anna lived. On
the threshold of a small brick house he was met
by an old woman. Her features had some distant
resemblance to Anna's; she had the same bluish-
black glitter in her eyes and a slightly hooked
nose, but her furrowed and earthy skin and her
sunken mouth betrayed her age.

"Are you Bunchuk?" she asked.

"Yes."

"Come in, won't you? My daughter has told
me about you."

She led him into a small room, showed him
where to put his things, and with rheumatically
contorted fingers pointed around the room.

"This is where you will sleep. That's your bed."

She spoke with a noticeably Jewish accent. Besides her in the house there was a young girl, rather frail but deep-eyed like Anna.

A little while later Anna herself arrived, bringing life and animation with her.

"Has anyone been? Has Bunchuk arrived?"

Her mother replied in Yiddish, and Anna strode firmly to the door of Bunchuk's room.

"May I come in?"

"Yes, yes." He rose from the chair and went to meet her.

"Well, is everything all right?"

She looked him over with a satisfied, smiling glance, and asked:

"Have you had anything to eat? Come into the other room."

She led him by his sleeve into the larger room, and said:

"Mother, this is my comrade." And she smiled.

During the night shots cracked like ripe acacia seed-pods over Rostov. Occasionally a machine-gun rattled; then the sound died away, and the night, the gracious, sombre February night, wrapped the streets again in silence. Bunchuk and Anna sat up late in his scrupulously tidy little room.

"I lived here with my little sister," she told him. "You see how modestly we lived—just like nuns. No cheap pictures, or photographs, nothing to show that I was a student in the high school."

"How did you manage?" he asked her.

Not without pride she replied: "I worked at a factory and gave lessons."

"And now?"

"Mother takes in sewing. The two of them need very little."

He told her the details of the capture of Novocherkassk, and the battles in which he had taken part since she left him. She gave him impressions of her work in Lugansk and Taganrog. At eleven o'clock, as soon as her mother had put out the light in her room, she said good-night and left him.

XX

Bunchuk was assigned to work in the Revolutionary Tribunal attached to the Don Revolutionary Committee. The tall chairman of the Tribunal, hollow-cheeked, his eyes faded with incessant work and sleepless nights, led Bunchuk to the window of his room. Fingering his wrist-watch (he was late for a conference) he asked:

"When did you join the Party? Aha, good! Well, you will be our commandant. Last night we sent our previous commandant to join Kaledin, because he was taking bribes. He was nothing but a sadist, a bestial swine, and we don't want that type in our ranks. It's dirty work we're doing, but we must retain full consciousness of our responsibility to the Party. Understand correctly what I'm saying." He laid extra emphasis on this phrase. "We must preserve our humanity. Of necessity we are physically exterminating the counter-revolutionaries, but we must not make a circus of the job. You understand me? Well, that's good. Now go and take over."

That same night Bunchuk, in charge of a squad of Red Guards, shot five counter-revolutionaries at midnight, taking them some three versts outside the town. Among them were two Cossacks, the rest inhabitants of Rostov. Almost every night thereafter they drove those sentenced to death out of the town in a lorry, and hasty graves were dug, some of the Red Guards and the condemned working side by side. Then Bunchuk would draw up his squad of Red Guards, and with a dull metallic ring in his voice gave the command:

"At the enemies of the Revolution ..." a wave of his revolver, "fire!"

After a week of this work, he withered and darkened, as though he had been rubbed with ashes. His eyes became sunken, and the nervously twitching eyelids failed to hide their cold, yearning glitter. Anna saw him only at night, for she was working in the Revolutionary Committee and came home late. But she always waited up until the familiar knock at the window told of his arrival.

One night he returned as usual after midnight. She opened the door and asked:

"Will you have some supper?"

He did not reply, but passed into his own room, stumbling drunkenly. He flung himself just as he was, in greatcoat, boots and cap, on to his bed. Anna went to him and glanced into his face: his eyes were stickily filmed, saliva glistened on his bared teeth, and his hair, thin after typhus, lay in damp strands over his forehead.

She sat down at his side. Pity and pain clawed at her heart. She whispered:

"Is it hard for you, Ilya?"

He squeezed her hand, clenched his teeth, and turned away to the wall. So he fell asleep, not saying a word. He muttered indistinctly and miserably in his sleep, and tried to jump up. She watched him in terror, and shuddered with unaccountable fear. He slept with eyes half-closed, and the prominent yellowish eye-balls gleamed feverishly under their lids.

"Give up this job!" she told him in the morning. "Go to the front. You're looking like nothing on earth, Ilya. You'll perish at this work."

"Shut up!" he shouted, his eyes blinking with rage.

"Don't shout! Have I offended you?"

He was quiet at once, as though his shout had released the fury pent up in his breast. He looked wearily at his palms, and said:

"The destruction of human filth is a filthy business. Shooting people is bad for the health and for the mind. Damn it all...." For the first time he cursed indescribably in her presence. "It's only fools and beasts, or fanatics, who volunteer for such filthy work. Isn't that so? We all want to live in a flowers garden. But damn it all! Before the flowers and trees can be planted the dirt must be cleared away. The earth must be dunged! You've got to get your hands dirty!" He raised his voice, although Anna had turned silently away. "The filth must be destroyed, and yet people are squeamish about the job!" he shouted, thundering his fists on the table and blinking his bloodshot eyes.

Anna's mother glanced into the room, and he recollected himself and spoke more quietly:

"I won't give up this work! I see, I feel positively that I am being of service here. I shall rake away the filth, I shall dung the earth, so that it will be more fertile. More fruitful. Some day happy people will walk this earth.... Perhaps my own son, that I haven't got, will walk here too!" He laughed gratingly and joylessly. "How many of these serpents, these ticks, have I shot! The tick is an insect that eats into the body. I've killed dozens with these hands." He stretched out his long-nailed, black-haired hands, clenched like a vulture's talons, then dropped them on to his knees and said in a whisper: "To hell with it all. We've got to burn, burn so there'll be no smoke to foul the air. . . . Only, I'm tired . . . that's true. A little more, and then I'll go off to the front. . . . You're right. . . ."

She said quietly: "Yes, go to the front or get on to other work. Do, Ilya, or you'll . . . go out of your mind."

He turned his back to her and drummed on the window.

"No . . . I'm strong enough. Don't think that there are any men made of iron. We're all made of the same stuff. In real life there isn't a man without fear in battle, and not a man who can kill people without feeling . . . without getting morally scarred. I don't feel any regret for the officers. They're class-conscious like you and me. But yesterday I had to shoot three Cossacks among the rest . . . three toilers. I began to untie one. . . ." His voice became hollow and indistinct, as though he were going farther and farther away. "I happened to touch his hand,

and it was as hard as book-leather, covered with calluses. A black palm, all cuts and lumps. . . . Well, I must be going." He broke off harshly and, turning away to avoid Anna's eyes, rubbed his throat that felt as if it were corded with a horsehair noose.

He pulled on his boots, drank a glass of milk and went out. In the passage Anna overtook him. She stood holding his heavy hand in her own, then she pressed it to her flaming cheek and ran out into the yard.

The weather turned warmer. Spring came knocking at the lands of the Don. At the beginning of April detachments of Ukrainian Red Guards driven back by the Haidamaks* and the Germans began to arrive in Rostov. Murders, pillaging, unauthorized requisitions occurred in the town. The Revolutionary Committee was compelled to disarm certain completely demoralized units. The task was not accomplished without conflicts and exchanges of fire. Around Novocherkassk the Cossacks were stirring. In March, like buds on the poplars, clashes broke out in the villages between the Cossacks and the aliens, risings rumbled here and there, and counter-revolutionary conspiracies were discov-

* Ukrainian nationalist forces.

ered. But Rostov went on living a passionate full-blooded life. Crowds of soldiers, sailors and workers promenaded up and down the main street of an evening. They held meetings, they husked sunflower seeds, spat on the wet pavements, and flirted with the women. As before, they worked, ate, drank, slept, died, gave birth, made love, hated, breathed the salty sea breeze, and lived in the grip of great and petty passions. Days sown with menace were approaching Rostov. The air was laden with the scent of the thawing black earth and the blood of imminent battles.

One sunny, pleasant day Bunchuk returned home earlier than usual, and was surprised to find Anna already there.

"But you're always so late; why are you early today?"

"I'm not feeling well."

She followed him into his room. He removed his outdoor clothes, and said with a smile that quivered with joy:

"Anna, after today I won't be working in the Tribunal."

"What? Where are you going?"

"To the Revolutionary Committee. I had a talk with Krivoshlykov today. He promised to send me somewhere into the district."

They had supper together, and afterwards he

lay down to sleep. In his agitation he could not get to sleep for a long time, but lay smoking, tossing on the hard mattress. He was greatly relieved to be leaving the Tribunal, for he had felt that it would not take much more for him to break down under the strain. He was finishing his fourth cigarette when he heard the light scrape of the door. Raising his head, he saw Anna. Barefoot, and wearing only her shift, she slipped across the threshold and quietly approached his bed. Through a chink in the shutter the misty green light of the moon fell on her bare shoulders. She bent over him and laid a warm hand on his lips.

"Move over.... Quiet...."

She lay down beside him.

She impatiently brushed back a strand of hair, as heavy as a bunch of grapes, from her forehead. Her eyes smoked with a bluish fire, and she whispered roughly, tormentedly:

"If not today, then tomorrow I may be deprived of you.... I want to love you with all my strength." She shuddered violently with her own resolution. "Well, be quick!"

Bunchuk kissed her, but with horror, with a great shame that overwhelmed his consciousness, he realized that he was impotent. His head shook and his cheeks flamed with his torture. After a moment Anna released herself and angrily thrust him off. With loathing and aversion in her voice she asked in a contemptuous whisper:

"Can't . . . can't you? Or are you . . . ill? Oh, how abominable. . .! Leave me alone!"

He squeezed her fingers so tightly that they cracked a little, stared into the misty blackness of her dilated, hostile eyes and stammeringly asked, his head twitching paralytically:

"Why? What are you condemning me for? Yes, I've burned myself out, to ashes . . .! Even for this I haven't the strength at the moment. I'm not ill. . . . Understand . . . try to understand! I've been drained to the dregs. . . ."

He gave a low moan, jumped out of bed and lit a cigarette. For a long time he stood by the window with sagging shoulders. Anna rose, silently embraced him, and as calmly as a mother kissed him on the brow.

But after a week, Anna, hiding her burning face under his arm, confessed:

"I thought . . . you had been with some other. . . . I didn't realize that the work had exhausted you so much."

And for long afterwards Bunchuk felt not only the caresses of a woman in love, but the warm, full-flowing care of a mother.

He was not sent into the country. Podtyolkov insisted that he be retained in Rostov. The Don Revolutionary Committee was seething with activity, preparing for a provincial Congress of Soviets and for a struggle against the counter-revolution that was raising its head in the Don area.

XXI

The frogs were croaking beyond the river-side willows. The sun was disappearing behind a low hill, and the cool of evening was soaking into the village of Syetrakov. Enormous slanting shadows cast by the houses fell athwart the dusty road. The village cattle were straggling slowly from the steppe. The Cossack women drove them on with twigs, exchanging gossip as they went. The barefoot children, already sun-burnt, were playing leap-frog in the side alleys. The old men were sitting with dignity on the ledges of the house walls.

The village had finished the spring sowing. Only here and there they were still sowing sun-flowers and millet.

A group of Cossacks was sitting on a pile of felled oak-trees close to one of the houses on the outskirts of the village. The master of the house, a pock-marked artilleryman, was telling of some incident in the German war. His audience, an old neighbour and his son-in-law, were listening in silence. The artilleryman's wife, a handsome woman, came down the steps. The sleeves of her rose-coloured blouse, tucked into her skirt, were rolled up to the elbows and revealed her dark, shapely arms. She was carrying a pitcher, and went to the cattle-yard with that free, sweeping, elegant stride peculiar to Cossack women. Her hair was escaping from its white kerchief (she had just been laying the stove for the morrow) and the sandals on her bare feet slapped along, pressing lightly on the young grass overgrowing the yard.

The sound of milk streaming into the pitcher came to the ears of the Cossacks. The mistress finished milking and, bending forward a little with her left arm curved upward like a swan's neck, carried the full pitcher of milk back to the house.

"Semyon, you'd better go and look for the calf," she called from the steps.

"And where's Mitka?" her husband asked.

"The devil knows; he's run off somewhere."

The Cossack rose unhurriedly and went to the corner of the street. The old man and his son-in-law turned to go home. But the Cossack called to them from the corner:

"Look, Dorofei Gavrilich! Come here!"

The two men went across to the Cossack, who silently pointed out into the steppe. In a ruddy cloud of dust a column of infantry, cavalry and wagons was advancing along the road.

"Soldiers, it seems," the old man screwed his eyes in astonishment and set his palm to his white eyebrows.

"Whose might they be?" the Cossack said with a note of alarm in his voice.

His wife came out of the yard gate, her jacket flung across her shoulders. She gazed into the steppe and gasped anxiously: "Who are they? Merciful Lord, how many there are!"

"They're not out for any good, that's certain. . . ."

The old man turned and went into the yard, shouting to his son-in-law:

"Come into the yard; there's no need to stand and stare."

Children and women came running to the corner, followed by groups of Cossacks. The column of soldiers wound along the road across the steppe about a verst from the village. The wind brought the sound of their voices, the snorting of horses, the rumble of wheels.

"They're not Cossacks; they're not our folk," the artilleryman's wife said to him. He shrugged his shoulders.

"Of course they're not Cossacks. Maybe they're Germans? No, they're Russians. Look, you can see their red flag. . . . So that's it. . . ."

A tall Cossack came up. He was evidently suffering from malaria, for he was a sandy yellow and was wrapped up in a sheepskin and felt boots. He raised his shaggy sheepskin cap and said:

"You see that flag? They're Bolsheviks."

"It's them all right."

Several riders broke away from the head of the column and galloped towards the village. The Cossacks exchanged glances and silently began to melt away; the girls and children scattered in all directions. In a few minutes the street was deserted. The group of riders galloped into the village and rode up to the oaks where a few minutes earlier the three Cossacks had been sitting. The artilleryman was standing by his gate. The leader of the riders, in a Kuban hat and with a great crimson silk scarf across his belted khaki tunic, rode up to him.

"Hullo there, Cossack! Open the gate!"

The Cossack turned pale and removed his cap.

"And who may you be?"

"Open the gate!" the soldier shouted.

The horse, with an evil look in its eye and champing at the bit, struck its fore-feet against the wattle fence. The Cossack opened the wicket-gate, and the riders rode into the yard in single file. Their leader jumped nimbly from his saddle and strode towards the steps. Before the others had dismounted he had reached them, seated himself, lit a cigarette and offered the Cossack his case. The man refused.

"Don't you smoke?"

"No, thank you."

"You're not Old Believers here?"

"No, we're Orthodox. And who may you be?"

"Who are we? Red Guards of the Second Socialist Army."

The other riders hurried towards the steps, leading their horses. They tied them to the railing. One of them, a tall man with hair falling like a horse's mane over his brow, went to the sheep-pen. He threw open the gate as though he were the master, bent down, fumbled at the partition of the pen, and dragged out a large sheep by its horns.

"Pyotr, come and give me a hand," he cried in a high falsetto voice.

A soldier in an Austrian greatcoat ran to help him. The Cossack master stroked his beard and looked about him as though he were in someone else's yard. He said nothing, and only grunted and went up the steps into the house when the sheep, its throat slit by a sabre, doubled up its thin legs.

The soldier in the Kuban hat and two others, one a Chinese, the other a Russian, followed him into the kitchen.

"Don't take offence, Cossack," the leader shouted carelessly as he crossed the threshold. "We'll pay good money."

He clapped his hand against the pocket of his trousers and laughed aloud. But the laugh suddenly died away as his eyes fell on the Cossack's wife. She was standing by the stove, her teeth clenched, staring at him with terrified eyes. His eyes shifting restlessly around the kitchen, he turned to the Chinese and said: "You go with this man," he pointed to the Cossack. "Go with him, he'll give you hay for the horses. Let us have some hay," he turned to the Cossack. "We'll pay good money for it. The Red Guard never pillages. Off you go, Cossack, off you go!" A steely note sounded in his voice.

Accompanied by the Chinese and another soldier, the Cossack went out of the house, glancing over his shoulder. He was going down the steps when he heard his wife calling in a weeping voice. He ran back into the passage and wrenched at the door. The catch gave way easily. The soldier had seized the woman's arm above the elbow and was dragging her into the twilit front room. She was resisting, pushing at his chest with her hands. He was on the point of putting his arms around her waist and carrying her off bodily, but at that moment the door flew open. The Cossack strode across the kitchen and placed himself in front of his wife. His voice was hard and low:

"You came as a guest into my home. . . . Why are you harming my woman? Leave her alone. I'm not afraid of your guns. Take whatever you want, steal everything, but don't lay hands on my wife. You'll do that across my body. And you, Nyura . . ." his nostrils quivering, he turned to his wife. "You go along to Uncle Dorofei. There's no point in your staying here."

Adjusting the straps across his shirt, the soldier smiled wrily.

"You get upset easily, Cossack. You won't even let a man have his little joke. I'm the joker of the whole company, don't you know? I did it on purpose. 'I'll just see what the woman's like,' I thought; but she started bawling. Are you letting us have some hay? Nothing doing? Well, has your neighbour got any?"

He went out whistling, vigorously waving his whip. Soon afterwards the entire detachment entered the village. There were about eight hundred bayonets and swords in all. The Red Guards prepared to spend the night outside the village. Evidently their commander did not trust his nondescript and undisciplined soldiers in the village at night.

Shaken in battles against the Haidamaks and the German army of occupation, the Tiraspol detachment of the Second Socialist Army had fought its way back to the Don, and, having abandoned the railway, was trying to make its way through to Voronezh in the north on foot. Demoralized under the influence of the criminal elements that flourished in the detachment, the Red Guards were roistering along the road. That night, despite the threats and orders of their command, they poured in crowds into the village, began to kill sheep, ravished two Cossack women on the outskirts, started shooting for no reason in the square, and wounded one of their own number. During the night they got drunk on the spirits they were carrying with them.

But meanwhile three mounted Cossacks had been dispatched from the village to raise the alarm in neighbouring villages. In the darkness of the night the Cossacks saddled their horses, armed themselves, and hastily assembled detachments of front-line Cossacks and older men. Under the command of officers and sergeant-majors living in the villages, they hurried towards Syetrakov, concealing themselves in ravines and behind mounds all round the Red Guard camp. During the night groups of men arrived from all the surrounding villages.

The stars of the Pleiad faded in the sky. At dawn avalanches of Cossack horsemen from all sides flung themselves with a roar on the Red Guards. A machine-gun rattled, and died away, broke into wild haphazard fire again, then was silent.

Within an hour the deed was accomplished; the detachment was wiped out; more than two hundred were shot and hewn down, some five hundred were taken prisoner. Two batteries of four field-guns apiece, twenty-six machine-guns, thousands of rifles and a large store of military equipment fell into the hands of the Cossacks.

Next day every road and track in the district blossomed with the red flags of galloping messengers. The villages seethed with excitement. The Soviets were thrown out head over heels, and atamans were hurriedly elected. By the beginning of May the upper districts of the Don Province had completely broken away from the Revolutionary Committee. The populous Vyeshenskaya was chosen as the centre of the new district, which was called the "Upper Don." And the Upper Don Region, drawing twelve Cossack and one Ukrainian districts into its orbit, began to live its own life, cut off from the main centre of the Don Province. A Cossack from the Yelanskaya District, a general named Zakhar Akimovich Alfyorov, was hurriedly elected Regional Ataman. It was said of him that he had worked his way up from indigent Cossack officer to the rank of general only thanks to his wife, an energetic and intelligent woman. It was said that she had dragged her ungifted consort by the ears and had given him no peace until, after failing three times, he passed into the military academy at the fourth attempt.

But if Alfyorov was talked about at all in these days, is was very little. The Cossacks' minds were occupied with other things.

XXII

The flood water was beginning to abate from the fields. By the garden fences the brown earth was laid bare and edged with borders of dry reeds, branches, and dead leaves left behind by the flood. The pussy-willows of the flooded Don-side woods were beginning to turn green, and the catkins hung in tassels. The poplars were ready to burst into bud. In the village farm-yards the sprigs of purple willow hung low over the pools, and their yellow buds, like fluffy ducklings' down, dabbled in the wind-ruffled water. At dawn and sunset flights of wild geese and ducks swam up to the fences in search of food, and copper-tongued grebes called in the backwaters. At noonday the wind-driven surface of the Don was fondling white-feathered teal.

There were many birds in transit that year. The Cossack fishermen, rowing out to their nets at dawn when the wine-red sunrise bloodied the water, had even seen wild swans resting in the wooded stretches of water. But the news brought back to the village by Christonya and old Matvei Kashulin was the greatest miracle of all. They had driven into the government forest to select a couple of young oaks for their farm needs, and as they were making their way through a thicket they disturbed a wild goat with a young kid. The lean, yellow-brown goat jumped out of a dell overgrown with thistles and thorns, and stood gazing for some seconds at them, her thin legs dancing nervously, the kid pressing against her. Hearing Christonya's gasp of astonishment, she sped off so fast through the oak saplings that the Cossacks hardly caught sight of her blue-grey hoofs and her short camel-brown tail.

"What was that?" Matvei Kashulin asked, dropping his axe in astonishment.

With inexplicable delight Christonya roared through the magically silent forest:

"It must have been a goat. A wild goat! I've seen them in the Carpathians."

"Then the war must have driven it into our steppe."

There was nothing left for Christonya but to

agree. "That must be it," he said. "And did you see the kid with her? A pretty sight, damn it! Just like a child with its mother."

All the way back to the village they were discussing this unprecedented visitor to the district. Old Matvei began to have his doubts.

"But if it was a goat, where were its horns?"

"And what do you want horns for?"

"I don't want the horns! I simply asked, if it was a goat why wasn't it like a goat? Have you ever seen a goat without horns? That's the point. Mebbe it was some kind of wild sheep?"

"Old man, you've lived past your time!" Christonya took offence. "Go and call on the Melekhovs. Their Grigory's got a whip made out of a goat's leg. Then will you admit it or not?"

Old Matvei made it his business to visit the Melekhovs the same day. Certainly the stock of Grigory's whip was covered with leather made from a wild goat's leg; even the tiny hoof at the end had been retained and was ingeniously shod with a copper shoe.

On the Wednesday in the last week of Lent Misha Koshevoi went out early in the morning to examine the nets he had set in the river by the forest. He left home before dawn. The earth, pinched by the morning frost, was crusted with fine ice, and scrunched under his feet. Misha walked along with a great oar over his shoulder, his cap thrust on the back of his head, his trousers gathered into white woollen stockings, breathing in the intoxicating morning air and the scent of the raw dampness. He pushed off his boat and rowed swiftly, standing and pulling strongly at the oar.

He examined his nets, took the fish from the last, and dropped the net back into the water, and then, as he rowed easily back, decided to have a smoke. The sky was reddening with the sunrise. In the east the mistily blue heaven looked as though it had been splashed from below with blood. The redness flowed over the horizon and turned a rusty gold. As he lit his cigarette Misha watched the slow flight of a grebe. The smoke curled and clung to the branches of the trees, and drifted off in clouds. Examining his catch—three young sterlet, some eight pounds of carp, and a heap of whitefish— he thought:

"Must sell some of it. Squinting Lukeshka will take it in exchange for some dried pears. Mother can stew them."

He rowed up to the landing stage. By the garden fences where he kept the boat a man was sitting. He wondered who it was as he drove the boat through the water with strong well-toned pulls. When he got a little nearer he saw that it was Knave, squatting on his haunches and smoking an enormous cigarette made of newspaper. His sly little eyes gleamed sleepily, and his cheeks were overgrown with a scrub of hair.

"What do you want?" Misha shouted to him. His voice went bouncing over the water like a ball.

"Row closer."

"Do you want some fish?"

"What should I want fish for?"

Knave shook with a fit of coughing, spat violently, and reluctantly stood up. His ill-fitting greatcoat hung on him like a coat on a scarecrow. His sharp, gristly ears were covered by the hanging flaps of his cap. He had only recently returned to the village, accompanied by the doubtful fame of having been a Red Guard. The Cossacks asked him where he had been since he was demobilized, but Knave gave evasive answers, avoiding the dangerous questions. To Ivan Alexeyevich and Misha Koshevoi he admitted that he had spent four months in a Red Guard detachment in the Ukraine, had been captured by the Ukrainian national troops, had escaped and joined the Red Army close to Rostov, and had now given himself furlough to get a rest and re-equip himself.

Knave took off his cap, stroked his bristling hair, looked round, then went to the boat and muttered:

"There's bad business afoot ... very bad! Chuck your fishing! Or we'll go on fishing and fishing and forget everything else."

"What's your news? Tell me!" Misha asked, squeezing Knave's hand in his own fishy paw, and smiling warmly. They had long been close friends.

"Yesterday Red Guards were smashed up at Migulinskaya. The struggle has begun, brother! The fur's beginning to fly!"

"What Red Guards? How did they get to Migulinskaya?"

"They were marching through the district, and the Cossacks set about them and have driven the prisoners to Kargin. They've already begun a field court martial there. Today they're going to mobilize everybody in Tatarsky. They'll be ringing the bell this morning."

Koshevoi tied up his boat, poured his fish into a basket, and walked away with great strides. Knave danced along in front like a young horse, his coat tails flying, his arms swinging.

"Ivan Alexeyevich told me. He's just relieved me; the mill's been working all night. And he had it straight from the horse's mouth. An of-

ficer from Vyeshenskaya has called at Mokhov's."

Across Misha's face, matured and faded with
the years of war, passed a look of anxiety. He
glanced sidelong at Knave. "Now what's going
to happen?"

"We must clear out of the village."

"Where to?"

"To Kamenskaya."

"But the Cossacks are White there."

"Then more to the left."

"How are you going to get through?"

"It can be done if you want to. And if not,
stay behind and the devil take you!" Knave
suddenly snarled. " 'Where to,' and 'where to'!
How am I to know? Look round a bit and you'll
find a hole for yourself."

"Don't get your rag out. What does Ivan
say?"

"While you're getting Ivan to move. . . ."

"Not so loud! There's a woman looking."

They glanced cautiously at a young woman
driving cows out of a yard. At the first cross-
road Misha turned back.

"Where are you going?" Knave asked in surprise.

Without looking back Misha muttered:

"I'm going to get my nets out."

"What for?"

"I don't want to lose them."

"So we'll be going?" Knave said in delight.

Misha waved his oar, and said as he walked away: "Go along to Ivan Alexeyevich, and I'll take my nets home and come along after."

Ivan Alexeyevich had already succeeded in passing the news on to the Cossacks who were friendly. He sent his little son to the Melekhovs, and Grigory came back with him. Christonya turned up without being warned, as though he had a presentiment of impending trouble. Soon Koshevoi also arrived, and they began to discuss the situation. They all talked at once, hurriedly, every moment expecting to hear the tocsin sound.

"We must clear out at once. Pack up our traps and go," Knave urged them excitedly.

"Give us your reasons. Why must we?" Christonya queried.

"What do you mean 'why must we'? They'll be ordering mobilization, and do you think you'll escape it?"

"I won't go, and that's all there is to it."

"They'll take you!"

"Let them try! I'm not a bullock at the plough."

Ivan Alexeyevich sent his cross-eyed wife out of the house, then snorted angrily:

"They'll take you. Knave's right there. Only where are we to go? That's the question."

"That's what I've already told him," Misha sighed.

"Well, do as you like. Do you think I want the lot of you?" Knave snarled. "I'll clear out by myself. I don't want any lily-livers with me. 'Yes, but why!' And 'Yes, but where!' They'll give it you hot and shove you into prison for Bolshevism. How can you sit here joking? In such times as these? Everything will go to the devil!"

Concentratedly, and with quiet anger, turning over in his hands a rusty nail torn out of the wall, Grigory Melekhov cut him short, saying drily: "Not so fast! Your position is different, there's nothing to keep you, you can go where you like! But we've got to think it over carefully. I've got a wife and two little children. I've tasted more gunpowder than you ever will!" He narrowed his black, angry eyes, bared his stout teeth, and shouted:

"You can wag your tongue, you whipper-snapper! You're just what you've always been. You've got nothing but a jacket to your name. . . ."

"Who are you snarling at?" Knave cried. "Showing off your officer's ways! Don't shout! I don't care a spit for you!" His sharp little face went white with rage and his tiny, bitter eyes glittered balefully.

Grigory had vented on him the anger he felt at having his peace disturbed by the news of the clashes between Cossacks and Red Guards in the district. He jumped up as though he had been struck, strode across to where Knave was fidgeting on his stool, and restraining with difficulty his desire to strike him, said:

"Shut up, you little snake! Lousy snot! You stump of a man. Who are you ordering about? Go where your arse takes you. Clear out so that you don't stink here! And shut up or I'll give you something to remember me by."

"Drop it, Grigory! That's not the way!" Koshevoi intervened, pushing Grigory's fist away from Knave's nose.

"You ought to chuck those Cossack habits! Aren't you ashamed? Shame on you, Melekhov! Shame on you!"

Coughing, Knave rose and went to the door. But at the threshold he could no longer contain himself, and turning round, stabbed the fiercely smiling Grigory with his tongue:

"And he was in the Red Guards! You gendarme! We shot men like you. . . ."

At that, Grigory could not restrain himself either. He thrust Knave out into the porch.

treading on the heels of his broken-down soldiers' boots, and threatened:

"Clear out, or I'll tear your legs off!"

"There's no need for all this. You're acting like a couple of kids." Ivan Alexeyevich shook his head disapprovingly and gave Grigory an unfriendly look. Misha sat silently biting his lips, evidently struggling to keep back the angry words that were on the tip of his tongue.

"Well, why did he take it on himself to tell other people what they've got to do?" not without embarrassment Grigory tried to justify his behaviour. Christonya gave him a sympathetic look, and under his gaze Grigory smiled a simple, boyish smile. "I nearly hit him! But what is there to hit? Hit him once, and there'd be nothing left!"

"Well, what do you think? We must come to some decision."

Ivan Alexeyevich fidgeted under the fixed gaze of Misha Koshevoi, who had asked the question, and answered with an effort:

"Well, Mikhail, Grigory's right in a way. How can we just pick up our things and fly? We've got our families to think of. Now wait a bit," he said hurriedly as he caught Misha's impatient gesture. "Maybe nothing will happen ... who knows? They've broken up the detachment at Syetrakov, and others won't come. We can wait a bit. I've got a wife and child, our clothes are worn out and we've got no flour. So how can I go off? Who's going to look after them?"

Misha, irritated, raised his eyebrows and fixed his eyes on the earthen floor.

"So you're not thinking of going?"

"I think it's better to wait. It's never too late to clear out. What do you think, Grigory, and you, Christonya?"

Finding unexpected support from Ivan and Christonya, Grigory spoke more animatedly:

"Why, of course; that's just what I said. That's what I fell out with Knave over. It isn't so easy. One, two and off we go? We've got to think it over... think it over, I say."

As he finished speaking there was a sudden clang from the bell in the church tower, and the sound flooded the square, the streets, the alleys. The clangour rolled over the brown surface of the flood waters, over the damp, chalky slopes of the hills, splitting into pea-like fragments and dying away in the forest. Then once more it broke out, now an incessant note of alarm:

"Dong, dong, dong, dong. . . ."

"There it goes!" Christonya blinked. "I'm off to my boat. Over to the other side and into the forest. Then let them find me!"

"Well, and what now?" Koshevoi rose heavily like an old man.

"We're not going now," Grigory answered for the others.

Misha once more raised his brows, and brushed the heavy lock of golden hair off his forehead.

"Well, good-bye . . ." he said. "Looks as if our roads lie in different directions."

Ivan Alexeyevich smiled apologetically.

"You're young, Misha, and fiery. You think they won't run together again? They will! Be sure of that!"

Koshevoi took leave of the others and went out. He struck across the yard to the neighbouring threshing-floor. Knave was crouching in the ditch. He must have sensed that Misha would go that way. He rose to meet him, and asked:

"Well?"

"They've refused."

"I knew they would all along. They're weak. . . . And Grisha—that friend of yours—is a rotten dog! He's a sour devil if ever there was one. He insulted me, the swine! Just because he's stronger. I hadn't a weapon with me, or I'd have killed him," he said in a choking voice.

Striding along at his side, Misha glanced at his bristling scrub of hair and thought: "And he would have too, the polecat!"

They walked swiftly, every beat of the bell whipping them along.

"Come to my place," Misha proposed. "We'll get some grub and be off. We'll go on foot; I'll leave my horse behind. You've got nothing to take?"

"I've got nothing," Knave said wrily. "I never saved enough to buy a mansion or an estate. I haven't even had any wages for the last fortnight. But let old pot-belly Mokhov get fatter by it! He'll dance with joy at not having to pay them."

The bell had stopped ringing. The drowsy silence was undisturbed. Chickens were pecking in the ashes along the roadside, calves were looking for herbage under the fences. Misha looked back: Cossacks were hurrying to the meeting in the square, some of them buttoning up their uniform tunics as they went. A rider sped across the square. A crowd was gathered by the school, the women in white kerchiefs and skirts, the men a mass of black.

A woman carrying pails halted in their path, superstitiously refusing to cross in front of them.

"Come on, come on!" she called angrily, "I don't want to cross your path."

Misha greeted her, and with a gleaming smile she asked:

"The Cossacks are all going to the meeting. Where are you off to? You're going the wrong way, Misha."

"I've got something to do at home."

They turned down a side alley. They could see the roof of Misha's house, the starling-box with a dry cherry-branch tied to it rocking in the wind. On the rise the sails of the windmill turned slowly, the torn sail-cloth flapping and the sheet-iron of the steep roof rattling a little.

The sun was not strong, but warm. A fresh breeze was blowing from the Don. In Bogatiryov's yard some women were plastering a large house with clay and whitewashing it in readiness for Easter. One of them was kneading the clay with dung. She walked round in a circle, her skirt raised high, dragging her full, white legs out of the sticky mess. She held her skirt in the tips of her fingers, showing the cotton garters that cut tightly into the flesh above her knees. She was fond of her appearance, and though the sun was still low on the horizon, had wrapped her face in her kerchief. The two other women, their faces wrapped to the eyes in kerchiefs, had clambered on ladders right under the reed-thatched roof, and were whitewashing. With sleeves tucked up above the elbows they worked the brushes backward and forward, and splashes of whitewash spattered over them. They sang as they worked. The elder, Marya, the widow of one of Bogatiryov's sons, was openly setting her cap at Misha. She was a freckled but good-looking woman. She struck up in a low voice, almost masculine in strength and famed throughout the village:

Ah, there's no one suffers more....

The other women joined in, and the three voices wove together skilfully in the bitter, naïvely complaining song:

Than my darling at the war.
A gunner-boy is he,
And he always thinks of me.

Misha and Knave passed close to the fence, listening to the song that mingled with the loud neighing of horses from the meadow:

Then a letter came that said
That my darling had been killed.
Oh, he's killed, my darling's killed
And beneath a bush lies he.

Marya, her warm grey eyes glittering under her kerchief, looked down and stared at Misha. Her bespattered face lighting up with a smile, she sang in a deep, amorous voice:

And his curls, his golden curls
In the wind were tossed about.
And his eyes, his deep brown eyes—
A black raven pecked them out.

Misha smiled at her in the tender way he had with women, and to Pelageya, who was kneading the clay, said:

"Lift your skirt a bit higher. We can't see properly over the fence."

She puckered her eyes at him.

"If you want to you can."

Marya stood on the ladder with her hands on her hips and, glancing round, asked in a drawling tone:

"Where have you been, dear?"

"Fishing."

"Don't go far, and we'll go into the barn and enjoy ourselves."

"You shameless hussy!"

Marya clicked her tongue, and with a laugh waved the wet brush at Misha. The drops of whitewash spattered over his jacket and cap.

"You might lend us Knave at least. He could help us clean up the house," the other woman cried after them, smiling and revealing her milky-white teeth. Marya whispered something to her and they burst into laughter.

"Lewd bitches!" Knave frowned, hastening his steps. But with a languishing and gentle smile Misha corrected him.

"Not lewd, only merry. I'm going off, but I'm leaving my darling behind," he added as he passed through the wicket-gate of his yard.

528

XXIII

After Koshevoi's departure the others sat for a little while without speaking. The tocsin bell rocked over the village and rattled the little window-panes of the house. Ivan Alexeyevich stared out through the window. A crumbly morning shadow cast by the shed fell over the ground. The dew lay greyly on the young grass. Even through the glass the sky showed azure. Ivan glanced at Christonya's drooping head.

"Maybe that will be the end of it? The Migulinskaya people have broken up the Reds, and they won't come farther...."

"No!" All Grigory's body twitched. "They've started, and they'll keep on. Well, shall we go to the square?"

Ivan Alexeyevich reached for his cap, and resolving his doubts, asked:

"Well, maybe we've got rusty after all? Mikhail's hot-headed, but he's an active lad. He's a reproach to us."

No one answered. They went out silently, and turned towards the square.

Ivan Alexeyevich walked along pensively, staring at the ground. He was oppressed with the thought that he had taken the wrong path and had not followed the dictates of his conscience. Knave and Misha were right, they all ought to have gone without hesitating. His attempts to justify his conduct were fruitless, and a deliberate, sneering voice inside him shattered them as a horse's hoof crushes the thin ice in the meadow. The one thing he firmly resolved upon was to desert to the Bolsheviks at the first opportunity. He came to the decision while he was walking to the square, but he told neither Grigory nor Christonya, realizing vaguely that they were passing through different struggles from his, and already in the depths of his heart afraid of them. They had all three jointly turned down Knave's proposal, each giving his family as the excuse. But each of them knew that the excuse was inconclusive and did not justify the decision. Now each felt embarrassed in the others' company, as though he had done something low and shameful. They were silent, but as they passed Mokhov's house Ivan Alexeyevich could endure the sickening silence no longer, and punishing himself and the others, he said:

"There's no point in hiding it. We came back from the front Bolsheviks, and now we're crawling into the bushes. Let others fight for us, but we'll stay with our women!"

"I've done my share of fighting, let others have a go," Grigory snapped and turned away.

"But how can they be like this?" Christonya

added. "A lot of robbers! Are we to join men like them? What sort of Red Guards do they call themselves? Raping women, robbing the Cossacks! We've got to see what we're doing. The blind man always falls over the chair."

"And have you seen all this, Christonya?" Ivan asked fiercely.

"People are talking about...."

"Ah... people...."

"Well, that's enough.... We don't want to be overheard."

The square was a rich blossom of Cossack trousers, caps, and here and there a shaggy black sheepskin cap. All the men of the village were assembled. No women were there, only the old men, and the Cossacks who had been at the war, and still younger men. The very oldest stood in front, leaning on their sticks: honorary judges, the members of the church council, the school managers, and the churchwarden. Grigory's eyes searched for his father's black and silver beard, and found him standing at the side of Miron Grigoryevich. In front of them, in his grey, full-dress tunic and medals, old Grishaka was leaning on his knobby stick. Together with Pantelei and Miron were all the elders of the village. Behind them stood the younger men, many of them comrades-in-arms of Grigory. On the other side of the ring he noticed his brother Pyotr, his shirt adorned with the orange and black ribbons of the cross of St. George. On his left was Mitka Korshunov, lighting his cigarette from Prokhor Zykov's. Prokhor was drawing hard to help him, pursing his lips and rounding his calf-like eyes. Behind were crowded the youngest Cossacks. In the centre of the ring, at a rickety table with its four legs pressed into the soft, still damp earth, sat the chairman of the village Revolutionary Committee. At his side stood a lieutenant whom Grigory did not know, dressed in a khaki cap with a cockade, a leather jacket with epaulettes, and khaki breeches. The chairman of the Revolutionary Committee was talking worriedly to him, and the officer stooped a little to listen with his large protruding ear close to the chairman's beard. The meeting hummed like a beehive. The Cossacks were talking and joking among themselves, but on all faces were looks of anxiety. Someone could wait no longer, and shouted:

"Let's start! What are you waiting for? Nearly everybody's here."

The officer straightened up, removed his cap, and said, as simply as though in his own family circle:

"Elders of the village, and you front-line Cossack brothers! You have all heard what happened at the village of Syetrakov, haven't you?"

"Who's that, where's he from?" Christonya boomed.

"From Vyeshenskaya. Soldatov I think his name is."

"A day or two ago," the lieutenant continued, "a detachment of Red Guards arrived at the village. The Germans have occupied the Ukraine, and as they moved towards the Don Province they threw the Red Guards back from the railway. The Reds entered Syetrakov and began to pillage the Cossacks' possessions, to ravish their women, to carry out unlawful arrests, and so on. When the neighbouring villages heard what had happened they fell on them with arms in hand. Half the detachment was destroyed, the remainder taken prisoner. The Cossacks got some fine spoils. Now the Migulinskaya and Kazanskaya districts have flung the Bolshevik government out of their areas. Young and old, the Cossacks have risen in defence of the quiet Don. In Vyeshenskaya the Revolutionary Committee has been flung out neck and crop, and a district ataman has been elected; and the same is true in most of the villages."

At this point in the speech the old men gave vent to a restrained mutter.

"Everywhere detachments are being formed. You also ought to form a detachment of front-line Cossacks, in order to defend the district from the arrival of new savage robber hordes. We must set up our own administration. We don't want the Red government, they bring only debauchery, and not liberty! And we shall not allow the muzhiks to violate our wives and sisters, to make a mockery of our Orthodox faith, to desecrate our holy churches, to plunder our possessions and property. Don't you agree, elders?"

The meeting thundered with the sudden "aye!" The officer began to read out a proclamation. Forgetting his papers, the chairman slipped away from the table. The crowd of elders listened without uttering a word. The front-line men behind muttered among themselves.

As soon as the officer began to read, Grigory slipped out of the crowd and turned to go home. Miron Grigoryevich noticed his departure, and nudged Pantelei with his elbow.

"Your younger son—he's slipping off!"

Pantelei limped out of the ring and shouted in a tone of imperative appeal:

"Grigory!"

His son turned half-round and halted without looking back.

"Come back, Son!"

"What are you going away for? Come back!" came a roar of voices from the crowd, and a wall of faces turned in Grigory's direction.

"And he's been an officer!"

"You needn't turn up your nose!"

"He was with the Bolsheviks himself."

"He's shed Cossack blood!"

"The Red devil!"

The shouts reached Grigory's ears. He listened with grating teeth, evidently struggling with himself. It seemed as though in another minute he would go off without a look back. But Pantelei and Pyotr gave sighs of relief as he wavered and then with downcast eyes returned to the crowd.

The old men overwhelmingly carried the day. With amazing speed Miron Grigoryevich was elected ataman. His freckled face greying, he went into the middle of the ring and confusedly received the symbol of his authority, the ataman's copper-headed staff, from his predecessor. He had never been ataman before, and when they called for him he had hesitated and refused the position, saying that he did not deserve such an honour, that he was uneducated. But now the old men insisted:

"Take up the staff, Grigoryevich, don't refuse."

"You're the best farmer in the village."

"You won't waste our goods."

"Mind you don't waste it on drink, like Semyon!"

"He wouldn't do that!"

"He's got plenty of his own we can take, if he does."

"We'll flay him like a sheep."

So unusual were the circumstances of the election and the state of semi-war in the district that Miron agreed without much persuasion. The election was not carried out as in former days, when the district ataman had arrived in the village, the Cossack heads of families had been summoned to a meeting, and a ballot had been taken. Now it was simply: "Those for Korshunov, step to the right," and the entire crowd had surged that way. Only the cobbler, who had a grudge against Korshunov, had remained standing alone in his place like a blasted oak in a meadow.

The perspiring Miron had hardly time to blink before the staff was thrust into his hand, and a roar went up:

"Now how about treating us?"

"Up into the air with the new ataman!"

But the officer intervened, and cleverly directed the meeting towards a business-like settlement of the remaining problems. He raised the question of electing a commander for the village detachment, and must have heard about Grigory in Vyeshenskaya, for he began by praising him, and through him the village.

"It would be well to have a commander who has been an officer. If we have to fight we shall do better and there will be fewer losses. And you've got plenty of heroes in your village. I cannot impose my will upon you, but for my part I recommend you to elect Cornet Melekhov."

"Which one? We've got two of them."

The officer ran his eyes over the crowd, noticed Grigory's bowed head and shouted with a smile:

"Grigory Melekhov! What do you think, Cossacks?"

"A good man!"

"Grigory Melekhov! He's a tough nut!"

"Come into the middle of the ring. The elders want to look at you."

Thrust forward from behind, Grigory, his face crimson, emerged into the middle of the ring and looked round him like a hunted animal.

"Lead our sons!" Matvei Kashulin rapped with his stick and crossed himself with a flourish of his arm. "Lead and guide them so that they will be with you like geese with a gander. As the gander defends its family and saves them from both man and beast, so you must

537

watch over them! Earn four more crosses, may God grant it!"

"Pantelei Prokofyevich, you've got a son!"

"And a fine brain in his head!"

"You lame devil, how about the drink?"

"Elders! Silence! Shall we carry out mobilization without calling for volunteers? Volunteers may go or they may not...."

"No, let's have volunteers!"

"You go yourself, what's holding you back?"

Meanwhile four elders from the upper part of the village who had been holding a whispered consultation with the newly-appointed ataman approached the officer. One of them, a little toothless old man, nicknamed "Wrinkle," was famous for having spent his life in petty legal wrangling. He visited the court so often that his one and only white mare knew the road well enough for her drunken master to be able to tumble into the cart and shout in his chirruping little voice: "To the court!" and she would set off in the right direction straight away. Wrinkle pulled his old cap off his head and went up to the lieutenant. The other old men, one of them a good farmer, Gerasim Boldyrev, much respected in the village, halted close by. Wrinkle, who besides his other merits, loved the sound of his own voice, was the first to speak:

"Your Honour, it looks as if you don't know very much about our village, or you wouldn't have picked Grigory Melekhov for a commander. We elders have got a complaint against the choice. It's our right to complain, you know. We've got an objection to make against him."

"What objection? What's the matter?"

"Well, how can we trust him when he himself's been in the Red Guards and one of their commanders, and it's only two months since he came back from them with a wound."

The officer flushed, and his ears seemed to swell with the influx of blood.

"Is that really true? I hadn't heard that. No one said anything about it to me."

"It's true, he's been with the Bolsheviks." another elder affirmed grimly. "We can't trust him!"

"Change him! What are our young Cossacks saying? They're saying that in the first battle he'll betray them."

"Elders!" the officer shouted, raising himself on his toes and addressing the elders, while cleverly ignoring the front-line men. "Elders! We've just elected Grigory Melekhov to be commander, but isn't there a danger in that? I've just been told that during the winter he was himself with the Red Guards. Can you entrust your sons and grandsons to him? And you, front-line brothers, can you follow his lead with quiet hearts?"

The Cossacks maintained a stupefied silence for a moment, then a tumult of conflicting shouts arose, and it was impossible to understand a word. When it died away old tufty-browed Bogatiryov stepped into the middle, took off his cap, and looked around.

"In my foolish mind I think this way. We can't give Grigory Panteleyevich this position. He's been on the wrong road, and we've all heard of that. Let him first earn our trust, make up for what he's done, and then we'll see. He's a good fighter, we know. . . . But we can't see the sun for mist; we can't see his past services; his work for the Bolsheviks is an eyesore to us."

"Let him go in the ranks," young Andrei Kashulin shouted fiercely.

"Make Pyotr Melekhov commander."

"Let Grisha go in the herd."

"A fine commander we'd have put over ourselves!"

"Yes, and I don't want the position! What the devil did you put me forward for?" Grigory shouted, flushing with excitement. Waving his hand he repeated: "I won't take the position if you want me to!" He thrust his hands into the depths of his trouser pockets, and with bowed head stalked away. Shouts followed him:

"Not so much of that!"

"The stinking filth! That's his Turkish blood coming out!"

"You're holding your hooked nose too high!"

"He won't keep quiet! He wouldn't keep his mouth shut even to the officers in the trenches."

"Come back!"

"After him! Hooh! Boo!"

"Why let him get away with it? Let's put him on trial ourselves!"

It was a long time before the meeting quietened down again. In the heat of argument someone jostled someone else, someone's nose began to bleed, one of the youngsters was suddenly enriched with a swelling under his eye. When peace was at last restored they elected Pyotr Melekhov commander, and he fairly glowed with pride. But now, like a mettlesome horse confronted with too high a fence, the officer took a tumble. When the next step of calling for volunteers was taken, no volunteers were forthcoming. The front-line men, who had been restrained in their attitude throughout the meeting, hesitated and were unwilling to enrol, passing it off as a joke.

"Why don't you go, Anikushka?"

But Anikushka muttered:

"I'm too young.... I haven't any whiskers yet."

"None of your jokes! Trying to make a laughing-stock of us?" old Kashulin howled right into his ear.

"You enrol your own son!" Anikushka retorted.

"Prokhor Zykov!" came a shout from the table. "Shall we put your name down?"

"I don't know . . ." he replied.

"We're putting you down."

Mitka Korshunov went up to the table with a serious face, and said curtly:

"Put me down."

"Well, who else? How about you, Fedot Bodovskov?"

"I've got rupture," Fedot muttered, dropping his Kalmyk eyes. The front-line men roared with laughter, and chaffed him unmercifully:

"Take your wife with you. If your rupture's troublesome, she'll put it right!"

And on the other side of the circle another joke fluttered over the crowd:

"We'll make you a cook. If your soup's rotten we'll fill you with it till your rupture comes out the other end."

"You'll be all right in a retreat, you won't run too fast."

But the elders got annoyed and began to curse:

"Enough, enough! What are you so merry for?"

"A fine time for showing their foolishness!"

"Shame on you, lads!" one of them shouted. "What of God? God won't overlook this! People are dying, and you.... Think of God!"

"Ivan Tomilin!" the officer looked round.

"I'm an artilleryman," Tomilin replied.

"Shall we put you down? We need artillerymen."

"Oh, all right, put me down then."

Anikushka and several others began to rally Tomilin.

"We'll carve you a gun out of a willow trunk. You'll fire pumpkins and potatoes instead of grape-shot."

With jesting and laughter some sixty men enrolled. The last was Christonya. He went up to the table and said deliberately:

"Write my name down. Only I warn you I shan't fight."

"Then why put yourself down?" the officer asked in irritation.

"I'll look on, officer. I want to have a look!"

"Put him down," the officer shrugged his shoulders.

The meeting did not end until nearly noon. It was decided to dispatch the detachment the very next day to the support of the Migulin-skaya villagers.

Next morning, out of the sixty volunteers only some forty turned up in the square. Pyotr, elegantly dressed in a greatcoat and high top boots, reviewed the Cossacks. Many of them had shoulder-straps with the numbers of their old regiments on them. Their saddles were loaded with saddle-bags containing food, linen, and cartridges brought back from the front. Not all of them had rifles, but the majority had cold steel.

A crowd of women, children and old men gathered in the square to see them off. Pyotr, on his prancing horse, drew up his half-company in ranks, inspected the motley collection of horses, the riders in greatcoats, tunics, and tarpaulin raincoats, and gave the order for departure. He walked the detachment up the hill. The Cossacks stared gloomily back at the village; someone in the last file fired a shot. At the top Pyotr drew on his gloves, stroked his wheaten whiskers, and turning his horse so that it advanced sideways, holding his cap on with his left hand, shouted:

"Squadron, trot!"

Standing in their stirrups, waving their whips, the Cossacks put their horses into a trot. The wind beat in their faces, shook the horses' tails and manes, and scattered a fine rain. They began to talk and joke. Christonya's raven horse stumbled, and he cursed and warmed it with lashes of the whip. The horse arched its neck, broke into a gallop and burst out of the ranks.

The Cossacks' gay mood did not desert them until they reached Kargin. They rode in the full conviction that there would be no war, that the Migulinskaya affair was only a fortuitous irruption of the Bolsheviks into Cossack territory.

XXIV

They reached Kargin in the late afternoon. There were no front-line men left in the district: they had all gone to Migulinskaya. Pyotr dismounted his detachment in the square, and went to the district ataman to arrange for billets. He was met by a tall, powerfully built, dark-faced officer. He wore a long voluminous shirt without any shoulder-straps, encircled with a Cossack belt, his striped Cossack *sharovari* were tucked into white woollen socks. A pipe hung from the corner of his thin lips. In his brown, glittering eyes there was a lowering crooked expression. He stood on the steps, smoking and watching Pyotr as he approached. The man's massive figure, the swelling, steely-strong chest and arm muscles showing beneath his shirt testified to his unusual strength.

35—1690

"Are you the district ataman?"

Puffing out a cloud of smoke from under his drooping whiskers, the officer replied in a deep baritone.

"Yes, I'm the district ataman. To whom have I the honour of speaking?"

Pyotr gave his name. Shaking his hand, the ataman bowed his head slightly.

"My name is Fyodor Dmitrievich Likhovidov."

Fyodor Dmitrievich Likhovidov, a Cossack of the Gusyno-Likhovidov village, was a man far removed from the ordinary. After completing his education at a Cadet college, he had for a long time completely disappeared. Several years later he suddenly reappeared in his village and with permission from the higher authorities began to recruit a force of volunteers from among the Cossacks who had served their term on the active list. In the region of what is now the stanitsa of Kargin he assembled a squadron of Cossack dare-devils and led them off to Persia, where they remained for a year as the shah's body-guard. During the Persian revolution Likhovidov fled with the shah and, having lost touch with most of his men, suddenly appeared again in Kargin. With him he brought the remnants of his detachment, three thoroughbred Arab horses from the shah's stable and much booty, rich carpets, precious ornaments, and exquisite silks. For a month he caroused and made merry, emptied the pockets of his *sharovari* of a large quantity of Persian gold, galloped about the village on a beautiful, slim-legged, snow-white horse that carried its head with the elegance of a swan, rode it up the steps of Levochkin's shop, chose and paid for his purchases without dismounting and rode out of the other door. Fyodor Likhovidov disappeared again as suddenly as he had come. His inseparable companion, his orderly, the Cossack dancer Pantelushka, disappeared with him; the horses and all that had been brought from Persia also disappeared.

Six months later Likhovidov turned up in Albania and his acquaintances in Kargin began to receive postcards of its blue mountains. Then he moved on to Italy, toured the Balkans, Rumania, and Western Europe; his travels took him nearly as far as Spain. Fyodor Likhovidov's name became invested with an aura of mystery. All kinds of speculation about him circulated in the village. All that was known of him for certain was that he was intimate with monarchist circles, had acquaintances among the high dignitaries of St. Petersburg, and was a prominent member of the "Alliance of the Russian People,"* but of the nature of his foreign missions no one had any knowledge whatsoever.

On his return from abroad Likhovidov established himself in Penza, at the house of the governor-general. Those of his acquaintances in Kargin who saw his photograph in the papers shook their heads and clicked their tongues in astonishment. "How Fyodor Dmitrievich is getting on! What people he has to do with, eh!" And there was Likhovidov, a smile on his dark hook-nosed Serbian face, taking the arm of the governor-general's wife to help her into her landau. The governor himself was smiling affectionately upon him as one of the family, the burly coachman held the reins in his finger tips, and the horses, about to plunge forward, were straining and champing at the bits. Likhovidov stood with one hand raised to his shaggy sheepskin hat, the other cupped under the elbow of the governor's wife.

At the end of 1917, after several years of absence, Likhovidov turned up in Kargin and made his home there, apparently for a long time. With him he brought a wife, either Ukrainian

* A monarchist organization in tsarist Russia whose activities included anti-semitic propaganda and pogroms and the murder of political opponents. It is now known that the Alliance received considerable financial support from the tsarist government.

or Polish, and a child; he took up residence in a small four-roomed house in the square and passed the winter making unknown plans. All the winter (and it was an unusually severe winter for the Don) the windows of his house remained wide open. Likhovidov was hardening himself and his family in a way that aroused great astonishment among the Cossacks.

In the spring of 1918, after the Syetrakov affair, he was elected ataman. And it was then that Fyodor Likhovidov's unlimited ability came to the fore. The stanitsa fell into a pair of hands so harsh that a week later even the old men were shaking their heads. He trained the Cossacks to such a pitch that after he spoke at a meeting (Likhovidov had a smooth tongue; nature had endowed him with brains as well as strength) the old men would bellow like a herd of bullocks: "Good luck to you, Your Honour! Our humblest regards! You're quite right!" Sternly the new ataman carried out his duties. His first step was to dispatch every front-line man in the district to Syetrakov the very day after the massacre of the Red Guards. The aliens, who composed a third of the inhabitants of the district, at first did not wish to go, while the soldiers protested. But Likhovidov insisted on having his way, and the elders signed his proposed decree that all muzhiks who took no part in the defence of the Don should be expelled from the district. The following day dozens of carts filled with soldiers singing and playing accordions were rolling along in the direction of Migulinskaya. Of the aliens only a few young soldiers fled to join the Red Guards.

As Pyotr approached, Likhovidov guessed by his walk that he was an officer risen from the ranks. So he did not invite him into his house, and spoke to him with a hint of benevolent familiarity:

"No, my lad, there's nothing for you to do in Migulinskaya. They've managed without you; we received a telegram yesterday evening. Ride back and await further orders. Stir up the Cossacks well! A large village like Tatarsky, and only forty fighters? Wring their withers, the scum! It's their skins that are at stake. Goodbye, and a good journey."

He went into his house, carrying his heavy body with unexpected ease, his simple Cossack sandals scraping on the wooden steps. Pyotr returned to his Cossacks in the square. They overwhelmed him with questions. Not attempting to hide his satisfaction, he smiled and answered:

"Home! They've managed without us!"

The Cossacks grinned and went in a crowd towards their horses. Christonya even sighed as though a great load had fallen from his back, and clapped Tomilin on the shoulders.

"So we're going home, gunner!"

After considering the situation they decided not to spend the night in Kargin, but to return at once. In scattered and disorderly groups they rode out of the village. They had ridden unwillingly to Kargin, rarely breaking into a trot, but on the way back they rode their horses hard. The earth, cracked with lack of rain, rumbled dully under their horses' hoofs. Beyond the Don and the distant range of hills blue lightning splintered on the horizon.

They arrived in Tatarsky at midnight. As they galloped down the hill Anikushka fired his Austrian rifle, and a salvo of shots rang out to announce their return. The dogs in the village gave tongue in reply, and scenting its home, one of the horses snorted and neighed. They scattered through the village in various directions.

As he said good-bye to Pyotr, Martin Shamil croaked with relief:

"Well, the fighting's over! That's good!"

Pyotr smiled in the darkness and rode off to his house. Pantelei came out and took his horse, unsaddled it and led it into the stable. He and Pyotr entered the house together.

"Is it all over?"

"Uh-huh!"

"Well, praise be! May we hear no more of it!"

Darya rose, hot from sleep. She went to get her husband some supper. Grigory came out half-dressed from the best room, scratching his hairy chest, and winked humorously at Pyotr.

"So you've overcome them already?"

"Now I'm overcoming the remains of the soup."

"You can overcome the soup all right, especially if I give you a hand!"

Until Easter there was not a sound or smell of war. But on Easter Saturday a messenger galloped into the village from Vyeshenskaya, left his lathered horse at Korshunov's gate, and ran into the porch.

"What news?" Miron Grigoryevich greeted him.

"I want the ataman. Is that you?"

"Yes."

"Arm the Cossacks at once. Podtyolkov is leading the Red Guards into Nagolinskaya District. Here's the order." He turned the sweaty lining of his cap inside out to get the packet.

At the sound of talking old Grishaka came out, harnessing a pair of spectacles on his nose. They read the order from the regional ataman. Leaning against the carved railing, the messenger rubbed the dust from his weather-beaten face with his sleeve.

On Easter Sunday, after breaking their fast, the mobilized Cossacks rode out of the village. General Alfyorov's order was strict: he threatened that all who refused to go would be deprived of the title of Cossack. So the detachment was composed not of forty men, as at first, but of a hundred and eight, including a number of older men who were possessed with the desire to have a smack at the Bolsheviks. The young men went because they had to, their elders in the heat of the chase.

Grigory Melekhov rode in the last rank with the hood of his rain-coat drawn over his cap. Rain was sprinkling from the hazy sky. Heavy clouds rolled above the green-clad steppe. An eagle was floating high under the cloudy ridge. With deliberate flaps of its wings it flew before the wind to the east, a gleaming brown speck fading into the distance.

The steppe glistened wetly. Here and there were snapdragons and clumps of last year's wormwood. Grey burial mounds stood guard on the slope.

As they dropped down into Kargin they were met by a youngster driving bullocks out to graze. He went slapping along with bare feet, waving his whip. Seeing the riders, he halted and attentively examined them and their mud-splashed horses.

"Where d'you come from?" Tomilin asked.

"Kargin," the lad boldly replied, smiling under the coat thrown over his head.

"Have your Cossacks gone?"

"They've gone. They've gone to smash the Red Guards. Have you got any tobacco for a cigarette, uncle?"

"Tobacco for you?" Grigory reined in his horse.

The lad went up to him. His tucked-up trouser-legs were wet, and the stripes were a shining red. He stared boldly into Grigory's face as Grigory pulled a pouch out of his pocket, and said:

"You'll be seeing some dead bodies in a minute, as soon as you go downhill. Yesterday our Cossacks drove the Red prisoners out and killed them. I was minding cattle over there by that bush, and saw them cut them down. Oh, it was terrible! When the swords began to swing they started screaming and running.... Afterwards I went and looked. One of them was cut down through the shoulder, and I could see the heart beating in his chest, and the blue kidneys.... It was terrible!" he repeated, astonished that the Cossacks were not frightened by his story. So at least he concluded as he stared at the cold unmoved faces of Grigory, Christonya and Tomilin.

He lit his cigarette, stroked the wet neck of Grigory's horse, said "Thank you" and ran off to his bullocks.

By the roadside, in a shallow hole washed with rain-water, only lightly sprinkled with earth, lay the bodies of the Red Guards. One leaden-blue face was visible, a crust of blood on its lips. And a bare foot with a blue quilted trouser-leg stuck out of the ground.

"Couldn't face up to the job of burying them! The swine!" Christonya muttered. He lashed his horse, overtook Grigory and galloped downhill.

"Well, so blood has flowed on the Don earth too!" Tomilin smiled, but his cheek was twitching.

XXV

Bunchuk's gunner was Maxim Gryaznov, the Cossack from Tatarsky village. He had lost his horse in a skirmish with Kutyopov's Volunteer Detachment, and since then had taken to heavy drinking and card-playing. When his horse (the one like a bull, with a streak of silver down its back) was killed under him he had unfastened the saddle and carried it three versts or so, then, seeing that at this rate he would not escape alive from the Volunteers, he had torn off the valuable metal pommel, removed the snaffles and left the other men in his unit to do the fighting. He had turned up in Rostov, quickly gambled away the silver-hilted sword he had taken from a captain cut down in battle, then lost the horse's equipment he had carried away with him, and even his trousers and kid boots. He was almost naked when he joined Bunchuk's machine-gun crew. He might have pulled himself together then, but in his very first battle a bullet struck him in the face, his blue eye dribbled on to his breast, and the blood spurted from the back of his head, that had been shattered like matchwood. Maxim Gryaznov, Tatarsky Cossack, former horse-stealer and of late a drunkard, had departed this life.

Bunchuk glanced at his body writhing in the throes of death, and carefully wiped the blood off the barrel of the machine-gun. Almost immediately afterward it became necessary to retreat. Bunchuk dragged back the machine-gun, leaving Maxim to stiffen on the hot earth. His swarthy body was exposed to the sun, for in his death struggles Maxim had pulled his shirt up over his head.

A platoon of Red Guards, all of them recently returned from the Turkish front, made a stand at the first cross-roads of the suburb. A soldier in a half-rotten fur cap helped Bunchuk to set up the machine-gun, and the others built rough barricades across the street, joking and shouting jibes in the direction of the enemy. Anna lay down at Bunchuk's side.

Suddenly there was a patter of feet along the next street to the right, and nine or ten Red Guards scuttled round the corner. One managed to shout:

"They're coming!"

In a moment the crossing became deserted and still. Then there was a whirl of dust, and a mounted Cossack with a white band across his hat, a carbine pressed to his side, charged round the corner. He pulled up his horse with such force that the animal sat down on its hind legs. Bunchuk fired a shot from his revolver. Bending low over his horse's neck, the Cossack galloped back. The soldiers behind the barricade hesitated irresolutely; two of them ran along under the wall and lay down by a gate. It was clear that in another minute the men would waver and retreat. The tense silence and their apprehensive glances did not promise steadiness. . . .

Of all that followed, Bunchuk remembered one moment indelibly and palpably. Anna, her kerchief thrust on the back of her head, dishevelled and agitated beyond recognition, jumped up with rifle at the trail, looked round, pointed to the house behind which the Cossack had disappeared, and in an unrecognizable, broken voice shouted: "Follow me!" With uncertain, stumbling feet she ran towards the corner.

Bunchuk raised himself off the ground. An unintelligible cry twisted his mouth. He seized a rifle from the nearest soldier and ran after Anna, panting, feeling an uncontrollable trembling in his legs, his face darkening as he strove powerlessly to shout, to call to her and turn her back. He heard the gasping breath of a few men pounding up behind him. In all his being he felt that something terrible, irreparable was about to happen. Even then he realized that the others would not follow her, that her action was senseless, reckless, doomed.

Near the corner he ran full tilt into the Cossacks as they galloped up. They fired a ragged volley. The whistle of bullets. A thin, miserable cry from Anna. Then he saw her crumpling to the road with outstretched hand and wild eyes. He did not see the Cossacks turn back, he did not see the Red soldiers chasing them, afire with belated enthusiasm for Anna's impulsive action. She, she alone was in his eyes, as she struggled at his feet. He turned her over to lift her and carry her away. But he saw blood streaming from her left side and the ragged edges of her blue blouse drooping limply round the wound; he realized that she had been struck by a dum-dum bullet and he knew that she was dying: he saw death lurking in her clouded eyes.

Someone thrust him aside, and they carried her into a yard and laid her in the cool of a lean-to shed.

A soldier pressed wads of cotton-wool into the wound and threw them away as they became soaked with blood. Mastering himself, Bunchuk unbuttoned the collar of her blouse, tore off a piece of his own shirt, and pressed it in a pad against the wound. But the blood came soaking through; he saw her face turning blue and her blackened lips quivering with agony. Her mouth gulped at the air, but her lungs could not breathe; the air came out again through her mouth and through the wound. He cut away her torn shirt and, feeling no shame, laid bare her body covered with the sweat of death. They managed to plug the wound a little, and a few minutes later she returned to consciousness. Her sunken eyes stared at Bunchuk out of their dark sockets for a moment, then the trembling lashes closed over them.

"Water! It's so hot!" she groaned, tossing about. She burst into tears. "I want to live! Ilya! My darling. . .! A-ah!"

Bunchuk put his swollen lips to her flaming cheek. He poured water over her chest. It brimmed the hollows under her collar-bones, but dried away in a moment. She was aflame with a mortal fire. She struggled and tore herself out of his hands.

"It's hot. . . . Fire. . .!"

As her strength failed she became a little cooler, and said articulately:

"Ilya, but why? Well, you see how simple it is. . . . You're a strange fellow. . . . It's terribly simple. . . . Ilya, dearest, you'll . . . there's Mother." She half-opened her eyes, which had been puckered as if in laughter, and striving to master her pain and horror, began to talk unintelligibly, as though something were choking her. "At first the feeling . . . a blow and a burning. . . . Now everything's on fire. . . . I feel . . . I'm dying." She frowned as she noticed his bitter gesture of denial. "Don't. . .! It's hard . . . ah, how hard it is to breathe!"

She talked in spasmodic outbursts, as though trying to tell him all that was burdening her. With horror he noticed that her face was becoming translucent and turning yellow at the temples. He turned his eyes to her hands lying lifelessly alongside her body, and saw the nails flooding with a rosy blue like ripening black plums.

"Water! My chest. . . . It's so hot!"

He ran to the house for water. As he returned he could no longer hear Anna's hoarse gasping from the shed. The setting sun was shining on her mouth as it contorted with a last spasm, and on the still warm, waxen hand pressed to the wound. Slowly putting his arms around her shoulders, he raised her, stared for a moment at the pinched, slightly freckled nose and the tiny dark lines between the eyes, and tried to catch the fading gleam of the pupils under the black brows. Her helplessly drooping head dropped lower, and in her slender girlish neck the pulse beat its last.

He pressed his cold lips to the black, half-closed eyelids, and called: "My friend! Dearest! Anna!"

Then he straightened up, turned sharply on his heel, and walked away unnaturally erect, not moving the arms pressed against his sides.

XXVI

In the days that followed Bunchuk lived as he had in the delirium of typhus. He still went about, did things, ate, slept, but always as if in a stupefying, narcotic doze. With frantic, swollen eyes he stared uncomprehendingly at the world around him, failed to recognize his friends, and looked as though he were heavily intoxicated or only just recovering from a wasting illness. From the moment of Anna's death feeling was temporarily atrophied in him: he wanted nothing, and thought of nothing. "Eat, Bunchuk!" his comrades pressed him; and he ate, his jaws working slowly and lazily. His comrades kept a watch on him and talked of sending him to hospital.

"Are you ill?" one of the machine-gunners asked the next day.

"No."

"What's the matter? Grief?"

"No."

"Well, let's have a smoke. You can't bring her back now, mate. It's no good trying."

When it was time to sleep they said to him: "Time to sleep!" and he lay down.

He spent four days in this state of withdrawal from the world of reality. On the fifth day Krivoshlykov. met him in the street, and caught hold of his arm.

"Aha, there you are! I've been looking for you," he said. Not knowing what had happened to Bunchuk, he gave him a friendly slap on the back and smiled anxiously. "What's the matter with you? You haven't been drinking, have you? Have you heard we're sending an expedition into the northern Don district, to mobilize the

Cossacks there? Podtyolkov will lead it. Our only hope is in the Cossacks of the north. Otherwise we'll be caught here. Will you go? We need agitators. You'll go, won't you?"

"Yes," Bunchuk replied shortly.

"Well, that's fine. We're leaving tomorrow."

In the same state of complete mental prostration Bunchuk prepared for departure, and rode off with the expedition the next day.

At this time the situation was extremely menacing for the Don Soviet Government. The German army of occupation was marching eastward from the Ukraine, and the districts of the lower Don were seething with counter-revolutionary revolts. Popov was lurking in the steppes beyond the Don, and threatening to attack Novocherkassk at any moment. The Provincial Congress of Soviets held in the middle of April was more than once interrupted in order to repel the revolting Cossacks threatening Rostov. Only in the north were the fires of the Revolution still burning, and towards those fires Podtyolkov and the others were involuntarily drawn as they lost hope of support on the lower Don. Mobilization there had failed. On Lagutin's initiative, Podtyolkov, recently elected chairman of the Don Council of People's Commissars, decided to go northward to mobilize three or four regiments of front-line men, and to throw them against the Germans and the counter-revolution in the lower districts. An Extraordinary Mobilization Commission of five, with Podtyolkov at its head, was appointed; ten million rubles in gold and tsarist money were withdrawn from the exchequer for the needs of the mobilization; a detachment consisting mainly of Cossacks from the Kamenskaya district was hastily scraped together to act as guard, and on May 1st the expedition set out northward, already under fire from German aircraft.

The railways were crowded with Red Guards retreating from the Ukraine. The insurgent Cossacks were blowing up bridges and wrecking trains. Every morning German aeroplanes flew along the railway from Novocherkassk to Kamenskaya, swooped low like flocks of vultures and opened machine-gun fire on the Red Guard detachments. The soldiers scattered out of the wagons, shots rang out sharply; at the stations the smell of the slag heaps was mingled with the reek of war and destruction. The aeroplanes soared away high into the air and the riflemen used up round after round of ammunition, littering the ground round the trains with empty cartridges till it was like an oak grove strewn with golden leaves in autumn. Everywhere were the signs of destruction. Burned-out and shattered wagons, broken wires

festooned around the telegraph poles, ruined
houses, and snow-fences swept away as though
by a hurricane.

For five days the expedition travelled slowly
along the railway line in the direction of Millerovo. On the sixth day Podtyolkov called a
meeting of the Mobilization Commission in his
wagon.

"We can't go on like this. I think we ought to
leave the wagons and march the rest of the
way."

"What?" Lagutin exclaimed. "While we're
plodding along on foot the Whites will sweep
right across us."

"It's a bit too far," Mrykhin said doubtfully.

Krivoshlykov sat silent, wrapped in his
greatcoat and yellow with malaria and quinine.
He sat huddled on a sack of sugar, taking no
part in the discussion. His eyes were hazy with
fever.

"Krivoshlykov!" Podtyolkov called to him
without raising his eyes.

"What's the question?"

"Aren't you listening? We must go on foot,
otherwise we'll be overtaken. What do you
think? You're more educated than the rest of
us."

"We could march," Krivoshlykov said slowly
and distinctly, but suddenly his teeth snapped

wolfishly and he began to tremble in a paroxysm of fever. "We could do it if we hadn't got so much to carry."

Podtyolkov unfolded a map by the door, and Mrykhin held it up by two corners. The wind blowing from the gloomy west tore at it, as though trying to snatch it away. "We'll take this road." Podtyolkov ran his nicotine-stained fingers over the map. "It might be a hundred and fifty to two hundred versts. Is that right?"

"Yes, we'd better walk it, blast their eyes!" Lagutin agreed.

"What do you say, Mikhail?"

Krivoshlykov, irritated, shrugged his shoulders. "I don't object."

"I'll tell the Cossacks to detrain at once. There's no point in losing time." Mrykhin looked around expectantly, and meeting with no opposition, jumped down from the wagon.

That sombre rainy morning the train carrying the Podtyolkov expedition was not far from Belaya Kalitva. Bunchuk was lying in his wagon with his head under his greatcoat. In the same wagon Cossacks were making tea, laughing and pulling one another's legs. Bunchuk kept his eyes closed. He was living over and over again the incidents of the past, feeling the same pain. Before his filmy eyes the snow-covered steppe lay fringed with the brown spines of forests on the horizon. He thought he could feel the cold wind, and Anna seemed to be standing at his side. He could see her black eyes, the strong yet tender lines of her mouth, the tiny freckles above her nose, the thoughtful furrow of her brow. He could not catch the words that came from her lips: they were inarticulate and interrupted by strange voices and laughter. But by the gleam of her eyes and the flutter of her eye-lashes he guessed what she was saying.

But then he saw a different Anna, her face a bluish yellow, the traces of tears on her cheeks, her nose pinched and her lips torturously writhing. He bent to kiss the dark hollows of her eyes. He groaned and clutched his throat to suppress his sobs. Anna did not leave him for a moment. Her features did not fade or darken with the passing of time. Her face, figure, walk, gestures, the sweep of her brows, all united to compose her living and whole. He recalled her words, her sentimentally romantic speeches, all he had lived through with her. And the vitality of this re-creation intensified his torment tenfold.

When the order came to detrain they aroused him. He got up, indifferently put his things together and went out. He helped to unload the baggage. With the same indifference he clambered on to a cart and rode off.

Rain was falling. The stunted grass along the roadside was wet. The open steppe, where the wind freely wandered over the slopes and hollows. Behind them the smoke of railway engines, the red blocks of the station buildings. The forty carts, hired from the nearest village, dragged along the road. The horses moved slowly. Soaked with rain, the clayey black earth hindered their movement. The mud clung to the wheels in black woolly clods. Before and behind them went crowds of miners fleeing with their wives and families and their miserable belongings eastward from the Cossack violence.

At a railway junction they were overtaken by the shattered remnants of two other Red Guard detachments. The men's faces were an earthy grey from the strain of fighting, lack of sleep, and privation. Shchadenko, their commander, came up to Podtyolkov. His handsome face with its clipped English moustache and thin hard nose was utterly exhausted. As Bunchuk went past he heard Shchadenko, his brows knitted, saying in a tired angry voice:

"Do you think I don't know my own lads? Things were bad enough before, and now we've got the Germans to reckon with, damn their hides. When shall I ever get my forces together again?"

After this talk Podtyolkov strode away to

catch up with his cart, frowning and apparently rather confused. Krivoshlykov came up and he started talking to him excitedly. Bunchuk saw Krivoshlykov sweep his arm downwards and volley out a few phrases. Podtyolkov brightened up and jumped on to the cart, making it creak with his weight. A lash from the driver on the horses' backs and the mud flew from the wheels.

"Faster!" shouted Podtyolkov, throwing his leather jacket open to the wind.

XXVII

For several days the expedition marched into the heart of the Don Province. The inhabitants of the Ukrainian villages welcomed them hospitably, glad to sell them provisions and gave them shelter. But no sooner was the question raised of hiring horses for the journey to Krasnokutsk than the Ukrainians began to scratch their heads and after some hesitation bluntly refused.

"You'll be getting good money, why turn up your noses at it?" Podtyolkov questioned one of them.

"Do you think I value money more than my own life?"

"We don't want your life, you just hire us out some horses and a cart."

"I can't do it."

"Why not?"

"You're going to the Cossacks, aren't you?"

"What about it?"

"Suppose something happens and I lose my horses. What shall I do then? How can I live without horses? No, man, leave me alone. I'm not going."

As they drew nearer to the Cossack lands, Podtyolkov and the other leaders began to grow apprehensive. They noticed a change in the attitude of the people, who now began to manifest open ill-will and alarm, selling their food reluctantly, and evading questions. The carts were no longer surrounded by a gay crowd of village youngsters. Hostile faces peered from the windows and the villagers hurried away out of sight.

"What are you, a lot of heathens?" the Cossacks of the expedition shouted. "Why are you staring at us like owls?"

Reduced to desperation by their cool reception, Vanka Boldyrev threw his cap to the ground in the village square and, glancing round in case one of the commanders should appear, roared:

"Are you men or devils? What are you standing silent for, damn you? We're pouring out our blood for your rights, and you just look through us! There is equality now, Comrades, there aren't any more Cossacks and khokhols, and nobody will lay hands on you. Bring us eggs and chickens at once, and we'll pay for everything in tsarist rubles."

Six Ukrainians stood listening to him, their heads drooping despondently like horses harnessed to ploughs. Not one of them responded to his fiery speech.

"You're just the same rotten khokhols that you've always been! May you burst, you pot-bellied bourgeois!" Boldyrev again hurled his well-worn cap to the ground and went purple in the face with scorn. "You wouldn't give away a shovelful of snow in winter!"

"You needn't yell!" was all the Ukrainians said as they dispersed in various directions.

In the same village an old Ukrainian woman questioned one of the Cossacks:

"Is it true you'll steal everything and cut us all to pieces?"

Without batting an eye-lash the Cossack replied:

"Yes, it's true. Maybe not everybody, but we'll cut up all the old men."

"Oh, my God! And what do you want to cut them up for?"

"We eat them with gruel. Mutton is off flavour now, it isn't sweet enough yet, so we put the old men into our pots and make a fine stew of them...."

"You wouldn't be joking, would you?"

"He's lying, Gran!" Mrykhin intervened, and turned on the jester:

"You learn how to joke and who to joke with! Podtyolkov would knock your head off for making jokes like that. What are you spreading those stories for? She'll go and tell everybody that we cut up the old men!"

Consumed with anxiety, Podtyolkov shortened the length of the halts and the nightly rests, and hurried the expedition onward. The day before their arrival in the Upper Don District he had a long talk with Lagutin.

"There's no point in our going too far, Ivan. We'll begin the mobilization as soon as possible. We'll proclaim an enrolment and offer good wages, but they'll have to bring their own horses and equipment, we can't throw the people's money down the drain. We'll gather men as we go along. By the time we get to Mikhailovka, we must have a division at our command. Do you think we'll get it?"

"We'll get them, provided everything is still quiet there."

"So you think the Whites may have begun already?"

"Who knows?" Lagutin stroked his scanty

beard and added despondently: "We're late. . . .
I'm afraid we'll fail. The officers are already
doing their work there. We must hurry. . . ."

"We are hurrying! And don't you be scared!
We mustn't be scared!" Podtyolkov replied, his
eyes gleaming harshly. "We have men following us, we can't afford to be afraid. We'll break
through! Within two weeks we'll be sweeping
the Germans and the Whites out of the Don."
Puffing hard at his cigarette, he gave expression to his own secret thoughts: "If we're too
late, we're lost and so is Soviet rule on the
Don. We mustn't be too late. If the officers
have organized a rising before we get there,
then that's the end!"

Towards evening of the following day they
set foot on Cossack territory. As they
approached the first village Podtyolkov, who
was riding with Lagutin and Krivoshlykov on
one of the foremost carts, saw a herd of cattle
in the steppe. "We'll go and question the herdsman," he proposed to Lagutin. Krivoshlykov
supported the idea.

Lagutin and Podtyolkov dismounted and
went over to the herd. The sun-scorched grass
of the common glistened brownly. The grass
was stunted and trampled and only near the
road was there a sturdy growth of rape and
wild oats rustling their bearded tops. Crush-

ing a sprig of old wormwood in his palm and breathing in its bitter scent, Podtyolkov went up to the herdsman.

"Hullo there, herdsman."

"Praise be."

"Looking after your herd?"

"Aye."

The old man lowered at them from under his bushy grey brows.

"Well, how're you getting on round here?"

"We manage, with God's help."

"What's the news?"

"There's nothing to tell. And who might you be?"

"We're soldiers going home."

"What village d'ye come from?"

"Ust-Khoperskaya."

"That Podtyolkov isn't with you, is he?"

"Yes."

The herdsman was obviously alarmed by the answer, and he turned pale.

"What's the matter, old man?" Podtyolkov inquired.

"Why, they say you're going to kill off all the Orthodox."

"Nonsense! Who's telling such stories?"

"The ataman said so at a meeting two days ago. Either he'd heard rumours or he'd had a message from the government saying Podtyolkov and the Kalmyks were coming to massacre us all."

"So you've got atamans again?" Lagutin asked, glancing at Podtyolkov, who bit into a stalk of grass with his strong yellow teeth.

"We elected an ataman some days ago. The Soviet has been closed down."

Lagutin would have asked more, but at that moment a little way off a huge bull jumped on one of the cows and crushed her to the ground.

"He'll break her back, the devil!" gasped the herdsman and with a speed that belied his years rushed away to his herd, shouting as he ran: "It's Nastyonka's. . . . He'll break her back. What are you up to, Baldy!"

Podtyolkov spread his arms and turned back to the cart. Lagutin, good farmer that he was, stared anxiously at the frail little cow that the bull had pinned to the earth and for a second the thought crossed his mind: "Yes, he could break her back, the devil!"

Only when he had made sure that the cow had survived the bull's onslaught with her spine intact did he return to the carts. "What shall we do? Surely they haven't got atamans again on the other side of the Don too?" he questioned himself. But his thoughts were again diverted by a thoroughbred bull standing by the roadside. The bull was sniffing at a big heavy-uddered black cow and shaking its massive bony head. Its great chest bulged to its knees and its long powerful body was taut as a violin string. The short legs were embedded in the ground like posts, and as Lagutin's eyes rested affectionately on the bull's dappled brown hide, jealously admiring its breeding, a single thought penetrated his worried mind: "We could do with a bull like that in our village. Ours are a poor lot." The thought took possession of him for a moment, then passed. As he walked up to the cart and glanced at the Cossacks' downcast faces, Lagutin was already considering what route they should take.

Wasted by fever, Krivoshlykov, the dreamer and poet, was saying to Podtyolkov:

"We are trying to get away from the wave of counter-revolution, but it's sweeping over us. It's coming on like the tide over a level shore. You can't race it."

Only Podtyolkov seemed to realize the full seriousness of the situation. He sat leaning forward in the cart and every minute shouted to the driver:

"Faster!"

Someone struck up a song at the back of the column but it died away abruptly. Laughter and shouts sounded above the rumble of the wheels.

The information obtained from the herdsman turned out to be correct. They passed a Cossack on his way to the village of Svechnikov with his wife. The man was wearing shoulder-straps and a cockade in his cap. Podtyolkov asked him a few questions and his face grew even darker.

Rain began to fall. The sky was overcast. Only to the east a deep-blue, sunlit scrap of sky peered through the clouds. As they were descending a slope into a little settlement they saw people running, and several carts racing along out of the farther side.

"They're running away. They're afraid of us ..." Lagutin said distractedly, eyeing the others.

"Get them back. Shout to them, the devils!" Podtyolkov exclaimed.

The Cossacks stood up in their carts and waved their hats. Someone shouted fiercely.

The carts of the expedition rattled down into the settlement. The wind was eddying along the broad, deserted street. In one of the yards an old Ukrainian woman, scolding the while, was throwing pillows into a cart, while her husband, barefoot and hatless, held the horses' bridles.

Here they learned that the man they had sent on ahead to arrange for quarters had been taken prisoner by a Cossack patrol and carried off. Evidently the Cossacks were not far away. At a short meeting the decision was taken to turn back. Podtyolkov, who had at first insisted on continuing their advance, still hesitated.

Krivoshlykov was again shaking with fever and kept silent.

"Maybe we could go on?" Podtyolkov asked Bunchuk, who had been present at the meeting.

Bunchuk shrugged indifferently. He did not care whether they went forward or back as long as they kept moving, moving away from the grief that dogged his footsteps. Podtyolkov paced up and down, talking of the advantages of going on to Ust-Medveditsa. But one of the Cossack agitators interrupted him sharply:

"You've taken leave of your senses! Where do you want to lead us to? To the counter-revolutionaries? We're going back! We don't want to die! What's that? See there?" He pointed to the slope above the village.

They all turned and gazed up the hill. On the crest the figures of three riders were clearly silhouetted against the sky.

"That's one of their patrols!" Lagutin exclaimed.

"And there, look!"

More groups of horsemen appeared, vanished beyond the hill, and re-appeared.

Podtyolkov gave the order to turn back. They

rode to the first Ukrainian village, only to find its inhabitants, evidently forewarned by the Cossacks, preparing to hide and flee.

Dusk began to fall. The fine, cold. rain soaked them to the skin. The men walked alongside the carts, holding their rifles at the ready. The road wound down into a valley, ran through it and climbed the rise beyond. On the hill-tops, the Cossack patrols appeared and disappeared. Their lurking presence made the nervous tension even greater.

Close to one of the ravines crossing the valley Podtyolkov jumped from his cart and curtly called to the men:

"Be ready!" He flicked up the safety catch on his cavalry carbine and walked forward beside the cart. Spring flood water showed blue in the ravine. It ran into a pond formed by a dam. The mud round the pond was pitted by the hoofprints of cattle that had come there to drink. The crumbling dam was fringed with sedges that drooped and rustled in the rain. Podtyolkov had expected an ambush at this spot, but the advance patrol failed to discover anybody.

"You needn't expect them here," Krivoshlykov whispered to him. "They won't attack now. They'll wait for night."

"I think so too."

XXVIII

The clouds gathered heavily in the west. Night fell. Far away towards the Don the sky was flickering, and the orange sheet-lightning quivered like a wounded bird. The sunset gleamed pallidly under a heavy pall of cloud. The steppe seemed to overflow with silence; mournful glimmers of the ebbing daylight lurked in the folds of the valley. There was an autumnal quality in that May evening. Even the grasses, not yet in flower, gave off an inexpressible odour of decay. Podtyolkov sniffed the mingled aroma of the saturated grasses as he walked along. Now and then he halted and stooped to scrape the mud from his boots, straightening up again and striding on wearily, his leather jacket thrown open and creaking with the damp.

They arrived at the next village after nightfall. The Cossacks of the expedition abandoned their carts and went to different houses for the night. Podtyolkov gave orders for pickets to be posted, but they had difficulty in getting men for the duty. Three flatly refused to go.

"Hold a comrades' court martial on them at once! Shoot them for refusing to obey orders!" Krivoshlykov fumed. But Podtyolkov made a bitter gesture.

"They've been demoralized by the journey. They won't defend themselves. We're done for, Misha!"

Somehow Lagutin managed to collect several Cossacks, and posted sentries outside the village. Podtyolkov made a round of the houses and spoke to the Cossacks upon whom he could most rely.

"Don't sleep, lads! Otherwise they'll get us!" he told them.

All through the night he sat at a table, his head on his hand, breathing heavily and hoarsely like a wounded animal. Just before dawn he was overcome with sleep, and dropped his head to the table. But almost immediately he was aroused to prepare for the further retreat. Day was breaking. He went out into the yard. The mistress of the house, just back from milking, met him in the porch.

"There are some horsemen riding on the hill," she informed him unconcernedly.

He ran into the yard. On the hill, beyond the pall of mist hanging over the village and the willows of the leas, large forces of Cossacks were visible. They were closing in on the village at a fast trot.

Cossacks from the other houses began to stream into the yard. One of them came up to Podtyolkov and called him aside:

"Comrade Podtyolkov ... delegates came in from them just now." He waved his hand towards the hill. "They told us to tell you that we are to lay down our arms and surrender at once. Otherwise they'll attack."

"You ... son of a bitch! How dare you. ..." Podtyolkov seized the man by his greatcoat collar, threw him aside and ran to the cart. He clutched his rifle by the barrel, and turned and shouted to the Cossacks in a hoarse, rough voice:

"Surrender? What talk can we have with the counter-revolution? We shall fight them! Follow me! To arms!"

A number of Cossacks rushed out of the yard behind him, and ran in a bunch to the end of the village. As they reached the last houses Podtyolkov was overtaken by Mrykhin.

"For shame, Podtyolkov!" he cried. "Are we to shed the blood of our brothers? Come back! We'll come to some agreement."

Seeing that only a small section of the expedition's force had followed him, and soberly realizing the inevitability of defeat in the event of a struggle, Podtyolkov silently took the bolt out of his rifle and let his hand drop to his side.

"It's no good, lads! Back to the village!"

They turned back. The entire expedition assembled in three adjacent yards. A few minutes later a group of forty Cossack horsemen entered the village. The main forces of the enemy remained in their positions on the low surrounding hills. Podtyolkov went to the end of the village to discuss the terms of the surrender. As he walked along the road he was overtaken by Bunchuk, who ran after him and stopped him.

"Are we surrendering?"

"Force will break a straw. What else are we to do?"

"Do you want to die?" Bunchuk shuddered from head to foot. "Tell them we won't surrender!" he cried in a toneless high-pitched voice, ignoring the Cossack veterans now surrounding Podtyolkov. "Tell them we won't hand over our arms!"

He turned on his heel and strode back, waving his revolver. He tried to persuade the Red Guards to attempt to break through and fight their way to the railway. But the majority were openly in favour of surrender. Some turned away, and others angrily declared:

"You go and fight. We're not going to shoot our own brothers!"

"We'll trust ourselves to them without our arms."

"Today's Easter Sunday, and you want us to shed blood?"

Bunchuk turned and went to his cart, threw his greatcoat underneath it, and lay down, gripping his revolver butt tightly in his hand. At first he thought of trying to escape. But he could not reconcile himself to flight and desertion, and he waited for Podtyolkov's return.

Podtyolkov came back some three hours later, bringing a great crowd of Cossacks with him into the village. He strode along firmly with head high. At his side was the commander of the White Cossack forces, Junior Captain Spiridonov, who happened to be a former artillery comrade of his. Spiridonov was saying something to him, smiling craftily. Behind him rode a Cossack pressing the rough staff of a white flag to his chest.

The streets and the yards where the carts of the expedition were gathered were dammed up with the Cossack newcomers. A roar of voices at once arose. Many of them were former comrades-in-arms of the Podtyolkov Cossacks, and as they recognized one another joyous exclamations and laughter broke out.

"Hullo, is that you, Prokhor? What brings you here?"

"We came very near to fighting you," Prokhor replied. "Remember how we chased the Austrians near Lvov?"

"Why, there's Cousin Danilo! Christ has risen, Cousin."

"Truly He has risen!" Danilo replied to the Easter greeting. There was the loud smack of kissing. Then the two Cossacks stood stroking their whiskers and staring at each other, smiling and clapping each other on the back.

"We haven't broken our fast yet ..." one of the Red Cossacks remarked.

"But you're Bolsheviks, what have you got to break your fast for?"

"Hm! Bolsheviks we may be, but we believe in God all the same."

"Ho! You're lying!"

"It's God's truth!"

"And do you wear a cross?"

"Of course. Here it is." The Red Guard unbuttoned the collar of his tunic and pulled out the tarnished copper cross that hung on his brown hairy chest.

The old men who had come out with pitchforks and axes to hunt the "rebel Podtyolkov" looked at one another in amazement.

"Why, they told us you had given up the Christian faith!" one of them declared. "We heard you were robbing the churches and killing the priests."

"That's all lies!" the broad-faced Red Guard assured them confidently. "They've been telling you lies. Why, before I came away from Rostov I went to church and took the sacrament."

"Well, I'm bothered!"

A puny little old man armed with a lance, which had been cut down to about half its former length, clapped his hands delightedly.

A buzz of animated talk went on in the street and the yards. But after half an hour several Cossacks strode down the street jostling aside the solid mass of men. "Those belonging to Podtyolkov's detachment, fall in for roll-call!" they shouted.

Behind them came Junior Captain Spiridonov. He removed his officer's cap, and called:

"All those belonging to Podtyolkov's detachment step to the left towards the fences. The others to the right. Brothers, front-line men! Together with your leaders we have decided that you must surrender all your weapons, for the people are afraid of you while you are armed. Put your rifles and the rest of your arms on your carts. We shall guard them jointly. We are going to send you to Krasnokutskaya, and there you will receive your arms back again."

A deep growl of discontent arose among the Red Guard Cossacks, and one of them shouted:

"We won't give up our arms!"

An uneasy mutter ran through the crowd packing the street and yards.

The Cossacks under Spiridonov's command surged to the right, leaving the Red Guards in a disorderly and spiritless mob in the middle of the street. Krivoshlykov looked around him like a hunted animal. Lagutin twisted his lips. Bunchuk, who was firmly resolved not to surrender his weapons, strode swiftly across to Podtyolkov, carrying his rifle at the trail.

"We mustn't give up our arms! Do you hear?"

"It's too late now," Podtyolkov whispered back, crushing the detachment roll nervously in his fingers.

The roll fell into the hands of Spiridonov, who glanced through it and asked: "There should be a hundred and twenty-eight men in the detachment. Where are the rest?"

"They dropped out on the way."

"So that's it. All right, tell them to surrender their arms."

Podtyolkov was the first to unfasten his revolver holster. As he gave it up he said huskily:

"My sabre and rifle are in the cart."

The disarming began. The Red Guards handed over their arms slackly, some of them attempting to hide their revolvers in the fences and yards.

"Anyone who doesn't give up his arms will be searched!" Spiridonov shouted, grinning cheerfully.

Led by Bunchuk, a number refused to give up their rifles, and the weapons were taken from them by force. One machine-gunner caused a stir by galloping out of the village, taking the breech-lock of his gun with him. In the general confusion several others hid themselves. Spiridonov at once set guards over Podtyolkov and the rest, searched them, and attempted to call a roll. But the prisoners answered reluctantly, and called out:

"What are you checking the list for? We're all here."

"Drive us to Krasnokutskaya."

"Put an end to this game."

The money chest was sealed up and sent off to Karginskaya under a strong guard. Then Spiridonov assembled the prisoners, and at once changing the tone of his voice and the expression on his face, gave the command:

"In double file! Left face! Forward march! Silence in the ranks!"

A mutter of discontent surged through the ranks of the Red Guards. They marched away unwillingly, quickly broke ranks and walked along in a disorderly crowd.

When Podtyolkov had called on his men to surrender their weapons, he probably still hoped for a favourable issue to the affair. But as soon as the prisoners were driven out of the village the Cossacks escorting them began to press on the outside men with their horses. Bunchuk was striding along on the left, and an old Cossack, with a flaming red beard and an earring black with age in his ear, needlessly struck him with his whip. The end lashed Bunchuk's cheek. He turned and clenched his fist, but a second, still fiercer blow forced him to push his way in to the crowd of prisoners. He did so involuntarily, driven by the elemental instinct for self-preservation; and for the first time since Anna's death a wry smile twisted his lips, as he realized with astonishment how strong and vital in man is the desire to live.

The Cossack escort began to beat up the prisoners. The old men, infuriated at the sight of their helpless enemies, rode their horses at them, and leaning out of their saddles, struck at them with their whips and the flat of their swords. Involuntarily those that had been struck struggled to get into the middle, jostling one another and crying out. Shaking his fists above his head, a tall Red Guard shouted:

"If you're out to kill us, kill us off at once, damn you! What are you torturing us for?"

"What about your promise?" Krivoshlykov shouted.

The old men grew less truculent. In reply to a prisoner's question, one of the escort muttered:

"Our orders are to drive you to Ponomaryov. Don't be afraid, brothers, no worse will happen to you."

When they arrived at the village of Ponomaryov, Spiridonov was standing at the door of a little shop, and as the prisoners passed inside one by one, he asked:

"Your surname? Christian name? Where were you born?"

It came to Bunchuk's turn. "Your surname?" Spiridonov asked, his pencil set expectantly to the paper. He glanced at the Red Guard's moody face, and seeing the man's lips pursed up ready to spit, he dodged swiftly and shouted:

"Move on, you swine! You'll die nameless."

Inspired by Bunchuk's example, two others following him refused to give their names, preferring to die unknown. When the last man had passed into the shop Spiridonov locked it up and posted guards around it.

While the spoils taken from the expedition's carts were being shared out close by the shop, a hurriedly organized field court martial, composed of representatives from all the villages participating in the capture, was held in a house close at hand. The chairman was a thick-set, yellow-haired captain, Vasily Popov. He sat under a mirror hung with the usual embroidered towels, his elbows sprawled over the table, his cap pushed to the back of his head. His oily, good-naturedly severe eyes turned interrogatively from one to another of the members of court and he repeated his question.

"What shall we do with them, elders?" he asked.

He bent over and whispered to a junior captain sitting at his side. The officer nodded hastily. Popov's eyes narrowed, the cheerfulness died out of them and was replaced by a cold and unrelenting gleam that his lowered lashes did little to hide. "What shall we do with these traitors to their country, who were coming to pillage our homes and destroy the Cossacks?"

An old man jumped to his feet like a released jack-in-the-box:

"Shoot them! Every one of them!" He shook his head as though possessed, and glanced around with fanatical eyes. Choking in the spittle that frothed from his lips, he shouted:

"No mercy for them, the Judases! Kill them!

Crucify them! Burn them! Kill the Jews among them!"

"Shall we send them into exile?" one of the members irresolutely proposed.

"Shoot them!"

"The death sentence!"

"Public execution!"

"The weeds have got to be rooted out!"

"Death to them!"

"Of course they must be shot. Why stop to discuss it?" Spiridonov declared indignantly.

The shouts drove the last vestige of good-natured complacency from the chairman's face. His lips set stonily.

"To be shot! Write that down!" he ordered the secretary.

"And Podtyolkov and Krivoshlykov? Are they to be shot too? That's too good for them!" a corpulent elderly Cossack sitting by the window shouted fiercely.

"They, as the ringleaders, must be hanged." the chairman curtly replied. Turning to the secretary, he ordered:

"Write this: 'Decree. We, the undersigned. . . .' "

The clerk, a distant relative of the chairman, bent his fair, smoothly combed head over the table and began scratching with his pen.

"Looks as if the lamp's running out of oil,"
someone said regretfully.

The lamp began to gutter, and the wick
smoked. In the silence the buzzing of a fly
caught in a spider-web on the ceiling, the scraping of the pen over the paper, and the heavy
asthmatic breathing of one of the members of
the court martial were clearly to be heard.

DECREE
April 27th (May 10th), 1918

We, the undersigned, elected representatives
of the villages in the Karginovskaya, Bokov-
skaya and Krasnokutskaya stanitsas:

representing	Vasilyevsky village	Stepan Maksayev
"	Bokovskoi village	Nikolai Kruzhilin
"	Fomin village	Fyodor Kumov
"	Verkhne-Yablon-ovsky village	Alexander Kukhtin
"	Nizhne-Dulensky village	Lev Sinev
"	Ilyinsky village	Semyon Volotskov
"	Konkovsky village	Mikhail Popov
"	Verkhne-Dulen-sky village	Yakov Rodin
"	Savostyanov village	Alexander Frolov
"	Milyutinskaya stanitsa	Maxim Fevralyov
"	Nikolayev village	Mikhail Groshev

representing	Krasnokutskaya stanitsa	Ilya Yelankin
"	Ponomaryov village	Ivan Dyachenko
"	Yevlantyev village	Nikolai Krivov
"	Malakhov village	Luka Yemelyanov
"	Novo-Zemtzevo village	Matvei Konovalov
"	Popov village	Mikhail Popov
"	Astakhov village	Vasily Shchegolkov
"	Orlov village	Fyodor Chekunov
"	Klimo-Fyodorov-sky village	Fyodor Chukarin

assembled here on April 27 (May 10), 1918, V. S. Popov presiding

Decree:

1) That the despoilers and betrayers of the toiling people, listed below, numbering eighty in all, be put to death by shooting, with the exception of two—Podtyolkov and Krivoshlykov—who, as the leaders of this group, shall be hanged.

2) That the Cossack Anton Kalitventsov from Mikhailovsky village be acquitted for lack of evidence.

3) That Konstantin Melnikov, Gavril Melnikov, Vasily Melnikov, Aksyonov and Vershinin, escaped from Podtyolkov's detachment and arrested in the stanitsa of Krasnokutskaya, be executed in accordance with article one of this decree.

4) That this decree be carried out tomorrow, April 28 (May 11), at 6 a.m.

5) That Lieutenant Senin be put in charge of the prisoners, and that by 11 p. m. two Cossacks from each village armed with rifles be assigned to his command. The members of the court shall be responsible for carrying out this article. The sentence shall be carried out by five Cossacks from each village, who shall be dispatched to the place of execution.

(Signed) V. S. Popov,
Chairman of the Military Section
A. F. Popov, Clerk

The clerk finished writing out the list of those condemned, and thrust the pen into the hand of his neighbour.

"Sign!"

The man took the inky pen in his stubby black fingers. "I'm not much of a hand at writing," he said with a sheepish smile.

The next man signed in the same uncertain manner, frowning and perspiring with the effort of concentration. Another made several false starts before signing, after which he withdrew his tongue that had remained hanging out during the process. Popov inscribed his signature and underlined it with a flourish, then rose, wiping his perspiring face with his hand-kerchief.

"Fix the list to it," he said with a yawn.

"Kaledin in the next world will thank us for this," one man smiled, watching as the clerk fixed the sheet of paper to the wall.

Nobody responded to the jest. They silently went out of the house.

"Lord Jesus . . ." someone sighed in the dark-ness of the porch.

XXIX

There was little sleep during that milkily starlit night for any of the prisoners locked up in the shop. Conversation quickly tailed away. The lack of air and their own anxiety choked them. All the evening one of them had been asking the guard:

"Open the door, Comrade, I want to go out-side. . . ."

He stood with his vest dangling out of his trousers, dishevelled and bare-footed, pressing his darkened face to the keyhole and repeating:

"Open up, Comrade!"

"None of your 'comrade,' " one of the guards replied at last.

"Open, brother!" the prisoner changed his style of address.

The guard set down his rifle, finished his cigarette, listened to the beat of wings as a flight of wild ducks flew out for the night's feed, then put his lips to the chink in the door and called:

"You can piss under yourself, you poor devil! Your trousers won't rot in the night, and at dawn they'll let you into heaven wet or dry. . . ."

"We're done for," the Red Guard exclaimed despairingly and turned away from the door.

They sat shoulder to shoulder. In one corner Podtyolkov, cursing to himself, was tearing up the money he had carried in his pockets. When he had finished with the money, he took off his boots and tapped Krivoshlykov on the shoulder.

"It's clear now . . . they've tricked us. Tricked us, the scum!" he said to his friend lying beside him. "It's galling, Mikhail. When I was a boy I used to go hunting in the forest with my father's flint-lock. You'd go along and the trees would be like a green roof over your head. I would shoot at the ducks and when I missed I used to get so annoyed with myself, I could have cried for shame. And here I have messed things up badly. If we'd left Rostov three days earlier we shouldn't have been facing our death here. We'd have turned their counter-revolution upside down."

Krivoshlykov's lips twisted painfully as he tried to smile, and he whispered back:

"Damn them, let them kill us! I'm not afraid to die yet. The only thing I'm afraid of is that in the next world we shan't recognize each other, like in the song. You and I will be there, Fyodor, but we'll meet as strangers.... I'm afraid of that!"

"Drop it!" Podtyolkov rumbled touchily, placing his big hot hands on his friend's shoulders. "That's not the trouble!"

Lagutin was telling someone about his village, and how his grandfather used to make fun of him because of his long head and how he had got a thrashing from the same grandfather for being caught on a neighbour's melon patch.

The disconnected snatches of talk followed various themes that night.

Bunchuk had found a place near the door, where he eagerly gasped in the draught coming through the chink. As his mind dwelt on the past he thought of his mother. Feeling a sharp prick of pain, he forced his thoughts in another direction, and turned to memories of Anna and more recent days. He found great relief and assuagement in this. He no longer felt the usual shiver down his spine or the inward ache of yearning at the thought that

598

he was about to be deprived of life. He looked
forward to death as a cheerless rest after a bitter and painful road, when weariness is so
great and the body aches so much that it is
impossible to feel any emotion at its end.

Near him a group of prisoners was talking
both gaily and sadly of women, of love, of the
great and petty joys which each had experienced. They spoke of their families, their relations, their friends. They noted the good quality of the young grain: the wheat was so tall
you couldn't even see the rooks in it. They
longed for vodka and for freedom, they cursed
Podtyolkov. But drowsiness covered many with
its black wing. Worn out physically and morally, they fell asleep lying, sitting, even standing.

Just as dawn was breaking, one of them,
whether awake or asleep, broke into tears. It
is terrible when rough, grown-up men, who
have forgotten the taste of salt tears since
childhood, begin to weep. At once several
voices disturbed the drowsy silence:

"Shut up, curse you!"

"Shut up or I'll tear your throat out."

"What a woman!"

"Here are men asleep, and he's lost all sense
of shame!"

The man snuffled, blew his nose, and lapsed
into silence. Here and there the gleaming red

points of cigarettes shone out, but nobody made a sound. The air was heavy with the scent of male sweat, of many healthy bodies pressed close together, of cigarette smoke and the dew which had fallen during the night.

In the village a cock heralded the sunrise. From outside the shop came the sound of footsteps and the clink of iron.

"Who goes there?" one of the guards called out.

"Friends! We're going to dig a grave for the Podtyolkov men," replied a young, eager voice.

In the shop everybody seemed to stir at once.

XXX

The detachment of Tatarsky Cossacks led by Pyotr Melekhov arrived in Ponomaryov at dawn of the same day. They found the village noisy with the clatter of Cossack boots, and the sound of horses being led to drink. Crowds were pouring towards the far end of the village. Pyotr halted his men in the centre of the village, and gave the order to dismount. Several Cossacks came up to them.

"Where are you from?" one of them asked.

"Tatarsky."

"You're a bit too late. We've caught Podtyolkov without your help. They're shut up over

there, like chickens in a coop." He laughed
and waved his hand towards the shop.

Christonya, Grigory, and several others went
closer to the man. "Where are they going to
send them?" Christonya inquired.

"To join the dead."

"What? You're lying!" Grigory seized the
man by his greatcoat.

"Well, invent a better lie, Your Honour!"
the man insolently retorted, and carefully freed
himself from Grigory's strong fingers. "Look
there; they've already built the gallows for
them." He pointed to two ropes hanging from
a cross-beam running between two stunted
willows.

"Stable the horses," Pyotr commanded.

The sky was overcast. A fine rain was falling. A dense mass of Cossacks and women had
gathered outside the village. Informed that the
execution would take place at six o'clock, the
inhabitants of Ponomaryov went along willingly as though to a rare and amusing spectacle. The women were dressed in holiday
clothes; many of them had their children with
them. The crowd swarmed over the pasture-
land, crowded around the gallows and the six-
foot-deep pit. The children clambered over the
raw clay of the mound thrown up on one side

of the pit; the men animatedly discussed the forthcoming execution; the women whispered sadly among themselves.

With traces of sleep still visible on his serious face the chairman of the court martial arrived. His strong teeth showed as he smoked and chewed at his cigarette. In a hoarse voice he ordered the Cossack guards:

"Drive the people back from the hole. Tell Spiridonov to send along the first batch." He glanced at his watch and stood on one side, watching the crowd being driven back by the guards in a colourful semicircle.

Spiridonov led a squad of Cossacks swiftly towards the shop. On the road he met Pyotr Melekhov.

"Any volunteers from your village?"

"Volunteers for what?"

"To act as a firing party."

"No, there aren't, and there won't be!" Pyotr roughly answered, passing round Spiridonov as he barred the road.

Nevertheless some of the Tatarsky men volunteered. Mitka Korshunov, stroking the hair falling below the peak of his cap, swung up to Pyotr and said, narrowing his green eyes:

"I'll volunteer. What did you say 'no' for? I'll be one. Give me some cartridges. I've only got one round."

He was joined by Andrei Kashulin, a tense evil expression on his pale face, and Fedot Bodovskov.

Whispers and muttering went up from the closely packed crowd when the first party of ten condemned prisoners, surrounded by a Cossack escort, set out from the shop.

Podtyolkov walked in front, barefoot, dressed in broad black breeches, his leather jerkin flung wide open. He set his great feet confidently on the muddy road, and when he slipped, raised his left arm slightly to keep his balance. At his side Krivoshlykov, deathly pale, could hardly drag himself along. His eyes gleamed feverishly, his mouth twitched with suffering. As he draped his greatcoat over his shoulders, he shivered as though perishing with cold. For some reason these two were left their clothes, but the others had been stripped down to their underlinen. Lagutin walked at the side of Bunchuk. Both of them were barefoot and wearing little more than their shirts. Lagutin's ragged drawers revealed his yellowish skin, and he sheepishly drew them around him. Bunchuk stared over the heads of the guards at the grey shroud of clouds in the distance. His cold, sober eyes blinked expectantly and tensely; his broad palm stroked his hairy chest under the open collar of his shirt. One would have thought he was looking forward to something unattainable, yet pleasant to think upon. Some of the others maintained expressions of stolid indifference; a grey-haired Bolshevik scornfully waved his hand and spat at the feet of the Cossack guards. But two or three had such dumb yearning in their eyes, such boundless terror in their distorted faces, that even the guards turned their eyes away as they met their gaze.

They strode along swiftly. Podtyolkov gave his arm to the stumbling Krivoshlykov. They drew near to the white kerchiefs and red and blue caps of the crowd. As he stared at them Podtyolkov cursed aloud. Catching Lagutin's eyes fixed on him, he abruptly asked:

"What's the matter?"

"You've gone grey during these last few days...."

"Isn't it enough to make you?" Podtyolkov breathed heavily, wiped the sweat from his narrow brow, and repeated: "Isn't it enough to make you? Even a wolf goes grey in a cage; and I'm a man."

Not another word did they say. The crowd surged forward in a solid mass. To the right stretched the long dark scar of the grave.

"Halt!" Spiridonov commanded.

Podtyolkov immediately took a step forward,

and wearily ran his eyes over the foremost ranks of the people. Most of them were grey-haired. The front-line men were somewhere at the back, pricked with conscience. Podtyolkov's drooping moustache stirred slightly as he said ponderously, yet distinctly:

"Elders! Allow me and Krivoshlykov to watch how our comrades will face their deaths. Hang us afterwards, but now we should like to see our friends and comrades, and to strengthen those who are weak of spirit."

The crowd was so quiet that the rain pattered audibly on their caps.

Captain Popov stood smiling in the rear, exposing his tobacco-stained teeth, but made no objection. The elders raggedly shouted their consent. Krivoshlykov and Podtyolkov stepped through the crowd, which divided and opened a narrow lane before them. A little way off from the pit they halted, hemmed in on all sides, watched by hundreds of eyes. They gazed as the Cossacks drew up the Red Guards in a ragged line with their backs to the pit. Podtyolkov could see perfectly, but Krivoshlykov had to stretch his lean neck and rise on his toes.

They recognized Bunchuk on the extreme left, standing with a slight stoop, breathing heavily, not raising his eyes from the ground. At his side stood Lagutin, still fumbling with his drawers. The man next in line was changed almost beyond recognition, and had aged at least twenty years. Two more approached the pit and turned round. One of them was smiling challengingly and impudently, furiously cursing and threatening the silent crowd with his clenched dirty fist. The last of the eight had to be carried. He threw himself back, dragged his feet lifelessly over the ground, clung to the Cossack guards, then, shaking his tear-stained face, started up and bellowed:

"Let me go, brothers! Let me go, for the love of God! Brothers! Brothers! What are you doing! I won four crosses in the German war. I have children. God, I'm innocent. Oh, why are you doing this...?"

A tall Cossack thrust his knee into the man's chest and drove him towards the pit. Only then did Podtyolkov recognize him, and his heart turned cold: it was one of the most fearless of his Red Guards, a man who had won all four classes of the Cross of St. George, a handsome, fair-haired young man. The Cossacks raised him upright; but he fell again and scrabbled at their feet, pressing his lips to their boots—to the boots which were kicking him in the face— and bellowing in an anguished, choking voice:

"Don't kill me! Have mercy! I have three

little children, one of them a girl ... my brothers, my friends!"

He embraced the tall Cossack's knees, but the man tore himself away, leaped back, and gave him a swinging kick on the ear with his iron-shod heel. Blood poured from the other ear and ran down his white collar.

"Stand him up!" Spiridonov shouted furiously.

Somehow they raised him, set him up and ran back. In the opposite rank the firing party brought their rifles to the ready. The crowd groaned and froze into stillness. A woman wailed hysterically.

Bunchuk wanted once more and yet once more to look at the grey pall of the sky, at the mournful earth over which he had wandered twenty-nine years. He raised his eyes, and saw the close rank of Cossacks some fifteen paces away. He saw one man, tall, with screwed-up green eyes, a lovelock falling over his narrow white brow, his lips compressed, his body leaning forward, aiming straight at Bunchuk's breast. Just before the volley rang out Bunchuk's ears were pierced by a long drawn-out shriek. He turned his head: a young, freckled woman ran out of the crowd and fled towards the village, one arm clutching a baby to her breast, the other hand covering its eyes.

After the irregular volley, when the eight men standing at the pit had fallen in a ragged line, the firing party ran towards the pit. Seeing that the Red Guard he had aimed at was still writhing and gnawing at his shoulder, Mitka Korshunov put another shot into him, and whispered to Andrei Kashulin:

"Look at that devil! He's bitten his shoulder until it's bleeding, and died like a wolf, without a groan."

Ten more of the condemned approached the pit, urged on by rifle-butts.

After the second volley the women in the crowd screamed and fled, jostling one another and dragging their children behind them. The men, too, began to move away. The loathsome scene of extermination, the screams and groans of the dying, the howling of those awaiting their turn were overwhelmingly oppressive, and the terrible spectacle was too much for the crowd. There remained only the front-line men, who had looked on death to their fill, and the most hardened of the elders.

Fresh groups of barefoot and unclothed Red Guards were brought up, new lines of volunteers confronted them, volleys spurted out, and single shots drily shook the air as the wounded were finished off. Hurriedly earth was shovelled over the first group of bodies in the trench.

Podtyolkov and Krivoshlykov went across to those awaiting their turn and endeavoured to encourage them. But their words had lost all significance: another power dominated these men whose lives in a minute or two were to be broken off like leaves withered at the stalk.

Grigory Melekhov pushed through the crowd to go back to the village, and came face to face with Podtyolkov. His former leader stepped back and stared at him.

"You here too, Melekhov?"

A bluish pallor overspread Grigory's cheeks, and he halted.

"Here. As you see. . . ."

"I see. . . ." Podtyolkov smiled wryly, staring with sudden hatred at Grigory's face. "Well, so you're shooting down your brothers? You've turned your coat? What a. . . ." He strode closer to Grigory and whispered: "So you serve us and them too, whoever pays most? Well, you are a. . . ."

Grigory seized his sleeve and asked breathlessly:

"Do you remember the battle at Glubokaya? Do you remember how they shot down the officers? Shot them down by your order? Huh? And now it's your turn. Don't moan! You're not the only one allowed to flay men's hides! You're finished, chairman of the Don commissars! You filthy swine, you sold the Cossacks to the Jews! Understand? Want to hear any more?"

Christonya put his arm around the raging Grigory and led him away. "Let's go back to the horses," he said. "There's nothing we can do here. God, what is coming over the people?"

But they halted as they heard Podtyolkov's voice raised passionately. Surrounded by old men and front-line men, he was shouting:

"You're blind ... ignorant! The officers have tricked you, they've forced you to kill your blood brothers. Do you think it will end with our death? No! Today you are on top, but to-morrow it will be your turn to be shot. The rule of the Soviets will be established all over Russia. Remember my words! You are shedding the blood of others in vain! You're a lot of fools."

"We'll manage any others who come!" an old man retorted.

"You won't shoot them all, Grandad!" Pod-tyolkov smiled. "You won't hang all Russia on the gallows! Look after your own head. You'll think better of it some day, but it will be too late."

"Don't threaten us!"

"I'm not threatening. I'm showing you the true path."

"You're blind yourself, Podtyolkov. Moscow's blinded your eyes."

Grigory did not stop to listen to any more, but almost ran to the yard where his horse was tethered. Tightening the saddle-girths, he and Christonya galloped out of the village and rode over the hill without a backward glance.

But still the slaughter of Cossack by Cossack went on in Ponomaryov. By the time all the Red Guards had been executed the trench was filled with bodies. Earth was heaped over them and stamped down with feet. Two officers in black masks took Podtyolkov and Krivoshlykov and led them to the gallows. Bravely, proudly lifting his head, Podtyolkov mounted the stool under the noose, unbuttoned the collar around his stout, swarthy neck, and without a tremor, himself set the soapy rope around his throat. One of the officers helped Krivoshlykov to mount his stool, and put the rope over his head.

"Allow us to say a last word before our deaths," Podtyolkov requested.

"Speak up! Go ahead!" the front-line men shouted.

He stretched his hands towards the little group that remained.

"See how few are left who wish to look on at our death!" Podtyolkov began. 'Their conscience has pricked them. On behalf of the toiling people, in their interests we have struggled against the rats of generals, not sparing our lives. And now we are perishing at your hands! But we do not curse you! You have been bitterly deceived. The revolutionary government will come, and you will realize on whose side was the truth. You have laid the finest sons of the quiet Don in that pit. . . ."

There was an increasing roar of voices, and his words were lost in the hubbub. Taking advantage of this, one of the officers kicked the stool from under his feet. Podtyolkov's great body fell and dangled, but his feet touched the ground. The knot gripping his throat choked him and forced him to draw himself upward. He rose on tiptoe, the toes of his bare feet digging into the damp earth, and gasped for air. Running his protruding eyes over the crowd, he said quietly:

"And you haven't even learned how to hang a man properly. . . . If I had the job, you wouldn't touch the ground, Spiridonov. . .!"

The spittle ran freely from his mouth. The masked officers and the nearest men raised the helpless, heavy body with difficulty on to the stool.

Krivoshlykov was not allowed to finish his speech. The stool flew from under his feet and crashed against an abandoned shovel. The lean, muscular body swung to and fro for a long time, contracting into a huddled ball until the knees touched his chin, then stretching again with a convulsive shudder. He was still struggling, his black, protruding tongue was still writhing, when the stool was kicked a second time from under Podtyolkov. Again the body fell heavily, the seam of the leather jerkin burst on the shoulder; but again the ends of the toes reached the ground. The crowd of Cossacks groaned; some of them crossed themselves and hurried away. So great were the dismay and confusion that for a minute all stood as though rooted to the spot, staring fearfully at Podtyolkov's blackened face.

But he was speechless; the knot gripped his throat too tightly. He only rolled his eyes, from which streams of tears were falling, and twisted his mouth. Striving to lighten his suffering, he stretched his whole body terribly and torturously upward.

Someone at last thought of a solution, and began with a shovel to dig away the earth below him. With each swing the body hung more stiffly, the neck lengthened and lengthened, and the head was drawn back on to his shoulders. The rope could hardly bear his great weight; it swung gently, creaking at the cross-beam. Yielding to its rhythmic movement, Podtyolkov swung also, turning in all directions as though to show his murderers his livid, blackening face and his chest, flooded with hot streams of spittle and tears.

XXXI

Misha Koshevoi and Knave left Kargin the second night after they had fled from Tatarsky. A mist enveloped the steppe, gathering in the hollows and crawling up the steep sides of the ravines. The quails were calling in the young grass. But in the lofty sky the moon floated like the fully opened blossom of a water-lily in a lake overgrown with reeds and sedges.

They kept on until dawn. The Milky Way began to fade in the sky. The dew was falling. They drew near to a village. But a few versts from the village they were overtaken by six Cossack horsemen. Misha and Knave would have turned off the road, but the grass was short and the moon was shining.

The Cossacks caught them and drove them back towards Kargin. They went some three hundred yards without speaking. Then a shot rang out. Knave stumbled over his feet and went sideways, sideways, like a horse afraid of its own shadow. He did not fall, but crumpled awkwardly to the ground, pressing his face into the grey wormwood.

For five minutes Misha walked on, stumbling, feeling nothing but a ringing in his ears. Then he asked:

"Why don't you shoot, you swine? Why make me suffer?"

"Get on, get on! Hold your tongue!" one of the Cossacks said kindly enough. "We killed the muzhik, but we had pity on you. You were in the Twelfth Regiment during the German war, weren't you?"

"Yes."

"Well, you'll serve again in the Twelfth. You're young yet. You've gone wrong a bit, but that's no great sin. We'll cure you."

Misha was "cured" three days later by a field court martial held at Kargin. In those days the court had two forms of punishment: shooting, and the birch. Those sentenced to be shot were driven out into the steppe at night. But those for whom there was hope of correction were birched publicly in the square.

On the Sunday morning the people began to assemble, filling all the square and climbing on to benches, sheds, roofs of houses and shops.

The first to be punished was the son of a priest. The man was an ardent Bolshevik and they would have shot him; but his father was a good priest, respected by all, and they decided to give his son a score of strokes. They pulled down his trousers, laid him bare over a bench and tied his hands together under it, a Cossack sat on his legs, and two others with bunches of willow switches stood at his side. They laid on. When they had finished the man rose, shook himself, pulled up his trousers, and bowed in all four directions. He was very glad to have escaped being shot, so he bowed and expressed his gratitude:

"Thank you, elders!"

"It was a pleasure!" someone answered.

And such a roar of laughter broke over the square that even the prisoners sitting a little way off in a shed also smiled.

In accordance with the sentence, they gave Misha twenty of the best. But still hotter was his shame. All the district, old and young, had assembled to watch. Misha pulled up his trousers, and all but weeping, said to the Cossack who had birched him:

"It isn't right!"

"What isn't?"

"It was my head that thought of it, and my arse has had to pay for it. I'm shamed for the rest of my life."

"Don't worry, shame isn't smoke; it won't

eat out your eyes," the Cossack consoled him, and in the desire to cheer his victim, he added:

"You're strong, my boy! Two of the strokes I gave you were real good ones. I wanted to see whether you would cry out, but I couldn't make you. Now, the other day they were birching a man and he couldn't hold himself. He must have had weak bowels."

The next day Misha was marched off to the front.

Knave was not buried until two days later. A couple of Cossacks from the nearest village were sent out by the ataman and dug a shallow grave. They sat smoking, their legs dangling in the hole.

"The earth's hard here," one said.

"Like iron. It's never been ploughed in my time. It's been set hard like this these many years."

"Yes, the lad will be lying in good earth, on a hill. There's wind here, and sun. It's dry. He won't rot quickly."

They glanced at Knave's body huddled in the grass, and rose.

"Shall we take his boots off?"

"Of course. They are good boots on his feet."

They laid him in the grave Christian fashion, with his head to the west, and shovelled the rich black earth on top of him.

"Shall we stamp it down?" the younger of the two asked when the earth was level with the edges.

"No need, let it be!" the other sighed. "When the angels sound the last trump he will be able to get to his feet more quickly."

Within two weeks the little mound was overgrown with burdock and wormwood; wild oats were dancing on it, rape was yellowing gaily at the side, clover was raising its head, and the air was scented with thyme, spurge and honey-dew.

Soon afterwards an old man drove out from the village, dug a little hole at the head of the grave, and set up a little shrine on a freshly cut oaken pole. The sorrowful features of the Virgin glowed softly under the little gable and on the base below her was painted an inscription in old Slavonic:

In the years of strife and trouble,
Brothers, judge not thy brother.

The old man rode away and the little shrine remained in the steppe to sadden the eyes of passing travellers with its eternally mournful aspect, and to stir in their hearts a strange and sad longing.

Later on, in May, two bustards fought around the shrine. They beat out a little bare patch in the blue wormwood, crushing the green flush of ripening quitch grass, fighting for the hen, for the right to life, for love and fertility. And again after a little while, under a mound, right by the shrine, in the shaggy shelter of the old wormwood a hen bustard laid nine speckled, smoky-blue eggs and sat on them, warming them with her body, and shielding them with her glossy wings.

Printed in the Union of Soviet Socialist Republics